Praise for #1 *New York Times* bestselling author

NORA ROBERTS

"Romance will never die as long as the megaselling Roberts keeps writing it."

—*Kirkus Reviews*

"Roberts nails her characters and settings with awesome precision, drawing readers into a vividly rendered world of family-centered warmth."

—*Library Journal*

"Roberts has a warm feel for her characters and an eye for the evocative detail."

—*Chicago Tribune*

"Roberts' bestselling novels are some of the best in the romance genre. They are thoughtfully plotted, well-written stories featuring fascinating characters."

—*USA TODAY*

"America's favorite writer."

—*The New Yorker*

"Nora Roberts is among the best."

—*The Washington Post*

NORA ROBERTS

THE COMING STORM

SILHOUETTE™

The Coming Storm

ISBN-13: 978-1-335-83222-1

Recycling programs
for this product may
not exist in your area.

Copyright © 2020 by Harlequin Books S.A.

The Welcoming
First published in 1989. This edition published in 2020.
Copyright © 1989 by Nora Roberts

The Art of Deception
First published in 1986. This edition published in 2020.
Copyright © 1986 by Nora Roberts

This edition published by arrangement with Harlequin Books S.A.

For questions and comments about the quality of this book,
please contact us at CustomerService@Harlequin.com.

Silhouette
22 Adelaide St. West, 40th Floor
Toronto, Ontario M5H 4E3, Canada
www.Harlequin.com

Printed in U.S.A.

CONTENTS

THE WELCOMING

For my friend Catherine Coulter,
because she's always good for a laugh.

Chapter 1

Everything he needed was in the backpack slung over his shoulders. Including his .38. If things went well he would have no use for it.

Roman drew a cigarette out of the crumpled pack in his breast pocket and turned away from the wind to light it. A boy of about eight raced along the rail of the ferry, cheerfully ignoring his mother's calls. Roman felt a tug of empathy for the kid. It was cold, certainly. The biting wind off Puget Sound was anything but springlike. But it was one hell of a view. Sitting in the glass-walled lounge would be cozier, but it was bound to take something away from the experience.

The kid was snatched by a blonde woman with pink cheeks and a rapidly reddening nose. Roman listened to them grumble at each other as she dragged the boy back inside. Families, he thought, rarely agreed on anything. Turning away, he leaned over the rail, lazily smoking as the ferry steamed by clumpy islands.

They had left the Seattle skyline behind, though the mountains of mainland Washington still rose up to amaze and impress the viewer. There was an aloneness here, despite the smattering of hardy passengers walking the slanting deck or bundling up in the patches of sunlight along wooden benches. He preferred the city, with its pace, its crowds, its energy. Its anonymity. He always had. For the life of him, he couldn't understand where this restless discontent he felt had come from, or why it was weighing so heavily on him.

The job. For the past year he'd been blaming it on the job. The pressure was something he'd always accepted, even courted. He'd always thought life without it would be bland and pointless. But just lately it hadn't been enough. He moved from place to place, taking little away, leaving less behind.

Time to get out, he thought as he watched a fishing boat chug by. Time to move on. And do what? he wondered in disgust, blowing out a stream of smoke. He could go into business for himself. He'd toyed with that notion a time or two. He could travel. He'd already been around the world, but it might be different to do it as a tourist.

Some brave soul came out on deck with a video camera. Roman turned, shifted, eased out of range. It was in all likelihood an unnecessary precaution; the move was instinctive. So was the watchfulness, and so was the casual stance, which hid a wiry readiness.

No one paid much attention to him, though a few of the women looked twice.

He was just over average height, with the taut, solid build of a lightweight boxer. The slouchy jacket and worn jeans hid well-toned muscles. He wore no hat and his thick black hair flew freely away from his tanned, hollow-cheeked face. It was unshaven, tough-featured. The eyes, a pale, clear green, might have softened the go-to-hell appearance, but they were intense, direct and, at the moment, bored.

It promised to be a slow, routine assignment.

Roman heard the docking call and shifted his pack. Routine or not, the job was his. He would get it done, file his report, then take a few weeks to figure out what he wanted to do with the rest of his life.

He disembarked with the smattering of other walking passengers. There was a wild, sweet scent of flowers now that competed with the darker scent of the water. The flowers grew in free, romantic splendor, many with blossoms as big as his fist. Some part of him appreciated their color and their charm, but he rarely took the time to stop and smell the roses.

Cars rolled off the ramp and cruised toward home or a day of sightseeing. Once the car decks were unloaded, the new passengers would board and set off for one of the other islands or for the longer, colder trip to British Columbia.

Roman pulled out another cigarette, lit it and took a casual look around—at the pretty, colorful gardens, the charming white hotel and restaurant, the signs that gave information on ferries and parking. It was all a matter of timing now. He ignored the patio café, though he would have dearly loved a cup of coffee, and wound his way to the parking area.

He spotted the van easily enough, the white-and-blue American model with Whale Watch Inn painted on the side. It was his job to talk himself onto the van and into the inn. If the details had been taken care of on this end, it would be routine. If not, he would find another way.

Stalling, he bent down to tie his shoe. The waiting cars were being loaded, and the foot passengers were already on deck. There were no more than a dozen vehicles in the parking area now, including the van. He was taking another moment to unbutton his jacket when he saw the woman.

Her hair was pulled back in a braid, not loose as it had been in the file picture. It seemed to be a deeper, richer blond in the sunlight. She wore tinted glasses, big-framed amber lenses that obscured half of her face, but he knew he wasn't mistaken. He could see the delicate line of her jaw, the small, straight nose, the full, shapely mouth.

His information was accurate. She was five-five, a hundred and ten pounds, with a small, athletic build. Her dress was casual—jeans, a chunky cream-colored cable-knit sweater over a blue shirt. The shirt would match her eyes. The jeans were tucked into suede ankle boots, and a pair of slim crystal earrings dangled at her ears.

She walked with a sense of purpose, keys jingling in one hand, a big canvas bag slung over her other shoulder. There was nothing flirtatious about the walk, but a man would notice it. Long, limber strides, a subtle swing at the hips, head up, eyes ahead.

Yeah, a man would notice, Roman thought as he flicked the cigarette away. He figured she knew it.

He waited until she reached the van before he started toward her.

Charity stopped humming the finale of Beethoven's *Ninth,* looked down at her right front tire and swore. Because she didn't think anyone was watching, she kicked it, then moved around to the back of the van to get the jack.

"Got a problem?"

She jolted, nearly dropped the jack on her foot, then whirled around.

A tough customer. That was Charity's first thought as she stared at Roman. His eyes were narrowed against the sun. He had one hand hooked around the strap of his backpack and the other tucked in his pocket. She put her own hand on her heart, made certain it was still beating, then smiled.

"Yes. I have a flat. I just dropped a family of four off for the ferry, two of whom were under six and candidates for reform school. My nerves are shot, the plumbing's on the fritz in unit 6, and my handyman just won the lottery. How are you?"

The file hadn't mentioned that she had a voice like café au lait, the rich, dark kind you drank in New Orleans. He noted that, filed it away, then nodded toward the flat. "Want me to change it?"

Charity could have done it herself, but she wasn't one to refuse help when it was offered. Besides, he could probably do it faster, and he looked as though he could use the five dollars she would give him.

"Thanks." She handed him the jack, then dug a

lemon drop out of her bag. The flat was bound to eat up the time she'd scheduled for lunch. "Did you just come in on the ferry?"

"Yeah." He didn't care for small talk, but he used it, and her friendliness, as handily as he used the jack. "I've been doing some traveling. Thought I'd spend some time on Orcas, see if I can spot some whales."

"You've come to the right place. I saw a pod yesterday from my window." She leaned against the van, enjoying the sunlight. As he worked, she watched his hands. Strong, competent, quick. She appreciated someone who could do a simple job well. "Are you on vacation?"

"Just traveling. I pick up odd jobs here and there. Know anyone looking for help?"

"Maybe." Lips pursed, she studied him as he pulled off the flat. He straightened, keeping one hand on the tire. "What kind of work?"

"This and that. Where's the spare?"

"Spare?" Looking into his eyes for more than ten seconds was like being hypnotized.

"Tire." The corner of his mouth quirked slightly in a reluctant smile. "You need one that isn't flat."

"Right. The spare." Shaking her head at her own foolishness, she went to get it. "It's in the back." She turned and bumped into him. "Sorry."

He put one hand on her arm to steady her. They stood for a moment in the sunlight, frowning at each other. "It's all right. I'll get it."

When he climbed into the van, Charity blew out a long, steadying breath. Her nerves were more ragged than she'd have believed possible. "Oh, watch out for the—" She grimaced as Roman sat back on his heels and peeled the remains of a cherry lollipop from his knee. Her laugh was spontaneous and as rich as her voice. "Sorry. A souvenir of Orcas Island from Jimmy 'The Destroyer' MacCarthy, a five-year-old delinquent."

"I'd rather have a T-shirt."

"Yes, well, who wouldn't?" Charity took the sticky mess from him, wrapped it in a tattered tissue and dropped it into her bag. "We're a family establishment," she explained as he climbed out with the spare. "Mostly everyone enjoys having children around, but once in a while you get a pair like Jimmy and Judy, the twin ghouls from Walla Walla, and you think about turning the place into a service station. Do you like children?"

He glanced up as he slipped the tire into place. "From a safe distance."

She laughed appreciatively at his answer. "Where are you from?"

"St. Louis." He could have chosen a dozen places. He couldn't have said why he'd chosen to tell the truth. "But I don't get back much."

"Family?"

"No."

The way he said it made her stifle her innate curiosity. She wouldn't invade anyone's privacy any more than she would drop the lint-covered lollipop on the ground. "I was born right here on Orcas. Every year I tell myself I'm going to take six months and travel. Anywhere." She shrugged as he tightened the last of the lug nuts. "I never seem to manage it. Anyway, it's beautiful here. If you don't have a deadline, you may find yourself staying longer than you planned."

"Maybe." He stood up to replace the jack. "If I can find some work, and a place to stay."

Charity didn't consider it an impulse. She had studied, measured and considered him for nearly fifteen minutes. Most job interviews took little more. He had a strong back and intelligent—if disconcerting—eyes, and if the state of his pack and his shoes was any indication he was down on his luck. As her name implied, she had been taught to offer people a helping hand. And if she could solve one of her more immediate and pressing problems at the same time...

"You any good with your hands?" she asked him.

He looked at her unable to prevent his mind from taking a slight detour. "Yeah. Pretty good."

Her brow—and her blood pressure—rose a little when she saw his quick survey. "I mean with tools. Hammer, saw, screwdriver. Can you do any carpentry, household repairs?"

"Sure." It was going to be easy, almost too easy. He wondered why he felt the small, unaccustomed tug of guilt.

"Like I said, my handyman won the lottery, a big one. He's gone to Hawaii to study bikinis and eat poi. I'd wish him well, except we were in the middle of renovating the west wing. Of the inn," she added, pointing to the logo on the van. "If you know your way around two-by-fours and drywall I can give you room and board and five an hour."

"Sounds like we've solved both our problems."

"Great." She offered a hand. "I'm Charity Ford."

"DeWinter." He clasped her hand. "Roman DeWinter."

"Okay, Roman." She swung her door open. "Climb aboard."

She didn't look gullible, Roman thought as he settled into the seat beside her. But then, he knew—better than most—that looks were deceiving. He was exactly where he wanted to be, and he hadn't had to resort to a song and dance. He lit a cigarette as she pulled out of the parking lot.

"My grandfather built the inn in 1938," she said, rolling down her window. "He added on to it a couple of times over the years, but it's still really an inn. We can't bring ourselves to call it a resort, even in the brochures. I hope you're looking for remote."

"That suits me."

"Me too. Most of the time." Talkative guy, she mused with a half smile. But that was all right. She could talk enough for both of them. "It's early in the season yet, so we're a long way from full." She cocked her elbow on the opened window and cheerfully took over the bulk of the conversation. The sunlight played on her earrings and refracted into brilliant colors. "You should have plenty of free time to knock around. The view from Mount Constitution's really spectacular. Or, if you're into it, the hiking trails are great."

"I thought I might spend some time in B.C."

"That's easy enough. Take the ferry to Sidney. We do pretty well with tour groups going back and forth."

"We?"

"The inn. Pop—my grandfather—built a half-dozen cabins in the sixties. We give a special package rate to tour groups. They can rent the cabins and have breakfast and dinner included. They're a little rustic, but the tourists really go for them. We get a group about once a week. During the season we can triple that."

She turned onto a narrow, winding road and kept the speed at fifty.

Roman already knew the answers, but he knew it might seem odd if he didn't ask the questions. "Do you run the inn?"

"Yeah. I've worked there on and off for as long as I can remember. When my grandfather died a couple of years ago I took over." She paused a moment. It still hurt; she supposed it always would. "He loved it. Not just the place, but the whole idea of meeting new people every day, making them comfortable, finding out about them."

"I guess it does pretty well."

She shrugged. "We get by." They rounded a bend where the forest gave way to a wide expanse of blue water. The curve of the island was clear, jutting out and tucking back in contrasting shades of deep green and brown. A few houses were tucked high in the cliffs beyond. A boat with billowing white sails ran with the wind, rippling the glassy water. "There are views like this all around the island. Even when you live here they dazzle you."

"And scenery's good for business."

She frowned a little. "It doesn't hurt," she said, and glanced back at him. "Are you really interested in seeing whales?"

"It seemed like a good idea since I was here."

She stopped the van and pointed to the cliffs. "If you've got patience and a good set of binoculars, up there's a good bet. We've spotted them from the inn, as I said. Still, if you want a close look, your best bet's out on a boat." When he didn't comment, she started the van again. He was making her jittery, she realized. He seemed to be looking not at the water or the forest but at her.

Roman glanced at her hands. Strong, competent, no-nonsense hands, he decided, though the fingers were beginning to tap a bit nervously on the wheel. She continued to drive fast, steering the van easily through the switchbacks. Another car approached. Without slackening speed, Charity lifted a hand in a salute.

"That was Lori, one of our waitresses. She works an early shift so she can be home when her kids get back from school. We usually run with a staff of ten, then add on five or six part-time during the summer."

They rounded the next curve, and the inn came into view. It was exactly what he'd expected, and yet it was more charming than the pictures he'd been shown. It was white clapboard, with weathered blue trim around arched and oval windows. There were fanciful turrets, narrow walkways and a wide skirting porch. A sweep of lawn led directly to the water, where a narrow, rickety dock jutted out. Tied to it was a small motorboat that swung lazily in the current.

A mill wheel turned in a shallow pond at the side of the inn, slapping the water musically. To the west, where the trees began to thicken, he could make out one of the cabins she had spoken of. Flowers were everywhere.

"There's a bigger pond out back." Charity drove around the side and pulled into a small graveled lot that was already half full. "We keep the trout there. The trail takes you to cabins 1, 2 and 3. Then it forks off to 4, 5 and 6." She stepped out and waited for him to join her. "Most everyone uses the back entrance. I can show you around the grounds later, if you like, but we'll get you settled in first."

"It's a nice place." He said it almost without thinking, and he meant it. There were two rockers on the square back porch, and an adirondack chair that needed its white paint freshened. Roman turned to study the view a guest would overlook from the empty seat. Part forest, part water, and very appealing. Restful. Welcoming. He thought of the pistol in his backpack. Appearances, he thought again, were deceiving.

With a slight frown, Charity watched him. He didn't seem to be looking so much as absorbing. It was an odd thought, but she would have sworn if anyone were to ask him to describe the inn six months later he would be able to, right down to the last pinecone.

Then he turned to her, and the feeling remained, more personal now, more intense. The breeze picked up, jingling the wind chimes that hung from the eaves.

"Are you an artist?" she asked abruptly.

"No." He smiled, and the change in his face was quick and charming. "Why?"

"Just wondering." You'd have to be careful of that smile, Charity decided. It made you relax, and she doubted he was a man it was wise to relax around.

The double glass doors opened up into a large, airy room that smelled of lavender and woodsmoke. There were two long, cushiony sofas and a pair of overstuffed chairs near a huge stone fireplace where logs crackled. Antiques were scattered throughout the room—a desk and chair with a trio of old inkwells, an oak hat-rack, a buffet with glossy carved doors. Tucked into a corner was a spinet with yellowing keys and the pair of wide arched windows that dominated the far wall made the water seem part of the room's decor. At a table near them, two women were playing a leisurely game of Scrabble.

"Who's winning today?" Charity asked.

Both looked up. And beamed. "It's neck and neck." The woman on the right fluffed her hair when she spotted Roman. She was old enough to be his grandmother, but she slipped her glasses off and straightened her thin shoulders. "I didn't realize you were bringing back another guest, dear."

"Neither did I." Charity moved over to add another log to the fire. "Roman DeWinter, Miss Lucy and Miss Millie."

His smile came again, smoothly. "Ladies."

"DeWinter." Miss Lucy put on her glasses to get a better look. "Didn't we know a DeWinter once, Millie?"

"Not that I recall." Millie, always ready to flirt, continued to beam at Roman, though he was hardly more than a myopic blur. "Have you been to the inn before, Mr. DeWinter?"

"No, ma'am. This is my first time in the San Juans."

"You're in for a treat." Millie let out a little sigh. It was really too bad what the years did. It seemed only yesterday that handsome young men had kissed her hand and asked her to go for a walk. Today they called her ma'am. She went wistfully back to her game.

"The ladies have been coming to the inn longer than I can remember," Charity told Roman as she led the way down a hall. "They're lovely, but I should warn you about Miss Millie. I'm told she had quite a reputation in her day, and she still has an eye for an attractive man."

"I'll watch my step."

"I get the impression you usually do." She took out a set of keys and unlocked the door. "This leads to the west wing." She started down another hall, brisk, businesslike. "As you can see, renovations were well under way before George hit the jackpot. The trim's been stripped." She gestured to the neat piles of wood along the freshly painted wall. "The doors need to be refinished yet, and the original hardware's in that box."

After taking off her sunglasses, she dropped them into her bag. He'd been right. The collar of her shirt matched her eyes almost exactly. He looked into them as she examined George's handiwork.

"How many rooms?"

"There are two singles, a double and a family suite in this wing, all in varying stages of disorder." She skirted a door that was propped against a wall, then walked into a room. "You can take this one. It's as close to being finished as I have in this section."

It was a small, bright room. Its window was bordered with stained glass and looked out over the mill wheel. The bed was stripped, and the floors were bare and in need of sanding. Wallpaper that was obviously new covered the walls from the ceiling down to a white chair rail. Below that was bare drywall.

"It doesn't look like much now," Charity commented.

"It's fine." He'd spent time in places that made the little room look like a suite at the Waldorf.

Automatically she checked the closet and the adjoining bath, making a mental list of what was needed. "You can start in here, if it'll make you more comfortable. I'm not particular. George had his own system. I never understood it, but he usually managed to get things done."

He hooked his thumbs in the front pockets of his jeans. "You got a game plan?"

"Absolutely."

Charity spent the next thirty minutes taking him through the wing and explaining exactly what she wanted. Roman listened, commenting little, and studied the setup. He knew from the blueprints he'd studied that the floor plan of this section mirrored that of the east wing. His position in it would give him easy access to the main floor and the rest of the inn.

He'd have to work, he mused as he looked at the half-finished walls and the paint tarps. He considered it a small bonus. Working with his hands was something he enjoyed and something he'd had little time for in the past.

She was very precise in her instructions. A woman who knew what she wanted and intended to have it. He appreciated that. He had no doubt that she was very good at what she did, whether it was running an inn… or something else.

"What's up there?" He pointed to a set of stairs at the end of the hallway.

"My rooms. We'll worry about them after the guest quarters are done." She jingled the keys as her thoughts went off in a dozen directions. "So, what do you think?"

"About what?"

"About the work."

"Do you have tools?"

"In the shed, the other side of the parking area."

"I can handle it."

"Yes." Charity tossed the keys to him. She was certain he could. They were standing in the octagonal parlor of the family suite. It was empty but for stacks of material and tarps. And it was quiet. She noticed all at once that they were standing quite close together and that she couldn't hear a sound. Feeling foolish, she took a key off her ring.

"You'll need this."

"Thanks." He tucked it in his pocket.

She drew a deep breath, wondering why she felt as though she'd just taken a long step with her eyes closed. "Have you had lunch?"

"No."

"I'll show you down to the kitchen. Mae'll fix you up." She started out, a little too quickly. She wanted to escape from the sensation that she was completely alone with him. And helpless. Charity moved her shoulders restlessly. A stupid thought, she told herself. She'd never been helpless. Still, she felt a breath of relief when she closed the door behind them.

She took him downstairs, through the empty lobby and into a large dining room decorated in pastels. There were small milk-glass vases on each table, with a handful of fresh flowers in each. Big windows opened onto a view of the water, and as if carrying through the theme, an aquarium was built into the south wall.

She stopped there for a moment, hardly breaking stride, scanning the room until she was satisfied that the tables were properly set for dinner. Then she pushed through a swinging door into the kitchen.

"And I say it needs more basil."

"I say it don't."

"Whatever you do," Charity murmured under her breath, "don't agree with either of them. Ladies," she said, using her best smile. "I brought you a hungry man."

The woman guarding the pot held up a dripping spoon. The best way to describe her was wide—face, hips, hands. She gave Roman a quick, squint-eyed survey. "Sit down, then," she told him, jerking a thumb in the direction of a long wooden table.

"Mae Jenkins, Roman DeWinter."

"Ma'am."

"And Dolores Rumsey." The other woman was holding a jar of herbs. She was as narrow as Mae was wide. After giving Roman a nod, she began to ease her way toward the pot.

"Keep away from that," Mae ordered, "and get the man some fried chicken."

Muttering, Dolores stalked off to find a plate.

"Roman's going to pick up where George left off," Charity explained. "He'll be staying in the west wing."

"Not from around here." Mae looked at him again, the way he imagined a nanny would look at a small, grubby child.

"No."

With a sniff, she poured him some coffee. "Looks like you could use a couple of decent meals."

"You'll get them here," Charity put in, playing peacemaker. She winced only a little when Dolores slapped a plate of cold chicken and potato salad in front of Roman.

"Needed more dill." Dolores glared at him, as if she were daring him to disagree. "She wouldn't listen."

Roman figured the best option was to grin at her and keep his mouth full. Before Mae could respond, the door swung open again.

"Can a guy get a cup of coffee in here?" The man stopped and sent Roman a curious look.

"Bob Mullins, Roman DeWinter. I hired him to finish the west wing. Bob's one of my many right hands."

"Welcome aboard." He moved to the stove to pour himself a cup of coffee, adding three lumps of sugar as Mae clucked her tongue at him. The sweet tooth didn't seem to have an effect on him. He was tall, perhaps six-two, and he couldn't weigh more than 160. His light brown hair was cut short around his ears and swept back from his high forehead.

"You from back east?" Bob asked between sips of coffee.

"East of here."

"Easy to do." He grinned when Mae flapped a hand to move him away from her stove.

"Did you get that invoice business straightened out with the greengrocer?" Charity asked.

"All taken care of. You got a couple of calls while you were out. And there's some papers you need to sign."

"I'll get to it." She checked her watch. "Now." She glanced over at Roman. "I'll be in the office off the lobby if there's anything you need to know."

"I'll be fine."

"Okay." She studied him for another moment. She couldn't quite figure out how he could be in a room with four other people and seem so alone. "See you later."

Roman took a long, casual tour of the inn before he began to haul tools into the west wing. He saw a young couple who had to be newlyweds locked in an embrace near the pond. A man and a young boy played one-on-one on a small concrete basketball court. The ladies, as he had come to think of them, had left their game to sit on the porch and discuss the garden. Looking exhausted, a family of four pulled up in a station wagon, then trooped toward the cabins. A man in a fielder's cap walked down the pier with a video camera on his shoulder.

There were birds trilling in the trees, and there was the distant sound of a motorboat. He heard a baby crying halfheartedly, and the strains of a Mozart piano sonata.

If he hadn't pored over the data himself he would have sworn he was in the wrong place.

He chose the family suite and went to work, wondering how long it would take him to get into Charity's rooms.

There was something soothing about working with his hands. Two hours passed, and he relaxed a little. A check of his watch had him deciding to take another, unnecessary trip to the shed. Charity had mentioned that wine was served in what she called the gathering room every evening at five. It wouldn't hurt for him to get another, closer look at the inn's guests.

He started out, then stopped by the doorway to his room. He'd heard something, a movement. Cautious, he eased inside the door and scanned the empty room.

Humming under her breath, Charity came out of the bath, where she'd just placed fresh towels. She unfolded linens and began to make the bed.

"What are you doing?"

Muffling a scream, she stumbled backward, then eased down on the bed to catch her breath. "My God, Roman, don't do that."

He stepped into the room, watching her with narrowed eyes. "I asked what you were doing."

"That should be obvious." She patted the pile of linens with her hand.

"You do the housekeeping, too?"

"From time to time." Recovered, she stood up and smoothed the bottom sheet on the bed. "There's soap and towels in the bath," she told him, then tilted her head. "Looks like you can use them." She unfolded the top sheet with an expert flick. "Been busy?"

"That was the deal."

With a murmur of agreement, she tucked up the corners at the foot of the bed the way he remembered his grandmother doing. "I put an extra pillow and blanket in the closet." She moved from one side of the bed to the other in a way that had him watching her with simple male appreciation. He couldn't remember the last time he'd seen anyone make a bed. It stirred thoughts in him that he couldn't afford. Thoughts of what it might be like to mess it up again—with her.

"Do you ever stop?"

"I've been known to." She spread a white wedding-ring quilt on the bed. "We're expecting a tour tomorrow, so everyone's a bit busy."

"Tomorrow?"

"Mmm. On the first ferry from Sidney." She fluffed his pillows, satisfied. "Did you—"

She broke off when she turned and all but fell against him. His hands went to her hips instinctively as hers braced against his shoulders. An embrace—unplanned, unwanted and shockingly intimate.

She was slender beneath the long, chunky sweater, he realized, even more slender than a man might expect. And her eyes were bluer than they had any right to be, bigger, softer. She smelled like the inn, smelled of that welcoming combination of lavender and woodsmoke. Drawn to it, he continued to hold her, though he knew he shouldn't.

"Did I what?" His fingers spread over her hips, drawing her just a fraction closer. He saw the dazed confusion in her eyes; her reaction tugged at him.

She'd forgotten everything. She could only stare, almost stupefied by the sensations that spiked through her. Involuntarily her fingers curled into his shirt. She got an impression of strength, a ruthless strength with the potential for violence. The fact that it excited her left her speechless.

"Do you want something?" he murmured.

"What?"

He thought about kissing her, about pressing his

mouth hard on hers and plunging into her. He would enjoy the taste, the momentary passion. "I asked if you wanted something." Slowly he ran his hands up under her sweater to her waist.

The shock of heat, the press of fingers, brought her back. "No." She started to back away, found herself held still, and fought her rising panic. Before she could speak again, he had released her. Disappointment. That was an odd reaction, she thought, when you'd just missed getting burned.

"I was—" She took a deep breath and waited for her scattered nerves to settle. "I was going to ask if you'd found everything you needed."

His eyes never left hers. "It looks like it."

She pressed her lips together to moisten them. "Good. I've got a lot to do, so I'll let you get back."

He took her arm before she could step away. Maybe it wasn't smart, but he wanted to touch her again. "Thanks for the towels."

"Sure."

He watched her hurry out, knowing her nerves were as jangled as his own. Thoughtfully he pulled out a cigarette. He couldn't remember ever having been thrown off balance so easily. Certainly not by a woman who'd done nothing more than look at him. Still, he made a habit of landing on his feet.

It might be to his advantage to get close to her, to play on the response he'd felt from her. Ignoring a wave of self-disgust, he struck a match.

He had a job to do. He couldn't afford to think about Charity Ford as anything more than a means to an end.

He drew smoke in, cursing the dull ache in his belly.

Chapter 2

It was barely dawn, and the sky to the east was fantastic. Roman stood near the edge of the narrow road, his hands tucked in his back pockets. Though he rarely had time for them, he enjoyed mornings such as this, when the air was cool and sparkling clear. A man could breathe here, and if he could afford the luxury he could empty his mind and simply experience.

He'd promised himself thirty minutes, thirty solitary, soothing minutes. The blooming sunlight pushed through the cloud formations, turning them into wild, vivid colors and shapes. Dream shapes. He considered lighting a cigarette, then rejected it. For the moment he wanted only the taste of morning air flavored by the sea.

There was a dog barking in the distance, a faint yap, yap, yap that only added to the ambience. Gulls, out for an early feeding, swooped low over the water, slicing the silence with their lonely cries. The fragrance of flowers, a celebration of spring, carried delicately on the quiet breeze.

He wondered why he'd been so certain he preferred the rush and noise of cities.

As he stood there he saw a deer come out of the trees and raise her head to scent the air. That was freedom, he thought abruptly. To know your place and to be content with it. The doe cleared the trees, picking her way delicately toward the high grass. Behind her came a gangly fawn. Staying upwind, Roman watched them graze.

He was restless. Even as he tried to absorb and accept the peace around him he felt the impatience struggling through. This wasn't his place. He had no place. That was one of the things that made him so perfect for his job. No roots, no family, no woman waiting for his return. That was the way he wanted it.

But he'd felt enormous satisfaction in doing the carpentry the day before, in leaving his mark on something that would last. All the better for his cover, he told himself. If he showed some skill and some care in the work he would be accepted more easily.

He was already accepted.

She trusted him. She'd given him a roof and a meal and a job, thinking he needed all three. She seemed to have no guile in her. Something had simmered between them the evening before, yet she had done nothing to provoke or prolong it. She hadn't—though he knew all females were capable of it from birth—issued a silent invitation that she might or might not have intended to keep.

She'd simply looked at him, and everything she felt had been almost ridiculously clear in her eyes.

He couldn't think of her as a woman. He couldn't think of her as ever being *his* woman.

He felt the urge for a cigarette again, and this time he deliberately suppressed it. If there was something you wanted that badly, it was best to pass it by. Once you gave in, you surrendered control.

He'd wanted Charity. For one brief, blinding instant the day before, he had craved her. A very serious error. He'd blocked the need, but it had continued to surface—when he'd heard her come into the wing for the night, when he'd listened to the sound of Chopin drifting softly down the stairway from her rooms. And again in the middle of the night, when he'd awakened to the deep country silence, thinking of her, imagining her.

He didn't have time for desires. In another place, at another time, they might have met and enjoyed each other for as long as enjoyments lasted. But now she was part of an assignment—nothing less, nothing more.

He heard the sound of running footsteps and tensed instinctively. The deer, as alert as he, lifted her head, then sprinted back into the trees with her young. His weapon was strapped just above his ankle, more out of habit than necessity, but he didn't reach for it. If he needed it it could be in his hand in under a second. Instead, he waited, braced, to see who was running down the deserted road at dawn.

Charity was breathing fast, more from the effort

of keeping pace with her dog than from the three-mile run. Ludwig bounded ahead, tugged to the right, jerked to the left, tangled and untangled in the leash. It was a daily routine, one that both of them were accustomed to. She could have controlled the little golden cocker, but she didn't want to spoil his fun. Instead, she swerved with him, adjusting her pace from a flat-out run to an easy jog and back again.

She hesitated briefly when she saw Roman. Then, because Ludwig sprinted ahead, she tightened her grip on the leash and kept pace.

"Good morning," she called out, then skidded to a halt when Ludwig decided to jump on Roman's shins and bark at him. "He doesn't bite."

"That's what they all say." But he grinned and crouched down to scratch between the dog's ears. Ludwig immediately collapsed, rolled over and exposed his belly for rubbing. "Nice dog."

"A nice spoiled dog," Charity added. "I have to keep him fenced because of the guests, but he eats like a king. You're up early."

"So are you."

"I figure Ludwig deserves a good run every morning, since he's so understanding about being fenced."

To show his appreciation, Ludwig raced once around Roman, tangling his lead around his legs.

"Now if I could only get him to understand the concept of a leash." She stooped to untangle Roman and to control the now-prancing dog.

Her light jacket was unzipped, exposing a snug T-shirt darkened with sweat between her breasts. Her hair, pulled straight, almost severely, back from her face, accented her bone structure. Her skin seemed almost translucent as it glowed from her run. He had an urge to touch it, to see how it felt under his fingertips. And to see if that instant reaction would rush out again.

"Ludwig, be still a minute." She laughed and tugged at his collar.

In response, the dog jumped up and lapped at her face. "He listens well," Roman commented.

"You can see why I need the fence. He thinks he can play with everyone." Her hand brushed Roman's leg as she struggled with the leash.

When he took her wrist, both of them froze.

He could feel her pulse skip, then sprint. It was a quick, vulnerable response that was unbearably arousing. Though it cost him, he kept his fingers loose. He had only meant to stop her before she inadvertently found his weapon. Now they crouched, knee to knee, in the center of the deserted road, with the dog trying to nuzzle between them.

"You're trembling." He said it warily, but he didn't release her. "Do you always react that way when a man touches you?"

"No." Because it baffled her, she kept still and waited to see what would happen next. "I'm pretty sure this is a first."

It pleased him to hear it, and it annoyed him, because he wanted to believe it. "Then we'll have to be careful, won't we?" He released her, then stood up.

More slowly, because she wasn't sure of her balance, she rose. He was angry. Though he was holding on to his temper, it was clear enough to see in his eyes. "I'm not very good at being careful."

His gaze whipped back to hers. There was a fire in it, a fire that raged and then was quickly and completely suppressed. "I am."

"Yes." The brief, heated glance had alarmed her, but Charity had always held her own. She tilted her head to study him. "I think you'd have to be, with that streak of violence you have to contend with. Who are you mad at, Roman?"

He didn't like to be read that easily. Watching her, he lowered a hand to pet Ludwig, who was resting his front paws on his knees. "Nobody at the moment," he told her, but it was a lie. He was furious—with himself.

She only shook her head. "You're entitled to your secrets, but I can't help wondering why you'd be angry with yourself for responding to me."

He took a lazy scan of the road, up, then down. They might have been alone on the island. "Would you like me to do something about it, here and now?"

He could, she realized. And he would. If he was pushed too far he would do exactly what he wanted, when he wanted. The frisson of excitement that passed through her annoyed her. Macho types were for other women, different women—not Charity Ford. Deliberately she looked at her watch.

"Thanks. I'm sure that's a delightful offer, but I have to get back and set up for breakfast." Struggling with the dog, she started off at what she hoped was a dignified walk. "I'll let you know if I can squeeze in, say, fifteen minutes later."

"Charity?"

She turned her head and aimed a cool look. "Yes?"

"Your shoe's untied."

She just lifted her chin and continued on.

Roman grinned at her back and tucked his thumbs in his pockets. Yes, indeed, the woman had one hell of a walk. It was too damn bad all around that he was beginning to like her.

He was interested in the tour group. It was a simple matter for Roman to loiter on the first floor, lingering over a second cup of coffee in the kitchen, passing idle conversation with the thick-armed Mae and the skinny Dolores. He hadn't expected to be put to work, but when he'd found himself with an armful of table linens he had made the best of it.

Charity, wearing a bright red sweatshirt with the inn's logo across the chest, meticulously arranged a folded napkin in a water glass. Roman waited a moment, watching her busy fingers smoothing and tapering the cloth.

"Where do you want these?"

She glanced over, wondering if she should still be annoyed with him, then decided against it. At the moment she needed every extra hand she could get. "On the tables would be a good start. White on the bottom, apricot on top, slanted. Okay?" She indicated a table that was already set.

"Sure." He began to spread the cloths. "How many are you expecting?"

"Fifteen on the tour." She held a glass up to the light and placed it on the table only after a critical inspection. "Their breakfast is included. Plus the guests already registered. We serve between seven-thirty and ten." She checked her watch, satisfied, then moved to another table. "We get some drop-ins, as well." After setting a chipped bread plate aside, she reached for another. "But it's lunch and dinner that really get hectic."

Dolores swooped in with a stack of china, then dashed out again when Mae squawked at her. Before the door had swung closed, the waitress they had passed on the road the day before rushed out with a tray of clanging silverware.

"Right," Roman murmured.

Charity rattled off instructions to the waitress, finished setting yet another table, then rushed over to a blackboard near the doorway and began to copy out the morning menu in a flowing, elegant hand.

Dolores, whose spiky red hair and pursed lips made Roman think of a scrawny chicken, shoved through the swinging door and set her fists on her skinny hips. "I don't have to take this, Charity."

Charity calmly continued to write. "Take what?"

"I'm doing the best that I can, and you know I told you I was feeling poorly."

Dolores was always feeling poorly, Charity thought as she added a ham-and-cheese omelet to the list. Especially when she didn't get her way. "Yes, Dolores."

"My chest's so tight that I can hardly take a breath."

"Um-hmm."

"Was up half the night, but I come in, just like always."

"And I appreciate it, Dolores. You know how much I depend on you."

"Well." Slightly mollified, Dolores tugged at her apron. "I guess I can be counted on to do my job, but you can just tell that woman in there—" She jerked a thumb toward the kitchen. "Just tell her to get off my back."

"I'll speak to her, Dolores. Just try to be patient. We're all a little frazzled this morning, with Mary Alice out sick again."

"Sick." Dolores sniffed. "Is that what they're calling it these days?"

Listening with only half an ear, Charity continued to write. "What do you mean?"

"Don't know why her car was in Bill Perkin's driveway all night again if she's sick. Now, with my condition—"

Charity stopped writing. Roman's brow lifted when he heard the sudden thread of steel in her voice. "We'll talk about this later, Dolores."

Deflated, Dolores poked out her lower lip and stalked back into the kitchen.

Storing her anger away, Charity turned to the waitress. "Lori?"

"Almost ready."

"Good. If you can handle the registered guests, I'll be back to give you a hand after I check the tour group in."

"No problem."

"I'll be at the front desk with Bob." Absently she pushed her braid behind her back. "If it gets too busy, send for me. Roman—"

"Want me to bus tables?"

She gave him a quick, grateful smile. "Do you know how?"

"I can figure it out."

"Thanks." She checked her watch, then rushed out.

He hadn't expected to enjoy himself, but it was hard not to, with Miss Millie flirting with him over her raspberry preserves. The scent of baking—something rich, with apples and cinnamon—the quiet strains of classical music and the murmur of conversation made it almost impossible not to relax. He carried trays to and from the kitchen. The muttered exchanges between Mae and Dolores were more amusing than annoying.

So he enjoyed himself. And took advantage of his position by doing his job.

As he cleared the tables by the windows, he watched a tour van pull up to the front entrance. He counted heads and studied the faces of the group. The guide was a big man in a white shirt that strained across his shoulders. He had a round, ruddy, cheerful face that smiled continually as he piloted his passengers inside. Roman moved across the room to watch them mill around in the lobby.

They were a mix of couples and families with small children. The guide—Roman already knew his name was Block—greeted Charity with a hearty smile and then handed her a list of names.

Did she know that Block had done a stretch in Leavenworth for fraud? he wondered. Was she aware that the man she was joking with had escaped a second term only because of some fancy legal footwork?

Roman's jaw tensed as Block reached over and flicked a finger at Charity's dangling gold earring.

As she assigned cabins and dealt out keys, two of the group approached the desk to exchange money. Fifty for one, sixty for the other, Roman noted as Canadian bills were passed to Charity's assistant and American currency passed back.

Within ten minutes the entire group was seated in the dining room, contemplating breakfast. Charity breezed in behind them, putting on an apron. She flipped open a pad and began to take orders.

She didn't look as if she were in a hurry, Roman noted. The way she chatted and smiled and answered questions, it was as though she had all the time in the world. But she moved like lightning. She carried three plates on her right arm, served coffee with her left hand and cooed over a baby, all at the same time.

Something was eating at her, Roman mused. It hardly showed…just a faint frown between her eyes. Had something gone wrong that morning that he'd missed? If there was a glitch in the system, it was up to him to find it and exploit it. That was the reason he was here on the inside.

Charity poured another round of coffee for a table of four, joked with a bald man wearing a paisley tie, then made her way over to Roman.

"I think the crisis has passed." She smiled at him, but again he caught something…. Anger? Disappointment?

"Is there anything you don't do around here?"

"I try to stay out of the kitchen. The restaurant has a three-star rating." She glanced longingly at the coffeepot. There would be time for that later. "I want to thank you for pitching in this morning."

"That's okay." He discovered he wanted to see her smile. Really smile. "The tips were good. Miss Millie slipped me a five."

She obliged him. Her lips curved quickly, and whatever had clouded her eyes cleared for a moment. "She likes the way you look in a tool belt. Why don't you take a break before you start on the west wing?"

"All right."

She grimaced at the sound of glass breaking. "I didn't think the Snyder kid wanted that orange juice." She hurried off to clean up the mess and listen to the parents' apologies.

The front desk was deserted. Roman decided that Charity's assistant was either shut up in the side office or out hauling luggage to the cabins. He considered slipping behind the desk and taking a quick look at the books but decided it could wait. Some work was better done in the dark.

An hour later Charity let herself into the west wing. She'd managed to hold on to her temper as she'd passed the guests on the first floor. She'd smiled and chatted with an elderly couple playing Parcheesi in the gathering room. But when the door closed behind her she let loose with a series of furious, pent-up oaths. She wanted to kick something.

Roman stepped into a doorway and watched her stride down the hall. Anger had made her eyes dark and brilliant.

"Problem?"

"Yes," she snapped. She stalked half a dozen steps past him, then whirled around. "I can take incompetence, and even some degree of stupidity. I can even tolerate an occasional bout of laziness. But I won't be lied to."

Roman waited a beat. Her anger was ripe and rich,

but it wasn't directed at him. "All right," he said, and waited.

"She could have told me she wanted time off, or a different shift. I might have been able to work it out. Instead she lies, calling in sick at the last minute five days out of the last two weeks. I was worried about her." She turned again, then gave in and kicked a door. "I hate being made a fool of. And I *hate* being lied to."

It was a simple matter to put two and two together. "You're talking about the waitress... Mary Alice?"

"Of course." She spun around. "She came begging me for a job three months ago. That's our slowest time, but I felt sorry for her. Now she's sleeping with Bill Perkin—or I guess it's more accurate to say she's not getting any sleep, so she calls in sick. I had to fire her." She let out a breath with a sound like an engine letting off steam. "I get a headache whenever I have to fire anybody."

"Is that what was bothering you all morning?"

"As soon as Dolores mentioned Bill, I knew." Calmer now, she rubbed at the insistent ache between her eyes. "Then I had to get through the check-in and the breakfast shift before I could call and deal with her. She cried." She gave Roman a long, miserable look. "I knew she was going to cry."

"Listen, baby, the best thing for you to do is take some aspirin and forget about it."

"I've already taken some."

"Give it a chance to kick in." Before he realized what he was doing, he lifted his hands and framed her face. Moving his thumbs in slow circles, he massaged her temples. "You've got too much going on in there."

"Where?"

"In your head."

She felt her eyes getting heavy and her blood growing warm. "Not at the moment." She tilted her head back and let her eyes close. Moving on instinct, she stepped forward. "Roman…" She sighed a little as the ache melted out of her head and stirred in the very center of her. "I like the way you look in a tool belt, too."

"Do you know what you're asking for?"

She studied his mouth. It was full and firm, and it would certainly be ruthless on a woman's. "Not exactly." Perhaps that was the appeal, she thought as she stared up at him. She didn't know. But she felt, and what she felt was new and thrilling. "Maybe it's better that way."

"No." Though he knew it was a mistake, he couldn't resist skimming his fingers down to trace her jaw, then her lips. "It's always better to know the consequences before you take the action."

"So we're being careful again."

He dropped his hands. "Yeah."

She should have been grateful. Instead of taking advantage of her confused emotions he was backing off, giving her room. She wanted to be grateful, but she felt only the sting of rejection. He had started it, she thought. Again. And he had stopped it. Again. She was sick and tired of being jolted along according to his whims.

"You miss a lot that way, don't you, Roman? A lot of warmth, a lot of joy."

"A lot of disappointment."

"Maybe. I guess it's harder for some of us to live

our lives aloof from others. But if that's your choice, fine." She drew in a deep breath. Her headache was coming back, doubled. "Don't touch me again. I make it a habit to finish whatever I start." She glanced into the room behind them. "You're doing a nice job here," she said briskly. "I'll let you get back to it."

He cursed her as he sanded the wood for the window trim. She had no right to make him feel guilty just because he wanted to keep his distance. Noninvolvement wasn't just a habit with him; it was a matter of survival. It was self-indulgent and dangerous to move forward every time you were attracted to a woman.

But it was more than attraction, and it was certainly different from anything he'd felt before. Whenever he was near her, his purpose became clouded with fantasies of what it would be like to be with her, to hold her, to make love with her.

And fantasies were all they were, he reminded himself. If things went well he would be gone in a matter of days. Before he was done he might very well destroy her life.

It was his job, he reminded himself.

He saw her, walking out to the van with those long, purposeful strides of hers, the keys jingling in her hand. Behind her were the newlyweds, holding hands, even though each was carrying a suitcase.

She would be taking them to the ferry, he thought. That would give him an hour to search her rooms.

He knew how to go through every inch of a room without leaving a trace. He concentrated first on the obvious—the desk in the small parlor. It was common for people to be careless in the privacy of their own homes. A slip of paper, a scribbled note, a name in an address book, were often left behind for the trained eye to spot.

It was an old desk, solid mahogany with a few rings and scratches. Two of the brass pulls were loose. Like the rest of the room, it was neat and well organized. Her personal papers—insurance documents, bills, correspondence—were filed on the left. Inn business took up the three drawers on the right.

He could see from a quick scan that the inn made a reasonable profit, most of which she funneled directly back into it. New linens, bathroom fixtures, paint. The stove Mae was so territorial about had been purchased only six months earlier.

She took a salary for herself, a surprisingly modest one. He didn't find, even after a more critical study, any evidence of her using any of the inn's finances to ease her own way.

An honest woman, Roman mused. At least on the surface.

There was a bowl of potpourri on the desk, as there was in every room in the inn. Beside it was a framed picture of Charity standing in front of the mill wheel with a fragile-looking man with white hair.

The grandfather, Roman decided, but it was Charity's image he studied. Her hair was pulled back in a ponytail, and her baggy overalls were stained at the knees. From gardening, Roman guessed. She was holding an armful of summer flowers. She looked as if she didn't have a care in the world, but he noted that her free arm was around the old man, supporting him.

He wondered what she had been thinking at that

moment, what she had done the moment after the picture had been snapped. He swore at himself and looked away from the picture.

She left notes to herself: Return wallpaper samples. New blocks for toy chest. Call piano tuner. Get flat repaired.

He found nothing that touched on his reason for coming to the inn. Leaving the desk, he meticulously searched the rest of the parlor.

Then he went into the adjoining bedroom. The bed, a four-poster, was covered with a lacy white spread and plumped with petit-point pillows. Beside it was a beautiful old rocker, its arms worn smooth as glass. In it sat a big purple teddy bear wearing yellow suspenders.

The curtains were romantic priscillas. She'd left the windows open, and the breeze came through billowing them. A woman's room, Roman thought, unrelentingly feminine with its lace and pillows, its fragile scents and pale colors. Yet somehow it welcomed a man, made him wish, made him want. It made him want one hour, one night, in that softness, that comfort.

He crossed the faded handhooked rug and, burying his self-disgust, went through her dresser.

He found a few pieces of jewelry he took to be heirlooms. They belonged in a safe, he thought, annoyed with her. There was a bottle of perfume. He knew exactly how it would smell. It would smell the way her skin did. He nearly reached for it before he caught himself. Perfume wasn't of any interest to him. Evidence was.

A packet of letters caught his eye. From a lover? he

wondered, dismissing the sudden pang of jealousy he felt as ridiculous.

The room was making him crazy, he thought as he carefully untied the slender satin ribbon. It was impossible not to imagine her there, curled on the bed, wearing something white and thin, her hair loose and the candles lit.

He shook himself as he unfolded the first letter. A room with a purple teddy bear wasn't seductive, he told himself.

The date showed him that they had been written when she had attended college in Seattle. From her grandfather, Roman realized as he scanned them. Every one. They were written with affection and humor, and they contained dozens of little stories about daily life at the inn. Roman put them back the way he'd found them.

Her clothes were casual, except for a few dresses hanging in the closet. There were sturdy boots, sneakers spotted with what looked like grass stains and two pairs of elegant heels on either side of fuzzy slippers in the shape of elephants. Like the rest of her rooms, they were meticulously arranged. Even in the closet he didn't find a trace of dust.

Besides an alarm clock and a pot of hand cream she had two books on her nightstand. One was a collection of poetry, the other a murder mystery with a gruesome cover. She had a cache of chocolate in the drawer and Chopin on her small portable stereo. There were candles, dozens of them, burned down to various heights. On one wall hung a seascape in deep, stormy blues and grays. On another was a collection of photos, most taken at the inn, many of her grandfather.

Roman searched behind each one. He discovered that her paint was fading, nothing more.

Her rooms were clean. Roman stood in the center of the bedroom, taking in the scents of candle wax, potpourri and perfume. They couldn't have been cleaner if she'd known they were going to be searched. All he knew after an hour was that she was an organized woman who liked comfortable clothes and Chopin and had a weakness for chocolate and lurid paperback novels.

Why did that make her fascinating?

He scowled and shoved his hands in his pockets, struggling for objectivity as he had never had to struggle before. All the evidence pointed to her being involved in some very shady business. Everything he'd discovered in the last twenty-four hours indicated that she was an open, honest and hardworking woman.

Which did he believe?

He walked toward the door at the far end of the room. It opened onto a postage-stamp-size porch with a long set of stairs that led down to the pond. He wanted to open the door, to step out and breathe in the air, but he turned his back on it and went out the way he had come in.

The scent of her bedroom stayed with him for hours.

Chapter 3

"I told you that girl was no good."

"I know, Mae."

"I told you you were making a mistake taking her on like you did."

"Yes, Mae." Charity bit back a sigh. "You told me."

"You keep taking in strays, you're bound to get bit."

Charity resisted—just barely—the urge to scream. "So you've told me."

With a satisfied grunt, Mae finished wiping off her pride and joy, the eight-burner gas range. Charity might run the inn, but Mae had her own ideas about who was in charge. "You're too softhearted, Charity."

"I thought you said it was hardheaded."

"That too." Because she had a warm spot for her young employer, Mae poured a glass of milk and cut a generous slab from the remains of her double chocolate cake. Keeping her voice brisk, she set both on the table. "You eat this now. My baking always made you feel better as a girl."

Charity took a seat and poked a finger into the icing. "I would have given her some time off."

"I know." Mae rubbed her wide-palmed hand on Charity's shoulder. "That's the trouble with you. You take your name too seriously."

"I hate being made a fool of." Scowling, Charity took a huge bite of cake. Chocolate, she was sure, would be a better cure for her headache than an entire bottle of aspirin. Her guilt was a different matter. "Do you think she'll get another job? I know she's got rent to pay."

"Types like Mary Alice always land on their feet. Wouldn't surprise me if she moved in lock, stock and barrel with that Perkin boy, so don't you be worrying about the likes of her. Didn't I tell you she wouldn't last six months?"

Charity pushed more cake into her mouth. "You told me," she mumbled around it.

"Now then, what about this man you brought home?"

Charity took a gulp of her milk. "Roman DeWinter."

"Screwy name." Mae glanced around the kitchen, surprised and a little disappointed that there was nothing left to do. "What do you know about him?"

"He needed a job."

Mae wiped her reddened hands on the skirt of her apron. "I expect there's a whole slew of pickpockets, cat burglars and mass murderers who need jobs."

"He's not a mass murderer," Charity stated. She

thought she had better reserve judgment on the other occupations.

"Maybe, maybe not."

"He's a drifter." She shrugged and took another bite of the cake. "But I wouldn't say aimless. He knows where he's going. In any case, with George off doing the hula, I needed someone. He does good work, Mae."

Mae had determined that for herself with a quick trip into the west wing. But she had other things on her mind. "He looks at you."

Stalling, Charity ran a fingertip up and down the side of her glass. "Everyone looks at me. I'm always here."

"Don't play stupid with me, young lady. I powdered your bottom."

"Whatever that has to do with anything," Charity answered with a grin. "So he looks?" She moved her shoulders again. "I look back." When Mae arched her brows, Charity just smiled. "Aren't you always telling me I need a man in my life?"

"There's men and there's men," Mae said sagely. "This one's not bad on the eyes, and he ain't afraid of working. But he's got a hard streak in him. That one's been around, my girl, and no mistake."

"I guess you'd rather I spent time with Jimmy Loggerman."

"Spineless worm."

After a burst of laughter, Charity cupped her chin in her hands. "You were right, Mae. I do feel better."

Pleased, Mae untied the apron from around her ample girth. She didn't doubt that Charity was a sensible girl, but she intended to keep an eye on Roman herself. "Good. Don't cut any more of that cake or you'll be up all night with a bellyache."

"Yes'm."

"And don't leave a mess in my kitchen," she added as she tugged on a practical brown coat.

"No, ma'am. Good night, Mae."

Charity sighed as the door rattled shut. Mae's leaving usually signaled the end of the day. The guests would be tucked into their beds or finishing up a late card game. Barring an emergency, there was nothing left for Charity to do until sunrise.

Nothing to do but think.

Lately she'd been toying with the idea of putting in a whirlpool. That might lure a small percentage of the resortgoers. She'd priced a few solarium kits, and in her mind she could already see the sunroom on the inn's south side. In the winter guests could come back from hiking to a hot, bubbling tub and top off the day with rum punch by the fire.

She would enjoy it herself, especially on those rare winter days when the inn was empty and there was nothing for her to do but rattle around alone.

Then there was her long-range plan to add on a gift shop supplied by local artists and craftsmen. Nothing too elaborate, she thought. She wanted to keep things simple, in keeping with the spirit of the inn.

She wondered if Roman would stay around long enough to work on it.

It wasn't wise to think of him in connection with any of her plans. It probably wasn't wise to think of him at all. He was, as she had said herself, a drifter. Men like Roman didn't light in one spot for long.

She couldn't seem to stop thinking about him. Almost from the first moment she'd felt something. Attraction was one thing. He was, after all, an attractive man, in a tough, dangerous kind of way. But there was more. Something in his eyes? she wondered. In his voice? In the way he moved? She toyed with the rest of her cake, wishing she could pin it down. It might simply be that he was so different from herself. Taciturn, suspicious, solitary.

And yet...was it her imagination, or was part of him waiting, to reach out, to grab hold? He needed someone, she thought, though he was probably unaware of it.

Mae was right, she mused. She had always had a weakness for strays and a hard-luck story. But this was different. She closed her eyes for a moment, wishing she could explain, even to herself, why it was so very different.

She'd never experienced anything like the sensations that had rammed into her because of Roman. It was more than physical. She could admit that now. Still, it made no sense. Then again, Charity had always thought that feelings weren't required to make sense.

For a moment out on the deserted road this morning she'd felt emotions pour out of him. They had been almost frightening in their speed and power. Emotions like that could hurt...the one who felt them, the one who received them. They had left her dazed and aching—and wishing, she admitted.

She thought she knew what his mouth would taste like. Not soft, not sweet, but pungent and powerful. When he was ready, he wouldn't ask, he'd take. It worried her that she didn't resent that. She had grown up knowing her own mind, making her own choices. A man like Roman would have little respect for a woman's wishes.

It would be better, much better, for them to keep their relationship—their short-term relationship, she added—on a purely business level. Friendly but careful. She let her chin sink into her hands again. It was a pity she had such a difficult time combining the two.

He watched her toy with the crumbs on her plate. Her hair was loose now and tousled, as if she had pulled it out of the braid and ran impatient fingers through it. Her bare feet were crossed at the ankles, resting on the chair across from her.

Relaxed. Roman wasn't sure he'd ever seen anyone so fully relaxed except in sleep. It was a sharp contrast to the churning energy that drove her during the day.

He wished she were in her rooms, tucked into bed and sleeping deeply. He'd wanted to avoid coming across her at all. That was personal. He needed her out of his way so that he could go through the office off the lobby. That was business.

He knew he should step back and keep out of sight until she retired for the night.

What was it about this quiet scene that was so appealing, so irresistible? The kitchen was warm and the scents of cooking were lingering, pleasantly overlaying those of pine and lemon from Mae's cleaning. There was a hanging basket over the sink that was almost choked with some leafy green plant. Every surface was scrubbed, clean and shiny. The huge refrigerator hummed.

She looked so comfortable, as if she were waiting

for him to come in and sit with her, to talk of small, inconsequential things.

That was crazy. He didn't want any woman waiting for him, and especially not her.

But he didn't step back into the shadows of the dining room, though he could easily have done so. He stepped toward her, into the light.

"I thought people kept early hours in the country."

She jumped but recovered quickly. She was almost used to the silent way he moved. "Mostly. Mae was giving me chocolate and a pep talk. Want some cake?"

"No."

"Just as well. If you had I'd have taken another piece and made myself sick. No willpower. How about a beer?"

"Yeah. Thanks."

She got up lazily and moved to the refrigerator to rattle off a list of brands. He chose one and watched her pour it into a pilsner glass. She wasn't angry, he noted, though she had certainly been the last time they were together. So Charity didn't hold grudges. She wouldn't, Roman decided as he took the glass from her. She would forgive almost anything, would trust everyone and would give more than was asked.

"Why do you look at me that way?" she murmured.

He caught himself, then took a long, thirsty pull on the beer. "You have a beautiful face."

She lifted a brow when he sat down and pulled out a cigarette. After taking an ashtray from a drawer, she sat beside him. "I like to accept compliments whenever I get them, but I don't think that's the reason."

"It's reason enough for a man to look at a woman." He sipped his beer. "You had a busy night."

Let it go, Charity told herself. "Busy enough that I need to hire another waitress fast. I didn't get a chance to thank you for helping out with the dinner crowd."

"No problem. Lose the headache?"

She glanced up sharply. But, no, he wasn't making fun of her. It seemed, though she couldn't be sure why the impression was so strong, that his question was a kind of apology. She decided to accept it.

"Yes, thanks. Getting mad at you took my mind off Mary Alice, and Mae's chocolate cake did the rest." She thought about brewing some tea, then decided she was too lazy to bother. "So, how was your day?"

She smiled at him in an easy offer of friendship that he found difficult to resist and impossible to accept. "Okay. Miss Millie said the door to her room was sticking, so I pretended to sand it."

"And made her day."

He couldn't prevent the smile. "I don't think I've ever been ogled quite so completely before."

"Oh, I imagine you have." She tilted her head to study him from a new angle. "But, with apologies to your ego, in Miss Millie's case it's more a matter of nearsightedness than lust. She's too vain to wear her glasses in front of any male over twenty."

"I'd rather go on thinking she's leering at me," he said. "She said she's been coming here twice a year since '52." He thought that over for a moment, amazed that anyone could return time after time to the same spot.

"She and Miss Lucy are fixtures here. When I was young I thought we were related."

"You been running this place long?"

"Off and on for all of my twenty-seven years." Smiling, she tipped back in her chair. She was a woman who relaxed easily and enjoyed seeing others relaxed. He seemed so now, she thought, with his legs stretched out under the table and a glass in his hand. "You don't really want to hear the story of my life, do you, Roman?"

He blew out a stream of smoke. "I've got nothing to do." And he wanted to hear her version of what he'd read in her file.

"Okay. I was born here. My mother had fallen in love a bit later in life than most. She was nearly forty when she had me, and fragile. There were complications. After she died, my grandfather raised me, so I grew up here at the inn, except for the periods of time when he sent me away to school. I loved this place." She glanced around the kitchen. "In school I pined for it, and for Pop. Even in college I missed it so much I'd ferry home every weekend. But he wanted me to see something else before I settled down here. I was going to travel some, get new ideas for the inn. See New York, New Orleans, Venice. I don't know…." Her words trailed off wistfully.

"Why didn't you?"

"My grandfather was ill. I was in my last year of college when I found out *how* ill. I wanted to quit, come home, but the idea upset him so much I thought it was better to graduate. He hung on for another three years, but it was…difficult." She didn't want to talk about the tears and the terror, or about the exhaustion of running the inn while caring for a near-invalid. "He was the bravest, kindest man I've ever known. He was so much a part of this place that there are still times when I expect to walk into a room and see him checking for dust on the furniture."

He was silent for a moment, thinking as much about what she'd left out as about what she'd told him. He knew her father was listed as unknown—a difficult obstacle anywhere, but especially in a small town. In the last six months of her grandfather's life his medical expenses had nearly driven the inn under. But she didn't speak of those things; nor did he detect any sign of bitterness.

"Do you ever think about selling the place, moving on?"

"No. Oh, I still think about Venice occasionally. There are dozens of places I'd like to go, as long as I had the inn to come back to." She rose to get him another beer. "When you run a place like this, you get to meet people from all over. There's always a story about a new place."

"Vicarious traveling?"

It stung, perhaps because it was too close to her own thoughts. "Maybe." She set the bottle at his elbow, then took her dishes to the sink. Even knowing that she was overly sensitive on this point didn't stop her from bristling. "Some of us are meant to be boring."

"I didn't say you were boring."

"No? Well, I suppose I am to someone who picks up and goes whenever and wherever he chooses. Simple, settled and naive."

"You're putting words in my mouth, baby."

"It's easy to do, *baby,* since you rarely put any there yourself. Turn off the lights when you leave."

He took her arm as she started by in a reflexive movement that he regretted almost before it was done. But it was done, and the sulky, defiant look she sent him began a chain reaction that raced through his system. There were things he could do with her, things he burned to do, that neither of them would ever forget.

"Why are you angry?"

"I don't know. I can't seem to talk to you for more than ten minutes without getting edgy. Since I normally get along with everyone, I figure it's you."

"You're probably right."

She calmed a little. It was hardly his fault that she had never been anywhere. "You've been around a little less than forty-eight hours and I've nearly fought with you three times. That's a record for me."

"I don't keep score."

"Oh, I think you do. I doubt you forget anything. Were you a cop?"

He had to make a deliberate effort to keep his face bland and fingers from tensing. "Why?"

"You said you weren't an artist. That was my first guess." She relaxed, though he hadn't removed his hand from her arm. Anger was something she enjoyed only in fast, brief spurts. "It's the way you look at people, as if you were filing away descriptions and any distinguishing marks. And sometimes when I'm with you I feel as though I should get ready for an interrogation. A writer, then? When you're in the hotel business you get pretty good at matching people with professions."

"You're off this time."

"Well, what are you, then?"

"Right now I'm a handyman."

She shrugged, making herself let it go. "Another trait of hotel people is respecting privacy, but if you turn out to be a mass murderer Mae's never going to let me hear the end of it."

"Generally I only kill one person at a time."

"That's good news." She ignored the suddenly very real anxiety that he was speaking the simple truth. "You're still holding my arm."

"I know."

So this was it, she thought, and struggled to keep her voice. "Should I ask you to let go?"

"I wouldn't bother."

She drew a deep, steadying breath. "All right. What do you want, Roman?"

"To get this out of the way, for both of us."

He rose. Her step backward was instinctive, and much more surprising to her than to him. "I don't think that's a good idea."

"Neither do I." With his free hand, he gathered up her hair. It was soft, as he'd known it would be. Thick and full and so soft that his fingers dived in and were lost. "But I'd rather regret something I did than something I didn't do."

"I'd rather not regret at all."

"Too late." He heard her suck in her breath as he yanked her against him. "One way or the other, we'll both have plenty to regret."

He was deliberately rough. He knew how to be gentle, though he rarely put the knowledge into practice. With her, he could have been. Perhaps because he knew that, he shoved aside any desire for tenderness. He wanted to frighten her, to make certain that when he let her go she would run, run away from him, because he wanted so badly for her to run to him.

Buried deep in his mind was the hope that he could make her afraid enough, repelled enough, to send him packing. If she did, she would be safe from him, and he from her. He thought he could accomplish it quickly. Then, suddenly, it was impossible to think at all.

She tasted like heaven. He'd never believed in heaven, but the flavor was on her lips, pure and sweet and promising. Her hand had gone to his chest in an automatic defensive movement. Yet she wasn't fighting him, as he'd been certain she would. She met his hard, almost brutal kiss with passion laced with trust.

His mind emptied. It was a terrifying experience for a man who kept his thoughts under such stringent control. Then it filled with her, her scent, her touch, her taste.

He broke away—for his sake now, not for hers. He was and had always been a survivor. His breath came fast and raw. One hand was still tangled in her hair, and his other was clamped tight on her arm. He couldn't let go. No matter how he chided himself to release her, to step back and walk away, he couldn't move. Staring at her, he saw his own reflection in her eyes.

He cursed her—it was a last quick denial—before he crushed his mouth to hers again. It wasn't heaven he was heading for, he told himself. It was hell.

She wanted to soothe him, but he never gave her the chance. As before, he sent her rushing into some hot, airless place where there was room only for sensation.

She'd been right. His mouth wasn't soft, it was hard and ruthless and irresistible. Without hesitation, without thought of self-preservation, she opened for him, greedily taking what was offered, selflessly giving what was demanded.

Her back was pressed against the smooth, cool surface of the refrigerator, trapped there by the firm, taut lines of his body. If it had been possible, she would have brought him closer.

His face was rough as it scraped against hers, and she trembled at the thrill of pleasure even that brought her. Desperate now, she nipped at his lower lip, and felt a new rush of excitement as he groaned and deepened an already bottomless kiss.

She wanted to be touched. She tried to murmur this new, compelling need against his mouth, but she managed only a moan. Her body ached. Just the anticipation of his hands running over her was making her shudder.

For a moment their hearts beat against each other in the same wild rhythm.

He tore away, aware that he had come perilously close to a line he didn't dare cross. He could hardly breathe, much less think. Until he was certain he could do both, he was silent.

"Go to bed, Charity."

She stayed where she was, certain that if she took a step her legs would give away. He was still close enough for her to feel the heat radiating from his body. But she looked into his eyes and knew he was already out of reach.

"Just like that?"

Hurt. He could hear it in her voice, and he wished he could make himself believe she had brought it on herself. He reached for his beer but changed his mind when he saw that his hand was unsteady. Only one thing was clear. He had to get rid of her, quickly, before he touched her again.

"You're not the type for quick sex on the kitchen floor."

The color that passion had brought to her cheeks faded. "No. At least I never have been." After taking a deep breath, she stepped forward. She believed in facing facts, even unpleasant ones. "Is that all this would have been, Roman?"

His hand curled into a fist. "Yes," he said. "What else?"

"I see." She kept her eyes on his, wishing she could hate him. "I'm sorry for you."

"Don't be."

"You're in charge of your feelings, Roman, not mine. And I am sorry for you. Some people lose a leg or a hand or an eye. They either deal with that loss or become bitter. I can't see what piece of you is missing, Roman, but it's just as tragic." He didn't answer; she hadn't expected him to. "Don't forget the lights."

He waited until she was gone before he fumbled for a match. He needed time to gain control of his head—and his hands—before he searched the office. What worried him was that it was going to take a great deal longer to gain control of his heart.

Nearly two hours later he hiked a mile and a half to use the pay phone at the nearest gas station. The road was quiet, the tiny village dark. The wind had come up, and it tasted of rain. Roman hoped dispassionately that it would hold off until he was back at the inn.

He placed the call, waited for the connection.

"Conby."

"DeWinter."

"You're late."

Roman didn't bother to check his watch. He knew it was just shy of 3:00 a.m. on the East Coast. "Get you up?"

"Am I to assume that you've established yourself?"

"Yeah, I'm in. Rigging the handyman's lottery ticket cleared the way. Arranging the flat gave me the opening. Miss Ford is…trusting."

"So we were led to believe. Trusting doesn't mean she's not ambitious. What have you got?"

A bad case of guilt, Roman thought as he lit a match. A very bad case. "Her rooms are clean." He paused and held the flame to the tip of his cigarette. "There's a tour group in now, mostly Canadians. A few exchanged money. Nothing over a hundred."

The pause was very brief. "That's hardly enough to make the business worthwhile."

"I got a list out of the office. The names and addresses of the registered guests."

There was another, longer pause, and a rustling sound that told Roman that his contact was searching for writing materials. "Let me have it."

He read them off from the copy he'd made. "Block's the tour guide. He's the regular, comes in once a week for a one-or two-night stay, depending on the package."

"Vision Tours."

"Right."

"We've got a man on that end. You concentrate on Ford and her staff." Roman heard the faint *tap-tap-tap* of Conby's pencil against his pad. "There's no way they can be pulling this off without someone on the inside. She's the obvious answer."

"It doesn't fit."

"I beg your pardon?"

Roman crushed the cigarette under his boot heel. "I said it doesn't fit. I've watched her. I've gone through her personal accounts, damn it. She's got under three thousand in fluid cash. Everything else goes into the place for new sheets and soap."

"I see." The pause again. It was maddening. "I suppose our Miss Ford hasn't heard of Swiss bank accounts."

"I said she's not the type, Conby. It's the wrong angle."

"I'll worry about the angles, DeWinter. You worry about doing your job. I shouldn't have to remind you that it's taken us nearly a year to come close to pinning this thing down. The Bureau wants this wrapped quickly, and that's what I expect from you. If you have a personal problem with this, you'd better let me know now."

"No." He knew personal problems weren't permitted. "You want to waste time, and the taxpayers' money, it's all the same to me. I'll get back to you."

"Do that."

Roman hung up. It made him feel a little better to scowl at the phone and imagine Conby losing a good night's sleep. Then again, his kind rarely did. He'd wake some hapless clerk up at six and have the list run through the computer. Conby would drink his coffee, watch the *Today* show and wait in his comfortable house in the D.C. suburbs for the results.

Grunt work and dirty work were left to others.

That was the way the game was played, Roman reminded himself as he started the long walk back to the inn. But lately, just lately, he was getting very tired of the rules.

Charity heard him come in. Curious, she glanced at the clock after she heard the door close below. It was after one, and the rain had started nearly thirty minutes before with a gentle hissing that promised to gain strength through the night.

She wondered where he had been.

His business, she reminded herself as she rolled over and tried to let the rain lull her to sleep. As long as he did his job, Roman DeWinter was free to come and go as he pleased. If he wanted to walk in the rain, that was fine by her.

How could he have kissed her like that and felt nothing?

Charity squeezed her eyes shut and swore at herself. It was her feelings she had to worry about, not Roman's. The trouble was, she always felt too much. This was one time she couldn't afford that luxury.

Something had happened to her when he'd kissed her. Something thrilling, something that had reached deep inside her and opened up endless possibilities. No, not possibilities, fantasies, she thought, shaking her head. If she were wise she would take that one moment of excitement and stop wanting more. Drifters made poor risks emotionally. She had the perfect example before her.

Her mother had turned to a drifter and had given him her heart, her trust, her body. She had ended up pregnant and alone. She had, Charity knew, pined for him for months. She'd died in the same hospital where her baby had been born, only days later. Betrayed, rejected and ashamed.

Charity had only discovered the extent of the shame after her grandfather's death. He'd kept the diary her mother had written. Charity had burned it, not out of shame but out of pity. She would always think of her mother as a tragic woman who had looked for love and had never found it.

But she wasn't her mother, Charity reminded herself as she lay awake listening to the rain. She was far, far less fragile. Love was what she had been named for, and she had felt its warmth all her life.

Now a drifter had come into her life.

He had spoken of regrets, she remembered. She was afraid that whatever happened—or didn't happen—between them, she would have them.

Chapter 4

The rain continued all morning, soft, slow, steady. It brought a chill, and a gloom that was no less appealing than the sunshine. Clouds hung over the water, turning everything to different shades of gray. Raindrops hissed on the roof and at the windows, making the inn seem all the more remote. Occasionally the wind gusted, rattling the panes.

At dawn Roman had watched Charity, bundled in a hooded windbreaker, take Ludwig out for his morning run. And he had watched her come back, dripping, forty minutes later. He'd heard the music begin to play in her room after she had come in the back entrance. She had chosen something quiet and floating with lots of violins this time. He'd been sorry when it had stopped and she had hurried down the hallway on her way to the dining room.

From his position on the second floor he couldn't hear the bustle in the kitchen below, but he could imagine it. Mae and Dolores would be bickering as waffle or muffin batter was whipped up. Charity would have grabbed a quick cup of coffee before rushing out to help the waitress set up tables and write the morning's menu.

Her hair would be damp, her voice calm as she smoothed over Dolores's daily complaints. She'd smell of the rain. When the early risers wandered down she would smile, greet them by name and make them feel as though they were sharing a meal at an old friend's house.

That was her greatest skill, Roman mused. Making a stranger feel at home.

Could she be as uncomplicated as she seemed? A part of him wanted badly to believe that. Another part of him found it impossible. Everyone had an angle, from the mailroom clerk dreaming of a desk job to the CEO wheeling another deal. She couldn't be any different.

He wouldn't have called the kiss they'd shared uncomplicated. There had been layers to it he couldn't have begun to peel away. It seemed contradictory that such a calm-eyed, smooth-voiced woman could explode with such towering passion. Yet she had. Perhaps her passion was as much a part of the act as her serenity.

It annoyed him. Just remembering his helpless response to her infuriated him. So he made himself dissect it further. If he was attracted to what she seemed to be, that was reasonable enough. He'd lived a solitary and often turbulent life. Though he had chosen to live that way, and certainly preferred it, it wasn't unusual that at some point he would find himself pulled toward a woman who represented everything he had never had. And had never wanted, Roman reminded himself as he tacked up a strip of molding.

He wasn't going to pretend he'd found any answers in Charity. The only answers he was looking for pertained to the job.

For now he would wait until the morning rush was over. When Charity was busy in her office, he would go down and charm some breakfast out of Mae. There was a woman who didn't trust him, Roman thought with a grin. There wasn't a naive bone in her sturdy body. And except for Charity there was no one, he was sure, who knew the workings of the inn better.

Yes, he'd put some effort into charming Mae. And he'd keep some distance between himself and Charity. For the time being.

"You're looking peaked this morning."

"Thank you very much." Charity swallowed a yawn as she poured her second cup of coffee. Peaked wasn't the word, she thought. She was exhausted right down to the bone. Her body wasn't used to functioning on three hours' sleep. She had Roman to thank for that, she thought, and shoved the just-filled cup aside.

"Sit." Mae pointed to the table. "I'll fix you some eggs."

"I haven't got time. I—"

"Sit," Mae repeated, waving a wooden spoon. "You need fuel."

"Mae's right," Dolores put in. "A body can't run on

coffee. You need protein and carbohydrates." She set a blueberry muffin on the table. "Why, if I don't watch my protein intake I get weak as a lamb. 'Course, the doctor don't say, but I think I'm hydroglycemic."

"Hypoglycemic," Charity murmured.

"That's what I said." Dolores decided she liked the sound of it. At the moment, however, it was just as much fun to worry about Charity as it was to worry about herself. "She could use some nice crisp bacon with those eggs, Mae. That's what I think."

"I'm putting it on."

Outnumbered, Charity sat down. The two women could scrap for days, but when they had common cause they stuck together like glue.

"I'm not peaked," she said in her own defense. "I just didn't sleep well last night."

"A warm bath before bed," Mae told her as the bacon sizzled. "Not hot, mind you. Lukewarm."

"With bath salts. Not bubbles or oils," Dolores added as she plunked down a glass of juice. "Good old-fashioned bath salts. Ain't that right, Mae?"

"Couldn't hurt," Mae mumbled, too concerned about Charity to think of an argument. "You've been working too hard, girl."

"I agree," Charity said, because it was easiest that way. "The reason I don't have time for a long, leisurely breakfast is that I have to see about hiring a new waitress so I don't have to work so hard. I put an ad in this morning's paper, so the calls should be coming in."

"Told Bob to cancel the ad," Mae announced, cracking an egg into the pan.

"What? Why?" Charity started to rise. "Damn it,

Mae, if you think I'm going to take Mary Alice back after she—"

"No such thing, and don't you swear at me, young lady."

"Testy." Dolores clucked her tongue. "Happens when you work too hard."

"I'm sorry," Charity mumbled, managing not to grind her teeth. "But, Mae, I was counting on setting up interviews over the next couple of days. I want someone in by the end of the week."

"My brother's girl left that worthless husband of hers in Toledo and came home." Keeping her back to Charity, Mae set the bacon to drain, then poked at the eggs. "She's a good girl, Bonnie is. Worked here a couple of summers while she was in school."

"Yes, I remember. She married a musician who was playing at one of the resorts in Eastsound."

Mae scowled and began to scoop up the eggs. "Saxophone player," she said, as if that explained it all. "She got tired of living out of a van and came home a couple weeks back. Been looking for work."

With a sigh, Charity pushed a hand through her bangs. "Why didn't you tell me before?"

"You didn't need anyone before." Mae set the eggs in front of her. "You need someone now."

Charity glanced over as Mae began wiping off the stove. The cook's heart was as big as the rest of her. "When can she start?"

Mae's lips curved, and she cleared her throat and wiped at a spill with more energy. "Told her to come in this afternoon so's you could have a look at her. Don't expect you to hire her unless she measures up."

"Well, then." Charity picked up her fork. Pleased at the thought of having one job settled, she stretched out her legs and rested her feet on an empty chair. "I guess I've got time for breakfast after all."

Roman pushed through the door and almost swore out loud. The dining room was all but empty. He'd been certain Charity would be off doing one of the dozens of chores she took on. Instead, she was sitting in the warm, fragrant kitchen, much as she had been the night before. With one telling difference, Roman reflected. She wasn't relaxed now.

Her easy smile faded the moment he walked in. Slowly she slipped her feet off the chair and straightened her back. He could see her body tense, almost muscle by muscle. Her fork stopped halfway to her lips. Then she turned slightly away from him and continued to eat. It was, he supposed, as close to a slap in the face as she could manage.

He rearranged his idea about breakfast and gossip in the kitchen. For now he'd make do with coffee.

"Wondered where you'd got to," Mae said as she pulled bacon out of the refrigerator again.

"I didn't want to get in your way." He nodded toward the coffeepot. "I thought I'd take a cup up with me."

"You need fuel." Dolores busied herself arranging a place setting across from Charity. "Isn't that right, Mae? Man can't work unless he has a proper breakfast."

Mae poured a cup. "He looks like he could run on empty well enough."

It was quite true, Charity thought. She knew what time he'd come in the night before, and he'd been up and working when she'd left the wing to oversee the breakfast shift. He couldn't have gotten much more sleep than she had herself, but he didn't look any the worse for wear.

"Meals are part of your pay, Roman." Though her appetite had fled, Charity nipped off a bite of bacon. "I believe Mae has some pancake batter left over, if you'd prefer that to eggs."

It was a cool invitation, so cool that Dolores opened her mouth to comment. Mae gave her a quick poke and a scowl. He accepted the coffee Mae shoved at him and drank it black.

"Eggs are fine." But he didn't sit down. The welcoming feel that was usually so much a part of the kitchen was not evident. Roman leaned against the counter and sipped while Mae cooked beside him.

She wasn't going to feel guilty, Charity told herself, ignoring a chastising look from Dolores. After all, she was the boss, and her business with Roman was…well, just business. But she couldn't bear the long, strained silence.

"Mae, I'd like some petits fours and tea sandwiches this afternoon. The rain's supposed to last all day, so we'll have music and dancing in the gathering room." Because breakfast seemed less and less appealing, Charity pulled a notepad out of her shirt pocket. "Fifty sandwiches should do if we have a cheese tray. We'll set up an urn of tea, and one of hot chocolate."

"What time?"

"At three, I think. Then we can bring out the wine at five for anyone who wants to linger. You can have your niece help out."

She began making notes on the pad.

She looked tired, Roman thought. Pale and heavy-eyed and surprisingly fragile. She'd apparently pulled her hair back in a hasty ponytail when it had still been damp. Little tendrils had escaped as they'd dried. They seemed lighter than the rest, their color more delicate than rich. He wanted to brush them away from her temples and watch the color come back into her cheeks.

"Finish your eggs," Mae told her. Then she nodded at Roman. "Yours are ready."

"Thanks." He sat down, wishing no more fervently than Charity that he was ten miles away.

Dolores began to complain that the rain was making her sinuses swell.

"Pass the salt," Roman murmured.

Charity pushed it in his direction. Their fingers brushed briefly, and she snatched hers away.

"Thanks."

"You're welcome." Charity poked her fork into her eggs. She knew from experience that it would be difficult to escape from the kitchen without cleaning her plate, and she intended to do it quickly.

"Nice day," he said, because he wanted her to look at him again. She did, and pent-up anger was simmering in her eyes. He preferred it, he discovered, to the cool politeness that had been there.

"I like the rain."

"Like I said—" he broke open his muffin "—it's a nice day."

Dolores blew her nose heartily. Amusement curved the corners of Charity's mouth before she managed to suppress it. "You'll find the paint you need—wall, ceiling, trim—in the storage cellar. It's marked for the proper rooms."

"All right."

"The brushes and pans and rollers are down there, too. Everything's on the workbench on the right as you come down the stairs."

"I'll find them."

"Good. Cabin 4 has a dripping faucet."

"I'll look at it."

She didn't want him to be so damn agreeable, Charity thought. She wanted him to be as tense and out of sorts as she was. "The window sticks in unit 2 in the east wing."

He sent her an even look. "I'll unstick it."

"Fine." Suddenly she noticed that Dolores had stopped complaining and was gawking at her. Even Mae was frowning over her mixing bowl. The hell with it, Charity thought as she shoved her plate away. So she was issuing orders like Captain Bligh. She damn well felt like Captain Bligh.

She took a ring of keys out of her pocket. She'd just put them on that morning, having intended to see to the minor chores herself. "Make sure to bring these back to the office when you've finished. They're tagged for the proper doors."

"Yes, ma'am." Keeping his eyes on hers, he dropped the ring into his breast pocket. "Anything else?"

"I'll let you know." She rose, took her plate to the sink and stalked out.

"What got into her?" Dolores wanted to know. "She looked like she wanted to chew somebody's head off."

"She just didn't sleep well." More concerned than

she wanted to let on, Mae set down the mixing bowl in which she'd been creaming butter and sugar. Because she felt like the mother of an ill-mannered child, she picked up the coffeepot and carried it over to Roman. "Charity's not feeling quite herself this morning," she told him as she poured him a second cup. "She's been overworked lately."

"I've got thick skin." But he'd felt the sting. "Maybe she should delegate more."

"Ha! That girl?" Pleased that he hadn't complained, she became more expansive. "It ain't in her. Feels responsible if a guest stubs his toe. Just like her grandpa." Mae added a stream of vanilla to the bowl and went back to her mixing. "Not a thing goes on around here she don't have a finger—more likely her whole hand— in. Except my cooking." Mae's wide face creased in a smile. "I shooed her out of here when she was a girl, and I can shoo her out of here today if need be."

"Girl can't boil water without scorching the pan," Dolores put in.

"She could if she wanted to," Mae said defensively, turning back to Roman with a sniff. "There's no need for her to cook when she's got me, and she's smart enough to know it. Everything else, though, from painting the porch to keeping the books, has to have her stamp on it. She's one who takes her responsibilities to heart."

Roman played out the lead she had offered him. "That's an admirable quality. You've worked for her a long time."

"Between Charity and her grandfather, I've worked

at the inn for twenty-eight years come June." She jerked her head in Dolores's direction. "She's been here eight."

"Nine," Dolores said. "Nine years this month."

"It sounds like when people come to work here they stay."

"You got that right," Mae told him.

"It seems the inn has a loyal, hardworking staff."

"Charity makes it easy." Competently Mae measured out baking powder. "She was just feeling moody this morning."

"She did look a little tired," Roman said slowly, ignoring a pang of guilt. "Maybe she'll rest for a while today."

"Not likely."

"The housekeeping staff seems tight."

"She'll still find a bed to make."

"Bob handles the accounts."

"She'll poke her nose in the books and check every column." There was simple pride in her voice as she sifted flour into the bowl. "Not that she don't trust those who work for her," Mae added. "It would just make her heart stop dead to have a bill paid late or an order mixed up. Thing is, she'd rather blame herself than somebody else if a mistake's made."

"I guess nothing much gets by her."

"By Charity?" With a snicker, Mae plugged in her electric mixer. "She'd know if a napkin came back from the laundry with a stain on it. Watch where you sneeze," she added as Dolores covered her face with a tissue. "Drink some hot water with a squeeze of lemon."

"Hot tea with honey," Dolores said.

"Lemon. Honey'll clog your throat."

"My mother always gave me hot tea with honey," Dolores told her.

They were still arguing about it when Roman slipped out of the kitchen.

He spent most of his time closed off in the west wing. Working helped him think. Though he heard Charity pass in and out a few times, neither of them sought the other's company. He could be more objective, Roman realized, when he wasn't around her.

Mae's comments had cemented his observations and the information that had been made available to him. Charity Ford ran the inn from top to bottom. Whatever went on in it or passed through it was directly under her eye. Logically that meant that she was fully involved with, perhaps in charge of, the operation he had come to destroy.

And yet...what he had said to Conby the night before still held true. It didn't fit.

The woman worked almost around the clock to make the inn a success. He'd seen her do everything from potting geraniums to hauling firewood. And, unless she was an astounding actress, she enjoyed it all.

She didn't seem the type who would want to make money the easy way. Nor did she seem the type who craved all the things easy money could buy. But that was instinct, not fact.

The problem was, Conby ran on facts. Roman had always relied heavily on instinct. His job was to prove her guilt, not her innocence. Yet, in less than two days, his priorities had changed.

It wasn't just a matter of finding her attractive. He had found other women attractive and had brought them down without a qualm. That was justice. One of the few things he believed in without reservation was justice.

With Charity he needed to be certain that his conclusions about her were based on more than the emotions she dragged out of him. Feelings and instincts were different. If a man in his position allowed himself to be swayed by feelings, he was useless.

Then what was it? No matter how long or how hard he thought it through, he couldn't pinpoint one specific reason why he was certain of her innocence. Because it was the whole of it, Roman realized. Her, the inn, the atmosphere that surrounded her. It made him want to believe that such people, such places, existed. And existed untainted.

He was getting soft. A pretty woman, big blue eyes, and he started to think in fairy tales. In disgust, he took the brushes and the paint pans to the sink to clean them. He was going to take a break, from work and from his own rambling thoughts.

In the gathering room, Charity was thinking just as reluctantly of him as she set a stack of records on the table between Miss Millie and Miss Lucy.

"What a lovely idea." Miss Lucy adjusted her glasses and peered at the labels. "A nice old-fashioned tea dance." From one of the units in the east wing came the unrelenting whine of a toddler. Miss Lucy sent a sympathetic glance in the direction of the noise. "I'm sure this will keep everyone entertained."

"It's hard for young people to know what to do with

themselves on a rainy day. It makes them cross. Oh, look." Miss Millie held up a 45. "Rosemary Clooney. Isn't this delightful?"

"Pick out your favorites." Charity gave the room a distracted glance. How could she prepare for a party when all she could think of was the way Roman had looked at her across the breakfast table? "I'm depending on you."

The long buffet and a small server had been cleared off to hold the refreshments. If she could count on Mae—and she always had—they should be coming up from the kitchen shortly.

Would Roman come in? she wondered. Would he hear the music and slip silently into the room? Would he look at her until her heart started to hammer and she forgot there was anything or anyone but him?

She was going crazy, Charity decided. She glanced at her watch. It was a quarter to three. Word had been passed to all the guests, and with luck she would be ready for them when they began to arrive. The ladies were deep in a discussion of Perry Como. Leaving them to it, Charity began to tug on the sofa.

"What are you doing?"

A squeal escaped her, and she cursed Roman in the next breath. "If you keep sneaking around I'm going to take Mae's idea of you being a cat burglar more seriously."

"I wasn't sneaking around. You were so busy huffing and puffing you didn't hear me."

"I wasn't huffing or puffing." She tossed her hair over her shoulder and glared at him. "But I am busy, so if you'd get out of my way—"

She waved a hand at him, and he caught it and held it. "I asked what you were doing."

She tugged, then tugged harder, struggling to control her temper. If he wanted to fight, she thought, she'd be happy to oblige him. "I'm knitting an afghan," she snapped. "What does it look like I'm doing? I'm moving the sofa."

"No, you're not."

She could, when the occasion called for, succeed in being haughty. "I beg your pardon?"

"I said you're not moving the sofa. It's too heavy."

"Thank you for your opinion, but I've moved it before." She lowered her voice when she noticed the interested glances the ladies were giving her. "And if you'd get the hell out of my way I'd move it again."

He stood where he was, blocking her. "You really do have to do everything yourself, don't you?"

"Meaning?"

"Where's your assistant?"

"The computer sprang a leak. Since Bob's better equipped to deal with that, he's playing with components and I'm moving furniture. Now—"

"Where do you want it?"

"I didn't ask you to—" But he'd already moved to the other end of the sofa.

"I said, where do you want it?"

"Against the side wall." Charity hefted her end and tried not to be grateful.

"What else?"

She smoothed down the skirt of her dress. "I've already given you a list of chores."

He hooked a thumb in his pocket as they stood on

either side of the sofa. He had an urge to put his hand over her angry face and give it a nice hard shove. "I've finished them."

"The faucet in cabin 4?"

"It needed a new washer."

"The window in unit 2?"

"A little sanding."

She was running out of steam. "The painting?"

"The first coat's drying." He angled his head. "Want to check it out?"

She blew out a breath. It was difficult to be annoyed when he'd done everything she'd asked. "Efficient, aren't you, DeWinter?"

"That's right. Got your second wind?"

"What do you mean?"

"You looked a little tired this morning." He skimmed a glance over her. The dark plum-colored dress swirled down her legs. Little silver buttons ranged down from the high neck to the hem, making him wonder how long it would take him to unfasten them. There was silver at her ears, as well, a fanciful trio of columns he remembered having seen in her drawer. "You don't now," he added, bringing his eyes back to hers.

She started to breathe again, suddenly aware that she'd been holding her breath since he'd started his survey. Charity reminded herself that she didn't have time to let him—or her feelings for him—distract her.

"I'm too busy to be tired." Relieved, she signaled to a waitress who was climbing the steps with a laden tray. "Just set it on the buffet, Lori."

"Second load's right behind me."

"Great. I just need to—" She broke off when the

first damp guests came through the back door. Giving up, she turned to Roman. If he was going to be in the way anyway, he might as well make himself useful. "I'd appreciate it if you'd roll up the rug and store it in the west wing. Then you're welcome to stay and enjoy yourself."

"Thanks. Maybe I will."

Charity greeted the guests, hung up their jackets, offered them refreshments and switched on the music almost before Roman could store the rug out of sight. Within fifteen minutes she had the group mixing and mingling.

She was made for this, he thought as he watched her. She was made for being in the center of things, for making people feel good. His place had always been on the fringe.

"Oh, Mr. DeWinter." Smelling of lilacs, Miss Millie offered him a cup and saucer. "You must have some tea. Nothing like tea to chase the blues away on a rainy day."

He smiled into her blurred eyes. If even she could see that he was brooding, he'd better watch his step. "Thanks."

"I love a party," she said wistfully as she watched a few couples dance to a bluesy Clooney ballad. "Why, when I was a girl, I hardly thought of anything else. I met my husband at a tea like this. That was almost fifty years ago. We danced for hours."

He would never have considered himself gallant, but she was hard to resist. "Would you like to dance now?"

The faintest of blushes tinted her cheeks. "I'd love to, Mr. DeWinter."

Charity watched Roman lead Miss Millie onto the floor. Her heart softened. She tried to harden it again but found it was a lost cause. It was a sweet thing to do, she thought, particularly since he was anything but a sweet man. She doubted that teas and dreamy little old ladies were Roman's style, but Miss Millie would remember this day for a long time.

What woman wouldn't? Charity mused. To dance with a strong, mysterious man on a rainy afternoon was a memory to be pressed in a book like a red rose. It was undoubtedly fortunate he hadn't asked her. She had already stored away too many memories of Roman. With a sigh, she herded a group of children into the television room and pushed a Disney movie into the VCR.

Roman saw her leave. And he saw her come back.

"That was lovely," Miss Millie told him when the music had stopped.

"What?" Quickly he brought himself back. "My pleasure." Then he made her pleasure complete by kissing her hand. By the time she had walked over to sigh with her sister he had forgotten her and was thinking of Charity.

She was laughing as an older man led her onto the floor. The music had changed. It was up-tempo now, something brisk and Latin. A mambo, he thought. Or a merengue. He wouldn't know the difference. Apparently Charity knew well enough. She moved through the complicated, flashy number as if she'd been dancing all her life.

Her skirt flared, wrapped around her legs, then flared again as she turned. She laughed, her face level and close to her partner's as they matched steps. The first prick of jealousy infuriated Roman and made him feel like a fool. The man Charity was matching steps with was easily old enough to be her father.

By the time the music ended he had managed to suppress the uncomfortable emotion but another had sprung up to take its place. Desire. He wanted her, wanted to take her by the hand and pull her out of that crowded room into someplace dim and quiet where all they would hear was the rain. He wanted to see her eyes go big and unfocused the way they had when he'd kissed her. He wanted to feel the incredible sensation of her mouth softening and heating under his.

"It's an education to watch her, isn't it?"

Roman jerked himself back as Bob eased over to pluck a sandwich from the tray. "What?"

"Charity. Watching her dance is an education." He popped the tiny sandwich into his mouth. "She tried to teach me once, hoping I'd be able to entertain some of the ladies on occasions like this. Trouble is, I not only have two left feet, I have two left legs." He gave a cheerful shrug and reached for another sandwich.

"Did you get the computer fixed?"

"Yeah. Just a couple of minor glitches." The little triangle of bread disappeared. Roman caught a hint of nerves in the way Bob's knuckle tapped against the server. "I can't teach Charity about circuit boards and software any more than she can teach me the samba. How's the work going?"

"Well enough." He watched as Bob poured a cup of tea and added three sugars to it. "I should be done in two or three weeks."

"She'll find something else for you to do." He

glanced over to where Charity and a new partner were dancing a fox-trot. "She's always got a new idea for this place. Lately she's been making noises about adding on a sunroom and putting in one of those whirlpool tubs."

Roman lit a cigarette. He was watching the guests now, making mental notes to pass on to Conby. There were two men who seemed to be alone, though they were chatting with other members of the tour group. Block stood by the doors, holding a plateful of sandwiches that he was dispatching with amazing ease and grinning at no one in particular.

"The inn must be doing well."

"Oh, it's stable." Bob turned his attention to the petits fours. "A couple of years ago things were a little rocky, but Charity would always find a way to keep the ship afloat. Nothing's more important to her."

Roman was silent for a moment. "I don't know much about the hotel business, but she seems to know what she's doing."

"Inside and out." Bob chose a cake with pink frosting. "Charity *is* the inn."

"Have you worked for her long?"

"About two and a half years. She couldn't really afford me, but she wanted to turn things around, modernize the bookkeeping. Pump new life into the place, was what she said." Someone put on a jitterbug, and he grinned. "She did just that."

"Apparently."

"So you're from back east." Bob paused for a moment, then continued when Roman made no comment. "How long are you planning to stay?"

"As long as it takes."

He took a long sip of tea. "As long as what takes?"

"The job." Roman glanced idly toward the west wing. "I like to finish what I start."

"Yeah. Well…" He arranged several petits fours on a plate. "I'm going to go offer these to the ladies and hope they let me eat them."

Roman watched him pass Block and exchange a quick word with him before he crossed the room. Wanting time to think, Roman slipped back into the west wing.

It was still raining when he came back hours later. Music was playing, some slow, melodic ballad from the fifties. The room was dimmer now, lit only by the fire and a glass-globed lamp. It was empty, too, except for Charity, who was busy tidying up, humming along with the music.

"Party over?"

She glanced around, then went hurriedly back to stacking cups and plates. "Yes. You didn't stay long."

"I had work to do."

Because she wanted to keep moving, she switched to emptying ashtrays. She'd held on to her guilt long enough. "I was tired this morning, but that's no excuse for being rude to you. I'm sorry if I gave you the impression that you couldn't enjoy yourself for a few hours."

He didn't want to accept an apology that he knew he didn't deserve. "I enjoy the work."

That only made her feel worse. "Be that as it may, I don't usually go around barking orders. I was angry with you."

"Was?"

She looked up, and her eyes were clear and direct. "Am. But that's my problem. If it helps, I'm every bit as angry with myself for acting like a child because you didn't let things get out of hand last night."

Uncomfortable, he picked up the wine decanter and poured a glass. "You didn't act like a child."

"A woman scorned, then, or something equally dramatic. Try not to contradict me when I'm apologizing."

Despite his best efforts, his lips curved against the rim of his glass. If he didn't watch himself he could find he was crazy about her. "All right. Is there more?"

"Just a little." She picked up one of the few petits fours that were left over, debated with herself, then popped it into her mouth. "I shouldn't let my personal feelings interfere with my running of the inn. The problem is, almost everything I think or feel connects with the inn."

"Neither of us were thinking of the inn last night. Maybe that's the problem."

"Maybe."

"Do you want the couch moved back?"

"Yes." Business as usual, Charity told herself as she walked over to lift her end. The moment it was in place she scooted around to plump the pillows. "I saw you dancing with Miss Millie. It thrilled her."

"I like her."

"I think you do," Charity said slowly, straightening and studying him. "You're not the kind of man who likes easily."

"No."

She wanted to go to him, to lift a hand to his cheek. That was ridiculous, she told herself. Apology notwithstanding, she was still angry with him for last night. "Has life been so hard?" she murmured.

"No."

With a little laugh, she shook her head. "Then again, you wouldn't tell me if it had been. I have to learn not to ask you questions. Why don't we call a truce, Roman? Life's too short for bad feelings."

"I don't have any bad feelings toward you, Charity."

She smiled a little. "It's tempting, but I'm not going to ask what kind of feelings you do have."

"I wouldn't be able to tell you, because I haven't figured it out." He was amazed that the words had come out. After draining the wine, he set the empty glass aside.

"Well." Nonplussed, she pushed her hair back with both hands. "That's the first thing you've told me I can really understand. Looks like we're in the same boat. Do I take it we have a truce?"

"Sure."

She glanced back as another record dropped onto the turntable. "This is one of my favorites. 'Smoke Gets in Your Eyes.'" She was smiling again when she looked back at him. "You never asked me to dance."

"No, I didn't."

"Miss Millie claims you're very smooth." She held out a hand in a gesture that was as much a peace offering as an invitation. Unable to resist, he took it in his. Their eyes stayed locked as he drew her slowly toward him.

Chapter 5

A fire simmered in the grate. Rain pattered against the windows. The record was old and scratchy, the tune hauntingly sad. Whether they wanted it or not, their bodies fitted. Her hand slid gently over his shoulder, his around her waist. With their faces close, they began to dance.

The added height from her heels brought her eyes level with his. He could smell the light fragrance that seemed so much a part of her. Seduced by it, he brought her closer, slowly. Their thighs brushed. Still closer. Her body melted against his.

It was so quiet. There was only the music, the rain, the hissing of the fire. Gloomy light swirled into the room. He could feel her heart beating against his, quick now, and not too steady.

His wasn't any too steady now, either.

Was that all it took? he wondered. Did he only have to touch her to think that she was the beginning and the end of everything? And to wish... His hand slid up her back, fingers spreading until they tangled in her hair. To wish she could belong to him.

He wasn't sure when that thought had sunk its roots in him. Perhaps it had begun the first moment he had seen her. She was—should have been—unattainable for him. But when she was in his arms, warm, just bordering on pliant, dozens of possibilities flashed through his head.

She wanted to smile, to make some light, easy comment. But she couldn't push the words out. Her throat was locked. The way he was looking at her now, as if she were the only woman he had ever seen or ever wanted to see, made her forget that the dance was supposed to be a gesture of friendship.

She might never be his friend, she knew, no matter how hard she tried. But with his eyes on hers she understood how easily she could be his lover.

Maybe it was wrong, but it didn't seem to matter as they glided across the floor. The song spoke of love betrayed, but she heard only poetry. She felt her will ebb away even as the music swelled inside her head. No, it didn't seem to matter. Nothing seemed to matter as long as she went on swaying in his arms.

She didn't even try to think, never attempted to reason. Following her heart, she pressed her lips to his.

Instant. Irresistible. Irrevocable. Emotions funneled from one to the other, then merged in a torrent of need. She didn't expect him to be gentle, though her kiss had offered comfort, as well as passion. He dived into it, into her, with a speed and force that left her reeling, then fretting for more.

So this was what drove people to do mad, desperate acts, she thought as their tongues tangled. This wild, painful pleasure, once tasted, would never be forgotten, would always be craved. She wrapped her arms around his neck as she gave herself to it.

With quick, rough kisses he drove them both to the edge. It was more than desire, he knew. Desire had never hurt, not deeply. It was like a scratch, soon forgotten, easily healed. This was a raw, deep wound.

Lust had never erased every coherent thought from his mind. Still, he could only think of her. Those thoughts were jumbled, and all of them were forbidden. Desperate, he ran his lips over her face, while wild fantasies of touching, of tasting every inch of her whirled in his head. It wouldn't be enough. It would never be enough. No matter how much he took from her, she would draw him back. And she could make him beg. The certainty of it terrified him.

She was trembling again, even as she strained against him. Her soft gasps and sighs pushed him toward the brink of reason. He found her mouth again and feasted on it.

He hardly recognized the change, could find no reason for it. All at once she was like glass in his arms, something precious, something fragile, something he needed to protect and defend. He lifted his hands to her face, his fingers light and cautiously caressing. His mouth, ravenous only a moment before, gentled.

Stunned, she swayed. New, vibrant emotions poured into her. Weak from the onslaught, she let her head fall back. Her arms slipped, boneless, to her sides. There was beauty here, a soft, shimmering beauty she had never known existed. Tenderness did what passion had not yet accomplished. As freely as a bird taking wing, her heart flew out to him.

Love, first experienced, was devastating. She felt tears burn the back of her eyes, heard her own quiet moan of surrender. And she tasted the glory of it as his lips played gently with hers.

She would always remember that one instant when the world changed—the music, the rain, the scent of fresh flowers. Nothing would ever be quite the same again. Nor would she ever want it to be.

Shaken, she drew back to lift a hand to her spinning head. "Roman—"

"Come with me." Unwilling to think, he pulled her against him again. "I want to know what it's like to be with you, to undress you, to touch you."

With a moan, she surrendered to his mouth again.

"Charity, Mae wants to—" Lori stopped on a dime at the top of the stairs. After clearing her throat, she stared at the painting on the opposite wall as if it fascinated her. "Excuse me. I didn't mean to…"

Charity had jerked back like a spring and was searching for composure. "It's all right. What is it, Lori?"

"It's, well… Mae and Dolores… Maybe you could come down to the kitchen when you get a minute." She rushed down the stairs, grinning to herself.

"I should…" Charity paused to draw in a steadying breath but managed only a shaky one. "I should go down." She retreated a step. "Once they get started, they need—" She broke off when Roman took her arm. He waited until she lifted her head and looked at him again.

"Things have changed."

It sounded so simple when he said it. "Yes. Yes, they have."

"Right or wrong, Charity, we'll finish this."

"No." She was far from calm, but she was very determined. "If it's right, we'll finish it. I'm not going to pretend I don't want you, but you're right when you say things have changed, Roman. You see, I know what I'm feeling now, and I have to get used to it."

He tightened his grip when she turned to go. "What are you feeling?"

She couldn't have lied if she'd wanted to. Dishonesty was abhorrent to her. When it came to feelings, she had neither the ability nor the desire to suppress them. "I'm in love with you."

His fingers uncurled from her arm. Very slowly, very carefully, as if he were retreating from some dangerous beast, he released her.

She read the shock on his face. That was understandable. And she read the distrust. That was painful. She gave him a last unsmiling look before she turned away.

"Apparently we both have to get used to it."

She was lying. Roman told himself that over and over as he paced the floor in his room. If not to him, then certainly to herself. People seemed to find love easy to lie about.

He stopped by the window and stared out into the

dark. The rain had stopped, and the moon was cruising in and out of the clouds. He jerked the window open and breathed in the damp, cool air. He needed something to clear his head.

She was working on him. Annoyed, he turned away from the view of trees and flowers and started pacing again. The easy smiles, the openhanded welcome, the casual friendliness...then the passion, the uninhibited response, the seduction. He wanted to believe it was a trap, even though his well-trained mind found the idea absurd.

She had no reason to suspect him. His cover was solid. Charity thought of him as a drifter, passing through long enough to take in some sights and pick up a little loose change. It was he who was setting the trap.

He dropped down on the bed and lit a cigarette, more out of habit than because he wanted one. Lies were part of his job, a part he was very good at. She hadn't lied to him, he reflected as he inhaled. But she was mistaken. He had made her want, and she had justified her desire for a relative stranger by telling herself she was in love.

But if it was true...

He couldn't allow himself to think that way. Leaning back against the headboard, he stared at the blank wall. He couldn't allow himself the luxury of wondering what it would be like to be loved, and especially not what it would be like to be loved by a woman to whom love would mean a lifetime. He couldn't afford any daydreams about belonging, about having someone belong to him. Even if she hadn't been part of his assignment he would have to sidestep Charity Ford.

She would think of love, then of white picket fences, Sunday dinners and evenings by the fire. He was no good for her. He would never be any good for her. Roman DeWinter, he thought with a mirthless smile. Always on the wrong side of the tracks. A questionable past, an uncertain future. There was nothing he could offer a woman like Charity.

But God, he wanted her. The need was eating away at his insides. He knew she was upstairs now. He imagined her curled up in the big four-poster, under white blankets, perhaps with a white candle burning low on the table.

He had only to climb the stairs and walk through the door. She wouldn't send him away. If she tried, it would take him only moments to break down her resistance. Believing herself in love, she would yield, then open her arms to him. He ached to be in them, to sink into that bed, into her, and let oblivion take them both.

But she had asked for time. He wasn't going to deny her what he needed himself. In the time he gave her he would use all his skill to do the one thing he knew how to do for her. He would prove her innocence.

Roman watched the tour group check out the following morning. Perched on a stepladder in the center of the lobby, he took his time changing bulbs in the ceiling fixture. The sun was out now, full and bright, bathing the lobby in light as a few members of the tour loitered after breakfast.

At the front desk, Charity was chatting with Block. He was wearing a fresh white shirt and his perpetual smile. Taking a calculator from his briefcase, he checked to see if Charity's tallies matched his own.

Bob poked his head out of the office and handed her a computer printout. Roman didn't miss the quick, uncertain look Bob sent in his direction before he shut himself away again.

Charity and Block compared lists. Still smiling, he took a stack of bills out of his briefcase. He paid in Canadian, cash. Having already adjusted the bill to take the exchange rate into account, Charity locked the cash away in a drawer, then handed Block his receipt.

"Always a pleasure, Roger."

"Your little party saved the day," he told her. "My people consider this the highlight of the tour."

Pleased, she smiled at him. "They haven't seen Mount Rainier yet."

"You're going to get some repeaters out of this." He patted her hand, then checked his watch. "Time to move them out. See you next week."

"Safe trip, Roger." She turned to make change for a departing guest, then sold a few postcards and a few souvenir key chains with miniature whales on them.

Roman replaced the globe on the ceiling fixture, taking his time until the lobby was clear again. "Isn't it strange for a company like that to pay cash?"

Distracted from her reservations list, Charity glanced up at him. "We never turn down cash." She smiled at him as she had promised herself she would. Her feelings, her problem, she reminded herself as he climbed down from the ladder. She only wished the hours she'd spent soul-searching the night before had resulted in a solution.

"It seems like they'd charge, or pay by check."

"It's their company policy. Believe me, with a small, independent hotel, a cash-paying customer like Vision can make all the difference."

"I'll bet. You've been dealing with them for a while?"

"A couple of years. Why?"

"Just curious. Block doesn't look much like a tour guide."

"Roger? No, I guess he looks more like a wrestler." She went back to her papers. It was difficult to make small talk when her feelings were so close to the surface. "He does a good job."

"Yeah. I'll be upstairs."

"Roman." There was so much she wanted to say, but she could feel, though they were standing only a few feet apart, that he had distanced himself from her. "We never discussed a day off," she began. "You're welcome to take Sunday, if you like."

"Maybe I will."

"And if you'd give Bob your hours at the end of the week, he generally takes care of payroll."

"All right. Thanks."

A young couple with a toddler walked out of the dining room. Roman left her to answer their questions on renting a boat.

It wasn't going to be easy to talk to him, Charity decided later. But she had to do it. She'd spent all morning on business, she'd double-checked the housekeeping in the cabins, she'd made every phone call on her list, and if Mae's comments were anything to go on she'd made a nuisance of herself in the kitchen.

She was stalling.

That wasn't like her. All her life she'd made a habit of facing her problems head-on and plowing through them. Not only with business, she thought now. Personal problems had always been given the same kind of direct approach. She had handled being parentless. Even as a child she had never evaded the sometimes painful questions about her background.

But then, she'd had her grandfather. He'd been so solid, so loving. He'd helped her understand that she was her own person. Just as he'd helped her through her first high-school crush, Charity remembered.

He wasn't here now, and she wasn't a fifteen-year-old mooning over the captain of the debating team. But if he had taught her anything, it was that honest feelings were nothing to be ashamed of.

Armed with a thermos full of coffee, she walked into the west wing. She wished it didn't feel so much like bearding the lion in his den.

He'd finished the parlor. The scent of fresh paint was strong, though he'd left a window open to air it out. The doors still had to be hung and the floors varnished, but she could already imagine the room with sheer, billowy curtains and the faded floral-print rug she'd stored in the attic.

From the bedroom beyond, she could hear the buzz of an electric saw. A good, constructive sound, she thought as she pushed the door open to peek inside.

His eyes were narrowed in concentration as he bent over the wood he had laid across a pair of sawhorses. Wood dust flew, dancing gold in the sunlight. His hands, and his arms where he'd rolled his sleeves up past the elbow, were covered with it. He'd used a bandanna to keep the hair out of his eyes. He didn't hum while he worked, as she did. Or talk to himself, she mused, as George had. But, watching him, she thought she detected a simple pleasure in doing a job and doing it well.

He could do things, she thought as she watched him measure the wood for the next cut. Good things, even important things. She was sure of it. Not just because she loved him, she realized. Because it was in him. When a woman spent all her life entertaining strangers in her home, she learned to judge, and to see.

She waited until he put the saw down before she pushed the door open. Before she could speak he whirled around. Her step backward was instinctive, defensive. It was ridiculous, she told herself, but she thought that if he'd had a weapon he'd have drawn it.

"I'm sorry." The nerves she had managed to get under control were shot to hell. "I should have realized I'd startle you."

"It's all right." He settled quickly, though it annoyed him to have been caught off guard. Perhaps if he hadn't been thinking of her he would have sensed her.

"I needed to do some things upstairs, so I thought I'd bring you some coffee on my way." She set the thermos on the stepladder, then wished she'd kept it, as her empty hands made her feel foolish. "And I wanted to check how things were going. The parlor looks great."

"It's coming along. Did you label the paint?"

"Yes. Why?"

"Because it was all done in this tidy printing on the lid of each can in the color of the paint. That seemed like something you'd do."

"Obsessively organized?" She made a face. "I can't seem to help it."

"I liked the way you had the paintbrushes arranged according to size."

She lifted a brow. "Are you making fun of me?"

"Yeah."

"Well, as long as I know." Her nerves were calmer now. "Want some of this coffee?"

"Yeah. I'll get it."

"You've got sawdust all over your hands." Waving him aside, she unscrewed the top. "I take it our truce is back on."

"I didn't realize it had been off."

She glanced back over her shoulder, then looked around and poured the coffee into the plastic cup. "I made you uncomfortable yesterday. I'm sorry."

He accepted the cup and sat down on a sawhorse. "You're putting words in my mouth again, Charity."

"I don't have to this time. You looked as if I'd hit you with a brick." Restless, she moved her shoulders. "I suppose I might have reacted the same way if someone had said they loved me out of the blue like that. It must have been pretty startling, seeing as we haven't known each other for long."

Finding he had no taste for it, he set the coffee aside. "You were reacting to the moment."

"No." She turned back to him, knowing it was important to talk face-to-face. "I thought you might think that. In fact, I even considered playing it safe and letting you. I'm lousy at deception. It seemed more fair to tell you that I'm not in the habit of...what I mean is, I don't throw myself at men as a rule. The truth is, you're the first."

"Charity." He dragged a hand through his hair, pulling out the bandanna and sending more wood dust scattering. "I don't know what to say to you."

"You don't have to say anything. The fact is, I came in here with my little speech all worked out. It was a pretty good one, too...calm, understanding, a couple of dashes of humor to keep it light. I'm screwing it up."

She kicked a scrap of wood into the corner before she paced to the window. Columbine and bluebells grew just below in a bed where poppies were waiting to burst into color. On impulse, she pushed up the window to breathe in their faint, fragile scents.

"The point is," she began, hating herself for keeping her back to him, "we can't pretend I didn't say it. I can't pretend I don't feel it. That doesn't mean I expect you to feel the same way, because I don't."

"What do you expect?"

He was right behind her. She jumped when his hand gripped her shoulder. Gathering her courage, she turned around. "For you to be honest with me." She was speaking quickly now, and she didn't notice his slight, automatic retreat. "I appreciate the fact that you don't pretend to love me. I may be simple, Roman, but I'm not stupid. I know it might be easier to lie, to say what you think I want to hear."

"You're not simple," he murmured, lifting a hand and brushing it against her cheek. "I've never met a more confusing, complicated woman."

Shock came first, then pleasure. "That's the nicest

thing you've ever said to me. No one's ever accused me of being complicated."

He'd meant to lower his hand, but she had already lifted hers and clasped it. "I didn't mean it as a compliment."

That made her grin. Relaxed again, she sat back on the windowsill. "Even better. I hope this means we're finished feeling awkward around each other."

"I don't know what I feel around you." He ran his hands up her arms to her shoulders, then down to the elbows again. "But awkward isn't the word for it."

Touched—much too deeply—she rose. "I have to go."

"Why?"

"Because it's the middle of the day, and if you kiss me I might forget that."

Already aroused, he eased her forward. "Always organized."

"Yes." She put a hand to his chest to keep some distance between them. "I have some invoices I have to go over upstairs." Holding her breath, she backed toward the door. "I do want you, Roman. I'm just not sure I can handle that part of it."

Neither was he, he thought after she shut the door. With another woman he would have been certain that physical release would end the tension. With Charity he knew that making love with her would only add another layer to the hold she had on him.

And she did have a hold on him. It was time to admit that, and to deal with it.

Perhaps he'd reacted so strongly to her declaration of love because he was afraid, as he'd never been afraid of anything in his life, that he was falling in love with her.

"Roman!" He heard the delight in Charity's voice when she called to him. He swung open the door and saw her standing on the landing at the top of the stairs. "Come up. Hurry. I want you to see them."

She disappeared, leaving him wishing she'd called him anyplace but that innocently seductive bedroom.

When he walked into her sitting room, she called again, impatience in her tone now. "Hurry. I don't know how long they'll stay."

She was sitting on the windowsill, her upper body out the opening, her long legs hooked just above the ankles. There was music playing, something vibrant, passionate. How was it he had never thought of classical music as passionate?

"Damn it, Roman, you're going to miss them. Don't just stand in the doorway. I didn't call you up to tie you to the bedposts."

Because he felt like a fool, he crossed to her. "There goes my night."

"Very funny. Look." She was holding a brass spy glass, and she pointed with it now, out to sea. "Orcas."

He leaned out the window and followed her guiding hand. He could see a pair of shapes in the distance, rippling the water as they swam. Fascinated, he took the spyglass from Charity's hand.

"There are three of them," he said. Delighted, he joined her on the windowsill. Their legs were aligned now, and he rested his hand absently on her knee. This time, instead of fire, there was simple warmth.

"Yes, there's a calf. I think it might be the same pod I spotted a few days ago." She closed a hand over his as they both stared out to sea. "Great, aren't they?"

"Yeah, they are." He focused on the calf, which was just visible between the two larger whales. "I never really expected to see any."

"Why? The island's named after them." She narrowed her eyes, trying to follow their path. She didn't have the heart to ask Roman for the glass. "My first clear memory of seeing one was when I was about four. Pop had me out on this little excuse for a fishing boat. One shot up out of the water no more than eight or ten yards away. I screamed my lungs out." Laughing, she leaned back against the window frame. "I thought it was going to swallow us whole, like Jonah or maybe Pinocchio."

Roman lowered the glass for a moment. "Pinocchio?"

"Yes, you know the puppet who wanted to be a real boy. Jiminy Cricket, the Blue Fairy. Anyway, Pop finally calmed me down. It followed us for ten or fifteen minutes. After that, I nagged him mercilessly to take me out again."

"Did he?"

"Every Monday afternoon that summer. We didn't always see something, but they were great days, the best days. I guess we were a pod, too, Pop and I." She turned her face into the breeze. "I was lucky to have him as long as I did, but there are times—like this— when I can't help wishing he were here."

"Like this?"

"He loved to watch them," she said quietly. "Even when he was ill, really ill, he would sit for hours at the window. One afternoon I found him sitting there with the spyglass on his lap. I thought he'd fallen asleep, but he was gone." There was a catch in her breath when she slowly let it out. "He would have wanted that, to just slip away while watching for his whales. I haven't been able to take the boat out since he died." She shook her head. "Stupid."

"No." He reached for her hand for the first time and linked his fingers with hers. "It's not."

She turned her face to his again. "You can be a nice man." The phone rang, and she groaned but slipped dutifully from the windowsill to answer it.

"Hello. Yes, Bob. What does he mean he won't deliver them? New management be damned, we've been dealing with that company for ten years. Yes, all right. I'll be right there. Oh, wait." She glanced up from the phone. "Roman, are they still there?"

"Yes. Heading south. I don't know if they're feeding or just taking an afternoon stroll."

She laughed and put the receiver at her ear again. "Bob— What? Yes, that was Roman." Her brow lifted. "That's right. We're in my room. I called Roman up here because I spotted a pod out my bedroom window. You might want to tell any of the guests you see around. No, there's no reason for you to be concerned. Why should there be? I'll be right down."

She hung up, shaking her head. "It's like having a houseful of chaperons," she muttered.

"Problem?"

"No. Bob realized that you were in my bedroom— or rather that we were alone in my bedroom—and got very big-brotherly. Typical." She opened a drawer and pulled out a fabric-covered band. In a few quick movements she had her hair caught back from her face. "Last year Mae threatened to poison a guest who made a pass at me. You'd think I was fifteen."

He turned to study her. She was wearing jeans and a sweatshirt with a silk-screened map of the island. "Yes, you would."

"I don't take that as a compliment." But she didn't have time to argue. "I have to deal with a small crisis downstairs. You're welcome to stay and watch the whales." She started toward the door, but then she stopped. "Oh, I nearly forgot. Can you build shelves?"

"Probably."

"Great. I think the parlor in the family suite could use them. We'll talk about it."

He heard her jog down the stairs. Whatever crisis there might be at the other end of the inn, he was sure she would handle it. In the meantime, she had left him alone in her room. It would be a simple matter to go through her desk again, to see if she'd left anything that would help him move his investigation forward.

It should be simple, anyway. Roman looked out to sea again. It should be something he could do without hesitation. But he couldn't. She trusted him. Sometime during the past twenty-four hours he reached the point where he couldn't violate that trust.

That made him useless. Swearing, Roman leaned back against the window frame. She had, without even being aware of it, totally undermined his ability to do his job. It would be best for him to call Conby and have himself taken off the case. It would simply be a matter of him turning in his resignation now, rather than at the end of the assignment. It was a question of duty.

He wasn't going to do that, either.

He needed to stay. It had nothing to do with being loved, with feeling at home. He needed to believe that. He also needed to finish his job and prove, beyond a shadow of a doubt, Charity's innocence. That was a question of loyalty.

Conby would have said that his loyalty belonged to the Bureau, not to a woman he had known for less than a week. And Conby would have been wrong, Roman thought as he set aside the spyglass. There were times, rare times, when you had a chance to do something good, something right. Something that proved you gave a damn. That had never mattered to him before, but it mattered now.

If the only thing he could give Charity was a clear name, he intended to give it to her. And then get out of her life.

Rising, he looked around the room. He wished he were nothing more than the out-of-work drifter Charity had taken into her home. If he were maybe he would have the right to love her. As it was, all he could do was save her.

Chapter 6

The weather was warming. Spring was busting loose, full of glory and color and scent. The island was a treasure trove of wildflowers, leafy trees and birdsong. At dawn, with thin fingers of fog over the water, it was a mystical, timeless place.

Roman stood at the side of the road and watched the sun come up as he had only days before. He didn't know the names of the flowers that grew in tangles on the roadside. He didn't know the song of a jay from that of a sparrow. But he knew Charity was out running with her dog and that she would pass the place he stood on her return.

He needed to see her, to talk to her, to be with her.

The night before, he had broken into her cash drawer and examined the bills she had neatly stacked and marked for today's deposit. There had been over two thousand dollars in counterfeit Canadian currency. His first impulse had been to tell her, to lay everything he knew and needed to know out in front of her. But he had quashed that. Telling her wouldn't prove her innocence to men like Conby.

He had enough to get Block. And nearly enough, he thought, to hang Bob along with him. But he couldn't get them without casting shadows on Charity. By her own admission, and according to the statements of her loyal staff, a pin couldn't drop in the inn without her knowing it.

If that was so, how could he prove that there had been a counterfeiting and smuggling ring going on under her nose for nearly two years?

He believed it, as firmly as he had ever believed anything. Conby and the others at the Bureau wanted facts. Roman drew on his cigarette and watched the fog melt away with the rising of the sun. He had to give them facts. Until he could, he would give them nothing.

He could wait and make sure Conby dropped the ax on Block on the guide's next trip to the inn. That would give Roman time. Time enough, he promised himself, to make certain Charity wasn't caught in the middle. When it went down, she would be stunned and hurt. She'd get over it. When it was over, and she knew his part in it, she would hate him. He would get over that. He would have to.

He heard a car and glanced over, then returned his gaze to the water. He wondered if he could come back someday and stand in this same spot and wait for Charity to run down the road toward him.

Fantasies, he told himself, pitching his half-finished

cigarette into the dirt. He was wasting too much time on fantasies.

The car was coming fast, its engine protesting, its muffler rattling. He looked over again, annoyed at having his morning and his thoughts disturbed.

His annoyance saved his life.

It took him only an instant to realize what was happening, and a heartbeat more to evade it. As the car barreled toward him, he leaped aside, tucking and rolling into the brush. A wave of displaced air flattened the grass before the car's rear tires gripped the roadbed again. Roman's gun was in his hand even as he scrambled to his feet. He caught a glimpse of the car's rear end as it sped around a curve. There wasn't even time to swear before he heard Charity's scream.

He ran, unaware of the fire in his thigh where the car had grazed him and the blood on his arm where he had rolled into a rock. He had faced death. He had killed. But he had never understood terror until this moment, with her scream still echoing in his head. He hadn't understood agony until he'd seen Charity sprawled beside the road.

The dog was curled beside her, whimpering, nuzzling her face with her nose. He turned at Roman's approach and began to growl, then stood, barking.

"Charity." Roman crouched beside her, and felt for a pulse, his hand shaking. "Okay, baby. You're going to be okay," he murmured to her as he checked for broken bones.

Had she been hit? A sickening vision of her being tossed into the air as the car slammed into her pulsed through his head. Using every ounce of control he possessed, he blocked it out. She was breathing. He held on to that. The dog whined as he turned her head and examined the gash on her temple. It was the only spot of color on her face. He stanched the blood with his bandanna, cursing when he felt its warmth on his fingers.

Grimly he replaced his weapon, then lifted her into his arms. Her body seemed boneless. Roman tightened his grip, half afraid she might melt through his arms. He talked to her throughout the half mile walk back to the inn, though she remained pale and still.

Bob raced out the front door of the inn. "My God! What happened? What the hell did you do to her?"

Roman paused just long enough to aim a dark, furious look at him. "I think you know better. Get me the keys to the van. She needs a hospital."

"What's all this?" Mae came through the door, wiping her hands on her apron. "Lori said she saw—" She went pale, but then she began to move with surprising speed, elbowing Bob aside to reach Charity. "Get her upstairs."

"I'm taking her to the hospital."

"Upstairs," Mae repeated, moving back to open the door for him. "We'll call Dr. Mertens. It'll be faster. Come on, boy. Call the doctor, Bob. Tell him to hurry."

Roman passed through the door, the dog at his heels. "And call the police," he added. "Tell them they've got a hit-and-run."

Wasting no time on words, Mae led the way upstairs. She was puffing a bit by the time she reached the second floor, but she never slowed down. When they moved into Charity's room, her color had returned.

"Set her on the bed, and be careful about it." She yanked the lacy coverlet aside and then just as efficiently, brushed Roman aside. "There, little girl, you'll be just fine. Go in the bathroom," she told Roman. "Get me a fresh towel." Easing a hip onto the bed, she cupped Charity's face with a broad hand and examined her head wound. "Looks worse than it is." She let out a long breath. After taking the towel Roman offered, she pressed it against Charity's temple. "Head wounds bleed heavy, make a mess. But it's not too deep."

He only knew that her blood was still on his hands. "She should be coming around."

"Give her time. I want you to tell me what happened later, but I'm going to undress her now, see if she's hurt anywhere else. You go on and wait downstairs."

"I'm not leaving her."

Mae glanced up. Her lips were pursed, and lines of worry fanned out from her eyes. After a moment, she simply nodded. "All right, then, but you'll be of some use. Get me the scissors out of her desk. I want to cut this shirt off."

So that was the way of it, Mae mused as she untied Charity's shoes. She knew a man who was scared to death and fighting his heart when she saw one. Well, she'd just have to get her girl back on her feet. She didn't doubt for a moment that Charity could deal with the likes of Roman DeWinter.

"You can stay," she told him when he handed her the scissors. "But whatever's been going on between the two of you, you'll turn your back till I make her decent."

He balled his hands into impotent fists and shoved

them into his pockets as he spun around. "I want to know where she's hurt."

"Just hold your horses." Mae peeled the shirt away and put her emotions on hold as she examined the scrapes and bruises. "Look in that top right-hand drawer and get me out a nightshirt. One with buttons. And keep your eyes to yourself," she added, "or I'll throw you out of here."

In answer, he tossed a thin white nightshirt onto the bed. "I don't care what she's wearing. I want to know how badly she's hurt."

"I know, boy." Mae's voice softened as she slipped Charity's limp arm into a sleeve. "She's got some bruises and scrapes, that's all. Nothing broken. The cut on her head's going to need some tending, but cuts heal. Why, she hurt herself worse when she fell out of a tree some time back. There's my girl. She's coming around."

He turned to look then, shirt or no shirt. But Mae had already done up the buttons. He controlled the urge to go to her—barely—and, keeping his distance, watched Charity's lashes flutter. The sinking in his stomach was pure relief. When she moaned, he wiped his clammy hands on his thighs.

"Mae?" As she struggled to focus her eyes, Charity reached out a hand. She could see the solid bulk of her cook, but little else. "What— Oh, God, my head."

"Thumping pretty good, is it?" Mae's voice was brisk, but she cradled Charity's hand in hers. She would have kissed it if she'd thought no one would notice. "The doc'll fix that up."

"Doctor?" Baffled, Charity tried to sit up, but the pain exploded in her head. "I don't want the doctor."

"Never did, but you're having him just the same."

"I'm not going to…" Arguing took too much effort. Instead, she closed her eyes and concentrated on clearing her mind. It was fairly obvious that she was in bed—but how the devil had she gotten there?

She'd been walking the dog, she remembered, and Ludwig had found a tree beside the road irresistible. Then…

"There was a car," she said, opening her eyes again. "They must have been drunk or crazy. It seemed like they came right at me. If Ludwig hadn't already been pulling me off the road, I—" She wasn't quite ready to consider that. "I stumbled, I think. I don't know."

"It doesn't matter now," Mae assured her. "We'll figure it all out later."

After a brisk knock, the outside door opened. A short, spry little man with a shock of white hair hustled in. He carried a black bag and was wearing grubby overalls and muddy boots. Charity took one look, then closed her eyes again.

"Go away, Dr. Mertens. I'm not feeling well."

"She never changes." Mertens nodded to Roman, then walked over to examine his patient.

Roman slipped quietly out into the sitting room. He needed a moment to pull himself together, to quiet the rage that was building now that he knew she would be all right. He had lost his parents, he had buried his best friend, but he had never, never felt the kind of panic he had experienced when he had seen Charity bleeding and unconscious beside the road.

Taking out a cigarette, he went to the open window. He thought about the driver of the old, rusted Chevy that had run her down. Even as his rage cooled, Roman understood one thing with perfect clarity. It would be his pleasure to kill whoever had hurt her.

"Excuse me." Lori was standing in the hall doorway, wringing her hands. "The sheriff's here. He wants to talk to you, so I brought him up." She tugged at her apron and stared at the closed door on the other side of the room. "Charity?"

"The doctor's with her," Roman said. "She'll be fine."

Lori closed her eyes and took a deep breath. "I'll tell the others. Go on in, sheriff."

Roman studied the paunchy man, who had obviously been called out of bed. His shirttail was only partially tucked into his pants, and he was sipping a cup of coffee as he came into the room.

"You Roman DeWinter?"

"That's right."

"Sheriff Royce." He sat, with a sigh, on the arm of Charity's rose-colored Queen Anne chair. "What's this about a hit-and-run?"

"About twenty minutes ago somebody tried to run down Miss Ford."

Royce turned to stare at the closed door just the way Lori had done. "How is she?"

"Banged up. She's got a gash on her head and some bruises."

"Were you with her?" He pulled out a pad and a stubby pencil.

"No. I was about a quarter mile away. The car

swerved at me, then kept going. I heard Charity scream. When I got to her, she was unconscious."

"Don't suppose you got a good look at the car?"

"Dark blue Chevy. Sedan, '67, '68. Muffler was bad. Right front fender was rusted through. Washington plates Alpha Foxtrot Juliet 847."

Royce lifted both brows as he took down the description. "You got a good eye."

"That's right."

"Good enough for you to guess if he ran you down on purpose?"

"I don't have to guess. He was aiming."

Without a flicker of an eye, Royce continued taking notes. He added a reminder to himself to do a routine check on Roman DeWinter. "He? Did you see the driver?"

"No," Roman said shortly. He was still cursing himself for that.

"How long have you been on the island, Mr. De-Winter?"

"Almost a week."

"A short time to make enemies."

"I don't have any—here—that I know of."

"That makes your theory pretty strange." Still scribbling, Royce glanced up. "There's nobody on the island who knows Charity and has a thing against her. If what you're saying's true, we'd be talking attempted murder."

Roman pitched his cigarette out the window. "That's just what we're talking about. I want to know who owns that car."

"I'll check it out."

"You already know."

Royce tapped his pad on his knee. "Yes, sir, you do have a good eye. I'll say this. Maybe I do know somebody who owns a car that fits your description. If I do, I know that that person wouldn't run over a rabbit on purpose, much less a woman. Then again, there's no saying you have to own a car to drive it."

Mae opened the connecting door, and he glanced up. "Well, now, Maeflower."

Mae's lips twitched slightly before she thinned them. "If you can't sit in a chair proper you can stand on your feet, Jack Royce."

Royce rose, grinning. "Mae and I went to school together," he explained. "She liked to bully me then, too. I don't suppose you've got any waffles on the menu today, Maeflower."

"Maybe I do. You find out who hurt my girl and I'll see you get some."

"I'm working on it." His face sobered again as he nodded toward the door. "Is she up to talking to me?"

"Done nothing but talk since she came around." Mae blinked back a flood of relieved tears. "Go ahead in."

Royce turned to Roman. "I'll be in touch."

"Doc said she could have some tea and toast." Mae sniffled, then made a production out of blowing her nose. "Hay fever," she said roughly. "I'm grateful you were close by when she was hurt."

"If I'd been closer she wouldn't have been hurt."

"And if she hadn't been walking that dog she'd have been in bed." She paused and gave Roman a level look. "I guess we could shoot him."

She surprised a little laugh out of him. "Charity might object to that."

"She wouldn't care to know you're out here brooding, either. Your arm's bleeding, boy."

He looked down dispassionately at the torn, blood-stained sleeve of his shirt. "Some."

"Can't have you bleeding all over the floor." She walked to the door, waving a hand. "Well, come on downstairs. I'll clean you up. Then you can bring the girl up some breakfast. I haven't got time to run up and down these steps all morning."

After the doctor had finished his poking and the sheriff had finished his questioning, Charity stared at the ceiling. She hurt everywhere there was to hurt. Her head especially, but the rest of her was throbbing right along in time.

The medication would take the edge off, but she wanted to keep her mind clear until she'd worked everything out. That was why she had tucked the pill Dr. Mertens had given her under her tongue until she'd been alone. As soon as she'd organized her thoughts she would swallow it and check into oblivion for a few hours.

She'd only caught a flash of the car, but it had seemed familiar. While she'd spoken with the sheriff she'd remembered. The car that had nearly run her over belonged to Mrs. Norton, a sweet, flighty lady who crocheted doilies and doll clothes for the local craft shops. Charity didn't think Mrs. Norton had ever driven over twenty-five miles an hour. That was a great deal less than the car had been doing when it had swerved at her that morning.

She hadn't seen the driver, not really, but she had the definite impression it had been a man. Mrs. Norton had been widowed for six years.

Then it was simple, Charity decided. Someone had gotten drunk, stolen Mrs. Norton's car, and taken it for a wild joyride around the island. They probably hadn't even seen her at the side of the road.

Satisfied, she eased herself up in the bed. The rest was for the sheriff to worry about. She had problems of her own.

The breakfast shift was probably in chaos. She thought she could rely on Lori to keep everyone calm. Then there was the butcher. She still had her list to complete for tomorrow's order. And she had yet to choose the photographs she wanted to use for the ad in the travel brochure. The deposit hadn't been paid, and the fireplace in cabin 3 was smoking.

What she needed was a pad, a pencil and a telephone. That was simple enough. She'd find all three at the desk in the sitting room. Carefully she eased her legs over the side of the bed. Not too bad, she decided, but she gave herself a moment to adjust before she tried to stand.

Annoyed with herself, she braced a hand on one of the bedposts. Her legs felt as though they were filled with Mae's whipped cream rather than muscle and bone.

"What the hell are you doing?"

She winced at the sound of Roman's voice, then

gingerly turned her head toward the doorway. "Nothing," she said, and tried to smile.

"Get back in bed."

"I just have a few things to do."

She was swaying on her feet, as pale as the nightshirt that buttoned modestly high at the neck and skimmed seductively high on her thighs. Without a word, he set down the tray he was carrying, crossed to her and scooped her up in his arms.

"Roman, don't. I—"

"Shut up."

"I was going to lie back down in a minute," she began. "Right after—"

"Shut up," he repeated. He laid her on the bed, then gave up. Keeping his arms around her, he buried his face against her throat. "Oh, God, baby."

"It's all right." She stroked a hand through his hair. "Don't worry."

"I thought you were dead. When I found you I thought you were dead."

"Oh, I'm sorry." She rubbed at the tension at the back of his neck, trying to imagine how he must have felt. "It must have been awful, Roman. But it's only some bumps and bruises. In a couple of days they'll be gone and we'll forget all about it."

"I won't forget." He pulled himself away from her. "Ever."

The violence she saw in his eyes had her heart fluttering. "Roman, it was an accident. Sheriff Royce will take care of it."

He bit back the words he wanted to say. It was best

that she believe it had been an accident. For now. He got up to get her tray. "Mae said you could eat."

She thought of the lists she had to make and decided she had a better chance getting around him if she co-operated. "I'll try. How's Ludwig?"

"Okay. Mae put him out and gave him a ham bone."

"Ah, his favorite." She bit into the toast and pretended she had an appetite.

"How's your head?"

"Not too bad." It wasn't really a lie, she thought. She was sure a blow with a sledgehammer would have been worse. "No stitches." She pulled back her hair to show him a pair of butterfly bandages. A bruise was darkening around them. "You want to hold up some fingers and ask me how many I see?"

"No." He turned away, afraid he would explode. The last thing she needed was another outburst from him, he reminded himself. He wasn't the kind to fall apart—at least he hadn't been until he'd met her.

He began fiddling with bottles and bowls set around the room. She loved useless little things, he thought as he picked up a wand-shaped amethyst crystal. Feeling clumsy, he set it down again.

"The sheriff said the car swerved at you." She drank the soothing chamomile tea, feeling almost human again. "I'm glad you weren't hurt."

"Damn it, Charity." He whirled, then made an effort to get a handle on his temper. "No, I wasn't hurt." And he was going to see to it that *she* wasn't hurt again. "I'm sorry. This whole business has made me edgy."

"I know what you mean. Want some tea? Mae sent up two cups."

He glanced at the pretty flowered pot. "Not unless you've got some whiskey to go in it."

"Sorry, fresh out." Smiling again, she patted the bed. "Why don't you come sit down?"

"Because I'm trying to keep my hands off you."

"Oh." Her smile curved wider. It pleased her that she was resilient enough to feel a quick curl of desire. "I like your hands on me, Roman."

"Bad timing." Because he couldn't resist, he crossed to the bed to take her hand in his. "I care about you, Charity. I want you to believe that."

"I do."

"No." His fingers tightened insistently on hers. He knew he wasn't clever with words, but he needed her to understand. "It's different with you than it's ever been with anyone." Fighting a fresh wave of frustration, he relaxed his grip. "I can't give you anything else."

She felt her heart rise up in her throat. "If I had known I could get that much out of you I might have bashed my head on a rock before."

"You deserve more." He sat down and ran a gentle finger under the bruise on her temple.

"I agree." She brought his hand to her lips and watched his eyes darken. "I'm patient."

Something was moving inside him, and he was helpless to prevent it. "You don't know enough about me. You don't know anything about me."

"I know I love you. I figured you'd tell me the rest eventually."

"Don't trust me, Charity. Not so much."

There was trouble here. She wanted to smooth it

from his face, but she didn't know how. "Have you done something so unforgivable, Roman?"

"I hope not. You should rest." Knowing he'd already said too much, he set her tray aside.

"I was going to, really. Right after I take care of a few things."

"The only thing you have to take care of today is yourself."

"That's very sweet of you, and as soon as I—"

"You're not getting out of bed for at least twenty-four hours."

"That's the most ridiculous thing I've ever heard. What possible difference does it make whether I'm lying down or sitting down?"

"According to the doctor, quite a bit." He picked up a tablet from the nightstand. "Is this the medication he gave you?"

"Yes."

"The same medication that you were supposed to take before he left?"

She struggled to keep from pouting. "I'm going to take it after I make a few phone calls."

"No phone calls today."

"Now listen, Roman, I appreciate your concern, but I don't take orders from you."

"I know. You give them to me."

Before she could respond, he lowered his lips to hers. Here was gentleness again, whisper-soft, achingly warm. With a little sound of pleasure, she sank into it.

He'd thought it would be easy to take one, only one, fleeting taste. But his hand curled into a fist as he fought the need to demand more. She was so fragile now. He wanted to soothe, not arouse…to comfort, not seduce. But in seconds he was both aroused and seduced.

When he started to pull back, she gave a murmur of protest and pressed him close again. She needed this sweetness from him, needed it more than any medication.

"Easy," he told her, clawing for his self-control. "I'm a little low on willpower, and you need rest."

"I'd rather have you."

She smiled at him, and his stomach twisted into knots. "Do you drive all men crazy?"

"I don't think so." Feeling on top of the world, she brushed his hair back from his brow. "Anyway, you're the first to ask."

"We'll talk about it later." Determined to do his best for her, he held out the pill. "Take this."

"Later."

"Uh-uh. Now."

With a sound of disgust, she popped the pill into her mouth, then picked up her cooling tea and sipped it. "There. Satisfied?"

He had to grin. "I've been a long way from satisfied since I first laid eyes on you, baby. Lift up your tongue."

"I beg your pardon?"

"You heard me. You're pretty good." He put a hand under her chin. "But I'm better. Let's have the pill."

She knew she was beaten. She took the pill out of her mouth, then made a production out of swallowing it. She touched the tip of her tongue to her lips. "It might still be in there. Want to search me for it?"

"What I want—" he kissed her lightly "—is for you to stay in bed." He shifted his lips to her throat. "No calls, no paperwork, no sneaking downstairs." He caught her earlobe between his teeth and felt her shudder, and his own. "Promise."

"Yes." Her lips parted as his brushed over them. "I promise."

"Good." He sat back and picked up the tray. "I'll see you later."

"But—" She set her teeth as he walked to the door. "You play dirty, DeWinter."

"Yeah." He glanced back at her. "And to win."

He left her, knowing she would no more break her word than she would fly out of the window. He had business of his own to attend to.

Chapter 7

An important part of Roman's training had been learning how to pursue an assignment in a thorough and objective manner. He had always found it second nature to do both. Until now. Still, for very personal reasons, he fully intended to be thorough.

When he left Charity, Roman expected to find Bob in the office, and he hoped to find him alone. He wasn't disappointed. Bob had the phone receiver at his ear and the computer monitor blinking above his fingers. After waving a distracted hand in Roman's direction, he went on with his conversation.

"I'll be happy to set that up for you and your wife, Mr. Parkington. That's a double room for the nights of the fifteenth and sixteenth of July."

"Hang up," Roman told him. Bob merely held up a finger, signaling a short wait.

"Yes, that's available with a private bath and includes breakfast. We'd be happy to help you arrange the rentals of kayaks during your stay. Your confirmation number is—"

Roman slammed a hand down on the phone, breaking the connection.

"What the hell are you doing?"

"Wondering if I should bother to talk to you or just kill you."

Bob sprang out of his chair and managed to put the desk between him and Roman. "Look, I know you've had an upsetting morning—"

"Do you?" Roman didn't bother to try to outmaneuver. He simply stood where he was and watched Bob sweat. "Upsetting. That's a nice, polite word for it. But you're a nice, polite man, aren't you, Bob?"

Bob glanced at the door and wondered if he had a chance of getting that far. "We're all a bit edgy because of Charity's accident. You could probably use a drink."

Roman moved over to a stack of computer manuals and unearthed a small silver flask. "Yours?" he said. Bob stared at him. "I imagine you keep this in here for those long nights when you're working late—and alone. Wondering how I knew where to find it?" He set it aside. "I came across it when I broke in here a couple of nights ago and went through the books."

"You broke in?" Bob wiped the back of his hand over suddenly dry lips. "That's a hell of a way to pay Charity back for giving you a job."

"Yeah, you're right about that. Almost as bad as using her inn to pass counterfeit bills and slip undesirables in and out of the country."

"I don't know what you're talking about." Bob took one cautious sideways step toward the door. "I want you out of here, DeWinter. When I tell Charity what you've done—"

"But you're not going to tell her. You're not going to tell her a damn thing—yet. But you're going to tell me." One look stopped Bob's careful movement cold. "Try for the door and I'll break your leg." Roman tapped a cigarette out of his pack. "Sit down."

"I don't have to take this." But he took a step back, away from the door, and away from Roman. "I'll call the police."

"Go ahead." Roman lit the cigarette and watched him through a veil of smoke. It was a pity Bob was so easily cowed. He'd have liked an excuse to damage him. "I was tempted to tell Royce everything I knew this morning. The problem with that was that it would have spoiled the satisfaction of dealing with you and the people you're with personally. But go ahead and call him." Roman shoved the phone across the desk in Bob's direction. "I can find a way of finishing my business with you once you're inside."

Bob didn't ask him to explain. He had heard the cell door slam the moment Roman had walked into the room. "Listen, I know you're upset...."

"Do I look upset?" Roman murmured.

No, Bob thought, his stomach clenching. He looked cold—cold enough to kill. Or worse. But there had to be a way out. There always was. "You said something about counterfeiting. Why don't you tell me what this is all about, and we'll try to settle this calm—" Before he got the last word out he was choking as Roman hauled him out of the chair by the collar.

"Do you want to die?"

"No." Bob's fingers slid helplessly off Roman's wrists.

"Then cut the crap." Disgusted, Roman tossed him back into the chair. "There are two things Charity doesn't do around here. Only two. She doesn't cook, and she doesn't work the computer. *Can't* would be a better word. She can't cook because Mae didn't teach her. Pretty easy to figure why. Mae wanted to rule in the kitchen, and Charity wanted to let her."

He moved to the window and casually lowered the shades so that the room was dim and private. "It's just as simple to figure why she can't work a basic office computer. You didn't teach her, or you made the lessons so complicated and contradictory she never caught on. You want me to tell you why you did that?"

"She was never really interested." Bob swallowed, his throat raw. "She can do the basics when she has to, but you know Charity—she's more interested in people than machines. I show her all the printouts."

"All? You and I know you haven't shown her all of them. Should I tell you what I think is on those disks you've got hidden in the file drawer?"

Bob pulled out a handkerchief with fumbling fingers and mopped at his brow. "I don't know what you're talking about."

"You keep the books for the inn, and for the little business you and your friends have on the side. I figure a man like you would keep backups, a little insurance in case the people you work for decided to cut you out." He opened a file drawer and dug out a disk. "We'll take a look at this later," he said, and tossed it onto the desk. "Two to three thousand a week washes through this place. Fifty-two weeks a year makes that a pretty good haul. Add that to the fee you charge to get someone back and forth across the border mixed with the tour group and you've got a nice, tidy sum."

"That's crazy." Barely breathing, Bob tugged at his collar. "You've got to know that's crazy."

"Did you know your references were still on file here?" Roman asked conversationally. "The problem is, they don't check out. You never worked for a hotel back in Ft. Worth, or in San Francisco."

"So I padded my chances a bit. That doesn't prove anything."

"I think we'll turn up something more interesting when we run your prints."

Bob stared down at the disk. Sometimes you could bluff, and sometimes you had to fold. "Can I have a drink?"

Roman picked up the flask, tossed it to him and waited while he twisted off the cap. "You made me for a cop, didn't you? Or you were worried enough to keep your ear to the ground. You heard me asking the wrong questions, were afraid I'd told Charity about the operation and passed it along to your friends."

"It didn't feel right." Bob wiped the vodka from his lips, then drank again. "I know a scam when I see one, and you made me nervous the minute I saw you."

"Why?"

"When you're in my business you get so you can spot cops. In the supermarket, on the street, buying underwear at a department store. It doesn't matter where, you get so you can make them."

Roman thought of himself and of the years he'd spent on the other side of the street. He'd made his share of cops, and he still could. "Okay. So what did you do?"

"I told Block I thought you were a plant, but he figured I was going loopy. I wanted to back off until you'd gone, but he wouldn't listen. Last night, when you went down for dinner, I looked through your room. I found a box of shells. No gun, just the shells. That meant you were wearing it. I called Block and told him I was sure you were a cop. You'd been spending a lot of time with Charity, so I figured she was working with you on it."

"So you tried to kill her."

"No, not me." Panicked, Bob pressed back in his chair. "I swear. I'm not a violent man, DeWinter. Hell, I like Charity. I wanted to pull out, take a breather. We'd already set up another place, in the Olympic Mountains. I figured we could take a few weeks, run legit, then move on it. Block just said he'd take care of it, and I thought he meant we'd handle next week's tour on the level. That would give me time to fix everything here and get out. If I'd known what he was planning…"

"What? Would you have warned her?"

"I don't know." Bob drained the flask, but the liquor did little to calm his nerves. "Look, I do scams, I do cons. I don't kill people."

"Who was driving the car?"

"I don't know. I swear it," he said. Roman took a step toward him, and he gripped the arms of his chair. "Listen, I got in touch with Block the minute this happened. He said he'd hired somebody. He couldn't have done it himself, because he was on the mainland. He said the guy wasn't trying to kill her. Block just wanted her out of the way for a few days. We've got a big shipment coming in and—" He broke off, knowing he was digging himself in deeper.

Roman merely nodded. "You're going to find out who was driving the car."

"Okay, sure." He made the promise without knowing if he could keep it. "I'll find out."

"You and I are going to work together for the next few days, Bob."

"But…aren't you going to call Royce?"

"Let me worry about Royce. You're going to go on doing what you do best. Lying. Only now you're going to lie to Block. You do exactly what you're told and you'll stay alive. If you do a good job I'll put in a word for you with my superior. Maybe you can make a deal, turn state's evidence."

After resting a hip on the desk, Roman leaned closer. "If you try to check out, I'll hunt you down. I'll find you wherever you hide, and when I'm finished you'll wish I'd killed you."

Bob looked into Roman's eyes. He believed him. "What do you want me to do?"

"Tell me about the next shipment."

Charity was sick of it. It was bad enough that she'd given her word to Roman and had to stay in bed all day. She couldn't even use the phone to call the office and see what was going on in the world.

She'd tried to be good-humored about it, poking

through the books and magazines that Lori had brought up to her. She'd even admitted—to herself—that there had been times, when things had gotten crazy at the inn, that she'd imagined having the luxury of an idle day in bed.

Now she had it, and she hated it.

The pill Roman had insisted she swallow had made her groggy. She drifted off periodically, only to wake later, annoyed that she didn't have enough control to stay awake and be bored. Because reading made her headache worse, she tried to work up some interest in the small portable television perched on the shelf across the room.

When she'd found *The Maltese Falcon* flickering in black and white she'd felt both pleasure and relief. If she had to be trapped in bed, it might as well be with Bogart. Even as Sam Spade succumbed to the Fat Man's drug, Charity's own medication sent her under. She awoke in a very poor temper to a rerun of a sitcom.

He'd made her promise to stay in bed, she thought, jabbing an elbow at her pillow. And he didn't even have the decency to spend five minutes keeping her company. Apparently he was too busy to fit a sickroom call into his schedule. That was fine for him, she decided, running around doing something useful while she was moldering between the sheets. It wasn't in her nature to do nothing, and if she had to do it for five minutes longer she was going to scream.

Charity smiled a bit as she considered that. Just what would he do if she let out one long bloodcurdling scream? It might be interesting to find out. Certainly more interesting, she decided, than watching a blond airhead jiggle around a set to the beat of a laugh track. Nodding, she sucked in her breath.

"What are you doing?"

She let it out again in a long huff as Roman pushed open the door. Pleasure came first, but she quickly buried it in resentment. "You're always asking me that."

"Am I?" He was carrying another tray. Charity distinctly caught the scent of Mae's prize chicken soup and her biscuits. "Well, what were you doing?"

"Dying of boredom. I think I'd rather be shot." After eyeing the tray, she decided to be marginally friendly. But not because she was glad to see him, she thought. It was dusk, and she hadn't eaten for hours. "Is that for me?"

"Possibly." He set the tray over her lap, then stayed close and took a long, hard look at her. There was no way for him to describe the fury he felt when he saw the bruises and the bandages. Just as there was no way for him to describe the sense of pleasure and relief he experienced when he saw the annoyance in her eyes and the color in her cheeks.

"I think you're wrong, Charity. You're going to live."

"No thanks to you." She dived into the soup. "First you trick a promise out of me, then you leave me to rot for the next twelve hours. You might have come up for a minute to see if I had lapsed into a coma."

He *had* come up, about the time Sam Spade had been unwrapping the mysterious bird, but she'd been sleeping. Nonetheless, he'd stayed for nearly half an hour, just watching her.

"I've been a little busy," he told her, and broke off half of her biscuit for himself.

"I'll bet." Feeling far from generous, she snatched it

back. "Well, since you're here, you might tell me how things are going downstairs."

"They're under control," he murmured, thinking of Bob and the phone calls that had already been made.

"It's only Bonnie's second day. She hasn't—"

"She's doing fine," he said, interrupting her. "Mae's watching her like a hawk. Where'd all these come from?" He gestured toward half a dozen vases of fresh flowers.

"Oh, Lori brought up the daisies with the magazines. Then the ladies came up. They really shouldn't have climbed all those stairs. They brought the wood violets." She rattled off more names of people who had brought or sent flowers.

He should have brought her some, Roman thought, rising and thrusting his hands into his pockets. It had never crossed his mind. Things like that didn't, he admitted. Not the small, romantic things a woman like Charity was entitled to.

"Roman?"

"What?"

"Did you come all the way up here to scowl at my peonies?"

"No." He hadn't even known the name for them. He turned away from the fat pink blossoms. "Do you want any more to eat?"

"No." She tapped the spoon against the side of her empty bowl. "I don't want any more to eat, I don't want any more magazines and I don't want anyone else to come in here, pat my hand and tell me to get plenty of rest. So if that's what you've got in mind you can leave."

"You're a charming patient, Charity." Checking his own temper, he removed the tray.

"No, I'm a miserable patient." Furiously, she tossed aside her self-control, and just as furiously tossed a paperback at his head. Fortunately for them both, her aim was off. "And I'm tired of being stuck in here as though I had some communicable disease. I have a bump on the head, damn it, not a brain tumor."

"I don't think a brain tumor's contagious."

"Don't be clever with me." Glaring at him, she folded her arms and dropped them over her chest. "I'm sick of being here, and sicker yet of being told what to do."

"You don't take that well, do you? No matter how good it is for you?"

When she was being unreasonable there was nothing she wanted to hear less than the truth. "I have an inn to run, and I can't do it from bed."

"Not tonight you don't."

"It's my inn, just like it's my body and my head." She tossed the covers aside. Even as she started to scramble out of bed her promise weighed on her like a chain. Swinging her legs up again, she fell back against the pillows.

Thumbs hooked in his pockets, he measured her. "Why don't you get up?"

"Because I promised. Now get out, damn it. Just get out and leave me alone."

"Fine. I'll tell Mae and the rest that you're feeling more like yourself. They've been worried about you."

She threw another book—harder—but had only the

small satisfaction of hearing it slap against the closing door.

The hell with him, she thought as she dropped her chin on her knees. The hell with everything.

The hell with her. He hadn't gone up there to pick a fight, and he didn't have to tolerate a bad-tempered woman throwing things at him, especially when he couldn't throw them back. Roman got halfway down the stairs, turned around and stalked back up again.

Charity was moping when he pushed open the door. She knew it, she hated it, and she wished everyone would leave her in peace to get on with it.

"What now?"

"Get up."

Charity straightened her spine against the headboard. "Why?"

"Get up," Roman repeated. "Get dressed. There must be a floor to mop or a trash can to empty around here."

"I said I wouldn't get up—" she set her chin "—and I won't."

"You can get out of bed on your own, or I can drag you out."

Temper had her eyes darkening and her chin thrusting out even farther. "You wouldn't dare." She regretted the words even as she spoke them. She'd already decided he was a man who would dare anything.

She was right. Roman crossed to the bed and grabbed her arm. Charity gripped one of the posts. Despite her hold, he managed to pull her up on her knees before she dug in. Before the tug-of-war could get much further she began to giggle.

"This is stupid." She felt her grip slipping and

hooked her arm around the bedpost. "Really stupid. Roman, stop. I'm going to end up falling on my face and putting another hole in my head."

"You wanted to get up. So get up."

"No, I wanted to feel sorry for myself. And I was doing a pretty good job of it, too. Roman, you're about to dislocate my shoulder."

"You're the most stubborn, hardheaded, unreasonable woman I've ever met," he said. But he released her.

"I have to go along with the first two, but I'm not usually unreasonable." Offering him a smile, she sat cross-legged. The storm was over. At least hers was, she thought. She recognized the anger that was still darkening his eyes. She let out a long sigh. "I guess you could say I was having a really terrific pity party for myself when you came in. I'm sorry I took it out on you."

"I don't need an apology."

"Yes, you do." She would have offered him a hand, but he didn't look ready to sign any peace treaties. "I'm not used to being cut off from what's going on. I'm hardly ever sick, so I haven't had much practice in taking it like a good little soldier." She idly pleated the sheet between her fingers as she slanted a look at him. "I really am sorry, Roman. Are you going to stay mad at me?"

"That might be the best solution." Anger had nothing to do with what he was feeling at the moment. She looked so appealing with that half smile on her face, her hair tousled, the nightshirt buttoned to her chin and skimming her thighs.

"Want to slug me?"

"Maybe." It was hopeless. He smiled and sat down beside her. He balled his hand into a fist and skimmed it lightly over her chin. "When you're back on your feet again I'll take another shot."

"It was nice of you to bring me dinner. I didn't even thank you."

"No, you didn't."

She leaned forward to kiss his cheek. "Thanks."

"You're welcome."

After blowing the hair out of her eyes, she decided to start over. "Did we have a good crowd tonight?"

"I bused thirty tables."

"I'm going to have to give you a raise. I guess Mae made her chocolate mousse torte."

"Yeah." Roman found his lips twitching again.

"I don't suppose there was any left over."

"Not a crumb. It was great."

"You had some?"

"Meals are part of my pay."

Feeling deprived, Charity leaned back against the pillows. "Right."

"Are you going to sulk again?"

"Just for a minute. I wanted to ask you if the sheriff had any news about the car."

"Not much. He found it about ten miles from here, abandoned." He reached over to smooth away a line between her brows. "Don't worry about it."

"I'm not. Not really. I'm just glad the driver didn't hurt anyone else. Lori said you'd cut your arm."

"A little." Their hands were linked. He didn't know whether he had taken hers or she had taken his.

"Were you taking a walk?"

"I was waiting for you."

"Oh." She smiled again.

"You'd better get some rest." He was feeling awkward again, awkward and clumsy. No other woman had ever drawn either reaction from him.

Reluctantly she released his hand. "Are we friends again?"

"I guess you could say that. Good night, Charity."

"Good night."

He crossed to the door and opened it. But he couldn't step across the threshold. He stood there, struggling with himself. Though it was only a matter of seconds, it seemed like hours to both of them.

"I can't." He turned back, shutting the door quietly behind him.

"Can't what?"

"I can't leave."

Her smile bloomed, in her eyes, on her lips. She opened her arms to him, as he had known she would. Walking back to her was nearly as difficult as walking away. He took her hands and held them hard in his.

"I'm no good for you, Charity."

"I think you're very good for me." She brought their joined hands to her cheek. "That means one of us is wrong."

"If I could, I'd walk out the door and keep going."

She felt the sting and accepted it. She'd never expected loving Roman to be painless. "Why?"

"For reasons I can't begin to explain to you." He stared down at their linked hands. "But I can't walk away. Sooner or later you're going to wish I had."

"No." She drew him down onto the bed. "Whatever happens, I'll always be glad you stayed." This time she smoothed the lines from his brow. "I told you before that this wouldn't happen unless it was right. I meant that." Lifting her hands, she linked them behind his neck. "I love you, Roman. Tonight is something I want, something I've chosen."

Kissing her was like sinking into a dream. Soft, drugging and too impossibly beautiful to be real. He wanted to take care, such complete, such tender care, not to hurt her now, knowing that he would have no choice but to hurt her eventually.

But tonight, for a few precious hours, there would be no future. With her he could be what he had never tried to be before. Gentle, loving, kind. With her he could believe it was possible for love to be enough.

He loved her. Though he'd never known he was capable of that strong and fragile emotion, he felt it with her. It streamed through him, painless and sweet, healing wounds he'd forgotten he had, soothing aches he'd lived with forever. How could he have known when he'd walked into her life that she would be his salvation? In the short time he had left he would show her. And in showing her he would give himself something he had never expected to have.

He made her feel beautiful. And delicate, Charity thought as his mouth whispered over hers. It was as though he knew that this first time together was to be savored and remembered. She heard her own sigh, then his, as her hands slid up his back. Whatever she had wished they could have together was nothing compared to this.

He laid her back gently, barely touching her, as the kiss lengthened. Even loving him as she did, she hadn't known he'd possessed such tenderness. Nor could she know that he had just discovered it in himself.

The lamplight glowed amber. He hadn't thought to light the candles. But he could see her in the brilliance of it, her eyes dark and on his, her lips curved as he brought his to meet them. He hadn't thought to set the music. But her nightshirt whispered as she brought her arms around him. It was a sound he would remember always. Air drifted in through the open window, stirring the scent of the flowers others had brought to her. But it was the fragrance of her skin that filled his head. It was the taste of it that he yearned for.

Lightly, almost afraid he might bruise her with a touch, he cupped her breasts in his hands. Her breath caught, then released on a moan against the side of his neck. He knew that nothing had ever excited him more.

Then her hands were on his shirt, her fingers undoing his buttons as her eyes remained on his. They were as dark, as deep, as vibrant, as the water that surrounded her home. He could read everything she felt in them.

"I want to touch you," she said as she drew the shirt from his shoulders. Her heart began to sprint as she looked at him, the taut muscles, the taut skin.

There was a strength in him that excited, perhaps because she understood that he could be ruthless. There was a toughness to his body, a toughness that made her realize he was a man who had fought, a man who would fight. But his hands were gentle on her now, almost hesitant. Her excitement leaped higher, and there was no fear in it.

"It seems I've wanted to touch you like this all my life." She ran her fingertips lightly over the bandage on his arm. "Does it hurt?"

"No." Every muscle in his body tensed when she

trailed her hands from his waist to his chest. It was impossible for him to understand how anyone could bring him peace and torment at the same time. "Charity…"

"Just kiss me again, Roman," she murmured.

He was helpless to refuse. He wondered what she would ask him for if she knew that he was powerless to deny her anything at this moment. Fighting back a flood of desperation, he kept his hands easy, sliding and stroking them over her until he felt the tremors begin.

He knew he could give her pleasure. The need to do so pulsed heavily inside him. He could ignite her passions. The drive to fan them roared through him like a brushfire. As he touched her he knew he could make her weak or strong, wild or limp. But it wasn't power that filled him at the knowledge. It was awe.

She would give him whatever he asked, without questions, without restrictions. This strong, beautiful, exciting woman was his. This wasn't a dream that would awaken him to frustration in the middle of the night. This wasn't a wish that he'd have to pretend he'd never made. It was real. She was real, and she was waiting for him.

He could have torn the nightshirt from her with one pull of his hand. Instead, he released button after tiny button, hearing her breath quicken, following the narrow path with soft, lingering kisses. Her fingers dug into his back, then went limp as her system churned. She could only groan as his tongue moistened her flesh, teasing and heating it. The night air whispered over her as he undressed her. Then he was lifting her, cradling her in his arms.

She was twined around him, her heart thudding frantically against his lips. He needed a moment to drag himself back, to find the control he wanted so that he could take her up, take her over. Murmuring to her, he used what skills he had to drive her past the edge of reason.

Her body was rigid against his. He watched her dazed eyes fly open. She gasped his name, and then he covered her mouth with his to capture her long, low moan as her body went limp.

She seemed to slide like water through his hands when he laid her down again. To his delight, her arousal burst free again at his lightest touch.

It was impossible. It was impossible to feel so much and still need more. Blindly she reached for him. Fresh pleasure poured into her until her arms felt too heavy to move. She was a prisoner, a gloriously willing prisoner, of the frantic sensations he sent tearing through her. She wanted to lock herself around him, to keep him there, always there. He was taking her on a long, slow journey to places she had never seen, places she never wanted to leave.

When he slid inside her she heard his low, breathless moan. So he was as much a captive as she.

With his face pressed against her neck, he fought the need to sprint toward release. He was trapped between heaven and hell, and he gloried in it. In her. In them. He heard her sob out his name, felt the strength pour into her. She was with him as no one had ever been.

Charity wrapped her arms around Roman to keep him from shifting away. "Don't move."

"I'm hurting you."

"No." She let out a long, long sigh. "No, you're not."

"I'm too heavy," he insisted, and compromised by gathering her close and rolling so that their positions were reversed.

"Okay." Satisfied, she rested her head on his shoulder. "You are," she said, "the most incredible lover."

He didn't even try to prevent the smile. "Thanks." He stroked a possessive hand down to her hip. "Have you had many?"

It was her turn to smile. The little trace of jealousy in his voice was a tremendous addition to an already-glorious night. "Define *many*."

Ignoring the quick tug of annoyance he felt, he played the game. "More than three. Three is a few. Anything more than three is many."

"Ah. Well, in that case." She almost wished she could lie and invent a horde. "I guess I've had less than a few. That doesn't mean I don't know an incredible one when I find him."

He lifted her head to stare at her. "I've done nothing in my life to deserve you."

"Don't be stupid." She inched up to kiss him briefly. "And don't change the subject."

"What subject?"

"You're clever, DeWinter, but not that clever." She lifted a brow and studied him in the lamplight. "It's my turn to ask you if you've had many lovers."

He didn't smile this time. "Too many. But only one who's meant anything."

The amusement faded from her eyes before she

closed them. "You'll make me cry," she murmured, lowering her head to his chest again.

Not yet, he thought, stroking her hair. Soon enough, but not yet. "Why haven't you ever gotten married?" he wondered aloud. "Had babies?"

"What a strange question. I haven't loved anyone enough before." She winced at her own words, then made herself smile as she lifted her head. "That wasn't a hint."

But it was exactly what he'd wanted to hear. He knew he was crazy to let himself think that way, even for a few hours, but he wanted to imagine her loving him enough to forgive, to accept and to promise.

"How about the traveling you said you wanted to do? Shouldn't that come first?"

She shrugged and settled against him again. "Maybe I haven't traveled because I know deep down I'd hate to go all those places alone. What good is Venice if you don't have someone to ride in a gondola with? Or Paris if there's no one to hold hands with?"

"You could go with me."

Already half-asleep, she laughed. She imagined Roman had little more than the price of a ferry ticket to his name. "Okay. Let me know when to pack."

"Would you?" He lifted her chin to look into her drowsy eyes.

"Of course." She kissed him, snuggled her head against his shoulder and went to sleep.

Roman switched off the lamp beside the bed. For a long time he held her and stared into the dark.

Chapter 8

Charity opened her eyes slowly, wondering why she couldn't move. Groggy, she stared into Roman's face. It was only inches from hers. He had pulled her close in his sleep, effectively pinning her arms and legs with his. Though his grip on her was somewhat guardlike, she found it unbearably sweet.

Ignoring the discomfort, she lay still and took advantage of the moment by looking her fill.

She'd always thought that people looked softer, more vulnerable, in sleep. Not Roman. He had the body of a fighter and the eyes of a man accustomed to facing trouble head-on. His eyes were closed now, and his body was relaxed. Almost.

Still, studying him, she decided that, asleep or awake, he looked tough as nails. Had he always been? she wondered. Had he had to be? It was true that smiling lent a certain charm to his face. It lightened the wariness in his eyes. In Charity's opinion, Roman smiled much too seldom.

She would fix that. Her own lips curved as she watched him. In time she would, gently, teach him to relax, to enjoy, to trust. She would make him happy. It wasn't possible to love as she had loved and not have it returned. And it wasn't possible to share what they had shared during the night without his heart being as lost as hers.

Sooner or later—sooner, if she had her way—he would come to accept how good they were together. And how much better they would become in all the years to follow. Then there would be time for promises and families and futures.

I'm not letting you go, she told him silently. *You don't realize it yet, but I've got a hold on you, and it's going to be mighty hard to break it.*

He had such a capacity for giving, she thought. Not just physically, though she wasn't ashamed to admit that his skill there had dazed and delighted her. He was a man full of emotions, too many of them strapped down. What had happened to him, she wondered, that had made him so wary of love, and so afraid to give it?

She loved him too much to demand an answer. It was a question he had to answer on his own…a question she knew he would answer as soon as he trusted her enough. When he did, all she had to do was show him that none of it mattered. All that counted, from this moment on, was what they felt for each other.

Inching over, she brushed a light kiss on his mouth. His eyes opened instantly. It took only a heartbeat longer for them to clear. Fascinated, Charity watched their expression change from one of suspicion to one of desire.

"You're a light sleeper," she began. "I just—"

Before she could complete the thought, his mouth, hungry and insistent, was on hers. She managed a quiet moan as she melted into his kiss.

It was the only way he knew to tell her what it meant to him to wake and find her close and warm and willing. Too many mornings he had woken alone in strange beds in empty rooms.

That was what he expected. For years he had deliberately separated himself from anyone who had tried to get close. The job. He'd told himself it was because of the job. But that was a lie, one of many. He'd chosen to remain alone because he hadn't wanted to risk losing again. Grieving again. Now, overnight, everything had changed.

He would remember it all, the pale fingers of light creeping into the room, the high echoing sound of the first birds calling to the rising sun, the scent of her skin as it heated against his. And her mouth…he would remember the taste of her mouth as it opened eagerly under his.

There were such deep, dark needs in him. She felt them, understood them, and met them unquestioningly. As dawn swept the night aside, he stirred her own until their needs mirrored each other's.

Slowly, easily, while his lips cruised over her face, he slipped inside her. With a sigh and a murmur, she welcomed him.

She felt as strong as an ox and as content as a cat with cream on its whiskers. With her eyes closed, Charity stretched her arms to the ceiling.

"And to think I used to consider jogging the best way to start the day." Laughing, she curled over against him again. "I have to thank you for showing me how very wrong I was."

"My pleasure." He could still feel his own heart thudding like a jackhammer against his ribs. "Give me a minute and I'll show you the best reason for staying in bed in the morning."

Lord, it was tempting. Before her blood could begin to heat she shook her head. She took a quick nip at his chin before she sat up. "Maybe if you've got some time when I get back."

He took her wrist but kept his fingers light. "From where?"

"From taking Ludwig for his run."

"No."

The hand that had lifted to push back her hair paused. Deliberately she continued to lift it to finger-comb the hair away from her face. "No, what?"

He recognized that tone. She was the boss again, despite the fact that her face was still glowing from lovemaking and she was naked to where the sheets pooled at her waist. This was the woman who didn't take orders. Roman decided he would have to show her again that she was wrong.

"No, you're not taking the dog out for a run."

Because she wanted to be reasonable, she added a smile. "Of course I am. I kept my promise and stayed in bed all day yesterday. And all night, for that matter. Now I'm going to get back to work."

Around the inn, that was fine. In fact, the sooner everything got back to normal the better it would be. But there was no way he was having her walking down a deserted road by herself. "You're in no shape to go for a mile hike."

"Three miles, and yes, I am."

"Three?" Lifting a brow, he stroked a hand over her thigh. "No wonder you've got such great muscle tone."

"That's not the point." She shifted away before his touch could weaken her.

"You have the most incredible body."

She shoved at his seeking hands. "Roman... I do?"

His lips curved. This was the way she liked them best. "Absolutely. Let me show you."

"No, I..." She caught his hands as they stroked her thighs. "We'll probably kill each other if we try this again."

"I'll risk it."

"Roman, I mean it." Her head fell back and she gasped when he scraped his teeth over her skin. It was impossible, she thought, impossible, for this deep, dark craving to take over again. "Roman—"

"Fabulous legs," he murmured, skimming his tongue behind her knee. "I didn't pay nearly enough attention to them last night."

"Yes, you—" She braced a hand against the mattress as she swayed. "You're trying to distract me."

"Yeah."

"You can't." She closed her eyes. He could, and he was. "Ludwig needs the run," she managed. "He enjoys it."

"Fine." He sat up and circled her waist with his hands. "I'll take him."

"You?" Wanting to catch her breath, she turned her head to avoid his kiss, then shuddered as his lips trailed down her throat. "It's not necessary. I'm perfectly... Roman." She said his name weakly as his thumbs circled her breasts.

"Yes, a truly incredible body," he murmured. "Long and lean and incredibly responsive. I can't seem to touch you and not want you."

She came up on her knees as he dragged another gasp out of her. "You're trying to seduce me."

"Nothing gets by you, does it?"

She was losing, weakening shamelessly. She knew it would infuriate her later, but for now all she could do was cling to him and let him have his way. "Is this your answer for everything?"

"No." He lifted her hips and brought her to him. "But it'll do."

Unable to resist, she wrapped her limbs around him and let passion take them both. When it was spent, she slid bonelessly down in the bed. She didn't argue when he drew the sheets over her shoulders.

"Stay here," he told her, kissing her hair. "I'll be back."

"His leash is on a hook under the steps," Charity murmured. "He gets two scoops of dog food when he gets back. And fresh water."

"I think I can handle a dog, Charity."

She yawned and tugged the blankets higher. "He likes to chase the Fitzsimmonses' cat. But don't worry, he can't catch her."

"That makes me breathe easier." He laced up his shoes. "Anything else I should know?"

"Mmm." She snuggled into the pillow. "I love you."

As always, it knocked him backward to hear her say it, to know she meant it. In silence, he stepped outside.

She wasn't tired, Charity thought as she stretched under the sheets. But Roman was right. Sleep wasn't the best reason for staying in bed in the morning. Despite her bumps and bruises, she knew she'd never felt better in her life.

Still, she indulged herself, lingering in bed, half dreaming, until guilt finally prodded her out.

Moving automatically, she turned on the stereo, then tidied the bed. In the parlor she glanced over the notes she'd left for herself, made a few more. Then she headed for the shower. She was humming along to Tchaikovsky's violin concerto when the curtain swished open.

"Roman!" She pressed both hands to her heart and leaned back against the tile. "You might as well shoot me as scare me to death. Didn't you ever hear of the Bates Motel?"

"I left my butcher knife in my other pants." She had her hair piled on top of her head and a cake of some feminine scented soap in her hand. Her skin was gleaming wet and already soapy. He pulled off his shirt and tossed it aside. "Did you ever consider teaching that dog to heel?"

"No." She grinned as she watched Roman unfasten his jeans. "I guess you could use a shower." Saying nothing, he tossed his jeans on top of his shirt. Charity took a moment to make a long, thorough survey. "Well, apparently that run didn't...tire you out." She was laughing when he stepped in with her.

It was nearly an hour later when Charity made it

down to the lobby. "I could eat one of everything." She pressed a hand to her stomach. "Good morning, Bob." She paused at the front desk to smile at him.

"Charity." Bob felt the sweat spring onto his palms when he spotted Roman behind her. "How are you feeling? It's awfully soon for you to be up and around."

"I'm fine." Idly she glanced at the papers on the desk. "Sorry I left you in the lurch yesterday."

"Don't be silly." Fear ground in his stomach as he eyed the wound on her temple. "We were worried about you."

"I appreciate that, but there's no need to worry anymore." She slanted a smile at Roman. "I've never felt better in my life."

Bob caught the look, and his stomach sank. If the cop was in love with her, he thought, things were going to be even stickier. "Glad to hear it. But—"

She stopped his protest by raising a hand. "Is there anything urgent?"

"No." He glanced at Roman again. "No, nothing."

"Good." After setting the papers aside again, Charity studied his face. "What's wrong, Bob?"

"Nothing. What could be wrong?"

"You look a little pale. You're not coming down with anything, are you?"

"No, everything's fine. Just fine. We got some new reservations. July's almost booked solid."

"Great. I'll look things over after breakfast. Get yourself some coffee." She patted his hand and walked into the dining room.

Three tables were already occupied, the patrons enjoying Mae's coffee cake before their meal was served.

Bonnie was busy taking orders. The breakfast menu was neatly listed on the board, and music was playing in the background, soft and soothing. The flowers were fresh, and the coffee was hot.

"Something wrong?" Roman asked her.

"No." Charity smoothed down the collar of her shirt. "What could be wrong? It looks like everything's just dandy." Feeling useless, she walked into the kitchen.

There was no bickering to referee. Mae and Dolores were working side by side, and Lori loaded up a tray with her first order.

"We need more butter for the French toast," Mae called out.

"Coming right up." Cheerful as a bird, Dolores began to scoop up neat balls of butter. As she offered the newly filled bowl to Lori, she spotted Charity standing inside the door. "Well, good morning." Her thin face creased with a smile. "Didn't expect to see you up."

"I'm fine."

"Sit down, girl." Hardly glancing around, Mae continued to sprinkle shredded cheese into an omelet. "Dolores will get you some tea."

Charity smiled with clenched teeth. "I don't want any tea."

"Want and need's two different things."

"Glad to see you're feeling better," Lori said as she rushed out with her tray.

Bonnie came in, pad in hand. "Oh, hi, Charity, we thought you'd rest another day. Feeling better?"

"I'm fine," Charity said tightly. "Just fine."

"Great. Two omelets with bacon, Mae. And an order of French toast with sausage. Two herb teas, an English muffin—crisp. And we're running low on coffee." After punching her order sheet on a hook by the stove, she took the fresh pot Dolores handed her and hurried out.

Charity walked over to get an apron, only to have Mae smack her hand away. "I told you to sit."

"And I told you I'm fine. That's *f-i-n-e*. I'm going to help take orders."

"The only orders you're taking today are from me. Now sit." She ran a hand up and down Charity's arm. Nobody recognized or knew how to deal with that stubborn look better than Mae. "Be a good girl, now. I won't worry so much if I know you've had a good breakfast. You don't want me to worry, do you?"

"No, of course not, but—"

"That's right. Now take a seat. I'll fix you some French toast. It's your favorite."

She sat down. Dolores set a cup of tea in front of her and patted her head. "You sure did give us all a fright yesterday. Have a seat, Roman. I'll get your coffee."

"Thanks. You're sulking," he murmured to Charity.

"I am not."

"Doc's coming by this morning to take another look at you."

"Oh, for heaven's sake, Mae—"

"You're not doing nothing till he gives the okay." With a nod, she began preparing Bonnie's order. "Fat lot of good you'll do if you're not a hundred percent. Things were hard enough yesterday."

Charity stopped staring into her tea and looked up. "Were they?"

"Everybody asking questions nobody had the answer to. Whole stacks of linens lost."

"Lost? But—"

"Found them." Mae made room at the stove for Dolores. "But it sure was confusing for a while. Then the dinner shift... Could have used an extra pair of hands for sure." Mae winked at Roman over Charity's head. "We'll all be mighty glad when the doc gives you his okay. Let that bacon crisp, Dolores."

"It is crisp."

"Not enough."

"Want me to burn it?"

Charity smiled and sipped her tea. It was good to be back.

It was midafternoon before she saw Roman again. She had a pencil behind her ear, a pad in one pocket and a dust cloth in another, and she was dashing down the hallway toward her rooms.

"In a hurry?"

"Oh." She stopped long enough to smile at him. "Yes. I have some papers up in my room that should be in the office."

"What's this?" He tugged at the dust cloth.

"One of the housekeepers came down with a virus. I sent her home." She looked at her watch and frowned. She thought she could spare about two minutes for conversation. "I really hope that's not what's wrong with Bob."

"What's wrong with Bob?"

"I don't know. He just doesn't look well." She tossed her hair back, causing the slender gold spirals in her ears to dance. "Anyway, we're short a housekeeper, and we've got guests checking into units 3 and 5 today. The

Garsons checked out of 5 this morning. They won't win any awards for neatness."

"The doctor said you were supposed to rest an hour this afternoon."

"Yes, but— How did you know?"

"I asked him." Roman pulled the dustcloth out of her pocket. "I'll clean 5."

"Don't be ridiculous. It's not your job."

"My job's to fix things. I'll fix 5." He took her chin in his hand before she could protest. "When I'm finished I'm going to go upstairs. If you aren't in bed I'm coming after you."

"Sounds like a threat."

He bent down and kissed her, hard. "It is."

"I'm terrified," she said, and dashed up the stairs.

It wasn't that she meant to ignore the doctor's orders. Not really. It was only that a nap came far down on her list of things to be done. Every phone call she made had to include a five-minute explanation of her injuries.

No, she was really quite well. Yes, it was terrible that someone had stolen poor Mrs. Norton's car and driven it so recklessly. Yes, she was sure the sheriff would get to the bottom of it. No, she had not broken her legs… her arm…her shoulder…. Yes, she intended to take good care of herself, thank you very much.

The goodwill and concern would have warmed her if she hadn't been so far behind in her work. To make it worse, Bob was distracted and disorganized. Worried that he was ill or dealing with a personal problem, Charity took on the brunt of his work.

Twice she'd fully intended to take a break and go up

to her rooms, and twice she'd been delayed by guests checking in. Taking it on faith that Roman had spruced up unit 5, she showed a young pair of newlyweds inside.

"You have a lovely view of the garden from here," Charity said as a cover while she made sure there were fresh towels. Roman had hung them on the rack, exactly where they belonged. The bed, with its heart-shaped white wicker headboard, was made up with a military precision she couldn't have faulted. It cost her, but she resisted the temptation to turn up the coverlet and check sheets.

"We serve complimentary wine in the gathering room every evening at five. We recommend that you make a reservation for dinner if you plan to join us, particularly since it's Saturday night. Breakfast is served between seven-thirty and ten. If you'd like to—" She broke off when Roman stepped into the room. "I'll be with you in a minute," she told him, and started to turn back to the newlyweds.

"Excuse me." Roman gave them both a friendly nod before he scooped Charity up in his arms. "Miss Ford is needed elsewhere. Enjoy your stay."

As the first shock wore off she began to struggle. "Are you out of your mind? Put me down."

"I intend to—when I get you to bed."

"You can't just…" The words trailed off into a groan as he carried her through the gathering room.

Two men sitting on the sofa stopped telling fish stories. A family coming in from a hike gawked from the doorway. Miss Millie and Miss Lucy halted their daily game of Scrabble by the window.

"Isn't that the most romantic thing?" Miss Millie said when they disappeared into the west wing.

"You have totally embarrassed me."

Roman shifted her weight in his arms and carried her upstairs. "You're lucky that's all I did."

"You had no right interrupting me when I was welcoming guests. Then, to make matters worse, you decide to play Rhett Butler."

"As I recall, he had something entirely different in mind when he carried another stubborn woman up to bed." He dropped her, none too gently, on the mattress. "You're going to rest."

"I'm tempted to tell you to go to hell."

He leaned down to cage her head between his hands. "Be my guest."

She'd be damned if she'd smile. "My manners are too ingrained to permit it."

"Aren't I the lucky one?" He leaned a little closer. There was amusement in his eyes now, enough of it so she had to bite her lip to keep from laughing. "I don't want you to get out of this bed for sixty minutes."

"Or?"

"Or… I'll sic Mae on you."

"A low blow, DeWinter."

He brushed a kiss just below the fresh bandage on her temple. "Tune out for an hour, baby. It won't kill you."

She reached up to toy with the top button of his shirt. "I'd like it better if you got in with me."

"I said tuned out, not turned on." When the phone in the parlor rang, he held her down with one hand. "Not a chance. Stay here and I'll get it."

She rolled her eyes behind his back as he walked into the adjoining room.

"Yes? She's resting. Tell him she'll get back to him in an hour. Hold her calls until four. That's right." He glanced down idly at a catalog she'd left open on her desk. She had circled a carved gold bracelet with a square-cut purple stone. "You handle whatever needs to be handled for the next hour. That's right."

"What was it?" Charity called from the next room.

"I'll tell you in an hour."

"Damn it, Roman."

He stopped in the doorway. "You want the message, I'll give it to you in an hour."

"But if it's important—"

"It's not."

She sent him a smoldering look. "How do you know?"

"I know it's not more important than you. Nothing is." He closed the door on her astonished expression.

He needed to keep Bob on a tight leash, he thought as he headed downstairs. As long as he was more afraid of him than of Block, things would be fine. He only had to keep the pressure on for a few more days. Block and Vision Tours would be checking in on Tuesday. When they checked out on Thursday morning he would lock the cage.

Roman pushed open the door of the office to find Bob staring at the computer screen and gulping coffee. "For somebody who's made his living from scams you're a mess."

Bob gulped more coffee. "I never worked with a cop looking over my shoulder before."

"Just think of me as your new partner," Roman advised him. He took the mug out of his hand and sniffed at it. "And lay off the booze."

"Give me a break."

"I'm giving you more of one than you deserve. Charity's worried that you're coming down with something—something other than a stretch in federal prison. I don't want her worrying."

"Look, you want me to carry on like it's business as usual. I'm lying to Block, setting him up." His hand shook as he passed it over his hair. "You don't know what he's capable of. *I* don't know what he's capable of." He looked at the mug, which Roman had set out of reach. "I need a little something to help me through the next few days."

"Let this get you through." Roman calmly lit a cigarette. "You pull this off and I'll go to bat for you. Screw up and I'll see to it that you're in a cage for a long time. Now take a break."

"What?"

"I said, take a break, go for a walk, get some real coffee." Roman tapped the ash from his cigarette into a little mosaic bowl.

"Sure." As he rose, Bob rubbed his palms on his thighs. "Look, DeWinter, I'm playing it straight with you. When this goes down, I expect you to keep Block off me."

"I'll take care of Block." That was a promise he intended to keep. When the door closed behind Bob, he picked up the phone. "DeWinter," he said when the connection was made.

"Make it quick," Conby told him. "I'm entertaining friends."

"I'll try not to let your martini get warm. I want to know if you've located the driver."

"DeWinter, an underling is hardly important at this point."

"It's important to me. Have you found him?"

"A man answering the description your informant gave you was detained in Tacoma this morning. He's being held for questioning by the local police." Conby put his hand over the receiver. Roman heard him murmur something that was answered by light laughter.

"We're using our influence to lengthen the procedure," Conby continued. "I'll be flying out there on Monday. By Tuesday afternoon I should be checked into the inn. I'm told I'll have a room overlooking a fish pond. It sounds very quaint."

"I want your word that Charity will be left out of this."

"As I explained before, if she's innocent she has nothing to worry about."

"It's not a matter of *if*." Struggling to hold his temper, Roman crushed out his cigarette. "She is innocent. We've got it on record."

"On the word of a whimpering little bookkeeper."

"She was damn near killed, and she doesn't even know why."

"Then keep a closer eye on her. We have no desire to see Miss Ford harmed, or to involve her any more deeply than necessary. There's a police officer out there who shares the same passionate opinion of Miss Ford as you do. Sheriff Royce managed to trace you to us."

"How?"

"He's a smart cop with connections. He has a cousin

or brother-in-law or some such thing with the Bureau. He wasn't at all pleased at being left in the dark."

"I'll bet."

"I imagine he'll be paying you a visit before long. Handle him carefully, DeWinter, but handle him."

Just as Roman heard the phone click in his ear the office door opened. For once, Roman thought, Conby was right on target. He replaced the receiver before settling back in his chair.

"Sheriff."

"I want to know what the hell's going on around here, Agent DeWinter."

"Close the door." Roman pushed back in the chair and considered half a dozen different ways of handling Royce. "I'd appreciate it if you'd drop the 'Agent' for now."

Royce just laid both palms on the surface of the desk. "I want to know what a federal agent is doing undercover in my territory."

"Following orders. Sit down?" He indicated a chair.

"I want to know what case you're working on."

"What did they tell you?"

Royce snorted disgustedly. "It got to the point where even my cousin started giving me the runaround, DeWinter, but I've got to figure that your being here had something to do with Charity being damn near run down yesterday."

"I'm here because I was assigned here." Roman waited a moment, sending Royce a long, direct look. "But my first priority is keeping Charity safe."

Royce hadn't been in law enforcement for nearly twenty years without being able to take the measure of a man. He took Roman's now, and was satisfied. "I got a load of bull from Washington about her being under investigation."

"She was. Now she's not. But she could be in trouble. Are you willing to help?"

"I've known that girl all her life." Royce took off his hat and ran his fingers through his hair. "Why don't you stop asking fool questions and tell me what's going on?"

Roman briefed him, pausing only once or twice to allow Royce to ask questions. "I don't have time to get into any more specifics. I want to know how many of your men you can spare Thursday morning."

"All of them," Royce said immediately.

"I only want your most experienced. I have information that Block will not only be bringing the counterfeit money, but also a man who'll register as Jack Marshall. His real name is Vincent Dupont. A week ago he robbed two banks in Ontario, killed a guard and wounded a civilian. Block will smuggle him out of Canada in the tour group, keep him here for a couple of days, then send him by short routes to South America. For his travel service to men like Dupont he takes a nice stiff fee. Both Dupont and Block are dangerous men. We'll have agents here at the inn, but we also have civilians. There's no way we can clear the place without tipping them off."

"It's a chancy game you're playing."

"I know." He thought of Charity dozing upstairs. "It's the only way I know how to play it."

Chapter 9

Charity drove back to the inn after dropping a trio of guests at the ferry. She was certain it was the most beautiful morning she'd ever seen. After the most wonderful night of her life, she thought. No, two of the most wonderful nights of her life.

Though she'd never considered herself terribly romantic, she'd always imagined what it would be like to really be in love. Her daydreams hadn't come close to what she was feeling now. This was solid and bewildering. It was simple and staggering. He filled her thoughts just as completely as he filled her heart. She couldn't wait to walk back into the inn, just knowing Roman would be there.

It seemed that every hour they spent together brought them closer. Gradually, step by step, she could feel the barriers he had placed around him lowering. She wanted to be there when they finally dropped completely.

He was in love with her. She was sure he was, whether he knew it or not. She could tell by the way he looked at her, by the way he touched her hair when he thought she was sleeping. By the way he held her so tightly all through the night, as if he were afraid she might somehow slip away from him. In time she would show him that she wasn't going anywhere—and that he wasn't going anywhere, either.

Something was troubling him. That was another thing she was sure of. Her eyes clouded as she drove along the water. There were times when she could feel the tension pulsing in him even when he was across the room. He seemed to be watching, waiting. But for what?

Since the accident he'd barely let her out of his sight. It was sweet, she mused. But it had to stop. She might love him, but she wouldn't be pampered. She was certain that if he had known she planned to drive to the ferry that morning he would have found a way to stop her.

She was right again. It had taken Roman some time to calm down after he had learned Charity wasn't in the office or the kitchen or anywhere else in the inn.

"She's driven up to drop some guests at the ferry," Mae told him, then watched in fascination as he let his temper loose.

"My, my," she said when the air was clear again. "You've got it bad, boy."

"Why did you let her go?"

"Let her go?" Mae let out a rich, appreciative laugh. "I haven't *let* that girl do anything since she could walk.

She just does it." She stopped stirring custard to study him. "Any reason she shouldn't drive to the ferry?"

"No."

"All right, then. Just cool your britches. She'll be back in half an hour."

He sweated and paced, nearly the whole time she was away. Mae and Dolores exchanged glances across the room. There would be plenty of gossip to pass around once they had the kitchen to themselves.

Mae thought of the way Charity had been smiling that morning. Why, the girl had practically danced into the kitchen. She kept her eye on Roman as he brooded over a cup of coffee and watched the clock. Yes, indeed, she thought, the boy had it bad.

"You got today off, don't you?" Mae asked him.

"What?"

"It's Sunday," she said patiently. "You got the day off?"

"Yeah, I guess."

"Nice day, too. Good weather for a picnic." She began slicing roast beef for sandwiches. "Got any plans?"

"No."

"Charity loves picnics. Yes, sir, she's mighty partial to them. You know, I don't think that girl's had a day away from this place in better than a month."

"Got any dynamite?"

Dolores piped up. "What's that?"

"I figure it would take dynamite to blast Charity out of the inn for a day."

It took her a minute, but Dolores finally got the joke. She chuckled. "Hear that, Mae? He wants dynamite."

"Pair of fools," Mae muttered as she cut generous pieces of chocolate cheesecake. "You don't move that girl with dynamite or threats or orders. Might as well bash your head against a brick wall all day." She tried not to sound pleased about it, and failed. "You want her to do something, you make her think she's doing you a favor. Make her think it's important to you. Dolores, you go on in that back room and get me the big wicker hamper. Boy, if you keep walking back and forth you're going to wear out my floor."

"She should have been back by now."

"She'll be back when she's back. You know how to run a boat?"

"Yes, why?"

"Charity always loved to picnic on the water. She hasn't been out in a boat in a long time. Too long."

"I know. She told me."

Mae turned around. Her face was set. "Do you want to make my girl happy?"

He tried to shrug it off, but he couldn't. "Yes. Yes, I do."

"Then you take her out on the boat for the day. Don't let her say no."

"All right."

Satisfied, she turned around again. "Go down in the cellar and get a bottle of wine. French. She likes the French stuff."

"She's lucky to have you."

Her wide face colored a bit, but she kept her voice brisk. "Around here, we got each other. You're all right," she added. "I wasn't sure of it when you first came around, but you're all right."

* * *

He was ready for her when she came back. Even as she stepped out of the van he was walking across the gravel lot, the wicker hamper in his hand.

"Hi."

"Hi." She greeted him with a smile and a quick kiss. Despite the two teenagers shooting hoops on the nearby court, Roman wrapped an arm around her and brought her hard against him for a longer, more satisfying embrace. "Well…" She had to take a deep breath and steady herself against the van. "Hello again." She noted then that he had pulled a loose black sweater over his jeans and was carrying a hamper. "What's this?"

"It's a basket," he told her. "Mae put a few things in it for me. It's my day off."

"Oh." She tossed her braid behind her back. "That's right. Where are you off to?"

"Out on the water, if I can use the boat."

"Sure." She glanced up at the sky, a bit wistfully. "It's a great day for it. Light wind, hardly a cloud."

"Then let's go."

"Let's?" He was already pulling her toward the pier. "Oh, Roman, I can't. I have dozens of things to do this afternoon. And I…" She didn't want to admit she wasn't ready to go out on the water again. "I can't."

"I'll have you back before the dinner shift." He laid a hand on her cheek. "I need you with me, Charity. I need to spend some time with you, alone."

"Maybe we could go for a drive. You haven't seen the mountains."

"Please." He set the hamper down to take both of her arms. "Do this for me."

Had he ever said "Please" before? she wondered. She didn't think so. With a sigh, she looked out at the boat rocking gently against the pier. "All right. Maybe for an hour. I'll go in and change."

The red sweater and jeans would keep her warm enough on the water, he decided. She would know that, too. She was stalling. "You look fine." He kept her hand in his as they walked down the pier. "This could use a little maintenance."

"I know. I keep meaning to." She waited until Roman stepped down into the boat. When he held up a hand, she hesitated, then forced herself to join him. "I have a key on my ring."

"Mae already gave me one."

"Oh." Charity sat down in the stern. "I see. A conspiracy."

It took him only two pulls to start the engine. Mae had told him Charity kept the boat for the staff to use. "From what you said to me the other day, I don't think he'd want you to grieve forever."

"No." As her eyes filled, she looked back toward the inn. "No, he wouldn't. But I loved him so much." She took a deep breath. "I'll cast off."

Before he sent the boat forward, Roman took her hand and drew her down beside him. After a moment she rested her head on his shoulder.

"Have you done much boating?"

"From time to time. When I was a kid we used to rent a boat a couple times each summer and take it on the river."

"Who's we?" She watched the shutters come down over his face. "What river?" she asked instead.

"The Mississippi." He smiled and slipped an arm over her shoulders. "I come from St. Louis, remember?"

"The Mississippi." Her mind was immediately filled with visions of steamboats and boys on wooden rafts. "I'd love to see it. You know what would be great? Taking a cruise all the way down, from St. Louis to New Orleans. I'll have to put that in my file."

"Your file?"

"The file I'm going to make on things I want to do." With a laugh, she waved to a passing sailboat before leaning over to kiss Roman's cheek. "Thanks."

"For what?"

"For talking me into this. I've always loved spending an afternoon out here, watching the other boats, looking at the houses. I've missed it."

"Have you ever considered that you give too much to the inn?"

"No. You can't give too much to something you love." She turned. If she shielded her eyes with her hand she could just see it in the distance. "If I didn't have such strong feelings for it, I would have sold it, taken a job in some modern hotel in Seattle or Miami or...or anywhere. Eight hours a day, sick leave, two weeks paid vacation." Just the idea made her laugh. "I'd wear a nice neat business suit and sensible shoes, have my own office and quietly go out of my mind." She dug into her bag for her sunglasses. "You should understand that. You have good hands and a sharp mind. Why aren't you head carpenter for some big construction firm?"

"Maybe when the time came I made the wrong choices."

With her head tilted, she studied him, her eyes narrowed and thoughtful behind the tinted lenses. "No, I don't think so. Not for you."

"You don't know enough about me, Charity."

"Of course I do. I've lived with you for a week. That probably compares with knowing someone on a casual basis for six months. I know you're very intense and internal. You have a wicked temper that you seldom lose. You're an excellent carpenter who likes to finish the job he starts. You can be gallant with little old ladies." She laughed a little and turned her face into the wind. "You like your coffee black, you're not afraid of hard work…and you're a wonderful lover."

"And that's enough for you?"

She lifted her shoulders. "I don't imagine you know too much more about me. I'm starving," she said abruptly. "Do you want to eat?"

"Pick a spot."

"Head over that way," she told him. "See that little jut of land? We can anchor the boat there."

The land she'd indicated was hardly more than a jumble of big, smooth rocks that fell into the water. As they neared it he could see a narrow stretch of sand crowded by trees. Cutting back the engine, he maneuvered toward the beach, Charity guiding him in with hand signals. As the current lapped at the sides of the boat, she pulled off her shoes and began to roll up her jeans.

"You'll have to give me a hand." As she said it she plunged into the knee-high water. "God, it's cold!" Then she was laughing and securing the line. "Come on."

The water was icy on his bare calves. Together they pulled the boat up onto a narrow spit of sand.

"I don't suppose you brought a blanket."

He reached into the boat and took out the faded red blanket Mae had given him. "This do?"

"Great. Grab the basket." She splashed through the shallows and onto the shore. After spreading the blanket at the base of the sheltering rocks she rolled down the damp legs of her jeans. "Lori and I used to come here when we were kids. To eat peanut butter sandwiches and talk about boys." Kneeling on the blanket, she looked around.

There were pines at her back, deep and green and thick all the way up the slope. A few feet away the water frothed at the rock, which had been worn smooth by wind and time. A single boat cruised in the distance, its sails full and white.

"It hasn't changed much." Smiling, she reached for the basket. "I guess the best things don't." She threw back the top and spotted a bottle of champagne. "Well." With a brow arched, she pulled it out. "Apparently we're going to have some picnic."

"Mae said you liked the French stuff."

"I do. I've never had champagne on a picnic."

"Then it's time you did." He took the bottle and walked back to dunk it in the water, screwing it down in the wet sand. "We'll let it chill a little more." He came back to her, taking her hand before she could explore deeper in the basket. He knelt. When they were thigh to thigh, he gathered her close and closed his mouth over hers.

Her quiet sound of pleasure came first, followed by a

gasp as he took the kiss deeper. Her arms came around him, then slid up until her hands gripped his shoulders. Desire was like a flood, rising fast to drag her under.

He needed…needed to hold her close like this, to taste the heat of passion on his lips, to feel her heart thud against him. He dragged his hands through her hair, impatiently tugging it free of the braids. All the while his mouth ravaged hers, gentleness forgotten.

There was a restlessness in him, and an anger that she couldn't understand. Responding to both, she pressed against him, unhesitatingly offering whatever he needed. Perhaps it would be enough. Slowly his mouth gentled. Then he was only holding her.

"That's a very nice way to start a picnic," Charity managed when she found her voice again.

"I can't seem to get enough of you."

"That's okay. I don't mind."

He drew away to frame her face in his hands. The crystal drops at her ears swung and shot out light. But her eyes were calm and deep and full of understanding. It would be better, he thought, and certainly safer, if he simply let her pull out the sandwiches. They could talk about the weather, the water, the people at the inn. There was so much he couldn't tell her. But when he looked into her eyes he knew he had to tell her enough about Roman DeWinter that she would be able to make a choice.

"Sit down."

Something in his tone sent a frisson of alarm down her spine. He was going to tell her he was leaving, she thought. "All right." She clasped her hands together, promising herself she'd find a way to make him stay.

"I haven't been fair with you." He leaned back against a rock. "Fairness hasn't been one of my priorities. There are things about me you should know, that you should have known before things got this far."

"Roman—"

"It won't take long. I did come from St. Louis. I lived in a kind of neighborhood you wouldn't even understand. Drugs, whores, Saturday night specials." He looked out at the water. The spiffy little sailboat had caught the wind. "A long way from here, baby."

So the trust had come, she thought. She wouldn't let him regret it. "It doesn't matter where you came from, Roman. It's where you are now."

"That's not always true. Part of where you come from stays with you." He closed a hand over hers briefly, then released it. It would be better, he thought, to break the contact now. "When he was sober enough, my father drove a cab. When he wasn't sober enough, he sat around the apartment with his head in his hands. One of my first memories is waking up at night hearing my mother screaming at him. Every couple of months she'd threaten to leave. Then he'd straighten up. We'd live in the eye of the hurricane until he'd stop off at the bar to have a drink. So she finally stopped threatening and did it."

"Where did you go?"

"I said she left."

"But...didn't she take you with her?"

"I guess she figured she was going to have it rough enough without dealing with a ten-year-old."

Charity shook her head and struggled with a deep, churning anger. It was hard for her to understand how a mother could desert her child. "She must have been very confused and frightened. Once she—"

"I never saw her again," Roman said. "You have to understand that not everyone loves unconditionally. Not everyone loves at all."

"Oh, Roman." She wanted to gather him close then, but he held her away from him.

"I stayed with my father another three years. One night he hit the gin before he got in the cab. He killed himself and his passenger."

"Oh, God." She reached for him, but he shook his head.

"That made me a ward of the court. I didn't much care for that, so I took off, hit the streets."

She was reeling from what he'd already told her, and she could barely take it all in. "At thirteen?"

"I'd been living there most of my life anyway."

"But how?"

He shook a cigarette out of his pack, lighting it and drawing deep before he spoke again. "I took odd jobs when I could find them. I stole when I couldn't. After a couple of years I got good enough at the stealing that I didn't bother much with straight jobs. I broke into houses, hot-wired cars, snatched purses. Do you understand what I'm telling you?"

"Yes. You were alone and desperate."

"I was a thief. Damn it, Charity, I wasn't some poor misguided youth. I stopped being a kid when I came home and found my father passed out and my mother gone. I knew what I was doing. I chose to do it."

She kept her eyes level with his, battling the need to take him in her arms. "If you expect me to condemn a child for finding a way to survive, I'll have to disappoint you."

She was romanticizing, he told himself, pitching his cigarette into the water.

"Do you still steal?"

"What if I told you I did?"

"I'd have to say you were stupid. You don't seem stupid to me, Roman."

He paused for a moment before he decided to tell her the rest. "I was in Chicago. I'd just turned sixteen. It was January, so cold your eyes couldn't water. I decided I needed to score enough to take a bus south. Thought I'd winter in Florida and fleece the rich tourists. That's when I met John Brody. I broke into his apartment and ended up with a .45 in my face. He was a cop." The memory of that moment still made him laugh. "I don't know who was more surprised. He gave me three choices. One, he could turn me over to Juvie. Two, he could beat the hell out of me. Three, he could give me something to eat."

"What did you do?"

"It's hard to play it tough when a two-hundred-pound man's pointing a .45 at your belt. I ate a can of soup. He let me sleep on the couch." Looking back, he could still see himself, skinny and full of bitterness, lying wakeful on the lumpy sofa.

"I kept telling myself I was going to rip off whatever I could and take off. But I never did. I used to tell myself he was a stupid bleeding heart, and that once it warmed up I'd split with whatever I could carry. The next thing I knew I was going to school." Roman paused a moment to look up at the sky. "He used to build things down in the basement of the building. He taught me how to use a hammer."

"He must have been quite a man."

"He was only twenty-five when I met him. He'd grown up on the South Side, running with the gangs. At some point he turned it around. Then he decided to turn me around. In some ways he did. When he got married a couple of years later he bought this old run-down house in the suburbs. We fixed it up room by room. He used to tell me there was nothing he liked better than living in a construction zone. We were adding on another room—it was going to be his workshop—when he was killed. Line of duty. He was thirty-two. He left a three-year-old son and a pregnant widow."

"Roman, I'm sorry." She moved to him and took his hands.

"It killed something in me, Charity. I've never been able to get it back."

"I understand." He started to pull away, but she held him fast. "I do. When you lose someone who was that much a part of your life, something's always going to be missing. I still think about Pop all the time. It still makes me sad. Sometimes it just makes me angry, because there was so much more I wanted to say to him."

"You're leaving out pieces. Look at what I was, where I came from. I was a thief."

"You were a child."

He took her shoulders and shook her. "My father was a drunk."

"I don't even know who my father was. Should I be ashamed of that?"

"It doesn't matter to you, does it? Where I've been, what I've done?"

"Not very much. I'm more interested in what you are now."

He couldn't tell her what he was. Not yet. For her own safety, he had to continue the deception for a few more days. But there was something he could tell her. Like the story he had just recounted, it was something he had never told anyone else.

"I love you."

Her hands went slack on his. Her eyes grew huge. "Would you—" She paused long enough to take a deep breath. "Would you say that again?"

"I love you."

With a muffled sob, she launched herself into his arms. She wasn't going to cry, she told herself, squeezing her eyes tight against the threatening tears. She wouldn't be red-eyed and weepy at this, the most beautiful and exciting moment of her life.

"Just hold me a moment, okay?" Overwhelmed, she pressed her face into his shoulder. "I can't believe this is happening."

"That makes two of us." But he was smiling. He could feel the stunned delight coil through him as he stroked her hair. It hadn't been so hard to say, he realized. In fact, he could easily get used to saying it several times a day.

"A week ago I didn't even know you." She tilted her head back until her lips met his. "Now I can't imagine my life without you."

"Don't. You might change your mind."

"Not a chance."

"Promise." Overwhelmed by a sudden sense of urgency, he gripped her hands. "I want you to make that a promise."

"All right. I promise. I won't change my mind about being in love with you."

"I'm holding you to that, Charity." He swooped her against him, then drained even happy thoughts from her mind. "Will you marry me?"

She jerked back, gaped, then sat down hard. "What? *What?*"

"I want you to marry me—now, today." It was crazy, and he knew it. It was wrong. Yet, as he pulled her up again, he knew he had to find a way to keep her. "You must know somebody, a minister, a justice of the peace, who could do it."

"Well, yes, but…" She held a hand to her spinning head. "There's paperwork, and licenses. God, I can't think."

"Don't think. Just say you will."

"Of course I will, but—"

"No buts." He crushed his mouth to hers. "I want you to belong to me. God, I need to belong to you. Do you believe that?"

"Yes." Breathless, she touched a hand to his cheek. "Roman, we're talking about marriage, a lifetime. I only intend to do this once." She dragged a hand through her hair and sat down again. "I guess everyone says that, but I need to believe it. It has to start off with more than a few words in front of an official. Wait, please," she said before he could speak again. "You've really thrown me off here, and I want to make you understand. I love you, and I can't think of anything I want more than to belong to you. When I marry you it has to be more than rushing to the J.P. and saying 'I do.' I don't have to have a big, splashy wedding, either. It's not a matter of long white trains and engraved invitations."

"Then what is it?"

"I want flowers and music, Roman. And friends." She took his face in her hands, willing him to understand. "I want to stand beside you knowing I look beautiful, so that everyone can see how proud I am to be your wife. If that sounds overly romantic, well, it should be."

"How long do you need?"

"Can I have two weeks?"

He was afraid to give her two days. But it was for the best, he told himself. He would never be able to hold her if there were still lies between them. "I'll give you two weeks, if you'll go away with me afterward."

"Where?"

"Leave it to me."

"I love surprises." Her lips curved against his. "And you…you're the biggest surprise so far."

"Two weeks." He took her hands firmly in his. "No matter what happens."

"You make it sound as though we might have to overcome a natural disaster in the meantime. I'm only going to take a few days to make it right." She brushed a kiss over his cheek and smiled again. "It will be right, Roman, for both of us. That's another promise. I'd like that champagne now."

She took out the glasses while he retrieved the bottle

from the water. As they sat together on the blanket, he released the cork with a pop and a hiss.

"To new beginnings," she said, touching her glass to his.

He wanted to believe it could happen. "I'll make you happy, Charity."

"You already have." She shifted so that she was cuddled against him, her head on his shoulder. "This is the best picnic I've ever had."

He kissed the top of her head. "You haven't eaten anything yet."

"Who needs food?" With a sigh, she reached up. He linked his hand with hers, and they both looked out toward the horizon.

Chapter 10

Check-in on Tuesday was as chaotic as it came. Charity barreled her way through it, assigning rooms and cabins, answering questions, finding a spare cookie for a cranky toddler, and waited for the first rush to pass.

She was the first to admit that she usually thrived on the noise, the problems and the healthy press of people that proved the inn's success. At the moment, though, she would have liked nothing better than having everyone, and everything settled.

It was hard to keep her mind on the business at hand when her head was full of plans for her wedding.

Should she have Chopin or Beethoven? She'd barely begun her list of possible selections. Would the weather hold so that they could have the ceremony in the gardens, or would it be best to plan an intimate and cozy wedding in the gathering room?

"Yes, sir, I'll be glad to give you information on renting bikes." She snatched up a pamphlet.

When was she going to find an afternoon free so that she could choose the right dress? It *had* to be the right dress, the perfect dress. Something ankle-length, with some romantic touches of lace. There was a boutique in Eastsound that specialized in antique clothing. If she could just—

"Aren't you going to sign that?"

"Sorry, Roger." Charity pulled herself back and offered him an apologetic smile. "I don't seem to be all here this morning."

"No problem." He patted her hand as she signed his roster. "Spring fever?"

"You could call it that." She tossed back her hair, annoyed that she hadn't remembered to braid it that morning. As long as she was smelling orange blossoms she'd be lucky to remember her own name. "We're a little behind. The computer's acting up again. Poor Bob's been fighting with it since yesterday."

"Looks like you've been in a fight yourself."

She lifted a hand to the healing cut on her temple. "I had a little accident last week."

"Nothing serious?"

"No, just inconvenient, really. Some idiot joyriding nearly ran me down."

"That's terrible." Watching her carefully, he pulled his face into stern lines. "Were you badly hurt?"

"No, only a few stitches and a medley of bruises. Scared me more than anything."

"I can imagine. You don't expect something like that around here. I hope they caught him."

"No, not yet." Because she'd already put the incident behind her, she gave a careless shrug. "To tell you the truth, I doubt they ever will. I imagine he got off the island as soon as he sobered up."

"Drunk drivers." Block made a sound of disgust. "Well, you've got a right to be distracted after something like that."

"Actually, I've got a much more pleasant reason. I'm getting married in a couple of weeks."

"You don't say!" His face split into a wide grin. "Who's the lucky man?"

"Roman DeWinter. I don't know if you met him. He's doing some remodeling upstairs."

"That's handy now, isn't it?" He continued to grin. The romance explained a lot. One look at Charity's face settled any lingering doubts. Block decided he'd have to have a nice long talk with Bob about jumping the gun. "Is he from around here?"

"No, he's from St. Louis, actually."

"Well, I hope he's not going to take you away from us."

"You know I'd never leave the inn, Roger." Her smile faded a bit. That was something she and Roman had never spoken of. "In any case, I promise to keep my mind on my work. You've got six people who want to rent boats." She took a quick look at her watch. "I can have them taken to the marina by noon."

"I'll round them up."

The door to the inn opened, and Charity glanced over. She saw a small, spare man with well-cut auburn hair, wearing a crisp sport shirt. He carried one small leather bag.

"Good morning."

"Good morning." He took a brief study of the lobby as he crossed to the desk. "Conby, Richard Conby. I believe I have a reservation."

"Yes, Mr. Conby. We're expecting you." Charity shuffled through the papers on the desk and sent up a quick prayer that Bob would have the computer humming along by the end of the day. "How was your trip?"

"Uneventful." He signed the register, listing his address as Seattle. Charity found herself both amused and impressed by his careful manicure. "I was told your inn is quiet, restful. I'm looking forward to relaxing for a day or two."

"I'm sure you'll find the inn very relaxing." She opened a drawer to choose a key. "Either Roman or I will drive your group to the marina, Roger. Have them in the parking lot at noon."

"Will do." With a cheerful wave, he sauntered off.

"I'll be happy to show you to your room, Mr. Conby. If you have any questions about the inn, or the island, feel free to ask me or any of the staff." She came around the desk and led the way to the stairs.

"Oh, I will," Conby said, following her. "I certainly will."

At precisely 12:05, Conby heard a knock and opened his door. "Prompt as always, DeWinter." He scanned down to Roman's tool belt. "Keeping busy, I see."

"Dupont's in cabin 3."

Conby decided to drop the sarcasm. This was a big one, much too big for him to let his personal feelings interfere. "You made a positive ID?"

"I helped him carry his bags."

"Very good." Satisfied, Conby finished arranging his ebony-handled clothes brush and shoe horn on the oak dresser. "We'll move in as planned on Thursday morning and take him before we close in on Block."

"What about the driver of the car who tried to kill Charity?"

Always fastidious, Conby walked into the adjoining bath to wash his hands. "You're inordinately interested in a small-time hood."

"Did you get a confession?"

"Yes." Conby unfolded a white hand towel bordered with flowers. "He admitted to meeting with Block last week and taking five thousand to—to put Miss Ford out of the picture. A very minor sum for a hit." His hands dry, Conby tossed the towel over the lip of the sink before walking back into the bedroom. "If Block had been more discerning, he might have had more success."

Taking him by the collar, Roman lifted Conby to his toes. "Watch your step," he said softly.

"It's more to the point for me to tell you to watch yours." Conby pulled himself free and straightened his shirt. In the five years since he had taken over as Roman's superior he had found Roman's methods crude and his attitude arrogant. The pity was, his results were invariably excellent. "You're losing your focus on this one, Agent DeWinter."

"No. It's taken me a while—maybe too long—but I'm focused just fine. You've got enough on Block to pin him with conspiracy to murder. Dupont's practically tied up with a bow. Why wait?"

"I won't bother to remind you who's in charge of this case."

"We both know who's in charge, Conby, but there's a difference between sitting behind a desk and calling the shots in the field. If we take them now, quietly, there's less risk of endangering innocent people."

"I have no intention of endangering any of the guests. Or the staff," he added, thinking he knew where Roman's mind was centered. "I have my orders on this, just as you do." He took a fresh handkerchief out of his drawer. "Since it's apparently so important to you, I'll tell you that we want to nail Block when he passes the money. We're working with the Canadian authorities on this, and that's the way we'll proceed. As for the conspiracy charges, we have the word of a bargain-basement hit man. It may take a bit more to make it stick."

"You'll make it stick. How many have we got?"

"We have two agents checking in tomorrow, and two more as backup. We'll take Dupont in his cabin, and Block in the lobby. Moving on Dupont any earlier would undoubtedly tip off Block. Agreed?"

"Yes."

"Since you've filled me in on the checkout procedures, it should go very smoothly."

"It better. If anything happens to her—anything— I'm holding you responsible."

Charity dashed into the kitchen with a loaded tray. "I don't know how things can get out of hand so fast. When have you ever known us to have a full house on a Wednesday night?" she asked the room at large, whipping out her pad. "Two specials with wild rice, one with baked potato, hold the sour cream, and one child's portion of ribs with fries." She rushed over to get the drinks herself.

"Take it easy, girl," Mae advised her. "They ain't going anywhere till they eat."

"That's the problem." She loaded up the tray. "What a time for Lori to get sick. The way this virus is bouncing around, we're lucky to have a waitress still standing. Whoops!" She backed up to keep from running into Roman. "Sorry."

"Need a hand?"

"I need two." She smiled and took the time to lean over the tray and kiss him. "You seem to have them. Those salads Dolores is fixing go to table 5."

"Girl makes me tired just looking at her," Mae commented as she filleted a trout. She lifted her head just long enough for her eyes to meet Roman's. "Seems to me she rushes into everything."

"Four house salads." Dolores was humming the "Wedding March" as she passed him a tray. "Looks like you didn't need that dynamite after all." Cackling, she went back to fill the next order.

Five minutes later he passed Charity in the doorway again. "Strange bunch tonight," she murmured.

"How so?"

"There's a man at table 2. He's so jumpy you'd think he'd robbed a bank or something. Then there's a couple at table 8, supposed to be on a second honeymoon. They're spending more time looking at everyone else than each other."

Roman said nothing. She'd made both Dupont and two of Conby's agents in less than thirty minutes.

"And then there's this little man in a three-piece suit

sitting at 4. Suit and tie," she added with a glance over her shoulder. "Came here to relax, he says. Who can relax in a three-piece suit?" Shifting, she balanced the tray on her hip. "Claims to be from Seattle and has an Eastern accent that could cut Mae's apple pie. Looks like a weasel."

"You think so?" Roman allowed himself a small smile at her description of Conby.

"A very well-groomed weasel," she added. "Check it out for yourself." With a small shudder, she headed toward the dining room again. "Anyone that smooth gives me the creeps."

Duty was duty though, and the weasel was sitting at her station. "Are you ready to order?" she asked Conby with a bright smile.

He took a last sip of his vodka martini. It was passable, he supposed. "The menu claims the trout is fresh."

"Yes, sir." She was particularly proud of that. The stocked pond had been her idea. "It certainly is."

"Fresh when it was shipped in this morning, no doubt."

"No." Charity lowered her pad but kept her smile in place. "We stock our own right here at the inn."

Lifting a brow, he tapped a finger against his empty glass. "Your fish may be superior to your vodka, but I have my doubts as to whether it is indeed fresh. Nonetheless, it appears to be the most interesting item on your menu, so I shall have to make do."

"The fish," Charity repeated, with what she considered admirable calm, "is fresh."

"I'm sure you consider it so. However, your conception of fresh and mine may differ."

"Yes, sir." She shoved the pad into her pocket. "If you'll excuse me a moment."

She might be innocent, Conby thought, frowning at his empty glass, but she was hardly efficient.

"Where's the fire?" Mae wanted to know when Charity burst into the kitchen.

"In my brain." She stopped a moment, hands on hips. "That—that insulting pipsqueak out there tells me our vodka's below standard, our menu's dull and our fish isn't fresh."

"A dull menu." Mae bristled down to her crepe-soled shoes. "What did he eat?"

"He hasn't eaten anything yet. One drink and a couple of crackers with salmon dip and he's a restaurant critic."

Charity took a turn around the kitchen, struggling with her temper. No urban wonder was going to stroll into her inn and pick it apart. Her bar was as good as any on the island, her restaurant had a triple-A rating, and her fish—

"Guy at table 4 wants another vodka martini," Roman announced as he carried in a loaded tray.

"Does he?" Charity whirled around. "Does he really?"

He couldn't recall ever seeing quite that glint in her eye. "That's right," he said cautiously.

"Well, I have something else to get him first." So saying, she strode into the utility room and then out again.

"Uh-oh," Dolores mumbled.

"Did I miss something?" Roman asked.

"Man's got a nerve saying the food's dull before he's even had a taste of it." Scowling, Mae scooped a helping of wild asparagus onto a plate. "I've a mind to add some curry to his entrée. A nice fat handful of it. We'll see about dull."

They all turned around when Charity strolled back in. She was still carrying the platter. On it flopped a very confused trout.

"My." Dolores covered her mouth with both hands, giggling. "Oh, my."

Grinning, Mae went back to her stove.

"Charity." Roman made a grab for her arm, but she evaded him and glided through the doorway. Shaking his head, he followed her.

A few of the diners looked up and stared as she carried the thrashing fish across the room. Weaving through the tables, she crossed to table 4 and held the tray under Conby's nose.

"Your trout, sir." She dropped the platter unceremoniously in front of him. "Fresh enough?" she asked with a small, polite smile.

In the archway Roman tucked his hands into his pockets and roared. He would have traded a year's salary for a photo of the expression on Conby's face as he and the fish gaped at each other.

When Charity glided back into the kitchen, she handed the tray and its passenger to Dolores. "You can put this back," she said. "Table 4 decided on the stuffed pork chops. I wish I had a pig handy." She let out a laughing squeal as Roman scooped her off the floor.

"You're the best." He pressed his lips to hers and held them there long after he'd set her down again. "The absolute best." He was still laughing as he gathered her close for a hug. "Isn't she, Mae?"

"She has her moments." She wasn't about to let them know how much good it did her to see them smiling at each other. "Now the two of you stop pawing each other in my kitchen and get back to work."

Charity lifted her face for one last kiss. "I guess I'd better fix that martini now. He looked like he could use one."

Because she wasn't one to hold a grudge, Charity treated Conby to attentive and cheerful service throughout the meal. Noting that he hadn't unbent by dessert, she brought him a serving of Mae's Black Forest cake on the house.

"I hope you enjoyed your meal, Mr. Conby."

It was impossible for him to admit that he'd never had better, not even in Washington's toniest restaurants. "It was quite good, thank you."

She offered an easy smile as she poured his coffee. "Perhaps you'll come back another time and try the trout."

Even for Conby, her smile was hard to resist. "Perhaps. You run an interesting establishment, Miss Ford."

"We try. Have you lived in Seattle long, Mr. Conby?"

He continued to add cream to his coffee, but he was very much on guard. "Why do you ask?"

"Your accent. It's very Eastern."

Conby deliberated only seconds. He knew that Dupont had already left the dining room, but Block was at a nearby table, entertaining part of his tour group with what Conby considered rather boring stories. "You have a good ear. I was transferred to Seattle eighteen months ago. From Maryland. I'm in marketing."

"Maryland." Deciding to forgive and forget, she

topped off his coffee. "You're supposed to have the best crabs in the country."

"I assure you, we do." The rich cake and the smooth coffee had mellowed him. He actually smiled at her. "It's a pity I didn't bring one along with me."

Laughing, Charity laid a friendly hand on his arm. "You're a good sport, Mr. Conby. Enjoy your evening."

Lips pursed, Conby watched her go. He couldn't recall anyone having accused him of being a good sport before. He rather liked it.

"We're down to three tables of diehards," Charity announced as she entered the kitchen again. "And I'm starving." She opened the refrigerator and rooted around for something to eat, but Mae snapped it closed again.

"You haven't got time."

"Haven't got time?" Charity pressed a hand to her stomach. "Mae, the way tonight went, I wasn't able to grab more than a stray French fry."

"I'll fix you a sandwich, but you had a call. Something about tomorrow's delivery."

"The salmon. Damn." She tilted her watch forward. "They're closed by now."

"Left an emergency number, I think. Message is upstairs."

"All right, all right. I'll be back in ten minutes." She cast a last longing glance at the refrigerator. "Make that two sandwiches."

To save time, she raced out through the utility room, rounded the side of the building and climbed the outside steps. When she opened the door, she could only stop and stare.

The music was pitched low. There was candlelight,

and there were flowers and a white cloth on a table at the foot of the bed. It was set for two. As she watched, Roman took a bottle of wine from a glass bucket and drew the cork.

"I thought you'd never get here."

She leaned back on the closed door. "If I'd known this was waiting, I'd have been here a lot sooner."

"You said you liked surprises."

"Yes." There was both surprise and delight in her eyes as she brushed her tumbled hair back from her forehead. "I like them a lot." Untying her apron, she walked to the table while he poured the wine. It glinted warm and gold in the candlelight. "Thanks," she murmured when he offered her a glass.

"I wanted to give you something." He gripped her hand, holding tight and trying not to remember that this was their last night together before all the questions had to be answered. "I'm not very good with romantic gestures."

"Oh, no, you're very good at them. Champagne picnics, late-night suppers." She closed her eyes for a moment. "Mozart."

"Picked at random," he admitted, feeling foolishly nervous. "I have something for you."

She looked at the table. "Something else?"

"Yes." He reached down to the seat of his chair and picked up a square box. "It just came today." It was the best he could do. He pushed the box into her hand.

"A present?" She'd always liked the anticipation as much as the gift itself, so she took a moment to study and shake the box. But the moment the lid was off she snatched the bracelet out. "Oh, Roman, it's gorgeous."

Thoroughly stunned, she turned the etched gold, watching the light glint off the metal and the square-cut amethyst. "It's absolutely gorgeous," she said again. "I'd swear I'd seen this before. Last week," she remembered. "In one of the magazines Lori brought me."

"You had it on your desk."

Overwhelmed, she nodded. "Yes, I'd circled this. I do that with beautiful things I know I'll never buy." She took a deep breath. "Roman, this is a wonderful, sweet and very romantic thing to do, but—"

"Then don't spoil it." He took the bracelet from the box and clasped it on her wrist. "I need the practice."

"No." She slipped her arms around him and rested her cheek against his shoulder. "I think you've got the hang of it."

He held her, letting the music, her scent, the moment, wash over him. Things could be different with her. He could be different with her.

"Do you know when I fell in love with you, Roman?"

"No." He kissed the top of her head. "I've thought more about why than when."

With a soft laugh, she snuggled against him. "I'd thought it was when you danced with me and you kissed me until every bone in my body turned to water."

"Like this?"

He turned his head, meeting her lips with his. Gently he set her on fire.

"Yes." She swayed against him, eyes closed. "Just like that. But that wasn't when. That was when I realized it, but it wasn't when I fell in love with you. Do you remember when you asked me about the spare?"

"The what?"

"The spare." Sighing, she tilted her head to give him easier access to her throat. "You wanted to know where the spare was so you could fix my flat." She leaned back to smile at his stunned expression. "I guess I can't call it love at first sight, since I'd already known you two or three minutes."

He ran his hands over her cheeks, through her hair, down her neck. "Just like that?"

"I'd never thought as much about falling in love and getting married as I suppose most people might. Because of Pop's being sick, and the inn. I always figured if it happened it would happen without me doing a lot of worrying or preparing. And I was right." She linked hands with him. "All I had to do was have a flat tire. The rest was easy."

A flat, Roman remembered, that had been deliberately arranged, just as her sudden need for a handyman had been arranged. As everything had been arranged, he thought, his grip tightening on her fingers. Everything except his falling in love with her.

"Charity…" He would have given anything to be able to tell her the truth, the whole truth. Anything but his knowledge that in ignorance there was safety. "I never meant for any of this to happen," he said carefully. "I never wanted to feel this way about anyone."

"Are you sorry?"

"About a lot of things, but not about being in love with you." He released her. "Your dinner's getting cold."

She tucked her tongue in her cheek. "If we found something else to do for an hour or so we could call it a midnight supper." She ran her hands up his chest to toy with the top button of his shirt. "Want to play Parcheesi?"

"No."

She flicked the button open and worked her way slowly, steadily down. "Scrabble?"

"Uh-uh."

"I know." She trailed a finger down the center of his body to the snap of his jeans. "How about a rip-roaring game of canasta?"

"I don't know how to play."

Grinning, she tugged the snap open. "Oh, I have a feeling you'd catch on." Her laugh was muffled against his mouth.

Her heated thoughts of seducing him spun away as he dragged her head back and plundered her mouth. Her hands, so confident an instant before, faltered, then fisted hard at the back of his shirt. This wasn't the gentle, persuasive passion he had shown her since the night they had become lovers. This was a raw, desperate need, and it held a trace of fury, and a hint of despair. Whirling from the feel of it, she strained against him, letting herself go.

He'd needed her before. Roman had already come to understand that he had needed her long before he'd ever met her. But tonight was different. He'd set the stage carefully—the wine, the candles, the music— wanting to give her the romance she made him capable of. Then he'd felt her cool fingertips on his skin. He'd seen the promising flicker of desire in her eyes. There was only tonight. In a matter of hours she would know everything. No matter how often he told himself he would set things right, he was very much afraid she wouldn't forgive him.

He had tonight.

Breathless, she clung to him as they tumbled onto the bed. Here was the restless, ruthless lover she had known existed alongside the gentle, patient one. And he excited her every bit as much. As frantic as he, she pulled the loosened shirt from his shoulders and gloried in the feel of his flesh under her hands.

He was as taut as wire, as explosive as gunpowder. She felt his muscles tense and tighten as his mouth raced hungrily over her face. With a throaty laugh she tugged at his jeans while they rolled over the bed. If this was a game they were playing, she was determined they would both win.

A broken moan escaped him as her seeking hands drove him toward delirium. With an oath, he snagged her wrists, yanking them over her head. Breath heaving, he watched her face as he hooked a hand in the top of her shirt and ripped it down the center.

She had only time for a gasp before his hot, open mouth lowered to her skin to torment and tantalize. Powerless against the onslaught, she arched against him. When her hands were free, she only pressed him closer, crying out as he sucked greedily at her breast.

There were sensations here, wild and exquisite, that trembled on but never crossed the thin line that separated pleasure from pain. She felt herself dragged under, deep, still deeper, to windmill helplessly down some dark, endless tunnel toward unreasonable pleasures.

She couldn't know what she was doing to him. He was skilled enough to be certain that she was trapped by her own senses. Yet her body wrapped around his, her hands sought, her lips hungered.

In the flickering light her skin was like white satin. Under his hands it flowed like lava, hot and dangerous. Passion heated her light floral scent and turned it into something secret and forbidden.

Impatient, he yanked her slacks down her hips, frantically tasting each new inch of exposed flesh. This new intimacy had her sobbing out his name, shuddering as climax slammed impossibly into climax.

She held on to him, her nails digging in, her palms sliding damply over his slick skin. Her mind was empty, wiped clear of all but sensation. His name formed on her lips again and again. She thought he spoke to her, some mad, frenzied words that barely penetrated her clouded brain. Perhaps they were promises, pleas or prayers. She would have answered all of them if she could.

Then his mouth was on hers, swallowing her cry of release, smothering her groan of surrender, as he drove himself into her.

Fast, hot, reckless, they matched rhythms. Far beyond madness, they clung. Driven by love, locked in desire, they raced. Even when they tumbled back to earth, they held each other close.

Chapter 11

With her eyes half closed, her lips curved, she gave a long, lazy sigh. "That was wonderful."

Roman topped off the wine in Charity's glass. "Are you talking about the meal or the preliminaries?"

She smiled. "Both." Before he could set the bottle down, she touched his hand. It was just a skimming of her fingertip over his skin. His pulse doubled. "I think we should make midnight suppers a regular event."

It was long past midnight. Even cold fish was delicious with wine and love. He hoped that if he held on hard enough it could always be like this. "The first time you looked at me like that I almost swallowed my tongue."

She kept her eyes on his. Even in candlelight they were the color of morning. "Like what?"

"Like you knew exactly what I was thinking, and

was trying not to think. Exactly what I wanted not to think. Exactly what I wanted, and was trying not to want. You scare the hell out of me."

Her lazy smile faltered. "I do?"

"You make too much difference. All the difference." He took both of her hands, wishing that just this once he had smooth words, a little poetry. "Every time you walk into a room…" But he didn't have smooth words, or poetry. "It makes a difference." He would have released her hands, but she turned them in his.

"I'm crazy about you. If I'd gone looking for someone to share my life, and my home, and my dreams, it would have been you."

She saw the shadow of concern in his eyes and willed it away. There was no room for worries in their lives tonight. With a quick, wicked smile, she nibbled on his fingers. "You know what I'd like?"

"More Black Forest cake."

"Besides that." Her eyes laughed at him over their joined hands. "I'd like to spend the night making love with you, talking with you, drinking wine and listening to music. I have a feeling I'd find it much more satisfying than the slumber parties I had as a girl."

She could, with a look and a smile, seduce him more utterly than any vision of black lace or white silk. "What would you like to do first?"

She had to laugh. It delighted her to see him so relaxed and happy. "Actually, there is something I want to talk with you about."

"I've already told you—I'll wear a suit, but no tuxedo."

"It's not about that." She smiled and traced a fingertip over the back of his hand. "Even though I know you'd look wonderful in a tux, I think a suit's more than adequate for an informal garden wedding. I'd like to talk to you about after the wedding."

"After-the-wedding plans aren't negotiable. I intend to make love with you for about twenty-four hours."

"Oh." As if she were thinking it through, she sipped her wine. "I guess I can go along with that. What I'd like to discuss is more long-range. It's something that Block said to me the other day."

"Block?" Alarm sprinted upward, then centered at the base of his neck.

"Just an offhand comment, but it made me think." She moved her shoulders in a quick, restless movement, then settled again. "I mentioned that we were getting married, and he said something about hoping you didn't take me away. It suddenly occurred to me that you might not want to spend your life here, on Orcas."

"That's it?" He felt the tension seep away.

"It's not such a little thing. I mean, I'm sure we can work it out, but you might not be crazy about the idea of living in a…well, a public kind of place, with people coming and going, and interruptions, and…" She let her words trail off, knowing she was rambling, as she did whenever she was nervous. "The point is, I need to know how you feel about staying on the island, living here, at the inn."

"How do you feel about it?"

"It isn't just a matter of what I feel any longer. It's what we feel."

It amazed him that she could so easily touch his heart. He supposed it always would. "It's been a long time since I've felt at home anywhere. I feel it here, with you."

She smiled and linked her fingers with his. "Are you tired?"

"No."

"Good." She rose and corked the wine. "Just let me get my keys."

"Keys to what?"

"The van," she told him as she walked into the next room.

"Are we going somewhere?"

"I know the best place on the island to watch the sun rise." She came back carrying a blanket and jiggling the keys. "Want to watch the sun come up with me, Roman?"

"You're only wearing a robe."

"Of course I am. It's nearly two in the morning. Don't forget the wine." With a laugh, she opened the door and crept down the steps. "Let's try not to wake anyone." She winced a little as she started across the gravel in her bare feet. With a muttered oath, Roman swung her up into his arms. "My hero," she murmured.

"Sure." He dumped her in the driver's seat of the van. "Where are we going, baby?"

"To the beach." She pushed her hair behind her shoulders as she started the van. Symphonic music blared from the radio before she twisted the knob. "I always play it too loud when I'm driving alone." She turned to look guiltily back at the inn. It remained dark and quiet. Slowly she drove out of the lot and onto the road. "It's a beautiful night."

"Morning."

"Whatever." She took a long, greedy gulp of air. "I haven't really had time for big adventures, so I have to take small ones whenever I get the chance."

"Is that what this is? An adventure?"

"Sure. We're going to drink the rest of the wine, make love under the stars and watch the sun come up over the water." She turned her head. "Is that all right with you?"

"I think I can live with it."

It was hours later when she curled up close to him. The bottle of wine was empty, and the stars were blinking out one by one.

"I'm going to be totally useless today." After a sleepy laugh, she nuzzled his neck. "And I don't even care."

He tugged the blanket over her. The mornings were still chilly. Though he hadn't planned it, the long night of loving had given him new hope. If he could convince her to sleep through the morning, he could complete his assignment, close the door on it and then explain everything. That would let him keep her out of harm's way and begin at the beginning.

"It's nearly dawn," she murmured.

They didn't speak as they watched day break. The sky paled. The night birds hushed. For an instant, time hung suspended. Then, slowly, regally, colors seeped into the horizon, bleeding up from the water, reflecting in it. Shadows faded, and the trees were tipped with gold. The first bird of the morning trumpeted the new day.

Roman gathered her to him to love her slowly under the lightening sky.

She dozed as he drove back to the inn. The sky was a pale, milky blue, but it was as quiet now as it had been when they'd left. When he lifted her out of the van, she sighed and nestled her head on his shoulder.

"I love you, Roman."

"I know." For the first time in his life he wanted to think about next week, next month, even next year—anything except the day ahead. He carried her up the stairs and into the inn. "I love you, Charity."

He had little trouble convincing her to snuggle between the sheets of the rumpled bed once he promised to take Ludwig for his habitual run.

Before he did, Roman went downstairs, strapped on his shoulder holster and shoved in his gun.

Taking Dupont was a study in well-oiled police work. By 7:45 his secluded cabin was surrounded by the best Sheriff Royce and the F.B.I. had to offer. Roman had ignored Conby's mutterings about bringing the locals into it and advised his superior to stay out of the way.

When the men were in position, Roman moved to the door himself, his gun in one hand, his shoulder snug against the frame. He rapped twice. When there was no response, he signaled for his men to draw their weapons and close in. Using the key he'd taken from Charity's ring, he unlocked the door.

Once inside, he scanned the room, legs spread, the gun held tight in both hands. The adrenaline was there, familiar, even welcome. With only a jerk of the head he signaled his backup. Guarding each other's flanks, they took a last circle.

Roman cautiously approached the bedroom. For the

first time, a smile—a grim smile—moved across his face. Dupont was in the shower. And he was singing.

The singing ended abruptly when Roman yanked the curtain aside.

"Don't bother to put your hands up," Roman told him as he blinked water out of his eyes. Keeping the gun level, he tossed his first prize a towel. "You're busted, pal. Why don't you dry off and I'll read you your rights?"

"Well done," Conby commented when the prisoner was cuffed. "If you handle the rest of this as smoothly, I'll see that you get a commendation."

"Keep it." Roman holstered his weapon. There was only one more hurdle before he could finally separate past and future. "When this is done, I'm finished."

"You've been in law enforcement for over ten years, DeWinter. You won't walk away."

"Watch me." With that, he headed back to the inn to finish what he had started.

When Charity awoke, it was full morning and she was quite alone. She was grateful for that, because she couldn't stifle a moan. The moment she sat up, her head, unused to the generous doses of wine and stingy amounts of sleep, began to pound.

She had no one but herself to blame, she admitted as she crawled out of bed. Her feet tangled in what was left of the shirt she'd been wearing the night before.

It had been worth it, she thought, gathering up the torn cotton. Well worth it.

But, incredible night or not, it was morning and she

had work to do. She downed some aspirin, allowed herself another groan, then dived into the shower.

Roman found Bob huddled in the office, anxiously gulping laced coffee. Without preamble, he yanked the mug away and emptied the contents into the trash can.

"I just needed a little something to get me through."

He'd had more than a little, Roman determined. His words were slurred, and his eyes were glazed. Even under the best of circumstances Roman found it difficult to drum up any sympathy for a drunk.

He dragged Bob out of his chair by the shirtfront. "You pull yourself together and do it fast. When Block comes in you're going to check him and his little group out. If you tip him off—if you so much as blink and tip him off—I'll hang you out to dry."

"Charity does the checkout," Bob managed through chattering teeth.

"Not today. You're going to go out to the desk and handle it. You're going to do a good job because you're going to know I'm in here and I'm watching you."

He stepped away from Bob just as the office door opened. "Sorry I'm late." Despite her heavy eyes, Charity beamed at Roman. "I overslept."

He felt his heart stop, then sink to his knees. "You didn't sleep enough."

"You're telling me." Her smile faded when she looked at Bob. "What's wrong?"

He grabbed at the thread of opportunity with both hands. "I was just telling Roman that I'm not feeling very well."

"You don't look well." Concerned, she walked over

to feel his brow. It was clammy and deepened the worry in her eyes. "You're probably coming down with that virus."

"That's what I'm afraid of."

"You shouldn't have come in at all today. Maybe Roman should drive you home."

"No, I can manage." He walked on shaking legs to the door. "Sorry about this, Charity." He turned to give her a last look. "Really sorry."

"Don't be silly. Just take care of yourself."

"I'll give him a hand," Roman muttered, and followed him out. They walked out into the lobby at the same time Block strolled in.

"Good morning." His face creased with his habitual smile, but his eyes were wary. "Is there a problem?"

"Virus." Bob's face was already turning a sickly green. Fear made a convincing cover. "Hit me pretty hard this morning."

"I called Dr. Mertens," Charity announced as she came in to stand behind the desk. "You go straight home, Bob. He'll meet you there."

"Thanks." But one of Conby's agents followed him out, and he knew he wouldn't be going home for quite a while.

"This virus has been a plague around here." She offered Block an apologetic smile. "I'm short a housekeeper, a waitress and now Bob. I hope none of your group had any complaints about the service."

"Not a one." Relaxed again, Block set his briefcase on the desk. "It's always a pleasure doing business with you, Charity."

Roman watched helplessly as they chatted and went

through the routine of checking lists and figures. She was supposed to be safe upstairs, sleeping deeply and dreaming of the night they'd spent together. Frustrated, he balled his hands at his side. Now, no matter what he did, she'd be in the middle.

He heard her laugh when Block mentioned the fish she'd carried into the dining room. And he imagined how her face would look when the agents moved in and arrested the man she thought of as a tour guide and a friend.

Charity read off a total. Roman steadied himself.

"We seem to be off by…22.50." Block began laboriously running the numbers through his calculator again. Brow furrowed, Charity went over her list, item by item.

"Good morning, dear."

"Hmm." Distracted, Charity glanced up. "Oh, good morning, Miss Millie."

"I'm just on my way up to pack. I wanted you to know what a delightful time we've had."

"We're always sorry to see you go. We were all pleased that you and Miss Lucy extended your stay for a few days."

Miss Millie fluttered her eyelashes myopically at Roman before making her way toward the stairs. At the top, he thought, there would now be an officer posted to see that she and the other guests were kept out of the way.

"I get the same total again, Roger." Puzzled, she tapped the end of her pencil on the list. "I wish I could say I'd run it through the computer, but…" She let her words trail off, ignoring her headache. "Ah, this might be it. Do you have the Wentworths in cabin 1 down for a bottle of wine? They charged it night before last."

"Wentworth, Wentworth…" With grating slowness, Block ran down his list. "No, nothing here."

"Let me find the tab." After opening a drawer, she flipped her way efficiently through the folders. Roman felt a bead of sweat slide slowly down his back. One of the agents strolled over to browse through some postcards.

"I've got both copies," she said with a shake of her head. "This virus is really hanging us up." She filed her copy of the receipt and handed Block his.

"No problem." Cheerful as ever, he noted the new charge, then added up his figures again. "That seems to match."

With the ease of long habit, Charity calculated the amount in Canadian currency. "That's 2,330.00." She turned the receipt around for Block's approval.

He clicked open his briefcase. "As always, it's a pleasure." He counted out the money in twenties. The moment Charity marked the bill Paid, Roman moved in.

"Put your hands up. Slow." He pressed the barrel of his gun into the small of Block's back.

"Roman!" Charity gaped at him, the key to the cash drawer in her hand. "What on earth are you doing?"

"Go around the desk," he told her. "Way around, and walk outside."

"Are you crazy? Roman, for God's sake—"

"Do it!"

Block moistened his lips, keeping his hands carefully aloft. "Is this a robbery?"

"Haven't you figured it out by now?" With his free hand, Roman pulled out his ID. After tossing it on the desk, he reached for his cuffs. "You're under arrest."

"What's the charge?"

"Conspiracy to murder, counterfeiting, transporting known felons across international borders. That'll do for a start." He yanked one of Block's arms down and slipped the cuff over his wrist.

"How could you?" Charity's voice was a mere whisper. She held his badge in her hand.

He took his eyes off Block for only a second to look at her. One second changed everything.

"How silly of me," Miss Millie muttered as she waltzed back into the lobby. "I was nearly upstairs when I realized I'd left my—"

For a man of his bulk, Block moved quickly. He dragged Miss Millie against him and had a knife to her throat before anyone could react. The cuffs dangled from one wrist. "It'll only take a heartbeat," he said quietly, staring into Roman's eyes. The gun was trained in the center of Block's forehead, and Roman's finger was twitching on the trigger.

"Think about it." Block's gaze swept the lobby, where other guns had been drawn. "I'll slice this nice little lady's throat. Don't move," he said to Charity. Shifting slightly, he blocked her way.

Wide-eyed, Miss Millie could only cling to Block's arm and whimper.

"Don't hurt her." Charity stepped forward, but she stopped quickly when she saw Block's grip tighten. "Please, don't hurt her." It had to be a dream, she told herself. A nightmare. "Someone tell me what's happening here."

"The place is surrounded." Roman kept his eyes and his weapon on Block. He waited in vain for one of his men to move in from the rear. "Hurting her isn't going to do you any good."

"It isn't going to do you any good, either. Think about it. Want a dead grandmother on your hands?"

"You don't want to add murder to your list, Block," Roman said evenly. And Charity was much too close, he thought. Much too close.

"It makes no difference to me. Now take it outside. All of you!" His voice rose as he scanned the room. "Toss down the guns. Toss them down and get out before I start slicing into her. Do it." He nicked Miss Millie's fragile throat with the blade.

"Please!" Again Charity took a step forward. "Let her go. I'll stay with you."

"Damn it, Charity, get back."

She didn't spare Roman a glance. "Please, Roger," she said again, taking another careful step forward. "She's old and frail. She might get sick. Her heart." Desperate, she stepped between him and Roman's gun. "I won't give you any trouble."

The decision took Block only a moment. He grabbed Charity and dug the point of the blade into her throat. Miss Millie slid bonelessly to the floor.

"Drop the gun." He saw the fear in Roman's eyes and smiled. Apparently he'd made a much better bargain. "Two seconds and it's over. I don't have anything to lose."

Roman held his hands up, letting his weapon drop. "We'll talk."

"We'll talk when I'm ready." Block shifted the knife so that the length of the blade lay across Charity's neck. She shut her eyes and waited to die. "Get out, now. The first time somebody tries to get back in she dies."

"Out." Roman pointed to the door. "Keep them back, Conby. All of them. There's my weapon," he said to Block. "I'm clean." He lifted his jacket cautiously to show his empty holster. "Why don't I hang around in here? You can have two hostages for the price of one. A federal agent ought to give you some leverage."

"Just the woman. Take off, DeWinter, or I'll kill her before you can think how to get to me. Now."

"For God's sake, Roman. Get her out of here. She needs a doctor." Charity sucked in her breath when the point of the knife pierced her skin.

"Don't." Roman held up his hands again, palms out, as he moved toward the crumpled form near the desk. Keeping his movements slow, he gathered the sobbing woman in his arms. "If you hurt her, you won't live long enough to regret it."

With that last frustrated threat he left Charity alone.

"Stay back." After bundling Miss Millie into waiting arms, he rushed off the porch, fighting to keep his mind clear. "Nobody goes near the doors or any of the windows. Get me a weapon." Before anyone could oblige him, he was yanking a gun away from one of Royce's deputies. With the smallest of gestures Royce signaled to his man to be silent.

"What do you want us to do?"

Roman merely stared down at the gun in his hand. It was loaded. He was trained. And he was helpless.

"DeWinter…" Conby began.

"Back off." When Conby started to speak again, Roman turned on him. "Back off."

He stared at the inn. He could hear Miss Millie crying softly as someone carried her to a car. The guests who had already been evacuated were being herded to safety. Roman imagined that Royce had arranged that. Charity would want to make sure they were well taken care of.

Charity.

Shoving the gun into his holster, he turned around. "Have the road blocked off a mile in each direction. Only official personnel in this area. We'll keep the inn surrounded from a distance of fifty feet. He'll be thinking again," Roman said slowly, "and when he starts thinking he's going to know he's blocked in."

He lifted both hands and rubbed them over his face. He'd been in hostage situations before. He was trained for them. With time and cool heads, the odds of getting a hostage out in a situation of this type were excellent. When the hostage was Charity, excellent wasn't nearly good enough.

"I want to talk to him."

"Agent DeWinter, under the circumstances I have serious reservations about you being in charge of this operation."

Roman rounded on him. "Get in my way, Conby, and I'll hang you up by your silk tie. Why the hell weren't there men positioned in the back, behind him?"

Because his palms were sweating, Conby's voice

was only more frigid. "I thought it best to have them outside, prepared if he attempted to run."

Roman battled the red wave of fury that burst behind his eyes. "When I get her out," he said softly, "I'm going to deal with you, you bastard. I need communication," he said to Royce. "Can you handle it?"

"Give me twenty minutes."

With a nod, Roman turned back to study the inn. Systematically he considered and rejected points of entry.

Inside, Charity felt some measure of relief when the knife was removed from her throat. Somehow the gun Block was pointing at her now seemed less personal.

"Roger—"

"Shut up. Shut up and let me think." He swiped a beefy forearm over his brow to dry it. It had all happened so fast, too fast. Everything up to now he had done on instinct. As Roman had calculated, he was beginning to think.

"They've got me trapped in here. I should've used you to get to one of the cars, should've taken off." Then he laughed, looking wildly around the lobby. "We're on a damn island. Can't drive off an island."

"I think if we—"

"Shut up!" He shouted and had her holding her breath as he leveled the gun at her. "I'm the one who needs to think. Feds. That sniveling little wart was right all along," he muttered, thinking of Bob. "He made DeWinter days ago. Did you?" As he asked, he grabbed her by the hair and yanked her head back to hold the barrel against her throat.

"No. I didn't know. I didn't. I still don't understand."

She could only give a muffled cry when he slammed her back against the wall. She'd never seen murder in a man's eyes before, but she recognized it. "Roger, think. If you kill me you won't have anything to bargain with." She tasted fear on her tongue as she forced the words out. "You need me."

"Yeah." He relaxed his grip. "You've been handy so far. You'll just have to go on being handy. How many ways in and out of this place?"

"I—I don't really know." She sucked in her breath when he gave her hair another cruel twist.

"You know how many two-by-fours are in this place."

"Five. There are five exits, not counting the windows. The lobby, the gathering room, the outside steps running to my quarters and a family suite in the east wing, and the back, through the utility room off the kitchen."

"That's good." Panting a bit, he considered the possibilities. "The kitchen. We'll take the kitchen. I'll have water and food there in case this takes a while. Come on." He kept a hand in her hair and the gun at the base of her neck.

His eyes on the inn, Roman paced back and forth behind the barricade of police cars. She was smart, he told himself. Charity was a smart, sensible woman. She wouldn't panic. She wouldn't do anything stupid.

Oh, God, she must be terrified. He lit a cigarette from the butt of another, but he didn't find himself soothed as the harsh smoke seared into him.

"Where's the goddamn phone?"

"Nearly ready." Royce pushed back his hat and straightened from where he'd been watching a lineman patch in a temporary line. "My nephew," he explained to Roman with a thin smile. "The boy knows his job."

"You got a lot of relatives."

"I'm lousy with them. Listen, I heard you and Charity were getting married. That part of the cover?"

"No." Roman thought of the picnic on the beach, that one clear moment in time. "No."

"In that case, I'm going to give you some advice. You're wrong," he said, before Roman could speak. "You do need it. You're going to have to get yourself calm, real calm, before you pick up that phone. A trapped animal reacts two ways. He either cowers back and gives up or he strikes out at anything in his way." Royce nodded toward the inn. "Block doesn't look like the type to give up easy, and Charity sure as hell's in his way. That line through yet, son?"

"Yes, sir." The young lineman's hands were sweaty with nerves and excitement. "You can dial right through." He passed the damp receiver to Roman.

"I don't know the number," Roman murmured. "I don't know the damn number."

"I know it."

Roman swung around to face Mae. In that one instant he saw everything he felt about himself mirrored in her eyes. There would be time for guilt later, he told himself. There would be a lifetime for it. "Royce, you were supposed to clear the area."

"Moving Maeflower's like moving a tank."

"I don't budge until I see Charity." Mae firmed her quivering lips. "She's going to need me when she comes out. Waste of time to argue," she added. "You want the number?"

"Yes."

She gave it to him. Tossing his cigarette aside, Roman dialed.

Charity jolted in the chair when the phone rang. Across the table, Block simply stared at it. He had had her pile everything she could drag or carry to block the two doors. Extra chairs, twenty-pound canisters of flour and sugar, the rolling butcher block, iron skillets, all sat in a jumble, braced against both entrances.

In the silent kitchen the phone sounded again and again, like a scream.

"Stay right where you are." Block moved across the room to answer it. "Yeah?"

"It's DeWinter. Thought you might be ready to talk about a deal."

"What kind of deal?"

"That's what we have to talk about. First I have to know you've still got Charity."

"Have you seen her come out?" Block spit into the phone. "You know damn well I've got her or you wouldn't be talking to me."

"I have to make sure she's still alive. Let me talk to her."

"You can go to hell."

Threats, abuse, curses, rose like bile in his throat. Still, when he spoke, his voice was dispassionate. "I verify that you still have a hostage, Block, or we don't deal."

"You want to talk to her?" Block gestured with the gun. "Over here," he ordered. "Make it fast. It's your boyfriend," he told Charity when she stood beside him. "He wants to know how you're doing. You tell him you're just fine." He brushed the gun up her cheek to rest it at her temple. "Understand?"

With a nod, she leaned into the phone. "Roman?"

"Charity." Too many emotions slammed into him for him to measure. He wanted to reassure her, to make promises, to beg her to be careful. But he knew he would have only seconds and that Block would be listening to every word spoken. "Has he hurt you?"

"No." She closed her eyes and fought back a sob. "No, I'm fine. He's going to let me fix some food."

"Hear that, DeWinter? She's fine." Deliberately Block dragged her arm behind her back until she cried out. "That can change anytime."

Roman gripped the phone helplessly as he listened to the sound of Charity's sobs. It took every ounce of control he had left to keep the terror out of his voice. "You don't have to hurt her. I said we'd talk about terms."

"We'll talk about terms, all right. My terms." He released Charity's arm and ignored her as she slid to the floor. "You get me a car. I want safe passage to the airport, DeWinter. Charity drives. I want a plane fueled up and waiting. She'll be getting on it with me, so any tricks and we're back to square one. When I get where I'm going, I turn her loose."

"How big a plane?"

"Don't try to stall me."

"Wait. I have to know. It's a small airport, Block. You know that. If you're going any distance—"

"Just get me a plane."

"Okay." Roman wiped the back of his hand over his mouth and forced his voice to level. He couldn't hear her any longer, and the silence was as anguishing as her sobbing. "I'm going to have to go through channels on this. That's how it works."

"The hell with your channels."

"Look, I don't have the authority to get you what you want. I need to get approval. Then I'll have to clear the airport, get a pilot. You'll have to give me some time."

"Don't yank my chain, DeWinter. You got an hour."

"I've got to get through to Washington. You know how bureaucrats are. It'll take me three, maybe four."

"The hell with that. You got two. After two I'm going to start sending her out in pieces."

Charity closed her eyes, lowered her head to her folded arms and wept out her terror.

Chapter 12

"We've got a couple of hours," Roman murmured, continuing to study the inn and the floor plan Royce had given him. "He's not as smart as I thought, or maybe he's too panicked to think it through."

"That could be to our advantage," Royce said when Roman shook his head at his offer of coffee. "Or it could work against us."

Two hours. Roman stared at the quiet clapboard building. He couldn't stand the idea of Charity being held at gunpoint for that long. "He wants a car, safe passage to the airport and a plane." He turned to Conby. "I want you to make sure he thinks he's going to get it."

"I'm aware of how to handle a hostage situation, DeWinter."

"Which one of your men is the best shot?" Roman asked Royce.

"I am." He kept his eyes steady on Roman's. "Where do you want me?"

"They're in the kitchen."

"He tell you that?"

"No, Charity. She told me he was going to let her fix some food. Since I doubt eating's on her mind, she was letting me know their position."

Royce glanced over to where Mae was pacing up and down the pier. "She's a tough girl. She's keeping her head."

"So far." But Roman remembered too well the sound of her muffled sobbing. "We need to shift two of the men around the back. I want them to keep their distance, stay out of sight. Let's see how close we can get." He turned to Conby again. "Give us five minutes, then call him again. Tell him who you are. You know how to make yourself sound important. Stall him, keep him on the phone as long as you can."

"You have two hours, DeWinter. We can call for a SWAT team from Seattle."

"We have two hours," Roman said grimly. "Charity may not."

"I can't take responsibility—"

Roman cut him off. "You'll damn well take it."

"Agent DeWinter, if this wasn't a crisis situation I would cite you for insubordination."

"Great. Just put it on my tab." He looked at the rifle Royce had picked up. It had a long-range telescopic sight. "Let's move."

She'd cried long enough, Charity decided, taking a long, deep breath. It wasn't doing her any good. Like her captor, she needed to think. Her world had whittled down to one room, with fear as her constant companion. This wouldn't do, she told herself, straightening her spine. Her life was being threatened, and she wasn't even sure why.

She rose from where she had been huddled on the floor. Block was still sitting at the table, holding the gun in one hand while the other tapped monotonously on the scrubbed wood. The dangling cuffs jangled. He was terrified, she realized. Perhaps every bit as much as she. There must be some way to use that to her advantage.

"Roger...would you like some coffee?"

"Yeah. That's good, that's a good idea." He took a firmer grip on the gun. "But don't get cute. I'm watching every move."

"Are they going to give you a plane?" She turned the burner on low. The kitchen was full of weapons, she thought. Knives, cleavers, mallets. Closing her eyes, she wondered if she had the courage to use one.

"They're going to give me anything I want as long as I have you."

"Why do they want you?" Stay calm, she told herself. She wanted to stay calm and alert and alive. "I don't understand." She poured the hot coffee into two cups. She didn't think she could swallow, but she hoped that sharing it would put him slightly more at ease. "They said something about counterfeiting."

It didn't matter what she knew. In any case, he had worked hard and was proud of it. "For over two years now I've been running a nice little game back and forth over the border. Twenties and tens in Canadian. I can stamp them out like bottle caps. But I'm careful, you know." He gulped at the coffee. "A couple thousand here, couple thousand there, with Vision as the front. We run a good tour, keep the clients happy."

"You've been paying me with counterfeit money?"

"You, and a couple other places. But you're the longest and most consistent." He smiled at her, as friendly as ever—if you didn't count the gun in his hand. "You have a special place here, Charity, quiet, remote, privately owned. You deal with a small local bank. It ran like a charm."

"Yes." She looked down at her cup, her stomach rolling. "I can see that." And Roman had come not to see the whales but to work on a case. That was all she had been to him.

"We were going to milk this route for a few more months," he continued. "Just lately Bob started getting antsy."

"Bob?" Her hand fisted on her lap. "Bob knew?"

"He was nothing but a nickel-and-dime con man before I took him on. Working scams and petty embezzlements. I set him up here and made him rich. Didn't do badly by you, either," he added with a grin. "You were on some shaky financial ground when I came along."

"All this time," she whispered.

"I'd decided to give it another six months, then move on, but Bob started getting real jumpy about your new handyman. The bastard set me up." He slammed the cup down. "Worked a deal with the feds. I should have caught it, the way he started falling apart after the hit-and-run."

"The accident—you tried to kill me."

"No." He patted her hand, and she cringed. "Truth is, I've always had a liking for you. But I wanted to get you out of the way for a while. Just testing the waters to see how DeWinter played it. He's good," Block mused. "Real good. Had me convinced he was only interested in you. The romance was a good touch. Threw me off."

"Yes." Devastated, she stared at the grain in the wood of the tabletop. "That was clever."

"Sucked me in," Block muttered. "I knew you weren't stringing me along. You haven't got it in you. But DeWinter... They've probably already taken Dupont."

"Who?"

"We don't just run the money. There are people, people who need to leave the country quietly, who pay a lot for our services. Looks like I'm going to have to take myself on as a client." He laughed and drained his cup. "How about some food? One of the things I'll miss most about this place is the food."

She rose silently and went to the refrigerator. It had all been a lie, she thought. Everything Roman had said, everything he'd done...

The pain cut deep and had her fighting back another bout of weeping. He'd made a fool of her, as surely and as completely as Roger Block had. They had used her, both of them, used her and her inn. She would never forgive. She rubbed her hands over her eyes to clear them. And she would never forget.

"How about that lemon meringue pie?" Relaxed, pleased with his own cleverness, Roger tapped the barrel of the gun on the table. "Mae outdid herself on that pie last night."

"Yes." Slowly Charity pulled it out. "There's a little left."

Block had ripped the frilly tiebacks from the sunny yellow curtains, but there was a space two inches wide at the center. Silently Roman eased toward it. He could see Charity reach into a cupboard, take out a plate.

There were tears drying on her cheeks. It tore at him to see them. Her hands were steady. That was something, some small thing to hold on to. He couldn't see Block, though he shifted as much as he dared.

Then, suddenly, as if she had sensed him, their eyes met through the glass. She braced, and in that instant he saw a myriad of emotions run across her face. Then it was set again. She looked at him as she would have looked at a stranger and waited for instructions.

He held up a hand, palm out, doing his best to signal her to hold on, to keep calm. Then the phone rang and he watched her jolt.

"About time," Block said. He was almost swaggering as he walked to the phone. "Yeah? Who the hell's this?" After listening a moment, he gave a pleased laugh. "I like dealing with a title. Where's my plane, Inspector Conby?"

As quickly as she dared, Charity tugged the curtain open another inch.

"Over here," Block ordered.

She dropped her hand, and the plate rattled to the counter. "What?"

He gestured with the gun. "I said over here."

Roman swore as she moved between him and a clear shot.

"I want them to know I'm keeping up my end."

Block took Charity by the arm, less roughly this time. "Tell the man I'm treating you fine."

"He hasn't hurt me," she said dully. She forced herself to keep her eyes away from the window. Roman was out there. He would do his best to get her out safely. That was his job.

"The plane'll be ready in a hour," Block told her after he hung up. "Just enough time for that pie and another cup of coffee."

"All right." She crossed to the counter again. Panic sprinted through her when she looked out the window and saw no one. He'd left. Because her fingers were unsteady, she fumbled with the pie. "Roger, are you going to let me go?"

He hesitated only an instant, but that was enough to tell her that his words were just another lie. "Sure. As soon as I'm clear."

So it came down to that. Her heart, her inn and now her life. She set the pie in front of him and studied his face. He was pleased with himself, she thought, and she hated him for it. But he was still sweating.

"I'll get your coffee." She walked to the stove. One foot, then the other. There was a buzzing in her ears. It was more than fear now, she realized as she turned the burner up under the pot. It was rage and despair and a strong, irresistible need to survive. Mechanically she switched the stove off. Then, taking a cloth, she took the pot by the handle.

He was still holding the gun, and he was shoveling pie into his mouth with his left hand. He thought she was a fool, Charity mused. Someone who could be used and duped and manipulated. She took a deep breath.

"Roger?"

He glanced up. Charity looked directly into his eyes.

"You forgot your coffee," she said calmly, then tossed the steaming contents into his face.

He screamed. She didn't think she'd ever heard a man scream like that before. He was half out of his chair, groping blindly for the gun. It happened quickly. No matter how often she played back the scene in her mind, she would never be completely sure what happened first.

She grabbed for the gun herself. Block's flailing hand caught her across the cheekbone. Even as she staggered backward there was the sound of glass breaking.

Roman was through the window. Charity landed on the floor, stunned by the blow, as he burst through. There were men breaking through the barricaded doors and rushing into the room. Someone dragged her from the floor and pulled her out.

Roman held the gun to Block's temple. They were kneeling on the shattered glass—or rather Roman was kneeling and supporting the moaning Block. There were already welts rising up on his wide face. "Please," Roman murmured. "Give me a reason."

"Roman." Royce laid a hand on his shoulder. "It's over."

But the rage clogged his throat. It made his finger slippery on the trigger of the gun. He remembered the way Charity had looked at him when she had seen him outside the window. Slowly he drew back and holstered his gun.

"Yeah. It's over. Get him the hell out of here." He rose and went to find Charity.

He found her in the lobby, wrapped in Mae's arms.

"I'm all right," Charity murmured. "Really." When she saw Roman, her eyes frosted over. "Everything's going to be fine now. I need to speak with Roman for a minute."

"You say your piece." Mae kissed both of her cheeks. "Then you're going to get in a nice hot tub."

"Okay." She squeezed Mae's hand. Strange, but it felt more like a dream now, as if she were pushing her way through layers and layers of gauzy gray curtains. "I think we'll have more privacy upstairs," she said to Roman. Then she turned without looking at him and started up the stairs.

He wanted to hold her. His fingers curled tight into his palms. He needed to lift her against him, touch her hair, her skin, and convince himself that the nightmare was over.

Her knees were shaking. Reaction was struggling to set in, but she fought it off. When she was alone, Charity promised herself. When she was finally alone, she would let it all out.

In her sitting room she turned to face him. She would not, could not, speak to him in the intimacy of her bedroom. "I imagine you have reports to file," she began. Was that her voice? she wondered. It sounded so thin and cold, so foreign. Deliberately she cleared her throat. "I've been told I'll have to make a statement, but I thought we should get this out of the way first."

"Charity." He started toward her, only to be brought up short when her hands whipped out.

"Don't." Her eyes were as cold as her voice. It wasn't a dream, she told herself. It was as harsh and as brutal a reality as she had ever known. "Don't touch me. Not now, not ever again."

His hands fell uselessly to his sides. "I'm sorry."

"Why? You accomplished exactly what you came to do. From what I've been able to gather, Roger and Bob had quite a system going. I'm sure your superiors will be delighted with you."

"It doesn't matter."

She dug his badge out of her pocket, where she had shoved it. "Yes." She threw it at him. "Yes, it does."

Struggling for calm, he pushed it into his pocket. He noted dispassionately that his hands were bleeding. "I couldn't tell you."

"Didn't tell me."

There was a faint bruise on her cheekbone. For a moment all his guilt and impotent fury centered there. "He hit you."

She ran a fingertip lightly across the mark. "I don't break easily."

"I want to explain."

"Do you?" She turned away for a moment. She wanted to keep her anger cold. "I think I get the picture."

"Listen, baby—"

"No, *you* listen, baby." Her composure cracking, she whirled around again. "You lied to me, you used me from the first minute to the last. It was all one huge, incredible lie."

"Not all."

"No? Let's see, how can we separate one from the

other? A convenient flat." She saw the anger in his eyes and shoved a chair out of her path. "And George, good old lucky George. I suppose it was worth a few thousand dollars to get him out of the way and leave you an opening. And Bob—you knew all about Bob, didn't you?"

"We couldn't be sure, not at first."

"Not at first," she repeated. As long as she kept her brain cold, she told herself, she could think. She could think and not feel. "I wonder, Roman, were you so sure of me? Or did you think I was part of it?" When he didn't answer, she spun around again. "You did. Oh, I see. I was under investigation all the time. And there you were, so conveniently on the scene. All you had to do was get close to me, and I made it so easy for you." With a laugh, she pressed her hands to her face. "My God, I threw myself at you."

"I wasn't supposed to get involved with you." Fighting desperation, he paced his words carefully. "It just happened. I fell in love with you."

"Don't say that to me." She lowered her hands. Her face was pale and cool behind them. "You don't even know what it means."

"I didn't, until you."

"You can't have love without trust, Roman. I trusted you. I didn't just give you my body. I gave you everything."

"I told you everything I could," he shot back. "Damn it, I couldn't tell you the rest. The things I told you about myself, about the way I grew up, the way I felt, they were all true."

"Do I have your word on that? Agent DeWinter?"

With an oath, he strode across the room and grabbed her arms. "I didn't know you when I took the assignment. I was doing a job. When things changed, the most important part of that job became proving your innocence and keeping you safe."

"If you had told me I would have proven my own innocence." She jerked out of his hold. "This is my inn, and these are my people. The only family I have left. Do you think I would risk it all for money?"

"No. I knew that, I trusted that, after the first twenty-four hours. I had orders, Charity, and my own instincts. If I had told you who I was and what was going on, you would never have been able to keep up a front."

"So I'm that stupid?"

"No. That honest." Digging deep, he found his control again. "You've been through a lot. Let me take you to the hospital."

"I've been through a lot," she repeated, and nearly laughed. "Do you know how it feels to know that for two years, *two years*, people I thought I knew were using me? I always thought I was such a good judge of character." Now she did laugh. She walked to the window. "They made a fool out of me week after week. I'm not sure I'll ever get over it. But that's nothing." She turned, wrapping her fingers around the windowsill. "That's nothing compared to what I feel when I think of how I let myself believe you were in love with me."

"If it was a lie, why am I here now, telling you that I do?"

"I don't know." Suddenly weary, she dragged her hair away from her face. "And it doesn't seem to matter. I'm wrung dry, Roman. For a while today I was sure he was going to kill me."

"Oh, Charity." He gathered her close, and when she didn't resist he buried his face in her hair.

"I thought he would kill me," she repeated, her arms held rigidly at her sides. "And I didn't want to die. In fact, nothing was quite so important to me as staying alive. When my mother fell in love and that love was betrayed, she gave up. I've never been much like her." She stepped stiffly out of his hold. "Maybe I'm gullible, but I've never been weak. I intend to pick up where I left off, before all of this. I'm going to keep the inn running. No matter what it takes, I'm going to erase you and these last weeks from my life."

"No." Furious, he took her face in his hands. "You won't, because you know I love you. And you made me a promise, Charity. No matter what happened, you wouldn't stop loving me."

"I made that promise to a man who doesn't exist." It hurt. She could feel the pain rip through her from one end to the other. "And I don't love the man who does." She took a small but significant step backward. "Leave me alone."

When he didn't move, she walked into the bedroom and flipped the lock.

Mae was busily sweeping up glass in the kitchen. For the first time in over twenty years the inn was closed. She figured it would open again soon enough, but for now she was content that her girl was safe upstairs in bed and the coffee-guzzling police were on their way out.

When Roman came in, she rested her arms on her broom. Mae had rocked Charity for nearly an hour while she'd cried over him. She'd been prepared to be cold and dismissive. It only took one look to change her mind.

"You look worn out."

"I…" Feeling lost, he glanced around the room. "I wanted to ask how she was before I left."

"She's miserable." She nodded, content with the anguish she saw in his eyes. "And stubborn. You got a few cuts."

Automatically he lifted a hand to rub at the nick on his temple. "Will you give her this number?" He dropped a card on the table. "She can reach me there if— She can reach me there."

"Sit down. Let me clean you up."

"No, it's all right."

"I said sit down." She went to a cupboard for a bottle of antiseptic. "She's had a bad shock."

He had a sudden mental image of Block holding the knife to her throat. "I know."

"She bounces back pretty quick from most things. She loves you."

Roman winced a little as she dabbed on the antiseptic, but not from the sting. "Did."

"Does," Mae said flatly. "She just doesn't want to right now. You been an agent for long?"

"Too long."

"Are you going to make sure that slimy worm Roger Block's put away?"

Roman's hands curled into fists. "Yes."

"Are you in love with Charity?"

He relaxed his hands. "Yes."

"I believe you, so I'm going to give you some advice." Puffing a bit, she sat down next to him. "She's hurt, real bad. Charity's the kind who likes to fix things herself. Give her a little time." She picked up the card and slipped it into her apron pocket. "I'll just hold on to this for now."

She was feeling stronger. And not just physically, Charity decided as she jogged along behind Ludwig. In every way. The sweaty dreams that had woken her night after night were fading. It wasn't nearly as difficult to talk, or to smile, or to pretend that she was in control again. She had promised herself she would put her life back together, and she was doing it.

She rarely thought of Roman. On a sigh, she relented. She would never get strong again if she began to lie to herself.

She *always* thought of Roman. It was difficult not to, and it was especially difficult today.

They were to have been married today. Charity veered into the grass as Ludwig explored. The ache came, spread and was accepted. Just after noon, with the music swelling and the sun streaming down on the garden, she would have put her hand in his. And promised.

A fantasy, she told herself, and nudged her dog back onto the shoulder of the road. It had been fantasy then, and it was a fantasy now.

And yet… With every day that passed she remembered more clearly the times they had spent together. His reluctance, and his anger. Then his tenderness and concern. She glanced down to where the bracelet shimmered on her wrist.

She'd tried to put it back in the box, to push it into some dark, rarely opened drawer. Every day she told herself she would. Tomorrow. And every day she remembered how sweet, how awkward and how wonderful he'd been when he'd given it to her.

If it had only been a job, why had he given her so much more than he had needed to? Not just the piece of jewelry, but everything the circle of gold had symbolized? He could have offered her friendship and respect, as Bob had, and she would have trusted him as much. He could have kept their relationship strictly physical. Her feelings would have remained the same.

But he had said he loved her. And at the end he had all but begged her to believe it.

She shook her head and increased her pace. She was being weak and sentimental. It was just the day… the beautiful spring morning that was to have been her wedding day.

What she needed was to get back to the inn and keep busy. This day would pass, like all the others.

At first she thought she was imagining it when she saw him standing beside the road, looking out at the sunrise over the water. Her feet faltered. Before she could think to prevent it, her knees weakened. Fighting her heart, she walked to him.

He'd heard her coming. As he'd stood in the growing light he'd remembered wondering if he came back, if he would stand just there and wait for Charity to run to him.

She wasn't running now. She was walking very

slowly, despite the eager dog. Could she know, he won-dered, that she held his life in her hands?

Nerves swarmed through her, making her fingers clench and unclench on the leash. She prayed as she stopped in front of him that her voice would be steadier.

"What do you want?"

He bent down to pat the squirming dog's head. "We'll get to that. How are you feeling?"

"I'm fine."

"You've been having nightmares." There were shad-ows under her eyes. He wouldn't make it easy on her by ignoring them.

She stiffened. "They're passing. Mae talks too much."

"At least she talks to me."

"We've already said all there is to say."

He closed a hand over her arm as she started by him. "Not this time. You had your say last time, and I had a lot of it coming. Now it's my turn." Reaching down, he unhooked the leash. Free, Ludwig bounded toward home. "Mae's waiting for him," Roman ex-plained before Charity could call the dog back.

"I see." She wrapped the leash around her fisted hand. "You two work all this out?"

"She cares about you. So do I."

"I have things to do."

"Yeah. This is first." He pulled her close and, ignor-ing her struggling, crushed his mouth to hers. It was like a drink after days in the desert, like a fire after a dozen long cold nights. He plundered, greedy, as though it were the first time. Or the last.

She couldn't fight him, or herself. Almost sobbing, she clung to him, hungry and hurting. No matter how strong she tried to be, she would never be strong enough to stand against her own heart.

Aching, she started to draw back, but he tightened his hold. "Give me a minute," he murmured, pressing his lips to her hair. "Every night I wake up and see him holding a knife at your throat. And there's nothing I can do. I reach for you, and you're not there. For a minute, one horrible minute, I'm terrified. Then I remember that you're safe. You're not with me, but you're safe. It's almost enough."

"Roman." With a helpless sigh, she stroked soothing hands over his shoulders. "It doesn't do any good to think about it."

"Do you think I could forget?" He pulled back, keeping his hands firm on her arms. "For the rest of my life I'll remember every second of it. I was responsible for you."

"No." The anger came quickly enough to surprise both of them. She shoved at his chest. "*I'm* responsible for me. I was and I am and I always will be. And I took care of myself."

"Yeah." He ran his palm over her cheek. The bruise had faded, even if the memory hadn't. "It was a hell of a way to serve coffee."

"Let's forget it." She shrugged out of his grip and walked toward the water. "I'm not particularly proud of letting myself be duped, so I'd rather not dwell on it."

"They were pros, Charity. You're not the first person they've used."

She pressed her lips together. "And you?"

"When you're undercover you lie, and you use, and you take advantage of anything that's offered." Her eyes were closed when he turned her around to face him. "I came here to do a job. It had been a long time since I'd let myself think beyond anything but the next day. Look at me. Please."

Taking a steadying breath, she opened her eyes. "We've been through this already, Roman."

"No. I'd hurt you. I'd disappointed you. You weren't ready to listen." Gently he brushed a tear from her lashes. "I hope you are now, because I can't make it much longer without you."

"I was too hard on you before." It took almost everything she had, but she managed a smile. "I was hurt, and I was a lot shakier than I knew from being locked up with Roger. After I gave my statement, Inspector Conby explained everything to me, more clearly. About how the operation had been working, what my responsibilities were, what you had to do."

"What responsibilities?"

"About the money. It's put us in somewhat of a hole, but at least we only have to pay back a percentage."

"I see." Roman laughed and shook his head. "He always was a prince."

"The merchant's responsible for the loss." She tilted her head. "You didn't know about the arrangements I've made with him?"

"No."

"But you work for him."

"Not anymore. I turned in my resignation when I got back to D.C."

"Oh, Roman, that's ridiculous. It's like throwing out the baby with the bathwater."

He smiled appreciatively at her innate practicality. "I decided I like carpentry better. Got any openings?"

Running the leash through her hands, she looked over the water. "I haven't given much thought to remodeling lately."

"I work cheap." He tilted her face to his. "All you have to do is marry me."

"Don't."

"Charity." Calling on patience he hadn't been aware he possessed, he held her still. "One of the things I most admire about you is your mind. You're real sharp. Look at me, really look. I figure you've got to know that I'm not beating my head against this same wall for entertainment. I love you. You've got to believe that."

"I'm afraid to," she whispered.

He felt the first true spark of hope. "Believe this. You changed my life. Literally changed it. I can't go back to the way it was before. I can't go forward unless you're with me. How long do you want me to stand here, waiting to start living again?"

With her arms wrapped around her chest, she walked a short distance away. The high grass at the water's edge was still misted with dew. She could smell it, and the fragile fragrances of wildflowers. It occurred to her then that she had blocked such small things out of her life ever since she'd sent him away.

If it was honesty she was demanding from him, how could she give him anything less?

"I've missed you terribly." She shook her head quickly before he could touch her again. "I tried not to wonder if you'd come back. I told myself I didn't want you to. When I saw you standing in the road, all I wanted to do was run to you. No questions, no explanations. But it's not that simple."

"No."

"I do love you, Roman. I can't stop. I have tried," she said, looking back at him. "Not very hard, but I have tried. I think I knew under all the anger and the hurt that you weren't lying about loving me back. I haven't wanted to forgive you for lying about the rest, but— That's just pride, really." Perhaps it was simple after all, she thought. "If I have to make a choice, I'd rather choose love." She smiled and opened her arms to him. "I guess you're hired."

She laughed when he caught her up in his arms and swung her around. "We'll make it work," he promised her, raining kisses all over her face. "Starting today."

"We were going to be married today."

"Are going to be." He hooked his arm under her legs to carry her.

"But we—"

"I have a license." Closing his mouth over hers, he swung her around again.

"A marriage license?"

"It's in my pocket, with two tickets to Venice."

"To—" Her hand slid limply from his shoulder. "To *Venice?* But how—?"

"And Mae bought you a dress yesterday. She wouldn't let me see it."

"Well." The thrill was too overwhelming to allow her to pretend annoyance. "You were awfully sure of yourself."

"No." He kissed her again, felt the curve of her lips, and the welcoming. "I was sure of you."

* * * * *

THE ART OF DECEPTION

For the Romance Writers of America,
in gratitude for the friends I've made
and the friends still to come.

Chapter 1

It was more like a castle than a house. The stone was gray, but beveled at the edges, Herodian-style, so that it shimmered with underlying colors. Towers and turrets jutted toward the sky, joined together by a crenellated roof. Windows were mullioned, long and narrow with diamond-shaped panes.

The structure—Adam would never think of it as anything so ordinary as a house—loomed over the Hudson, audacious and eccentric and, if such things were possible, pleased with itself. If the stories were true, it suited its owner perfectly.

All it required, Adam decided as he crossed the flagstone courtyard, was a dragon and a moat.

Two grinning gargoyles sat on either side of the wide stone steps. He passed by them with a reservation natural to a practical man. Gargoyles and turrets could be accepted in their proper place—but not in rural New York, a few hours' drive out of Manhattan.

Deciding to reserve judgment, he lifted the heavy brass knocker and let it fall against a door of thick Honduras mahogany. After a third pounding, the door creaked open. With strained patience, Adam looked down at a small woman with huge gray eyes, black braids and a soot-streaked face. She wore a rumpled sweatshirt and jeans that had seen better days. Lazily, she rubbed her nose with the back of her hand and stared back.

"Hullo."

He bit back a sigh, thinking that if the staff ran to half-witted maids, the next few weeks were going to be very tedious. "I'm Adam Haines. Mr. Fairchild is expecting me," he enunciated.

Her eyes narrowed with curiosity or suspicion, he couldn't be sure. "Expecting you?" Her accent was broad New England. After another moment of staring, she frowned, shrugged, then moved aside to let him in.

The hall was wide and seemingly endless. The paneling gleamed a dull deep brown in the diffused light. Streaks of sun poured out of a high angled window and fell over the small woman, but he barely noticed. Paintings. For the moment, Adam forgot the fatigue of the journey and his annoyance. He forgot everything else but the paintings.

Van Gogh, Renoir, Monet. A museum could claim no finer exhibition. The power pulled at him. The hues, the tints, the brush strokes, and the overall magnificence they combined to create, tugged at his senses. Perhaps, in some strange way, Fairchild had been right to house them in something like a fortress. Turning,

Adam saw the maid with her hands loosely folded, her huge gray eyes on his face. Impatience sprang back.

"Run along, will you? Tell Mr. Fairchild I'm here."

"And who might you be?" Obviously impatience didn't affect her.

"Adam Haines," he repeated. He was a man accustomed to servants—and one who expected efficiency.

"Ayah, so you said."

How could her eyes be smoky and clear at the same time? he wondered fleetingly. He gave a moment's thought to the fact that they reflected a maturity and intelligence at odds with her braids and smeared face. "Young lady…" He paced the words, slowly and distinctly. "Mr. Fairchild is expecting me. Just tell him I'm here. Can you handle that?"

A sudden dazzling smile lit her face. "Ayah."

The smile threw him off. He noticed for the first time that she had an exquisite mouth, full and sculpted. And there was something…something under the soot. Without thinking, he lifted a hand, intending to brush some off. The tempest hit.

"I can't do it! I tell you it's impossible. A travesty!" A man barreled down the long, curved stairs at an alarming rate. His face was shrouded in tragedy, his voice croaked with doom. "This is all your fault." Coming to a breathless stop, he pointed a long, thin finger at the little maid. "It's on your head, make no mistake."

Robin Goodfellow, Adam thought instantly. The man was the picture of Puck, short with a spritely build, a face molded on cherubic lines. The spare thatch of light hair nearly stood on end. He seemed to dance. His thin legs lifted and fell on the landing as he waved the long finger at the dark-haired woman. She remained serenely undisturbed.

"Your blood pressure's rising every second, Mr. Fairchild. You'd better take a deep breath or two before you have a spell."

"Spell!" Insulted, he danced faster. His face glowed pink with the effort. "I don't have spells, girl. I've never had a spell in my life."

"There's always a first time." She nodded, keeping her fingers lightly linked. "Mr. Adam Haines is here to see you."

"Haines? What the devil does Haines have to do with it? It's the end, I tell you. The climax." He placed a hand dramatically over his heart. The pale blue eyes watered so that for one awful moment, Adam thought he'd weep. "Haines?" he repeated. Abruptly he focused on Adam with a brilliant smile. "I'm expecting you, aren't I?"

Cautiously Adam offered his hand. "Yes."

"Glad you could come, I've been looking forward to it." Still showing his teeth, he pumped Adam's hand. "Into the parlor," he said, moving his grip from Adam's hand to his arm. "We'll have a drink." He walked with the quick bouncing stride of a man who hadn't a worry in the world.

In the parlor Adam had a quick impression of antiques and old magazines. At a wave of Fairchild's hand he sat on a horsehair sofa that was remarkably uncomfortable. The maid went to an enormous stone fireplace and began to scrub out the hearth with quick, tuneful little whistles.

"I'm having Scotch," Fairchild decided, and reached for a decanter of Chivas Regal.

"That'll be fine."

"I admire your work, Adam Haines." Fairchild offered the Scotch with a steady hand. His face was calm, his voice moderate. Adam wondered if he'd imagined the scene on the stairs.

"Thank you." Sipping Scotch, Adam studied the little genius across from him.

Small networks of lines crept out from Fairchild's eyes and mouth. Without them and the thinning hair, he might have been taken for a very young man. His aura of youth seemed to spring from an inner vitality, a feverish energy. The eyes were pure, unfaded blue. Adam knew they could see beyond what others saw.

Philip Fairchild was, indisputably, one of the greatest living artists of the twentieth century. His style ranged from the flamboyant to the elegant, with a touch of everything in between. For more than thirty years, he'd enjoyed a position of fame, wealth and respect in artistic and popular circles, something very few people in his profession achieved during their lifetime.

Enjoy it he did, with a temperament that ranged from pompous to irascible to generous. From time to time he invited other artists to his house on the Hudson, to spend weeks or months working, absorbing or simply relaxing. At other times, he barred everyone from the door and went into total seclusion.

"I appreciate the opportunity to work here for a few weeks, Mr. Fairchild."

"My pleasure." The artist sipped Scotch and sat, gesturing with a regal wave of his hand—the king granting benediction.

Adam successfully hid a smirk. "I'm looking forward to studying some of your paintings up close. There's such incredible variety in your work."

"I live for variety," Fairchild said with a giggle. From the hearth came a distinct snort. "Disrespectful brat," Fairchild muttered into his drink. When he scowled at her, the maid tossed a braid over her shoulder and plopped her rag noisily into the bucket. "Cards!" Fairchild bellowed, so suddenly Adam nearly dumped the Scotch in his lap.

"I beg your pardon?"

"No need for that," Fairchild said graciously and shouted again. At the second bellow the epitome of butlers walked into the parlor.

"Yes, Mr. Fairchild." His voice was grave, lightly British. The dark suit he wore was a discreet contrast to the white hair and pale skin. He held himself like a soldier.

"See to Mr. Haines's car, Cards, and his luggage. The Wedgwood guest room."

"Very good, sir," the butler agreed after a slight nod from the woman at the hearth.

"And put his equipment in Kirby's studio," Fairchild added, grinning as the hearth scrubber choked. "Plenty of room for both of you," he told Adam before he scowled. "My daughter, you know. She's doing sculpture, up to her elbows in clay or chipping at wood and marble. I can't cope with it." Gripping his glass in both hands, Fairchild bowed his head. "God knows I try. I've put my soul into it. And for what?" he demanded, jerking his head up again. "For what?"

"I'm afraid I—"

"Failure!" Fairchild moaned, interrupting him. "To

have to deal with failure at my age. It's on your head," he told the little brunette again. "You have to live with it—if you can."

Turning, she sat on the hearth, folded her legs under her and rubbed more soot on her nose. "You can hardly blame me if you have four thumbs and your soul's lost." The accent was gone. Her voice was low and smooth, hinting of European finishing schools. Adam's eyes narrowed. "You're determined to be better than I," she went on. "Therefore, you were doomed to fail before you began."

"Doomed to fail! Doomed to fail, am I?" He was up and dancing again, Scotch sloshing around in his glass. "Philip Fairchild will overcome, you heartless brat. He shall triumph! You'll eat your words."

"Nonsense." Deliberately, she yawned. "You have your medium, Papa, and I have mine. Learn to live with it."

"Never." He slammed a hand against his heart again. "Defeat is a four-letter word."

"Six," she corrected, and, rising, commandeered the rest of his Scotch.

He scowled at her, then at his empty glass. "I was speaking metaphorically."

"How clever." She kissed his cheek, transferring soot.

"Your face is filthy," Fairchild grumbled.

Lifting a brow, she ran a finger down his cheek. "So's yours."

They grinned at each other. For a flash, the resemblance was so striking, Adam wondered how he'd missed it. Kirby Fairchild, Philip's only child, a well-respected artist and eccentric in her own right. Just what, Adam wondered, was the darling of the jet set doing scrubbing out hearths?

"Come along, Adam." Kirby turned to him with a casual smile. "I'll show you to your room. You look tired. Oh, Papa," she added as she moved to the door, "this week's issue of *People* came. It's on the server. That'll keep him entertained," she said to Adam as she led him up the stairs.

He followed her slowly, noting that she walked with the faultless grace of a woman who'd been taught how to move. The pigtails swung at her back. Jeans, worn white at the stress points, had no designer label on the back pocket. Her canvas Nikes had broken shoelaces.

Kirby glided along the second floor, passing half a dozen doors before she stopped. She glanced at her hands, then at Adam. "You'd better open it. I'll get the knob filthy."

He pushed open the door and felt like he was stepping back in time. Wedgwood blue dominated the color scheme. The furniture was all Middle Georgian—carved armchairs, ornately worked tables. Again there were paintings, but this time, it was the woman behind him who held his attention.

"Why did you do that?"

"Do what?"

"Put on that act at the door." He walked back to where she stood at the threshold. Looking down, he calculated that she barely topped five feet. For the second time he had the urge to brush the soot from her face to discover what lay beneath.

"You looked so polished, and you positively glowered." She leaned a shoulder against the doorjamb.

There was an elegance about him that intrigued her, because his eyes were sharp and arrogant. Though she didn't smile, the amusement in her expression was soft and ripe. "You were expecting a dimwitted parlor maid, so I made it easy for you. Cocktails at seven. Can you find your way back, or shall I come for you?"

He'd make do with that for now. "I'll find it."

"All right. *Ciao,* Adam."

Unwillingly fascinated, he watched her until she'd turned the corner at the end of the hall. Perhaps Kirby Fairchild would be as interesting a nut to crack as her father. But that was for later.

Adam closed the door and locked it. His bags were already set neatly beside the rosewood wardrobe. Taking the briefcase, Adam spun the combination lock and drew up the lid. He pulled out a small transmitter and flicked a switch.

"I'm in."

"Password," came the reply.

He swore, softly and distinctly. "Seagull. And that is, without a doubt, the most ridiculous password on record."

"Routine, Adam. We've got to follow routine."

"Sure." There'd been nothing routine since he'd stopped his car at the end of the winding uphill drive. "I'm in, McIntyre, and I want you to know how much I appreciate your dumping me in this madhouse." With a flick of his thumb, he cut McIntyre off.

Without stopping to wash, Kirby jogged up the steps to her father's studio. She opened the door, then slammed it so that jars and tubes of paint shuddered on their shelves.

"What have you done this time?" she demanded.

"I'm starting over." Wispy brows knit, he huddled over a moist lump of clay. "Fresh start. Rebirth."

"I'm not talking about your futile attempts with clay. Adam Haines," she said before he could retort. Like a small tank, she advanced on him. Years before, Kirby had learned size was of no consequence if you had a knack for intimidation. She'd developed it meticulously. Slamming her palms down on his worktable, she stood nose to nose with him. "What the hell do you mean by asking him here and not even telling me?"

"Now, now, Kirby." Fairchild hadn't lived six decades without knowing when to dodge and weave. "It simply slipped my mind."

Better than anyone else, Kirby knew nothing slipped his mind. "What're you up to now, Papa?"

"Up to?" He smiled guilelessly.

"Why did you ask him here now, of all times?"

"I've admired his work. So've you," he pointed out when her mouth thinned. "He wrote such a nice letter about *Scarlet Moon* when it was exhibited at the Metropolitan last month."

Her brow lifted, an elegant movement under a layer of soot. "You don't invite everyone who compliments your work."

"Of course not, my sweet. That would be impossible. One must be…selective. Now I must get back to my work while the mood's flowing."

"Something's going to flow," she promised. "Papa, if you've a new scheme after you promised—"

"Kirby!" His round, smooth face quivered with emotion. His lips trembled. It was only one of his talents. "You'd doubt the word of your own father? The seed that spawned you?"

"That makes me sound like a gardenia, and it won't work." She crossed her arms over her chest. Frowning, Fairchild poked at the unformed clay.

"My motives are completely altruistic."

"Hah."

"Adam Haines is a brilliant young artist. You've said so yourself."

"Yes, he is, and I'm sure he'd be delightful company under different circumstances." She leaned forward, grabbing her father's chin in her hand. "Not now."

"Ungracious," Fairchild said with disapproval. "Your mother, rest her soul, would be very disappointed in you."

Kirby ground her teeth. "Papa, the Van Gogh!"

"Coming along nicely," he assured her. "Just a few more days."

Knowing she was in danger of tearing out her hair, she stalked to the tower window. "Oh, bloody murder."

Senility, she decided. It had to be senility. How could he consider having that man here now? Next week, next month, but now? That man, Kirby thought ruthlessly, was nobody's fool.

At first glance she'd decided he wasn't just attractive—very attractive—but sharp. Those big camel's eyes gleamed with intelligence. The long, thin mouth equaled determination. Perhaps he was a bit pompous in his bearing and manner, but he wasn't soft. No, she was certain instinctively that Adam Haines would be hard as nails.

She'd like to do him in bronze, she mused. The straight nose, the sharp angles and planes in his face. His hair was nearly the color of deep, polished bronze, and just a tad too long for convention. She'd want to capture his air of arrogance and authority. But not now!

Sighing, she moved her shoulders. Behind her back, Fairchild grinned. When she turned back to him, he was studiously intent on his clay.

"He'll want to come up here, you know." Despite the soot, she dipped her hands in her pockets. They had a problem; now it had to be dealt with. For the better part of her life, Kirby had sorted through the confusion her father gleefully created. The truth was, she'd have had it no other way. "It would seem odd if we didn't show him your studio."

"We'll show him tomorrow."

"He mustn't see the Van Gogh." Kirby planted her feet, prepared to do battle on this one point, if not the others. "You're not going to make this more complicated than you already have."

"He won't see it. Why should he?" Fairchild glanced up briefly, eyes wide. "It has nothing to do with him."

Though she realized it was foolish, Kirby was reassured. No, he wouldn't see it, she thought. Her father might be a little…unique, she decided, but he wasn't careless. Neither was she. "Thank God it's nearly finished."

"Another few days and off it goes, high into the mountains of South America." He made a vague, sweeping gesture with his hands.

Moving over, Kirby uncovered the canvas that stood on an easel in the far corner. She studied it as an artist, as a lover of art and as a daughter.

The pastoral scene was not peaceful but vibrant. The brush strokes were jagged, almost fierce, so that the simple setting had a frenzied kind of motion. No, it didn't sit still waiting for admiration. It reached out and grabbed by the throat. It spoke of pain, of triumph, of agonies and joys. Her lips tilted because she had no choice. Van Gogh, she knew, could have done no better.

"Papa." When she turned her head, their eyes met in perfect understanding. "You are incomparable."

By seven, Kirby had not only resigned herself to their house guest, but was prepared to enjoy him. It was a basic trait of her character to enjoy what she had to put up with. As she poured vermouth into a glass, she realized she was looking forward to seeing him again, and to getting beneath the surface gloss. She had a feeling there might be some fascinating layers in Adam Haines.

She dropped into a high-backed chair, crossed her legs and tuned back in to her father's rantings.

"It hates me, fails me at every turn. Why, Kirby?" He spread his hands in an impassioned plea. "I'm a good man, loving father, faithful friend."

"It's your attitude, Papa." She shrugged a shoulder as she drank. "Your emotional plane's faulty."

"There's nothing wrong with my emotional plane." Sniffing, Fairchild lifted his glass. "Not a damn thing wrong with it. It's the clay that's the problem, not me."

"You're cocky," she said simply. Fairchild made a sound like a train straining up a long hill.

"Cocky? *Cocky?* What the devil kind of word is that?"

"Adjective. Two syllables, five letters."

Adam heard the byplay as he walked toward the parlor. After a peaceful afternoon, he wondered if he was ready to cope with another bout of madness. Fairchild's voice was rising steadily, and as Adam paused in the doorway, he saw that the artist was up and shuffling again.

McIntyre was going to pay for this, Adam decided. He'd see to it that revenge was slow and thorough. When Fairchild pointed an accusing finger, Adam followed its direction. For an instant he was totally and uncharacteristically stunned.

The woman in the chair was so completely removed from the grimy, pigtailed chimney sweep, he found it nearly impossible to associate the two. She wore a thin silk dress as dark as her hair, draped at the bodice and slit up the side to show off one smooth thigh. He studied her profile as she watched her father rant. It was gently molded, classically oval with a very subtle sweep of cheekbones. Her lips were full, curved now in just a hint of a smile. Without the soot, her skin was somewhere between gold and honey with a look of luxurious softness. Only the eyes reminded him this was the same woman—gray and large and amused. Lifting one hand, she tossed back the dark hair that covered her shoulders.

There was something more than beauty here. Adam knew he'd seen women with more beauty than Kirby

Fairchild. But there was something… He groped for the word, but it eluded him.

As if sensing him, she turned—just her head. Again she stared at him, openly and with curiosity, as her father continued his ravings. Slowly, very slowly, she smiled. Adam felt the power slam into him.

Sex, he realized abruptly. Kirby Fairchild exuded sex the way other women exuded perfume. Raw, unapologetic sex.

With a quick assessment typical of him, Adam decided she wouldn't be easy to deceive. However he handled Fairchild, he'd have to tread carefully with Fairchild's daughter. He decided as well that he already wanted to make love to her. He'd have to tread *very* carefully.

"Adam." She spoke in a soft voice that nonetheless carried over her father's shouting. "You seem to have found us. Come in, Papa's nearly done."

"Done? I'm undone. And by my own child." Fairchild moved toward Adam as he entered the room. "Cocky, she says. I ask you, is that a word for a daughter to use?"

"An aperitif?" Kirby asked. She rose with a fluid motion that Adam had always associated with tall, willowy women.

"Yes, thank you."

"Your room's agreeable?" His face wreathed in smiles again, Fairchild plopped down on the sofa.

"Very agreeable." The best way to handle it, Adam decided, was to pretend everything was normal. Pretenses were, after all, part of the game. "You have an… exceptional house."

"I'm fond of it." Content, Fairchild leaned back. "It was built near the turn of the century by a wealthy and insane English lord. You'll take Adam on a tour tomorrow, won't you, Kirby?"

"Of course." As she handed Adam a glass, she smiled into his eyes. Diamonds, cold as ice, glittered at her ears. He could feel the heat rise.

"I'm looking forward to it." Style, he concluded. Whether natural or developed, Miss Fairchild had style.

She smiled over the rim of her own glass, thinking precisely the same thing about Adam. "We aim to please."

A cautious man, Adam turned to Fairchild again. "Your art collection rivals a museum's. The Titian in my room is fabulous."

The Titian, Kirby thought in quick panic. How could she have forgotten it? What in God's name could she do about it? No difference. It made no difference, she reassured herself. It couldn't, because there was nothing to be done.

"The Hudson scene on the west wall—" Adam turned to her just as Kirby was telling herself to relax "—is that your work?"

"My... Oh, yes." She smiled as she remembered. She'd deal with the Titian at the first opportunity. "I'd forgotten that. It's sentimental, I'm afraid. I was home from school and had a crush on the chauffeur's son. We used to neck down there."

"He had buck teeth," Fairchild reminded her with a snort.

"Love conquers all," Kirby decided.

"The Hudson River bank is a hell of a place to lose

your virginity," her father stated, suddenly severe. He swirled his drink, then downed it.

Enjoying the abrupt paternal disapproval, she decided to poke at it. "I didn't lose my virginity on the Hudson River bank." Amusement glimmered in her eyes. "I lost it in a Renault in Paris."

Love conquers all, Adam repeated silently.

"Dinner is served," Cards announced with dignity from the doorway.

"And about time, too." Fairchild leaped up. "A man could starve in his own home."

With a smile at her father's retreating back, Kirby offered Adam her hand. "Shall we go in?"

In the dining room, Fairchild's paintings dominated. An enormous Waterford chandelier showered light over mahogany and crystal. A massive stone fireplace thundered with flame and light. There were scents of burning wood, candles and roasted meat. There was Breton lace and silver. Still, his paintings dominated.

It appeared he had no distinct style. Art was his style, whether he depicted a sprawling, light-filled landscape or a gentle, shadowy portrait. Bold brush strokes or delicate ones, oils streaked on with a pallet knife or misty watercolors, he'd done them all. Magnificently.

As varied as his paintings were his opinions on other artists. While they sat at the long, laden table, Fairchild spoke of each artist personally, as if he'd been transported back in time and had developed relationships with Raphael, Goya, Manet.

His theories were intriguing, his knowledge was impressive. The artist in Adam responded to him. The

practical part, the part that had come to do a job, remained cautious. The opposing forces made him uncomfortable. His attraction to the woman across from
him made him itchy.

He cursed McIntyre.

Adam decided the weeks with the Fairchilds might
be interesting despite their eccentricities. He didn't care
for the complications, but he'd allowed himself to be
pulled in. For now, he'd sit back and observe, waiting
for the time to act.

The information he had on them was sketchy. Fairchild was just past sixty, a widower of nearly twenty
years. His art and his talent were no secrets, but his
personal life was veiled. Perhaps due to temperament.
Perhaps, Adam mused, due to necessity.

About Kirby, he knew almost nothing. Professionally, she'd kept a low profile until her first showing
the year before. Though it had been an unprecedented
success, both she and her father rarely sought publicity for their work. Personally, she was often written
up in the glossies and tabloids as she jetted to Saint
Moritz with this year's tennis champion or to Marti-
nique with the current Hollywood golden boy. He knew
she was twenty-seven and unmarried. Not for lack of
opportunity, he concluded. She was the type of woman
men would constantly pursue. In another century, duels
would have been fought over her. Adam thought she'd
have enjoyed the melodrama.

From their viewpoint, the Fairchilds knew of Adam
only what was public knowledge. He'd been born under
comfortable circumstances, giving him both the time
and means to develop his talent. At the age of twenty,

his reputation as an artist had begun to take root. A dozen years later, he was well established. He'd lived in Paris, then in Switzerland, before settling back in the States.

Still, during his twenties, he'd traveled often while painting. With Adam, his art had always come first. However, under the poised exterior, under the practicality and sophistication, there was a taste for adventure and a streak of cunning. So there had been McIntyre.

He'd just have to learn control, Adam told himself as he thought of McIntyre. He'd just have to learn how to say no, absolutely no. The next time Mac had an inspiration, he could go to hell with it.

When they settled back in the parlor with coffee and brandy, Adam calculated that he could finish the job in a couple of weeks. True, the place was immense, but there were only a handful of people in it. After his tour he'd know his way around well enough. Then it would be routine.

Satisfied, he concentrated on Kirby. At the moment she was the perfect hostess—charming, personable. All class and sophistication. She was, momentarily, precisely the type of woman who'd always appealed to him—well-groomed, well-mannered, intelligent, lovely. The room smelled of hothouse roses, wood smoke and her own tenuous scent, which seemed to blend the two. Adam began to relax with it.

"Why don't you play, Kirby?" Fairchild poured a second brandy for himself and Adam. "It helps clear my mind."

"All right." With a quick smile for Adam, Kirby

moved to the far end of the room, running a finger over a wing-shaped instrument he'd taken for a small piano.

It took only a few notes for him to realize he'd been wrong. A harpsichord, he thought, astonished. The tinny music floated up. Bach. Adam recognized the composer and wondered if he'd fallen down the rabbit hole. No one—no one normal—played Bach on a harpsichord in a castle in the twentieth century.

Fairchild sat, his eyes half closed, one thin finger tapping, while Kirby continued to play. Her eyes were grave, her mouth was faintly moist and sober. Suddenly, without missing a note or moving another muscle, she sent Adam a slow wink. The notes flowed into Brahms. In that instant, Adam knew he was not only going to take her to bed. He was going to paint her.

"I've got it!" Fairchild leaped up and scrambled around the room. "I've got it. Inspiration. The golden light!"

"Amen," Kirby murmured.

"I'll show you, you wicked child." Grinning like one of his gargoyles, Fairchild leaned over the harpsichord. "By the end of the week, I'll have a piece that'll make anything you've ever done look like a doorstop."

Kirby raised her brows and kissed him on the mouth. "Goat droppings."

"You'll eat your words," he warned as he dashed out of the room.

"I sincerely hope not." Rising, she picked up her drink. "Papa has a nasty competitive streak." Which constantly pleased her. "More brandy?"

"Your father has a…unique personality." An emerald flashed on her hand as she filled her glass again. He saw her hands were narrow, delicate against the hard glitter of the stone. But there'd be strength in them, he reminded himself as he moved to the bar to join her. Strength was indispensable to an artist.

"You're diplomatic." She turned and looked up at him. There was the faintest hint of rose on her lips. "You're a very diplomatic person, aren't you, Adam?"

He'd already learned not to trust the nunlike expression. "Under some circumstances."

"Under most circumstances. Too bad."

"Is it?"

Because she enjoyed personal contact during any kind of confrontation, she kept her eyes on his while she drank. Her irises were the purest gray he'd ever seen, with no hint of other colors. "I think you'd be a very interesting man if you didn't bind yourself up. I believe you think everything through very carefully."

"You see that as a problem?" His voice had cooled. "It's a remarkable observation after such a short time."

No, he wouldn't be a bore, she decided, pleased with his annoyance. It was lack of emotion Kirby found tedious. "I could've come by it easily enough after an hour, but I'd already seen your work. Besides talent, you have self-control, dignity and a strong sense of the conventional."

"Why do I feel as though I've been insulted?"

"Perceptive, too." She smiled, that slow curving of lips that was fascinating to watch. When he answered it, she made up her mind quickly. She'd always found it the best way. Still watching him, she set down her brandy. "I'm impulsive," she explained. "I want to see what it feels like."

Her arms were around him, her lips on his, in a

move that caught him completely off balance. He had a very brief impression of wood smoke and roses, of incredible softness and strength, before she drew back. The hint of a smile remained as she picked up her brandy and finished it off. She'd enjoyed the brief kiss, but she'd enjoyed shocking him a great deal more.

"Very nice," she said with borderline approval. "Breakfast is from seven on. Just ring for Cards if you need anything. Good night."

She turned to leave, but he took her arm. Kirby found herself whirled around. When their bodies collided, the surprise was hers.

"You caught me off guard," he said softly. "I can do much better than nice."

He took her mouth swiftly, molding her to him. Soft to hard, thin silk to crisp linen. There was something primitive in her taste, something…ageless. She brought to his mind the woods on an autumn evening—dark, pungent and full of small mysteries.

The kiss lengthened, deepened without plan on either side. Her response was instant, as her responses often were. It was boundless as they often were. She moved her hands from his shoulders, to his neck, to his face, as if she were already sculpting. Something vibrated between them.

For the moment, blood ruled. She was accustomed to it; he wasn't. He was accustomed to reason, but he found none here. Here was heat and passion, needs and desires without questions or answers.

Ultimately, reluctantly, he drew back. Caution, because he was used to winning, was his way.

She could still taste him. Kirby wondered, as she felt

his breath feather over her lips, how she'd misjudged him. Her head was spinning, something new for her. She understood heated blood, a fast pulse, but not the clouding of her mind.

Not certain how long he'd have the advantage, Adam smiled at her. "Better?"

"Yes." She waited until the floor became solid under her feet again. "That was quite an improvement." Like her father, she knew when to dodge and weave. She eased herself away and moved to the doorway. She'd have to do some thinking, and some reevaluating. "How long are you here, Adam?"

"Four weeks," he told her, finding it odd she didn't know.

"Do you intend to sleep with me before you go?"

Torn between amusement and admiration, he stared at her. He respected candor, but he wasn't used to it in quite so blunt a form. In this case, he decided to follow suit. "Yes."

She nodded, ignoring the little thrill that raced up her spine. Games—she liked to play them. To win them. Kirby sensed one was just beginning between her and Adam. "I'll have to think about that, won't I? Good night."

Chapter 2

Shafts of morning light streamed in the long windows of the dining room and tossed their diamond pattern on the floor. Outside the trees were touched with September. Leaves blushed from salmon to crimson, the colors mixed with golds and rusts and the last stubborn greens. The lawn was alive with fall flowers and shrubs that seemed caught on fire. Adam had his back to the view as he studied Fairchild's paintings.

Again, Adam was struck with the incredible variety of styles Fairchild cultivated. There was a still life with the light and shadows of a Goya, a landscape with the frantic colors of a Van Gogh, a portrait with the sensitivity and grace of a Raphael. Because of its subject, it was the portrait that drew him.

A frail, dark-haired woman looked out from the canvas. There was an air of serenity, of patience, about her. The eyes were the same pure gray as Kirby's, but the features were gentler, more even. Kirby's mother had been a rare beauty, a rare woman who looked like she'd had both strength and understanding. While she wouldn't have scrubbed at a hearth, she would have understood the daughter who did. That Adam could see this, be certain of it, without ever having met Rachel Fairchild, was only proof of Fairchild's genius. He created life with oil and brush.

The next painting, executed in the style of Gainsborough, was a full-length portrait of a young girl. Glossy black curls fell over the shoulders of a white muslin dress, tucked at the bodice, belled at the skirt. She wore white stockings and neat black buckle shoes. Touches of color came from the wide pink sash around her waist and the dusky roses she carried in a basket. But this was no demure *Pinky*.

The girl held her head high, tilting it with youthful arrogance. The half smile spoke of devilment while the huge gray eyes danced with both. No more than eleven or twelve, Adam calculated. Even then, Kirby must have been a handful.

"An adorable child, isn't she?" Kirby stood at the doorway as she had for five full minutes. She'd enjoyed watching and dissecting him as much as Adam had enjoyed dissecting the painting.

He stood very straight—prep school training, Kirby decided. Yet his hands were dipped comfortably in his pockets. Even in a casual sweater and jeans, there was an air of formality about him. Contrasts intrigued her, as a woman and as an artist.

Turning, Adam studied her as meticulously as he

had her portrait. The day before, he'd seen her go from grubby urchin to sleek sophisticate. Today she was the picture of the bohemian artist. Her face was free of cosmetics and unframed as her hair hung in a ponytail down her back. She wore a shapeless black sweater, baggy, paint-streaked jeans and no shoes. To his annoyance, she continued to attract him.

She turned her head and, by accident or design, the sunlight fell over her profile. In that instant, she was breathtaking. Kirby sighed as she studied her own face. "A veritable angel."

"Apparently her father knew better."

She laughed, low and rich. His calm, dry voice pleased her enormously. "He did at that, but not everyone sees it." She was glad he had, simply because she appreciated a sharp eye and a clever mind. "Have you had breakfast?"

He relaxed. She'd turned again so that the light no longer illuminated her face. She was just an attractive, friendly woman. "No, I've been busy being awed."

"Oh, well, one should never be awed on an empty stomach. It's murder on the digestion." After pressing a button, she linked her arm through his and led him to the table. "After we've eaten, I'll take you through the house."

"I'd like that." Adam took the seat opposite her. She wore no fragrance this morning but soap—clean and sexless. It aroused nonetheless.

A woman clumped into the room. She had a long bony face, small mud-brown eyes and an unfortunate nose. Her graying hair was scraped back and bundled at the nape of her neck. The deep furrows in her brow indicated her pessimistic nature. Glancing over, Kirby smiled.

"Good morning, Tulip. You'll have to send a tray up to Papa, he won't budge out of the tower." She drew a linen napkin from its ring. "Just toast and coffee for me, and don't lecture. I'm not getting any taller."

After a grumbling disapproval, Tulip turned to Adam. His order of bacon and eggs received the same grumble before she clumped back out again.

"Tulip?" Adam cocked a brow as he turned to Kirby.

"Fits beautifully, doesn't it?" Lips sober, eyes amused, she propped her elbows on the table and dropped her face in her hands. "She's really a marvel as far as organizing. We've had a running battle over food for fifteen years. Tulip insists that if I eat, I'll grow. After I hit twenty, I figured I'd proved her wrong. I wonder why adults insist on making such absurd statements to children."

The robust young maid who'd served dinner the night before brought in coffee. She showered sunbeam smiles over Adam.

"Thank you, Polly." Kirby's voice was gentle, but Adam caught the warning glance and the maid's quick blush.

"Yes, ma'am." Without a backward glance, Polly scurried from the room. Kirby poured the coffee herself.

"Our Polly is very sweet," she began. "But she has a habit of becoming, ah, a bit too matey with two-thirds of the male population." Setting down the silver coffee urn, Kirby smiled across the table. "If you've a taste for slap and tickle, Polly's your girl. Otherwise, I wouldn't encourage her. I've even had to warn her off Papa."

The picture of the lusty young Polly with the Puck-like Fairchild zipped into Adam's mind. It lingered there a moment with perfect clarity until he roared with laughter.

Well, well, well, Kirby mused, watching him. A man who could laugh like that had tremendous potential. She wondered what other surprises he had tucked away. Hopefully she'd discover quite a few during his stay.

Picking up the cream pitcher, he added a stream to his coffee. "You have my word, I'll resist temptation."

"She's built stupendously," Kirby observed as she sipped her coffee black.

"Really?" It was the first time she'd seen his grin— quick, crooked and wicked. "I hadn't noticed."

Kirby studied him while the grin did odd things to her nervous system. Surprise again, she told herself, then reached for her coffee. "I've misjudged you, Adam," she murmured. "A definite miscalculation. You're not precisely what you seem."

He thought of the small transmitter locked in his dignified briefcase. "Is anyone?"

"Yes." She gave him a long and completely guileless look. "Yes, some people are precisely what they seem, for better or worse."

"You?" He asked because he suddenly wanted to know badly who and what she was. Not for McIntyre, not for the job, but for himself.

She was silent a moment as a quick, ironic smile moved over her face. He guessed, correctly, that she was laughing at herself. "What I seem to be today is what I am—today." With one of her lightning changes, she threw off the mood. "Here's breakfast."

They talked a little as they ate, inconsequential things, polite things that two relative strangers speak about over a meal. They'd both been raised to handle such situations—small talk, intelligent give-and-take that skimmed over the surface and meant absolutely nothing.

But Kirby found herself aware of him, more aware than she should have been. More aware than she wanted to be.

Just what kind of man was he, she wondered as he sprinkled salt on his eggs. She'd already concluded he wasn't nearly as conventional as he appeared to be— or perhaps as he thought himself to be. There was an adventurer in there, she was certain. Her only annoyance stemmed from the fact that it had taken her so long to see it.

She remembered the strength and turbulence of the kiss they'd shared. He'd be a demanding lover. And a fascinating one. Which meant she'd have to be a great deal more careful. She no longer believed he'd be easily managed. Something in his eyes…

Quickly she backed off from that line of thought. The point was, she had to manage him. Finishing off her coffee, she sent up a quick prayer that her father had the Van Gogh well concealed.

"The tour begins from bottom to top," she said brightly. Rising, she held out her hand. "The dungeons are marvelously morbid and damp, but I think we'll postpone that in respect of your cashmere sweater."

"Dungeons?" He accepted her offered arm and walked from the room with her.

"We don't use them now, I'm afraid, but if the vibrations are right, you can still hear a few moans and rattles." She said it so casually, he nearly believed her. That, he realized, was one of her biggest talents. Making the ridiculous sound plausible. "Lord Wickerton, the original owner, was quite dastardly."

"You approve?"

"Approve?" She weighed this as they walked. "Perhaps not, but it's easy to be intrigued by things that happened nearly a hundred years ago. Evil can become romantic after a certain period of time, don't you think?"

"I've never looked at it quite that way."

"That's because you have a very firm grip on what's right and what's wrong."

He stopped and, because their arms were linked, Kirby stopped beside him. He looked down at her with an intensity that put her on guard. "And you?"

She opened her mouth, then closed it again before she could say something foolish. "Let's just say I'm flexible. You'll enjoy this room," she said, pushing open a door. "It's rather sturdy and staid."

Taking the insult in stride, Adam walked through with her. For nearly an hour they wandered from room to room. It occurred to him that he'd underestimated the sheer size of the place. Halls snaked and angled, rooms popped up where they were least expected, some tiny, some enormous. Unless he got very, very lucky, Adam concluded, the job would take him a great deal of time.

Pushing open two heavy, carved doors, Kirby led him into the library. It had two levels and was the size of an average two-bedroom apartment. Faded Persian rugs were scattered over the floor. The far wall was glassed in the small diamond panes that graced most of the windows in the house. The rest of the walls were lined floor to ceiling with books. A glance showed Chaucer standing beside D. H. Lawrence. Stephen King leaned against Milton. There wasn't even the pretense of organization, but there was the rich smell of leather, dust and lemon oil.

The books dominated the room and left no space for paintings. But there was sculpture.

Adam crossed the room and lifted a figure of a stallion carved in walnut. Freedom, grace, movement, seemed to vibrate in his hands. He could almost hear the steady heartbeat against his palm.

There was a bronze bust of Fairchild on a high, round stand. The artist had captured the puckishness, the energy, but more, she'd captured a gentleness and generosity Adam had yet to see.

In silence, he wandered the room, examining each piece as Kirby looked on. He made her nervous, and she struggled against it. Nerves were something she felt rarely, and never acknowledged. Her work had been looked at before, she reminded herself. What else did an artist want but recognition? She linked her fingers and remained silent. His opinion hardly mattered, she told herself, then moistened her lips.

He picked up a piece of marble shaped into a roaring mass of flames. Though the marble was white, the fire was real. Like every other piece he'd examined, the mass of marble flames was physical. Kirby had inherited her father's gift for creating life.

For a moment, Adam forgot all the reasons he was

there and thought only of the woman and the artist. "Where did you study?"

The flip remark she'd been prepared to make vanished from her mind the moment he turned and looked at her with those calm brown eyes. "école des Beaux-Arts formally. But Papa taught me always."

He turned the marble in his hands. Even a pedestrian imagination would've felt the heat. Adam could all but smell it. "How long have you been sculpting?"

"Seriously? About four years."

"Why the hell have you only had one exhibition? Why are you burying it here?"

Anger. She lifted her brow at it. She'd wondered just what sort of a temper he'd have, but she hadn't expected to see it break through over her work. "I'm having another in the spring," she said evenly. "Charles Larson's handling it." Abruptly uncomfortable, she shrugged. "Actually, I was pressured into having the other. I wasn't ready."

"That's ridiculous." He held up the marble as if she hadn't seen it before. "Absolutely ridiculous."

Why should it make her feel vulnerable to have her work in the palm of his hand? Turning away, Kirby ran a finger down her father's bronze nose. "I wasn't ready," she repeated, not sure why, when she never explained herself to anyone, she was explaining such things to him. "I had to be sure, you see. There are those who say—who'll always say—that I rode on Papa's coattails. That's to be expected." She blew out a breath, but her hand remained on the bust of her father. "I had to know differently. *I* had to know."

He hadn't expected sensitivity, sweetness, vulnerability. Not from her. But he'd seen it in her work, and he'd heard it in her voice. It moved him, every bit as much as her passion had. "Now you do."

She turned again, and her chin tilted. "Now I do." With an odd smile, she crossed over and took the marble from him. "I've never told anyone that before—not even Papa." When she looked up, her eyes were quiet, soft and curious. "I wonder why it should be you."

He touched her hair, something he'd wanted to do since he'd seen the morning sun slant on it. "I wonder why I'm glad it was."

She took a step back. There was no ignoring a longing so quick and so strong. There was no forgetting caution. "Well, we'll have to think about it, I suppose. This concludes the first part of our tour." She set the marble down and smiled easily. "All comments and questions are welcome."

He'd dipped below the surface, Adam realized, and she didn't care for it. That he understood. "Your home's...overwhelming," he decided, and made her smile broaden into a grin. "I'm disappointed there isn't a moat and dragon."

"Just try leaving your vegetables on your plate and you'll see what a dragon Tulip can be. As to the moat..." She started to shrug an apology, then remembered. "Toadstools, how could I have forgotten?"

Without waiting for an answer, she grabbed his hand and dashed back to the parlor. "No moat," she told him as she went directly to the fireplace. "But there are secret passageways."

"I should've known."

"It's been quite a while since I—" She broke off and

began to mutter to herself as she pushed and tugged at the carved oak mantel. "I swear it's one of the flowers along here—there's a button, but you have to catch it just right." With an annoyed gesture, she flicked the ponytail back over her shoulder. Adam watched her long, elegant fingers push and prod. He saw that her nails were short, rounded and unpainted. A schoolgirl's nails, or a nun's. Yet the impression of sexual vitality remained. "I know it's here, but I can't quite... *Et voilà*." Pleased with herself, Kirby stepped back as a section of paneling slid creakily aside. "Needs some oil," she decided.

"Impressive," Adam murmured, already wondering if he'd gotten lucky. "Does it lead to the dungeons?"

"It spreads out all over the house in a maze of twists and turns." Moving to the entrance with him, she peered into the dark. "There's an entrance in nearly every room. A button on the other side opens or closes the panel. The passages are horribly dark and moldy." With a shudder, she stepped back. "Perhaps that's why I forgot about them." Suddenly cold, she rubbed her hands together. "I used to haunt them as a child, drove the servants mad."

"I can imagine." But he saw the quick dread in her eyes as she looked back into the dark.

"I paid for it, I suppose. One day my flashlight went out on me and I couldn't find my way out. There're spiders down there as big as schnauzers." She laughed, but took another step back. "I don't know how long I was in there, but when Papa found me I was hysterical. Needless to say, I found other ways to terrorize the staff."

"It still frightens you."

She glanced up, prepared to brush it off. For the second time the quiet look in his eyes had her telling the simple truth. "Yes. Yes, apparently it does. Well, now that I've confessed my neurosis, let's move on."

The panel closed, grumbling in protest as she pushed the control. Adam felt rather than heard her sigh of relief. When he took her hand, he found it cold. He wanted to warm it, and her. Instead he concentrated on just what the passages could mean to him. With them he'd have access to every room without the risk of running into one of the staff or one of the Fairchilds. When an opportunity was tossed in your lap, you took it for what it was worth. He'd begin tonight.

"A delivery for you, Miss Fairchild."

Both Kirby and Adam paused on the bottom landing of the stairs. Kirby eyed the long white box the butler held in his hands. "Not again, Cards."

"It would appear so, miss."

"Galoshes." Kirby sniffed, scratched a point just under her jaw and studied the box. "I'll just have to be more firm."

"Just as you say, miss."

"Cards..." She smiled at him, and though his face remained inscrutable, Adam would have sworn he came to attention. "I know it's rude, but give them to Polly. I can't bear to look at another red rose."

"As you wish, miss. And the card?"

"Details," she muttered, then sighed. "Leave it on my desk, I'll deal with it. Sorry, Adam." Turning, she started up the stairs again. "I've been bombarded with roses for the last three weeks. I've refused to become Jared's mistress, but he's persistent." More exasperated than annoyed, she shook her head as they rounded the first curve. "I suppose I'll have to threaten to tell his wife."

"Might work," Adam murmured.

"I ask you, shouldn't a man know better by the time he hits sixty?" Rolling her eyes, she bounced up the next three steps. "I can't imagine what he's thinking of."

She smelled of soap and was shapeless in the sweater and jeans. Moving behind her to the second story, Adam could imagine very well.

The second floor was lined with bedrooms. Each was unique, each furnished in a different style. The more Adam saw of the house, the more he was charmed. And the more he realized how complicated his task was going to be.

"The last room, my boudoir." She gave him the slow, lazy smile that made his palms itchy. "I'll promise not to compromise you as long as you're aware my promises aren't known for being kept." With a light laugh, she pushed open the door and stepped inside. "Fish fins."

"I beg your pardon?"

"Whatever for?" Ignoring him, Kirby marched into the room. "Do you see that?" she demanded. In a gesture remarkably like her father's, she pointed at the bed. A scruffy dog lay like a lump in the center of a wedding ring quilt. Frowning, Adam walked a little closer.

"What is it?"

"A dog, of course."

He looked at the gray ball of hair, which seemed to have no front or back. "It's possible."

A stubby tail began to thump on the quilt.

"This is no laughing matter, Montique. I take the heat, you know."

Adam watched the bundle shift until he could make out a head. The eyes were still hidden behind the mop of fur, but there was a little black nose and a lolling tongue. "Somehow I'd've pictured you with a brace of Afghan hounds."

"What? Oh." Giving the mop on the bed a quick pat, she turned back to Adam. "Montique doesn't belong to me, he belongs to Isabelle." She sent the dog an annoyed glance. "She's going to be very put out."

Adam frowned at the unfamiliar name. Had McIntyre missed someone? "Is she one of the staff?"

"Good grief, no." Kirby let out a peal of laughter that had Montique squirming in delight. "Isabelle serves no one. She's… Well, here she is now. There'll be the devil to pay," she added under her breath.

Shifting his head, Adam looked toward the doorway. He started to tell Kirby there was no one there when a movement caught his eye. He looked down on a large buff-colored Siamese. Her eyes were angled, icily blue and, though he hadn't considered such things before, regally annoyed. The cat crossed the threshold, sat and stared up at Kirby.

"Don't look at me like that," Kirby tossed out. "I had nothing to do with it. If he wanders in here, it has nothing to do with me." Isabelle flicked her tail and made a low, dangerous sound in her throat. "I won't tolerate your threats, and I will not keep my door locked." Kirby folded her arms and tapped a foot on the Aubusson carpet. "I refuse to change a habit of a lifetime for your convenience. You'll just have to keep a closer eye on him."

As he watched silently, Adam was certain he saw genuine temper in Kirby's eyes—the kind of temper one person aims toward another person. Gently he placed a hand on her arm and waited for her to look at him. "Kirby, you're arguing with a cat."

"Adam." Just as gently, she patted his hand. "Don't worry. I can handle it." With a lift of her brow, she turned back to Isabelle. "Take him, then, and put him on a leash if you don't want him wandering. And the next time, I'd appreciate it if you'd knock before you come into my room."

With a flick of her tail, Isabelle moved to the bed and stared up at Montique. He thumped his tail, tongue lolling, before he leaped clumsily to the floor. With a kind of jiggling trot, he followed the gliding cat from the room.

"He went with her," Adam murmured.

"Of course he did," Kirby retorted. "She has a beastly temper."

Refusing to be taken for a fool, Adam gave Kirby a long, uncompromising look. "Are you trying to tell me that the dog belongs to that cat?"

"Do you have a cigarette?" she countered. "I rarely smoke, but Isabelle affects me that way." She noted that his eyes never lost their cool, mildly annoyed expression as he took one out and lit it for her. Kirby had to swallow a chuckle. Adam was, she decided, remarkable. She drew on the cigarette and blew out the smoke without inhaling. "Isabelle maintains that Montique followed her home. I think she kidnapped him. It would be just like her."

Games, he thought again. Two could play. "And to whom does Isabelle belong?"

"Belong?" Kirby's eyes widened. "Isabelle belongs to no one but herself. Who'd want to lay claim to such a wicked creature?"

And he could play as well as anyone. Taking the cigarette from her, Adam drew in smoke. "If you dislike her, why don't you just get rid of her?"

She nipped the cigarette from his fingers again. "I can hardly do that as long as she pays the rent, can I? There, that's enough," she decided after another drag. "I'm quite calm again." She handed him back the cigarette before she walked to the door. "I'll take you up to Papa's studio. We'll just skip over the third floor, everything's draped with dustcovers."

Adam opened his mouth, then decided that some things were best left alone. Dismissing odd cats and ugly dogs, he followed Kirby back into the hall again. The stairs continued up in a lazy arch to the third floor, then veered sharply and became straight and narrow. Kirby stopped at the transition point and gestured down the hall.

"The floor plan is the same as the second floor. There's a set of stairs at the opposite side that lead to my studio. The rest of these rooms are rarely used." She gave him the slow smile as she linked hands. "Of course, the entire floor's haunted."

"Of course." He found it only natural. Without a word, he followed her to the tower.

Chapter 3

Normalcy. Tubes of paint were scattered everywhere, brushes stood in jars. The scent of oil and turpentine hung in the air. This Adam understood—the debris and the sensuality of art.

The room was rounded with arching windows and a lofty ceiling. The floor might have been beautiful at one time, but now the wood was dull and splattered and smeared with paints and stains. Canvases were in the corners, against the walls, stacked on the floor.

Kirby gave the room a swift, thorough study. When she saw all was as it should be, the tension eased from her shoulders. Moving across the room, she went to her father.

He sat, motionless and unblinking, staring down at a partially formed mound of clay. Without speaking, Kirby walked around the worktable, scrutinizing the clay from all angles. Fairchild's eyes remained riveted on his work. After a few moments, Kirby straightened, rubbed her nose with the back of her hand and pursed her lips.

"Mmm."

"That's only your opinion," Fairchild snapped.

"It certainly is." For a moment, she nibbled on her thumbnail. "You're entitled to another. Adam, come have a look."

He sent her a killing glance that caused her to grin. Trapped by manners, he crossed the studio and looked down at the clay.

It was, he supposed, an adequate attempt—a partially formed hawk, talons exposed, beak just parted. The power, the life, that sung in his paints, and in his daughter's sculptures, just wasn't there. In vain, Adam searched for a way out.

"Hmm," he began, only to have Kirby pounce on the syllable.

"There, he agrees with me." Kirby patted her father's head and looked smug.

"What does he know?" Fairchild demanded. "He's a painter."

"And so, darling Papa, are you. A brilliant one."

He struggled not to be pleased and poked a finger into the clay. "Soon, you hateful brat, I'll be a brilliant sculptor, as well."

"I'll get you some Play-Doh for your birthday," she offered, then let out a shriek as Fairchild grabbed her ear and twisted. "Fiend." With a sniff, she rubbed at the lobe.

"Mind your tongue or I'll make a Van Gogh of you."

As Adam watched, the little man cackled; Kirby, however, froze—face, shoulders, hands. The fluidity he'd noticed in her even when she was still vanished. It wasn't annoyance, he thought, but…fear? Not of Fairchild. Kirby, he was certain, would never be afraid of a man, particularly her father. *For* Fairchild was more feasible, and just as baffling.

She recovered quickly enough and tilted her chin. "I'm going to show Adam my studio. He can settle in."

"Good, good." Because he recognized the edge to her voice, Fairchild patted her hand. "Damn pretty girl, isn't she, Adam?"

"Yes, she is."

As Kirby heaved a gusty sigh, Fairchild patted her hand again. The clay on his smeared onto hers. "See, my sweet, aren't you grateful for those braces now?"

"Papa." With a reluctant grin, Kirby laid her cheek against his balding head. "I never wore braces."

"Of course not. You inherited your teeth from me." He gave Adam a flashing smile and a wink. "Come back when you've got settled, Adam. I need some masculine company." He pinched Kirby's cheek lightly. "And don't think Adam's going to sniff around your ankles like Rick Potts."

"Adam's nothing like Rick," Kirby murmured as she picked up a rag and wiped the traces of clay from her hands. "Rick is sweet."

"She inherited her manners from the milkman," Fairchild observed.

She shot a look at Adam. "I'm sure Adam can be sweet, too." But there was no confidence in her voice. "Rick's forte is watercolor. He's the sort of man women want to mother. I'm afraid he stutters a bit when he gets excited."

"He's madly in love with our little Kirby." Fairchild would've cackled again, but for the look his daughter sent him.

"He just thinks he is. I don't encourage him."

"What about the clinch I happened in on in the library?" Pleased with himself, Fairchild turned back to Adam. "I ask you, when a man's glasses are steamed, isn't there a reason for it?"

"Invariably." He liked them, damn it, whether they were harmless lunatics or something more than harmless. He liked them both.

"You know very well that was totally one-sided." Barely shifting her stance, she became suddenly regal and dignified. "Rick lost control, temporarily. Like blowing a fuse, I suppose." She brushed at the sleeve of her sweater. "Now that's quite enough on the subject."

"He's coming to stay for a few days next week." Fairchild dropped the bombshell as Kirby walked to the door. To her credit, she barely broke stride. Adam wondered if he was watching a well-plotted game of chess or a wild version of Chinese checkers.

"Very well," Kirby said coolly. "I'll tell Rick that Adam and I are lovers and that Adam's viciously jealous, and keeps a stiletto in his left sock."

"Good God," Adam murmured as Kirby swept out of the door. "She'll do it, too."

"You can bank on it," Fairchild agreed, without disguising the glee in his voice. He loved confusion. A man of sixty was entitled to create as much as he possibly could.

* * *

The structure of the second tower studio was identical to the first. Only the contents differed. In addition to paints and brushes and canvases, there were knives, chisels and mallets. There were slabs of limestone and marble and lumps of wood. Adam's equipment was the only spot of order in the room. Cards had stacked his gear personally.

A long wooden table was cluttered with tools, wood shavings, rags and a crumpled ball of material that might've been a paint smock. In a corner was a high-tech stereo component system. An ancient gas heater was set into one wall with an empty easel in front of it.

As with Fairchild's tower, Adam understood this kind of chaos. The room was drenched with sun. It was quiet, spacious and instantly appealing.

"There's plenty of room," Kirby told him with a sweeping gesture. "Set up where you're comfortable. I don't imagine we'll get in each other's way," she said doubtfully, then shrugged. She had to make the best of it. Better for him to be here, in her way, than sharing her father's studio with the Van Gogh. "Are you temperamental?"

"I wouldn't say so," Adam answered absently as he began to unpack his equipment. "Others might. And you?"

"Oh, yes." Kirby plopped down behind the work-table and lifted a piece of wood. "I have tantrums and fits of melancholia. I hope it won't bother you." He turned to answer, but she was staring down at the wood in her hands, as if searching for something hidden inside. "I'm doing my emotions now. I can't be held responsible."

Curious, Adam left his unpacking to walk to the shelf behind her. On it were a dozen pieces in various stages. He chose a carved piece of fruitwood that had been polished. "Emotions," he murmured, running his fingers over the wood.

"Yes, that's—"

"*Grief,*" he supplied. He could see the anguish, feel the pain.

"Yes." She wasn't sure if it pleased her or not to have him so in tune—particularly with that one piece that had cost her so much. "I've done *Joy* and *Doubt,* as well. I thought to save *Passion* for last." She spread her hands under the wood she held and brought it to eye level. "This is to be *Anger.*" As if to annoy it, she tapped the wood with her fingers. "One of the seven deadly sins, though I've always thought it mislabeled. We need anger."

He saw the change in her eyes as she stared into the wood. Secrets, he thought. She was riddled with them. Yet as she sat, the sun pouring around her, the unformed wood held aloft in her hands, she seemed to be utterly, utterly open, completely readable, washed with emotion. Even as he began to see it, she shifted and broke the mood. Her smile when she looked up at him was teasing.

"Since I'm doing *Anger,* you'll have to tolerate a few bouts of temper."

"I'll try to be objective."

Kirby grinned, liking the gloss of politeness over the sarcasm. "I bet you have bundles of objectivity."

"No more than my share."

"You can have mine, too, if you like. It's very small."
Still moving the wood in her hands, she glanced toward his equipment. "Are you working on anything?"

"I was." He walked around to stand in front of her.
"I've something else in mind now. I want to paint you."

Her gaze shifted from the wood in her hands to his face. With some puzzlement, he saw her eyes were wary. "Why?"

He took a step closer and closed his hand over her chin. Kirby sat passively as he examined her from different angles. But she felt his fingers, each individual finger, as it lay on her skin. Soft skin, and Adam didn't bother to resist the urge to run his thumb over her cheek. The bones seemed fragile under his hands, but her eyes were steady and direct.

"Because," he said at length, "your face is fascinating. I want to paint that, the translucence, and your sexuality."

Her mouth heated under the careless brush of his fingers. Her hands tightened on the fruitwood, but her voice was even. "And if I said no?"

That was another thing that intrigued him, the trace of hauteur she used sparingly—and very successfully. She'd bring men to their knees with that look, he thought. Deliberately he leaned over and kissed her. He felt her stiffen, resist, then remain still. She was, in her own way, in her own defense, absorbing the feelings he brought to her. Her knuckles had whitened on the wood, but he didn't see. When he lifted his head, all Adam saw was the deep, pure gray of her eyes.

"I'd paint you anyway," he murmured. He left the room, giving them both time to think about it.

She did think about it. For nearly thirty minutes, Kirby sat perfectly still and let her mind work. It was a curious part of her nature that such a vibrant, restless woman could have such a capacity for stillness. When it was necessary, Kirby could do absolutely nothing while she thought through problems and looked for answers. Adam made it necessary.

He stirred something in her that she'd never felt before. Kirby believed that one of the most precious things in life was the original and the fresh. This time, however, she wondered if she should skirt around it.

She appreciated a man who took the satisfaction of his own desires for granted, just as she did. Nor was she averse to pitting herself against him. But... She couldn't quite get past the *but* in Adam's case.

It might be safer—smarter, she amended—if she concentrated on the awkwardness of Adam's presence with respect to the Van Gogh and her father's hobby. The attraction she felt was ill-timed. She touched her tongue to her top lip and thought she could taste him. Ill-timed, she thought again. And inconvenient.

Her father had better be prudent, she thought, then immediately sighed. Calling Philip Fairchild prudent was like calling Huck Finn studious. The blasted, brilliant Van Gogh was going to have to make a speedy exit. And the Titian, she remembered, gnawing on her lip. She still had to handle that.

Adam was huddled with her father, and there was nothing she could do at the moment. Just a few more days, she reminded herself. There'd be nothing more to worry about. The smile crept back to her mouth. The rest of Adam's visit might be fun. She thought of him, the serious brown eyes, the strong, sober mouth.

Dangerous fun, she conceded. But then, what was life without a bit of danger? Still smiling, she picked up her tools.

She worked in silence, in total concentration. Adam, her father, the Van Gogh were forgotten. The wood in her hand was the center of the universe. There was life there; she could feel it. It only waited for her to find the key to release it. She would find it, and the soaring satisfaction that went hand in hand with the discovery.

Painting had never given her that. She'd played at it, enjoyed it, but she'd never possessed it. She'd never been possessed by it. Art was a lover that demanded complete allegiance. Kirby understood that.

As she worked, the wood seemed to take a tentative breath. She felt suddenly, clearly, the temper she sought pushing against the confinement. Nearly—nearly free.

At the sound of her name, she jerked her head up. "Bloody murder!"

"Kirby, I'm so sorry."

"Melanie." She swallowed the abuse, barely. "I didn't hear you come up." Though she set down her tools, she continued to hold the wood. She couldn't lose it now. "Come in. I won't shout at you."

"I'm sure you should." Melanie hesitated at the doorway. "I'm disturbing you."

"Yes, you are, but I forgive you. How was New York?" Kirby gestured to a chair as she smiled at her oldest friend.

Pale blond hair was elegantly styled around a heart-shaped face. Cheekbones, more prominent than Kirby's, were tinted expertly. The Cupid's-bow mouth was carefully glossed in deep rose. Kirby decided, as she did regularly, that Melanie Burgess had the most perfect profile ever created.

"You look wonderful, Melly. Did you have fun?"

Melanie wrinkled her nose as she brushed off the seat of her chair. "Business. But my spring designs were well received."

Kirby brought up her legs and crossed them under her. "I'll never understand how you can decide in August what we should be wearing next April." She was losing the power of the wood. Telling herself it would come back, she set it on the table, within reach. "Have you done something nasty to the hemlines again?"

"You never pay any attention anyway." She gave Kirby's sweater a look of despair.

"I like to think of my wardrobe as timeless rather than trendy." She grinned, knowing which buttons to push. "This sweater's barely twelve years old."

"And looks every day of it." Knowing the game and Kirby's skill, Melanie switched tactics. "I ran into Ellen Parker at 21."

"Did you?" After lacing her hands, Kirby rested her chin on them. She never considered gossiping rude, particularly if it was interesting. "I haven't seen her for months. Is she still spouting French when she wants to be confidential?"

"You won't believe it." Melanie shuddered as she pulled a long, slender cigarette from an enameled case. "I didn't believe it myself until I saw it with my own eyes. Jerry told me. You remember Jerry Turner, don't you?"

"Designs women's underwear."

"Intimate apparel," Melanie corrected with a sigh. "Really, Kirby."

"Whatever. I appreciate nice underwear. So what did he tell you?"

Melanie pulled out a monogrammed lighter and flicked it on. She took a delicate puff. "He told me that Ellen was having an affair."

"There's news," Kirby returned dryly. With a yawn, she stretched her arms to the ceiling and relieved the stiffness in her shoulder blades. "Is this number two hundred and three, or have I missed one?"

"But, Kirby—" Melanie tapped her cigarette for emphasis as she leaned forward "—she's having this one with her son's orthodontist."

It was the sound of Kirby's laughter that caused Adam to pause on his way up the tower steps. It rang against the stone walls, rich, real and arousing. He stood as it echoed and faded. Moving quietly, he continued up.

"Kirby, really. An orthodontist." Even knowing Kirby as well as she did, Melanie was stunned by her reaction. "It's so—so middle-class."

"Oh, Melanie, you're such a wonderful snob." She smothered another chuckle as Melanie gave an indignant huff. When Kirby smiled, it was irresistible. "It's perfectly acceptable for Ellen to have any number of affairs, as long as she keeps her choice socially prominent but an orthodontist goes beyond good taste?"

"It's not acceptable, of course," Melanie muttered,

finding herself caught in the trap of Kirby's logic. "But if one is discreet, and…"

"Selective?" Kirby supplied good-naturedly. "Actually, it is rather nasty. Here's Ellen carrying on with her son's orthodontist, while poor Harold shells out a fortune for the kid's overbite. Where's the justice?"

"You say the most astonishing things."

"Orthodonture work is frightfully expensive."

With an exasperated sigh, Melanie tried another change of subject. "How's Stuart?"

Though he'd been about to enter, Adam stopped in the doorway and kept his silence. Kirby's smile had vanished. The eyes that had been alive with humor were frigid. Something hard, strong and unpleasant came into them. Seeing the change, Adam realized she'd make a formidable enemy. There was grit behind the careless wit, the raw sexuality and the eccentric-rich-girl polish. He wouldn't forget it.

"Stuart," Kirby said in a brittle voice. "I really wouldn't know."

"Oh, dear." At the arctic tone, Melanie caught her bottom lip between her teeth. "Have you two had a row?"

"A row?" The smile remained unpleasant. "One might put it that way." Something flared—the temper she'd been prodding out of the wood. With an effort, Kirby shrugged it aside. "As soon as I'd agreed to marry him, I knew I'd made a mistake. I should've dealt with it right away."

"You'd told me you were having doubts." After stubbing out her cigarette, Melanie leaned forward to take

Kirby's hands. "I thought it was nerves. You'd never let any relationship get as far as an engagement before."

"It was an error in judgment." No, she'd never let a relationship get as far as an engagement. Engagements equaled commitment. Commitments were a lock, perhaps the only lock, Kirby considered sacred. "I corrected it."

"And Stuart? I suppose he was furious."

The smile that came back to Kirby's lips held no humor. "He gave me the perfect escape hatch. You know he'd been pressuring me to set a date?"

"And I know that you'd been putting him off."

"Thank God," Kirby murmured. "In any case, I'd finally drummed up the courage to renege. I think it was the first time in my life I've felt genuine guilt." Moving her shoulders restlessly, she picked up the wood again. It helped to steady her, helped her to concentrate on temper. "I went by his place, unannounced. It was a now-or-never sort of gesture. I should've seen what was up as soon as he answered the door, but I was already into my neat little speech when I noticed a few—let's say articles of intimate apparel tossed around the room."

"Oh, Kirby."

Letting out a long breath, Kirby went on. "That part of it was my fault, I suppose. I wouldn't sleep with him. There was just no driving urge to be intimate with him. No…" She searched for a word. "Heat," she decided, for lack of anything better. "I guess that's why I knew I'd never marry him. But, I was faithful." The fury whipped through her again. "I was faithful, Melly."

"I don't know what to say." Distress vibrated in her voice. "I'm so sorry, Kirby."

Kirby shook her head at the sympathy. She never looked for it. "I wouldn't have been so angry if he hadn't stood there, telling me how much he loved me, when he had another woman keeping the sheets warm. I found it humiliating."

"You have nothing to be humiliated about," Melanie returned with some heat. "He was a fool."

"Perhaps. It would've been bad enough if we'd stuck to the point, but we got off the track of love and fidelity. Things got nasty."

Her voice trailed off. Her eyes clouded over. It was time for secrets again. "I found out quite a bit that night," she murmured. "I've never thought of myself as a fool, but it seems I'd been one."

Again, Melanie reached for her hand. "It must have been a dreadful shock to learn Stuart was unfaithful even before you were married."

"What?" Blinking, Kirby brought herself back. "Oh, that. Yes, that, too."

"Too? What else?"

"Nothing." With a shake of her head, Kirby swept it all aside. "It's all dead and buried now."

"I feel terrible. Damn it, I introduced you."

"Perhaps you should shave your head in restitution, but I'd advise you to forget it."

"Can you?"

Kirby's lips curved up, her brow lifted. "Tell me, Melly, do you still hold André Fayette against me?"

Melanie folded her hands primly. "It's been five years."

"Six, but who's counting?" Grinning, Kirby leaned forward. "Besides, who expects an oversexed French art student to have any taste?"

Melanie's pretty mouth pouted. "He was very attractive."

"But base." Kirby struggled with a new grin. "No class, Melly. You should thank me for luring him away, however unintentionally."

Deciding it was time to make his presence known, Adam stepped inside. Kirby glanced up and smiled without a trace of the ice or the fury. "Hello, Adam. Did you have a nice chat with Papa?"

"Yes."

Melanie, he decided as he glanced in her direction, was even more stunning at close quarters. Classic face, classic figure draped in a pale rose dress cut with style and simplicity. "Am I interrupting?"

"Just gossip. Melanie Burgess, Adam Haines. Adam's our guest for a few weeks."

Adam accepted the slim rose-tipped hand. It was soft and pampered, without the slight ridge of callus that Kirby's had just under the fingers. He wondered what had happened in the past twenty-four hours to make him prefer the untidy artist to the perfectly groomed woman smiling up at him. Maybe he was coming down with something.

"*The* Adam Haines?" Melanie's smile warmed. She knew of him, the irreproachable lineage and education. "Of course you are," she continued before he could comment. "This place attracts artists like a magnet. I have one of your paintings."

"Do you?" Adam lit her cigarette, then one of his own. "Which one?"

"A Study in Blue." Melanie tilted her face to smile into his eyes, a neat little feminine trick she'd learned soon after she'd learned to walk.

From across the table, Kirby studied them both. Two extraordinary faces, she decided. The tips of her fingers itched to capture Adam in bronze. A year before, she'd done Melanie in ivory—smooth, cool and perfect. With Adam, she'd strive for the undercurrents.

"I wanted the painting because it was so strong," Melanie continued. "But I nearly let it go because it made me sad. You remember, Kirby. You were there."

"Yes, I remember." When she looked up at him, her eyes were candid and amused, without the traces of flirtation that flitted in Melanie's. "I was afraid she'd break down and disgrace herself, so I threatened to buy it myself. Papa was furious that I didn't."

"Uncle Philip could practically stock the Louvre already," Melanie said with a casual shrug.

"Some people collect stamps," Kirby returned, then smiled again. "The still life in my room is Melanie's work, Adam. We studied together in France."

"No, don't ask," Melanie said quickly, holding up her hand. "I'm not an artist. I'm a designer who dabbles."

"Only because you refuse to dig your toes in."

Melanie inclined her head, but didn't agree or refute. "I must go. Tell Uncle Philip I said hello. I won't risk disturbing him, as well."

"Stay for lunch, Melly. We haven't seen you in two months."

"Another time." She rose with the grace of one who'd been taught to sit and stand and walk. Adam stood with her, catching the drift of Chanel. "I'll see you this weekend at the party." With another smile, she offered Adam her hand. "You'll come, too, won't you?"

"I'd like that."

"Wonderful." Snapping open her bag, Melanie drew out thin leather gloves. "Nine o'clock, Kirby. Don't forget. Oh!" On her way to the door, she stopped, whirling back. "Oh, God, the invitations were sent out before I... Kirby, Stuart's going to be there."

"I won't pack my derringer, Melly." She laughed, but it wasn't quite as rich or quite as free. "You look as though someone's just spilled caviar on your Saint Laurent. Don't worry about it." She paused, and the chill passed quickly in and out of her eyes. "I promise you, I won't."

"If you're sure..." Melanie frowned. It was, however, not possible to discuss such a thing in depth in front of a guest. "As long as you won't be uncomfortable."

"I won't be the one who suffers discomfort." The careless arrogance was back.

"Saturday, then." Melanie gave Adam a final smile before she slipped from the room.

"A beautiful woman," Adam commented, coming back to the table.

"Yes, exceptional." The simple agreement had no undertones of envy or spite.

"How do two women, two exceptional women, of totally different types, remain friends?"

"By not attempting to change one another." She

picked up the wood again and began to roll it around in her hands. "I overlook what I see as Melanie's faults, and she overlooks mine." She saw the pad and pencil in his hand and lifted a brow. "What're you doing?"

"Some preliminary sketches. What are your faults?"

"Too numerous to mention." Setting the wood down again, she leaned back.

"Any good points?"

"Dozens." Perhaps it was time to test him a bit, to see what button worked what switch. "Loyalty," she began breezily. "Sporadic patience and honesty."

"Sporadic?"

"I'd hate to be perfect." She ran her tongue over her teeth. "And I'm terrific in bed."

His gaze shifted to her bland smile. Just what game was Kirby Fairchild playing? His lips curved as easily as hers. "I bet you are."

Laughing, she leaned forward again, chin cupped in her hands. "You don't rattle easily, Adam. It makes me all the more determined to keep trying."

"Telling me something I'd already concluded isn't likely to rattle me. Who's Stuart?"

The question had her stiffening. She'd challenged him, Kirby conceded, now she had to meet one of his. "A former fiancé," she said evenly. "Stuart Hiller."

The name clicked, but Adam continued to sketch. "The same Hiller who runs the Merrick Gallery?"

"The same." He heard the tightening in her voice. For a moment he wanted to drop it, to leave her to her privacy and her anger. The job came first.

"I know him by reputation," Adam continued. "I'd

planned to see the gallery. It's about twenty miles from here, isn't it?"

She paled a bit, which confused him, but when she spoke her voice was steady. "Yes, it's not far. Under the circumstances, I'm afraid I can't take you."

"You may mend your differences over the weekend." Prying wasn't his style. He had a distaste for it, particularly when it involved someone he was beginning to care about. When he lifted his gaze, however, he didn't see discomfort. She was livid.

"I think not." She made a conscious effort to relax her hands. Noting the gesture, Adam wondered how much it cost her. "It occurred to me that my name would be Fairchild-Hiller." She gave a slow, rolling shrug. "That would never do."

"The Merrick Gallery has quite a reputation."

"Yes. As a matter of fact, Melanie's mother owns it, and managed it until a couple of years ago."

"Melanie? Didn't you say her name was Burgess?"

"She was married to Carlyse Burgess—Burgess Enterprises. They're divorced."

"So, she's Harriet Merrick's daughter." The cast of players was increasing. "Mrs. Merrick's given the running of the gallery over to Hiller?"

"For the most part. She dips her hand in now and then."

Adam saw that she'd relaxed again, and concentrated on the shape of her eyes. Round? Not quite, he decided. They were nearly almond shaped, but again, not quite. Like Kirby, they were simply unique.

"Whatever my personal feelings, Stuart's a knowledgeable dealer." She gave a quick, short laugh. "Since she hired him, she's had time to travel. Harriet's just back from an African safari. When I phoned her the other day, she told me she'd brought back a necklace of crocodile teeth."

To his credit, Adam closed his eyes only briefly. "Your families are close, then. I imagine your father's done a lot of dealing through the Merrick Gallery."

"Over the years. Papa had his first exhibition there, more than thirty years ago. It sort of lifted his and Harriet's careers off at the same time." Straightening in her chair, Kirby frowned across the table. "Let me see what you've done."

"In a minute," he muttered, ignoring her outstretched hand.

"Your manners sink to my level when it's convenient, I see." Kirby plopped back in her chair. When he didn't comment, she screwed her face into unnatural lines.

"I wouldn't do that for long," Adam advised. "You'll hurt yourself. When I start in oil, you'll have to behave or I'll beat you."

Kirby relaxed her face because her jaw was stiffening. "Corkscrews, you wouldn't beat me. You have the disadvantage of being a gentleman, inside and out."

Lifting his head, he pinned her with a look. "Don't bank on it."

The look alone stopped whatever sassy rejoinder she might have made. It wasn't the look of a gentleman, but of a man who made his own way however he chose. Before she could think of a proper response, the sound of shouting and wailing drifted up the tower steps and through the open door. Kirby made no move to spring up and investigate. She merely smiled.

"I'm going to ask two questions," Adam decided. "First, what the hell is that?"

"Which that is that, Adam?" Her eyes were dove gray and guileless.

"The sound of mourning."

"Oh, that." Grinning, she reached over and snatched his sketch pad. "That's Papa's latest tantrum because his sculpture's not going well—which of course it never will. Does my nose really tilt that way?" Experimentally she ran her finger down it. "Yes, I guess it does. What was your other question?"

"Why do you say 'corkscrews' or something equally ridiculous when a simple 'hell' or 'damn' would do?"

"It has to do with cigars. You really must show these sketches to Papa. He'll want to see them."

"Cigars." Determined to have her full attention, Adam grabbed the pad away from her.

"Those big, nasty, fat ones. Papa used to smoke them by the carload. You needed a gas mask just to come in the door. I begged, threatened, even tried smoking them myself." She swallowed on that unfortunate memory. "Then I came up with the solution. Papa is a sucker."

"Is that so?"

"That is, he just can't resist a bet, no matter what the odds." She touched the wood again, knowing she'd have to come back to it later. "My language was, let's say, colorful. I can swear eloquently in seven languages."

"Quite an accomplishment."

"It has its uses, believe me. I bet Papa ten thousand

dollars that I could go longer without swearing than he could without smoking. Both my language and the ozone layer have been clean for three months." Rising, Kirby circled the table. "I have the gratitude of the entire staff." Abruptly she dropped in his lap. Letting her head fall back, she wound her arms around his neck. "Kiss me again, will you? I can't resist."

There can't be another like her, Adam thought as he closed his mouth over hers. With a low sound of pleasure, Kirby melted against him, all soft demand.

Then neither of them thought, but felt only.

Desire was swift and sharp. It built and expanded so that they could wallow in it. She allowed herself the luxury, for such things were too often brief, too often hollow. She wanted the speed, the heat, the current. A risk, but life was nothing without them. A challenge, but each day brought its own. He made her feel soft, giddy, senseless. No one else had. If she could be swept away, why shouldn't she be? It had never happened before.

She needed what she'd never realized she needed from a man before: strength, solidity.

Adam felt the initial stir turn to an ache—something deep and dull and constant. It wasn't something he could resist, but something he found he needed. Desire had always been basic and simple and painless. Hadn't he known she was a woman who would make a man suffer? Knowing it, shouldn't he have been able to avoid it? But he hurt. Holding her soft and pliant in his arms, he hurt. From wanting more.

"Can't you two wait until after lunch?" Fairchild demanded from the doorway.

With a quiet sigh, Kirby drew her lips from Adam's. The taste lingered as she knew now it would. Like the wood behind her, it would be something that pulled her back again and again.

"We're coming," she murmured, then brushed Adam's mouth again, as if in promise. She turned and rested her cheek against his in a gesture he found impossibly sweet. "Adam's been sketching me," she told her father.

"Yes, I can see that." Fairchild gave a quick snort. "He can sketch you all he chooses after lunch. I'm hungry."

Chapter 4

Food seemed to soothe Fairchild's temperament. As he plowed his way through poached salmon, he went off on a long, technical diatribe on surrealism. It appeared breaking conventional thought to release the imagination had appealed to him to the extent that he'd given nearly a year of his time in study and application. With a good-humored shrug, he confessed that his attempts at surrealistic painting had been poor, and his plunge into abstraction little better.

"He's banished those canvases to the attic," Kirby told Adam as she poked at her salad. "There's one in shades of blue and yellow, with clocks of all sizes and shapes sort of melting and drooping everywhere and two left shoes tucked in a corner. He called it *Absence of Time.*"

"Experimental," Fairchild grumbled, eyeing Kirby's uneaten portion of fish.

"He refused an obscene amount of money for it and locked it, like a mad relation, in the attic." Smoothly she transferred her fish to her father's plate. "He'll be sending his sculpture to join it before long."

Fairchild swallowed a bite of fish, then ground his teeth. "Heartless brat." In the blink of an eye he changed from amiable cherub to gnome. "By this time next year, Philip Fairchild's name will be synonymous with sculpture."

"Horse dust," Kirby concluded, and speared a cucumber. "That shade of pink becomes you, Papa." Leaning over, she placed a loud kiss on his cheek. "It's very close to fuchsia."

"You're not too old to forget my ability to bring out the same tone on your bottom."

"Child abuser." As Adam watched, she stood and wrapped her arms around Fairchild's neck. In the matter of love for her father, the enigma of Kirby Fairchild was easily solvable. "I'm going out for a walk before I turn yellow and dry up. Will you come?"

"No, no, I've a little project to finish." He patted her hand as she tensed. Adam saw something pass between them before Fairchild turned to him. "Take her for a walk and get on with your…sketching," he said with a cackle. "Have you asked Kirby if you can paint her yet? They all do." He stabbed at the salmon again. "She never lets them."

Adam lifted his wine. "I told Kirby I was going to paint her."

The new cackle was full of delight. Pale blue eyes lit with the pleasure of trouble brewing. "A firm hand, eh? She's always needed one. Don't know where she got such a miserable temper." He smiled artlessly. "Must've come from her mother's side."

Adam glanced up at the serene, mild-eyed woman in the portrait. "Undoubtedly."

"See that painting there?" Fairchild pointed to the portrait of Kirby as a girl. "That's the one and only time she modeled for me. I had to pay the brat scale." He gave a huff and a puff before he attacked the fish again. "Twelve years old and already mercenary."

"If you're going to discuss me as if I weren't here, I'll go fetch my shoes." Without a backward glance, Kirby glided from the room.

"Hasn't changed much, has she?" Adam commented as he drained his wine.

"Not a damn bit," Fairchild agreed proudly. "She'll lead you a merry chase, Adam, my boy. I hope you're in condition."

"I ran track in college."

Fairchild's laugh was infectious. Damn it, Adam thought again, I like him. It complicated things. From the other room he heard Kirby in a heated discussion with Isabelle. He was beginning to realize complication was the lady's middle name. What should've been a very simple job was developing layers he didn't care for.

"Come on, Adam." Kirby poked her head around the doorway. "I've told Isabelle she can come, but she and Montique have to keep a distance of five yards at all times. Papa—" she tossed her ponytail back "—I really think we ought to try raising the rent. She might look for an apartment in town."

"We should never have agreed to a long-term lease,"

Fairchild grumbled, then gave his full attention to Kirby's salmon.

Deciding not to comment, Adam rose and went outside.

It was warm for September, and breezy. The grounds around the house were alive with fall. Beds of zinnias and mums spread out helter-skelter, flowing over their borders and adding a tang to the air. Near a flaming maple, Adam saw an old man in patched overalls. With a whimsical lack of dedication, he raked at the scattered leaves. As they neared him, he grinned toothlessly.

"You'll never get them all, Jamie."

He made a faint wheezing sound that must've been a laugh. "Sooner or later, missy. There be plenty of time."

"I'll help you tomorrow."

"Ayah, and you'll be piling them up and jumping in 'em like always." He wheezed again and rubbed a frail hand over his chin. "Stick to your whittling and could be I'll leave a pile for you."

With her hands hooked in her back pockets, she scuffed at a leaf. "A nice big one?"

"Could be. If you're a good girl."

"There's always a catch." Grabbing Adam's hand, she pulled him away.

"Is that little old man responsible for the grounds?" Three acres, he calculated. Three acres if it was a foot.

"Since he retired."

"Retired?"

"Jamie retired when he was sixty-five. That was before I was born." The breeze blew strands of hair into her face and she pushed at them. "He claims to be ninety-two, but of course he's ninety-five and won't admit it." She shook her head. "Vanity."

Kirby pulled him along until they stood at a dizzying height above the river. Far below, the ribbon of water seemed still. Small dots of houses were scattered along the view. There was a splash of hues rather than distinct tones, a melding of textures.

On the ridge where they stood there was only wind, river and sky. Kirby threw her head back. She looked primitive, wild, invincible. Turning, he looked at the house. It looked the same.

"Why do you stay here?" Blunt questions weren't typical of him. Kirby had already changed that.

"I have my family, my home, my work."

"And isolation."

Her shoulders moved. Though her lashes were lowered, her eyes weren't closed. "People come here. That's not isolation."

"Don't you want to travel? To see Florence, Rome, Venice?"

From her stance on a rock, she was nearly eye level with him. When she turned to him, it was without her usual arrogance. "I'd been to Europe five times before I was twelve. I spent four years in Paris on my own when I was studying."

She looked over his shoulder a moment, at nothing or at everything, he couldn't be sure. "I slept with a Breton count in a chateau, skied in the Swiss Alps and hiked the moors in Cornwall. I've traveled, and I'll travel again. But…" He knew she looked at the house now, because her lips curved. "I always come home."

"What brings you back?"

"Papa." She stopped and smiled fully. "Memories, familiarity. Insanity."

"You love him very much." She could make things impossibly complicated or perfectly simple. The job he'd come to do was becoming more and more of a burden.

"More than anything or anyone." She spoke quietly, so that her voice seemed a part of the breeze. "He's given me everything of importance: security, independence, loyalty, friendship, love—and the capability to give them back. I'd like to think someday I'll find someone who wants that from me. My home would be with him then."

How could he resist the sweetness, the simplicity, she could show so unexpectedly? It wasn't in the script, he reminded himself, but reached a hand to her face, just to touch. When she brought her hand to his, something stirred in him that wasn't desire, but was just as potent.

She felt the strength in him, and sensed a confusion that might have been equal to her own. Another time, she thought. Another time, it might have worked. But now, just now, there were too many other things. Deliberately she dropped her hand and turned back to the river. "I don't know why I tell you these things," she murmured. "It's not in character. Do people usually let you in on their personal thoughts?"

"No. Or maybe I haven't been listening."

She smiled and, in one of her lightning changes of mood, leaped from the rock. "You're not the type people would confide in." Casually she linked her arm through his. "Though you seem to have strong, sturdy shoulders. You're a little aloof," she decided. "And just a tad pompous."

"Pompous?" How could she allure him one instant and infuriate him the next? "What do you mean, pompous?"

Because he sounded dangerously like her father, she swallowed. "Just a tad," she reminded him, nearly choking on a laugh. "Don't be offended, Adam. Pomposity certainly has its place in the world." When he continued to scowl down at her, she cleared her throat of another laugh. "I like the way your left brow lifts when you're annoyed."

"I'm not pompous." He spoke very precisely and watched her lips tremble with fresh amusement.

"Perhaps that was a bad choice of words."

"It was a completely incorrect choice." Just barely, he caught himself before his brow lifted. Damn the woman, he thought, and swore he wouldn't smile.

"Conventional." Kirby patted his cheek. "I'm sure that's what I meant."

"I'm sure those two words mean the same thing to you. I won't be categorized by either."

Tilting her head, she studied him. "Maybe I'm wrong," she said, to herself as much as him. "I've been wrong before. Give me a piggyback ride."

"What?"

"A piggyback ride," Kirby repeated.

"You're crazy." She might be sharp, she might be talented, he'd already conceded that, but part of her brain was permanently on holiday.

With a shrug, she started back toward the house. "I

knew you wouldn't. Pompous people never give or receive piggyback rides. It's the law."

"Damn." She was doing it to him, and he was letting her. For a moment, he stuck his hands in his pockets and stood firm. Let her play her games with her father, Adam told himself. He wasn't biting. With another oath, he caught up to her. "You're an exasperating woman."

"Why, thank you."

They stared at each other, him in frustration, her in amusement, until he turned his back. "Get on."

"If you insist." Nimbly she jumped on his back, blew the hair out of her eyes and looked down. "Wombats, you're tall."

"You're short," he corrected, and hitched her to a more comfortable position.

"I'm going to be five-seven in my next life."

"You'd better add pounds as well as inches to your fantasy." Her hands were light on his shoulders, her thighs firm around his waist. Ridiculous, he thought. Ridiculous to want her now, when she's making a fool of both of you. "What do you weigh?"

"An even hundred." She sent a careless wave to Jamie.

"And when you take the ball bearings out of your pocket?"

"Ninety-six, if you want to be technical." With a laugh, she gave him a quick hug. Her laughter was warm and distracting at his ear. "You might do something daring, like not wearing socks."

"The next spontaneous act might be dropping you on your very attractive bottom."

"Is it attractive?" Idly she swung her feet back and

forth. "I see so little of it myself." She held him for a moment longer because it felt so right, so good. Keep it light, she reminded herself. And watch your step. As long as she could keep him off balance, things would run smoothly. Leaning forward, she caught the lobe of his ear between her teeth. "Thanks for the lift, sailor."

Before he could respond, she'd jumped down and dashed into the house.

It was night, late, dark and quiet, when Adam sat alone in his room. He held the transmitter in his hand and found he wanted to smash it into little pieces and forget it had ever existed. No personal involvements. That was rule number one, and he'd always followed it. He'd never been tempted not to.

He'd wanted to follow it this time, he reminded himself. It just wasn't working that way. Involvement, emotion, conscience; he couldn't let any of it interfere. Staring at Kirby's painting of the Hudson, he flicked the switch.

"McIntyre?"

"Password."

"Damn it, this isn't a chapter of Ian Fleming."

"Procedure," McIntyre reminded him briskly. After twenty seconds of dead air, he relented. "Okay, okay, what've you found out?"

I've found out I'm becoming dangerously close to being crazy about a woman who makes absolutely no sense to me, he thought. "I've found out that the next time you have a brainstorm, you can go to hell with it."

"Trouble?" McIntyre's voice snapped into the receiver. "You were supposed to call in if there was trouble."

"The trouble is I like the old man and the daughter's...unsettling." An apt word, Adam mused. His system hadn't settled since he'd set eyes on her.

"It's too late for that now. We're committed."

"Yeah." He let out a breath between his teeth and blocked Kirby from his mind. "Melanie Merrick Burgess is a close family friend and Harriet Merrick's daughter. She's a very elegant designer who doesn't seem to have any deep interest in painting. At a guess I'd say she'd be very supportive of the Fairchilds. Kirby recently broke off her engagement to Stuart Hiller."

"Interesting. When?"

"I don't have a date," Adam retorted. "And I didn't like pumping her about something that sensitive." He struggled with himself as McIntyre remained silent. "Sometime during the last couple months, I'd say, no longer. She's still smoldering." And hurting, he said to himself. He hadn't forgotten the look in her eyes. "I've been invited to a party this weekend. I should meet both Harriet Merrick and Hiller. In the meantime, I've had a break here. The place is riddled with secret passages."

"With what?"

"You heard me. With some luck, I'll have easy access throughout the house."

McIntyre grunted in approval. "You won't have any trouble recognizing it?"

"If he's got it, and if it's in the house, *and* if by some miracle I can find it in this anachronism, I'll recognize it." He switched off and, resisting the urge to throw the transmitter against the wall, dropped it back in the briefcase.

Clearing his mind, Adam rose and began to search the fireplace for the mechanism.

It took him nearly ten minutes, but he was rewarded with a groaning as a panel slid halfway open. He squeezed inside with a flashlight. It was both dank and musty, but he played the light against the wall until he found the inside switch. The panel squeaked closed and left him in the dark.

His footsteps echoed and he heard the scuttering sound of rodents. He ignored both. For a moment he stopped at the wall of Kirby's room. Telling himself he was only doing his job, he took the time to find the switch. But he wondered if she was already sleeping in the big four-poster bed, under the wedding ring quilt.

He could press the button and join her. The hell with McIntyre and the job. The hell with everything but what lay beyond the wall. Procedure, he thought on an oath. He was sick to death of procedure. But Kirby had been right. Adam had a very firm grip on what was right and what was wrong.

He turned and continued down the passage.

Abruptly the corridor snaked off, with steep stone steps forking to the left. Mounting them, he found himself in another corridor. A spider scrambled on the wall as he played his light over it. Kirby hadn't exaggerated much about the size. The third story, he decided, was as good a place to start as any.

He turned the first mechanism he found and slipped through the opening. Dust and dustcovers. Moving quietly, he began a slow, methodical search.

Kirby was restless. While Adam had been standing on the other side of the wall, fighting back the urge to open the panel, she'd been pacing her room. She'd considered going up to her studio. Work might calm her—but any work she did in this frame of mind would be trash. Frustrated, she sank down on the window seat. She could see the faint reflection of her own face and stared at it.

She wasn't completely in control. Almost any other flaw would've been easier to admit. Control was essential and, under the current circumstances, vital. The problem was getting it back.

The problem was, she corrected, Adam Haines.

Attraction? Yes, but that was simple and easily dealt with. There was something more twisted into it that was anything but simple. He could involve her, and once involved, nothing would be easily dealt with.

Laying her hands on the sill, she rested her head on them. He could hurt her. That was a first—a frightening first. Not a superficial blow to the pride or ego, Kirby admitted, but a hurt down deep where it counted; where it wouldn't heal.

Obviously, she told herself, forewarned was forearmed. She just wouldn't let him involve her, therefore she wouldn't let him hurt her. And that little piece of logic brought her right back to the control she didn't have. While she struggled to methodically untangle her thoughts, the beam of headlights distracted her.

Who'd be coming by at this time of night? she wondered without too much surprise. Fairchild had a habit of asking people over at odd hours. Kirby pressed her nose to the glass. A sound, not unlike Isabelle's growl, came from her throat.

"Of all the nerve," she muttered. "Of all the bloody nerve."

Springing up, she paced the floor three times before she grabbed a robe and left the room.

Above her head, Adam was about to reenter the passageway when he, too, saw the beams. Automatically he switched off his flashlight and stepped beside the window. He watched the man step from a late-model Mercedes and walk toward the house. Interesting, Adam decided. Abandoning the passageway, he slipped silently into the hall.

The sound of voices drifted up as he eased himself into the cover of a doorway and waited. Footsteps drew nearer. From his concealment, Adam watched Cards lead a slim, dark man up to Fairchild's tower studio.

"Mr. Hiller to see you, sir." Cards gave the information as if it were four in the afternoon rather than after midnight.

"Stuart, so nice of you to come." Fairchild's voice boomed through the doorway. "Come in, come in."

After counting to ten, Adam started to move toward the door Cards had shut, but just then a flurry of white scrambled up the stairs. Swearing, he pressed back into the wall as Kirby passed, close enough to touch.

What the hell is this? he demanded, torn between frustration and the urge to laugh. Here he was, trapped in a doorway, while people crept up tower steps in the middle of the night. While he watched, Kirby gathered the skirt of her robe around her knees and tiptoed up to the tower.

It was a nightmare, he decided. Women with floating hair sneaking around drafty corridors in filmy white. Secret passages. Clandestine meetings. A normal, sensible man wouldn't be involved in it for a minute. Then again, he'd stopped being completely sensible when he'd walked in the front door.

After Kirby reached the top landing, Adam moved closer. Her attention was focused on the studio door. Making a quick calculation, Adam moved up the steps behind her, then melted into the shadows in the corner. With his eyes on her, he joined Kirby in the eavesdropping.

"What kind of fool do you think I am?" Stuart demanded. He stood beside Adam with only the wall separating them.

"Whatever kind you prefer. Makes no difference to me. Have a seat, my boy."

"Listen to me, we had a deal. How long did you think it would take before I found out you'd double-crossed me?"

"Actually I didn't think it would take you quite so long." Smiling, Fairchild rubbed a thumb over his clay hawk. "Not as clever as I thought you were, Stuart. You should've discovered the switch weeks ago. Not that it wasn't superb," he added with a touch of pride. "But a smart man would've had the painting authenticated."

Because the conversation confused her, Kirby pressed even closer to the door. She tucked her hair behind her ear as if to hear more clearly. Untended, her robe fell open, revealing a thin excuse for a nightgown and a great deal of smooth golden skin. In his corner, Adam shifted and swore to himself.

"We had a deal—" Stuart's voice rose, but Fairchild cut him off with no more than a wave of his hand.

"Don't tell me you believe in that nonsense about honor among thieves? Time to grow up if you want to play in the big leagues."

"I want the Rembrandt, Fairchild."

Kirby stiffened. Because his attention was now fully focused on the battle in the tower, Adam didn't notice. By God, he thought grimly, the old bastard did have it.

"Sue me," Fairchild invited. Kirby could hear the shrug in his voice.

"Hand it over, or I'll break your scrawny neck."

For a full ten seconds, Fairchild watched calmly as Stuart's face turned a deep, dull red. "You won't get it that way. And I should warn you that threats make me irritable. You see…" Slowly he picked up a rag and began to wipe some excess clay from his hands. "I didn't care for your treatment of Kirby. No, I didn't care for it at all."

Abruptly he was no longer the harmless eccentric. He was neither cherub nor gnome, but a man. A dangerous one. "I knew she'd never go as far as marrying you. She's far too bright. But your threats, once she told you off, annoyed me. When I'm annoyed, I tend to be vindictive. A flaw," he said amiably. "But that's just the way I'm made." The pale eyes were cold and calm on Stuart's. "I'm still annoyed, Stuart. I'll let you know when I'm ready to deal. In the meantime, stay away from Kirby."

"You're not going to get away with this."

"I hold all the cards." In an impatient gesture, he brushed Stuart aside. "I have the Rembrandt, and only I know where it is. If you become a nuisance, which you're dangerously close to becoming, I may decide to

keep it. Unlike you, I have no pressing need for money."
He smiled, but the chill remained in his eyes. "One
should never live above one's means, Stuart. That's
my advice."

Impotent, intimidated, Stuart loomed over the little
man at the worktable. He was strong enough, and furious enough, to have snapped Fairchild's neck with
his hands. But he wouldn't have the Rembrandt, or
the money he so desperately needed. "Before we're
done, you'll pay," Stuart promised. "I won't be made
a fool of."

"Too late," Fairchild told him easily. "Run along
now. You can find your way out without disturbing
Cards, can't you?"

As if he were already alone, Fairchild went back
to his hawk.

Swiftly, Kirby looked around for a hiding place.
For one ridiculous moment, Adam thought she'd try to
ease herself into the corner he occupied. The moment
she started to cross the hall toward him, the handle of
the door turned. She'd left her move too late. With her
back pressed against the wall, Kirby closed her eyes
and pretended to be invisible.

Stuart wrenched open the door and stalked from
the room, blind with rage. Without a backward glance
he plunged down the steps. His face, Adam noted as
he passed, was murderous. At the moment, he lacked
a weapon. But if he found one, he wouldn't hesitate.

Kirby stood, still and silent, as the footsteps receded. She sucked in a deep breath, then let it out on a
huff. What now? *What now?* she thought, and wanted
to just bury her face in her hands and surrender. In-

stead, she straightened her shoulders and went in to confront her father.

"Papa." The word was quiet and accusing. Fairchild's head jerked up, but his surprise was quickly masked by a genial smile.

"Hello, love. My hawk's beginning to breathe. Come have a look."

She took another deep breath. All of her life she'd loved him, stood by him. Adored him. None of that had ever stopped her from being angry with him. Slowly, keeping her eyes on him, she crossed the front panels of her robe and tied the sash. As she approached, Fairchild thought she looked like a gunslinger buckling on his six-gun. She wouldn't, he thought with a surge of pride, intimidate like Hiller.

"Apparently you haven't kept me up to date," she began. "A riddle, Papa. What do Philip Fairchild, Stuart Hiller and Rembrandt have in common?"

"You've always been clever at riddles, my sweet."

"*Now,* Papa."

"Just business." He gave her a quick, hearty smile as he wondered just how much he'd have to tell her.

"Let's be specific, shall we?" She moved so that only the table separated them. "And don't give me that blank, foolish look. It won't work." Bending over, she stared directly into his eyes. "I heard quite a bit while I was outside. Tell me the rest."

"Eavesdropping." He made a disapproving tsk-tsk. "Rude."

"I come by it honestly. Now tell me or I'll annihilate your hawk." Sweeping up her arm, she held her palm three inches above his clay.

"Vicious brat." With his bony fingers, he grabbed her wrist, each knowing who'd win if it came down to it. He gave a windy sigh. "All right."

With a nod, Kirby removed her hand then folded her arms under her breasts. The habitual gesture had him sighing again.

"Stuart came to me with a little proposition some time ago. You know, of course, he hasn't a cent to his name, no matter what he pretends."

"Yes, I know he wanted to marry me for my money." No one but her father would've detected the slight tightening in her voice.

"I didn't bring that up to hurt you." His hand reached for hers in the bond that had been formed when she'd taken her first breath.

"I know, Papa." She squeezed his hand, then stuck both of hers in the pockets of her robe. "My pride suffered. It has to happen now and again, I suppose. But I don't care for humiliation," she said with sudden fierceness. "I don't care for it one bloody bit." With a toss of her head, she looked down at him. "The rest."

"Well." Fairchild puffed out his cheeks, then blew out the breath. "Among his other faults, Stuart's greedy. He needed a large sum of money, and didn't see why he had to work for it. He decided to help himself to the Rembrandt self-portrait from Harriet's gallery."

"He *stole* it?" Kirby's eyes grew huge. "Great buckets of bedbugs! I wouldn't have given him credit for that much nerve."

"He thought himself clever." Rising, Fairchild walked to the little sink in the corner to wash off his hands. "Harriet was going on her safari, and there'd be no one to question the disappearance for several weeks. Stuart's a bit dictatorial with the staff at the gallery."

"It's such a treat to flog underlings."

"In any case—" lovingly, Fairchild draped his hawk for the night "—he came to me with an offer—a rather paltry offer, too—if I'd do the forgery for the Rembrandt's replacement."

She hadn't thought he could do anything to surprise her. Certainly nothing to hurt her. "Papa, it's Harriet's Rembrandt," she said in shock.

"Now, Kirby, you know I'm fond of Harriet. Very fond." He put a comforting arm around her shoulders. "Our Stuart has a very small brain. He handed over the Rembrandt when I said I needed it to do the copy." Fairchild shook his head. "There wasn't any challenge to it, Kirby. Hardly any fun at all."

"Pity," she said dryly and dropped into a chair.

"Then I told him I didn't need the original any longer, and gave him the copy instead. He never suspected." Fairchild linked his hands behind his back and stared up at the ceiling. "I wish you'd seen it. It was superlative. It was one of Rembrandt's later works, you know. Rough textures, such luminous depth—"

"Papa!" Kirby interrupted what would've become a lecture.

"Oh, yes, yes." With an effort, Fairchild controlled himself. "I told him it'd take just a little more time to complete the copy and treat it for the illusion of age. He bought it. Gullibility," Fairchild added and clucked his tongue. "It's been almost three weeks, and he just got around to having the painting tested. I made certain it wouldn't stand up to the most basic of tests, of course."

"Of course," Kirby murmured.

"Now he has to leave the copy in the gallery. And I have the original."

She gave herself a moment to absorb all he'd told her. It didn't make any difference in how she felt. Furious. "Why, Papa? Why did you do this! It isn't like all the others. It's Harriet."

"Now, Kirby, don't lose control. You've such a nasty temper." He did his best to look small and helpless. "I'm much too old to cope with it. Remember my blood pressure."

"Blood pressure be hanged." She glared up at him with fury surging into her eyes. "Don't think you're going to get around me with that. Old?" she tossed back. "You're still your youngest child."

"I feel a spell coming on," he said, inspired by Kirby's own warning two days before. He pressed a trembling hand to his heart and staggered. "I'll end up a useless heap of cold spaghetti. Ah, the paintings I might have done. The world's losing a genius."

Clenching her fists, Kirby beat them on his worktable. Tools bounced and clattered while she let out a long wail. Protective, Fairchild placed his hands around his hawk and waited for the crisis to pass. At length, she slumped back in the chair, breathless.

"You used to do better than that," he observed. "I think you're mellowing."

"Papa." Kirby clamped her teeth to keep from grinding them. "I know I'll be forced to beat you about the head and ears, then I'll be arrested for patricide. You know I've a terror of closed-in places. I'd go mad in prison. Do you want that on your conscience?"

"Kirby, have I ever given you cause for one moment's worry?"

"Don't force me into a recital, Papa, it's after midnight. What have you done with the Rembrandt?"

"Done with it?" He frowned and fiddled with the cover of his hawk. "What do you mean, done with it?"

"Where is it?" she asked, carefully spacing the words. "You can't leave a painting like that lying around the house, particularly when you've chosen to have company."

"Company? Oh, you mean Adam. Fine boy. I'm fond of him already." His eyebrows wiggled twice. "You seem to be finding him agreeable."

Kirby narrowed her eyes. "Leave Adam out of this."

"Dear, dear, dear." Fairchild grinned lavishly. "And I thought you'd brought him up."

"Where *is* the Rembrandt?" All claim to patience disintegrated. Briefly, she considered banging her head on the table, but she'd given up that particular ploy at ten.

"Safe and secure, my sweet." Fairchild's voice was calm and pleased. "Safe and secure."

"Here? In the house?"

"Of course." He gave her an astonished look. "You don't think I'd keep it anywhere else?"

"Where?"

"You don't need to know everything." With a flourish, he whipped off his painting smock and tossed it over a chair. "Just content yourself that it's safe, hidden with appropriate respect and affection."

"Papa."

"Kirby." He smiled—a gentle father's smile. "A

child must trust her parent, must abide by the wisdom
of his years. You do trust me, don't you?"

"Yes, of course, but—"

He cut her off with the first bars of "Daddy's Little
Girl" in a wavering falsetto.

Kirby moaned and lowered her head to the table.
When would she learn? And how was she going to deal
with him this time? He continued to sing until the gig-
gles welled up and escaped. "You're incorrigible." She
lifted her head and took a deep breath. "I have this terrible feeling that you're leaving out a mountain of details and that I'm going to go along with you anyway."

"Details, Kirby." His hand swept them aside. "The
world's too full of details, they clutter things up. Remember, art reflects life, and life's an illusion. Come
now, I'm tired." He walked to her and held out his hand.
"Walk your old papa to bed."

Defeated, she accepted his hand and stood. Never,
never would she learn. And always, always would she
adore him. Together they walked from the room.

Adam watched as they started down the steps, arm
in arm.

"Papa…" Only feet away from Adam's hiding place,
Kirby stopped. "There is, of course, a logical reason
for all this?"

"Kirby." Adam could see the mobile face move into
calm, sober lines. "Have I ever done anything without
a sensible, logical reason?"

She started with a near-soundless chuckle. In moments, her laughter rang out, rich and musical. It
echoed back, faint and ghostly, until she rested her head
against her father's shoulder. In the half-light, with her

eyes shining, Adam thought she'd never looked more alluring. "Oh, my papa," she began in a clear contralto. "To me he is so wonderful." Linking her arm through Fairchild's, she continued down the steps.

Rather pleased with himself, and with his offspring, Fairchild joined her in his wavery falsetto. Their mixed voices drifted over Adam until the distance swallowed them.

Leaving the shadows, he stood at the head of the stairway. Once he heard Kirby's laugh, then there was silence.

"Curiouser and curiouser," he murmured.

Both Fairchilds were probably mad. They fascinated him.

Chapter 5

In the morning the sky was gray and the rain sluggish. Adam was tempted to roll over, close his eyes and pretend he was in his own well-organized home, where a housekeeper tended to the basics and there wasn't a gargoyle in sight. Partly from curiosity, partly from courage, he rose and prepared to deal with the day.

From what he'd overheard the night before, he didn't count on learning much from Kirby. Apparently she'd known less about the matter of the Rembrandt than he. Adam was equally sure that no matter how much he prodded and poked, Fairchild would let nothing slip. He might look innocent and harmless, but he was as shrewd as they came. And potentially dangerous, Adam mused, remembering how cleanly Fairchild had dealt with Hiller.

The best course of action remained the nightly

searches with the aid of the passages. The days he determined for his own sanity to spend painting.

I shouldn't be here in the first place, Adam told himself as he stood in the shower under a strong cold spray of water. If it hadn't been for the fact that Mac tantalized me with the Rembrandt, I *wouldn't* be here. The last time, he promised himself as he toweled off. The very last time.

Once the Fairchild hassle was over, painting would not only be his first order of business, it would be his only business.

Dressed, and content with the idea of ending his secondary career in a few more weeks, Adam walked down the hallway thinking of coffee. Kirby's door was wide open. As he passed, he glanced in. Frowning, he stopped, walked back and stood in the doorway.

"Good morning, Adam. Isn't it a lovely day?" She smiled, upside down, as she stood on her head in the corner.

Deliberately he glanced at the window to make sure he was on solid ground. "It's raining."

"Don't you like the rain? I do." She rubbed her nose with the back of her hand. "Look at it this way, there must be dozens of places where the sun's shining. It's all relative. Did you sleep well?"

"Yes." Even in her current position, Adam could see that her face glowed, showing no signs of a restless night.

"Come in and wait a minute, I'll go down to breakfast with you."

He walked over to stand directly in front of her. "Why are you standing on your head?"

"It's a theory of mine." She crossed her ankles against the wall while her hair pooled onto the carpet. "Could you sit down a minute? It's hard for me to talk to you when your head's up there and mine's down here."

Knowing he'd regret it, Adam crouched. Her sweater had slipped up, showing a thin line of smooth midriff.

"Thanks. My theory is that all night I've been horizontal, and most of the day I'll be right side up. So…" Somehow she managed to shrug. "I stand on my head in the morning and before bed. That way the blood can slosh around a bit."

Adam rubbed his nose between his thumb and forefinger. "I think I understand. That terrifies me."

"You should try it."

"I'll just let my blood stagnate, thanks."

"Suit yourself. You'd better stand back, I'm coming up."

She dropped her feet and righted herself with a quick athletic agility that surprised him. Facing him, she pushed at the hair that floated into her eyes. As she tossed it back she gave him a long, slow smile.

"Your face is red," he murmured, more in his own defense than for any other reason.

"Can't be helped, it's part of the process." She'd spent a good many hours arguing with herself the night before. This morning she'd decided to let things happen as they happened. "It's the only time I blush," she told him. "So, if you'd like to say something embarrassing…or flattering…?"

Against his better judgment, he touched her, circling her waist with his hands. She didn't move back, didn't move forward, but simply waited. "Your blush is already fading, so it seems I've missed my chance."

"You can give it another try tomorrow. Hungry?"

"Yes." Her lips made him hungry, but he wasn't ready to test himself quite yet. "I want to go through your clothes after breakfast."

"Oh, really?" She drew out the word, catching her tongue between her teeth.

His brow lifted, but only she was aware of the gesture. "For the painting."

"You don't want to do a nude." The humor in her eyes faded into boredom as she drew away. "That's the usual line."

"I don't waste my time with lines." He studied her—the cool gray eyes that could warm with laughter, the haughty mouth that could invite and promise with no more than a smile. "I'm going to paint you because you were meant to be painted. I'm going to make love with you for exactly the same reason."

Her expression didn't change, but her pulse rate did. Kirby wasn't foolish enough to pretend even to herself it was anger. Anger and excitement were two different things. "How decisive and arrogant of you," she drawled. Strolling over to her dresser, she picked up her brush and ran it quickly through her hair. "I haven't agreed to pose for you, Adam, nor have I agreed to sleep with you." She flicked the brush through a last time then set it down. "In fact, I've serious doubts that I'll do either. Shall we go?"

Before she could get to the door, he had her. The speed surprised her, if the strength didn't. She'd hoped to annoy him, but when she tossed her head back to look at him, she didn't see temper. She saw cool, patient determination. Nothing could have been more unnerving.

Then he had her close, so that his face was a blur and his mouth was dominant. She didn't resist. Kirby rarely resisted what she wanted. Instead she let the heat wind through her in a slow continuous stream that was somehow both terrifying and peaceful.

Desire. Wasn't that how she'd always imagined it would be with the right man? Wasn't that what she'd been waiting for since the first moment she'd discovered herself a woman? It was here now. Kirby opened her arms to it.

His heartbeat wasn't steady, and it should have been. His mind wasn't clear, and it had to be. How could he win with her when he lost ground every time he was around her? If he followed through on his promise—or threat—that they'd be lovers, how much more would he lose? And gain, he thought as he let himself become steeped in her. The risk was worth taking.

"You'll pose for me," he said against her mouth. "And you'll make love with me. There's no choice."

That was the word that stopped her. That was the phrase that forced her to resist. She'd always have a choice. "I don't—"

"For either of us," Adam finished as he released her. "We'll decide on the clothes after breakfast." Because he didn't want to give either of them a chance to speak, he propelled her from the room.

An hour later, he propelled her back.

She'd been serene during the meal. But he hadn't been fooled. Livid was what she was, and livid was exactly how he wanted her. She didn't like to be outmaneuvered, even on a small point. It gave him a surge of satisfaction to be able to do so. The defiant, sulky look in her eyes was exactly what he wanted for the portrait.

"Red, I think," he stated. "It would suit you best."

Kirby waved a hand at her closet and flopped backward onto her bed. Staring up at the ceiling, she thought through her position. It was true she'd always refused to be painted, except by her father. She hadn't wanted anyone else to get that close to her. As an artist, she knew just how intimate the relationship was between painter and subject, be the subject a person or a bowl of fruit. She'd never been willing to share herself with anyone to that extent.

But Adam was different. She could, if she chose, tell herself it was because of his talent, and because he wanted to paint her, not flatter her. It wasn't a lie, but it wasn't quite the truth. Still, Kirby was comfortable with partial truths in certain cases. If she was honest, she had to admit that she was curious to see just how she'd look from his perspective, and yet she wasn't entirely comfortable with that.

Moving only her eyes, she watched him as he rummaged through her closet.

He didn't have to know what was going on in her head. Certainly she was skilled in keeping her thoughts to herself. It might be a challenge to do so under the sharp eyes of an artist. It might be interesting to see just how difficult she could make it for him. She folded her hands demurely on her stomach.

While Kirby was busy with her self-debate, Adam looked through an incredible variety of clothes. Some were perfect for an orphan, others for an eccentric teenager. He wondered if she'd actually worn the purple miniskirt and just how she'd looked in it. Elegant gowns from Paris and New York hung haphazardly with army surplus. If clothes reflected the person, there was more than one Kirby Fairchild. He wondered just how many she'd show him.

He discarded one outfit after another. This one was too drab, that one too chic. He found a pair of baggy overalls thrown over the same hanger with a slinky sequin dress with a two-thousand-dollar label. Pushing aside a three-piece suit perfect for an assistant D.A., he found it.

Scarlet silk. It was undoubtedly expensive, but not chic in the way he imagined Melanie Burgess would design. The square-necked bodice tapered to a narrow waist before the material flared into a full skirt. There were flounces at the hem and underskirts of white and black and fuchsia. The sleeves were short and puffed, running with stripes of the same colors. It was made for a wealthy gypsy. It was perfect.

"This." Adam carried it to the bed and stood over Kirby. With a frown, she continued to stare up at the ceiling. "Put it on and come up to the studio. I'll do some sketches."

She spoke without looking at him. "Do you realize that not once have you asked me to pose for you? You told me you wanted to paint me, you told me you were going to paint me, but you've never *asked* if you could paint me." With her hands still folded, one finger began to tap. "Instinct tells me you're basically a gentleman, Adam. Perhaps you've just forgotten to say please."

"I haven't forgotten." He tossed the dress across the bottom of the bed. "But I think you hear far too many pleases from men. You're a woman who brings men to their knees with the bat of an eye. I'm not partial to kneeling." No, he wasn't partial to kneeling, and it was becoming imperative that he handle the controls, for both of them. Bending over, he put his hands on either side of her head then sat beside her. "And I'm just as used to getting my own way as you are."

She studied him, thinking over his words and her position. "Then again, I haven't batted my eyes at you yet."

"Haven't you?" he murmured.

He could smell her, that wild, untamed fragrance that was suited to isolated winter nights. Her lips pouted, not by design, but mood. It was that that tempted him. He had to taste them. He did so lightly, as he'd intended. Just a touch, just a taste, then he'd go about his business. But her mouth yielded to him as the whole woman hadn't. Or perhaps it conquered.

Desire scorched him. Fire was all he could relate to. Flames and heat and smoke. That was her taste. Smoke and temptation and a promise of unreasonable delights.

He tasted, but it was no longer enough. He had to touch.

Her body was small, delicate, something a man might fear to take. He did, but no longer for her sake. For his own. Small and delicate she might be, but she could slice a man in two. Of that he was certain. But as he touched, as he tasted, he didn't give a damn.

Never had he wanted a woman more. She made him feel like a teenager in the back seat of a car, like a man paying for the best whore in a French bordello, like a husband nuzzling into the security of a wife. Her complexities were more erotic than satin and lace and smoky light—the soft, agile mouth, the strong, determined hands. He wasn't certain he'd ever escape from either. In possessing her, he'd invite an endless cycle of complications, of struggles, of excitement. She was an opiate. She was a dive from a cliff. If he wasn't careful, he was going to overdose and hit the rocks.

It cost him more than he would have believed to draw back. She lay with her eyes half closed, her mouth just parted. Don't get involved, he told himself frantically. Get the Rembrandt and walk away. That's what you came to do.

"Adam…" She whispered his name as if she'd never said it before. It felt so beautiful on her tongue. The only thought that stayed with her was that no one had ever made her feel like this. No one else ever would. Something was opening inside her, but she wouldn't fight it. She'd give. The innocence in her eyes was real, emotional not physical. Seeing it, Adam felt desire flare again.

She's a witch, he told himself. Circe. Lorelei. He had to pull back before he forgot that. "You'll have to change."

"Adam…" Still swimming, she reached up and touched his face.

"Emphasize your eyes." He stood before he could take the dive.

"My eyes?" Mind blank, body throbbing, she stared up at him.

"And leave your hair loose." He strode to the door as she struggled up to her elbows. "Twenty minutes."

She wouldn't let him see the hurt. She wouldn't allow herself to feel the rejection. "You're a cool one, aren't you?" she said softly. "And as smooth as any I've ever run across. You might find yourself on your knees yet."

She was right—he could've strangled her for it. "That's a risk I'll have to take." With a nod, he walked through the door. "Twenty minutes," he called back.

Kirby clenched her fists together then slowly relaxed them. "On your knees," she promised herself. "I swear it."

Alone in Kirby's studio, Adam searched for the mechanism to the passageway. He looked mainly from curiosity. It was doubtful he'd need to rummage through a room that he'd been given free run in, but he was satisfied when he located the control. The panel creaked open, as noisily as all the others he'd found. After a quick look inside, he shut it again and went back to the first order of business—painting.

It was never a job, but it wasn't always a pleasure. The need to paint was a demand that could be soft and gentle, or sharp and cutting. Not a job, but work certainly, sometimes every bit as exhausting as digging a trench with a pick and shovel.

Adam was a meticulous artist, as he was a meticulous man. Conventional, as Kirby had termed him, perhaps. But he wasn't rigid. He was as orderly as she wasn't, but his creative process was remarkably similar to hers. She might stare at a piece of wood for an hour until she saw the life in it. He would do the same with a canvas. She would feel a jolt, a physical release the moment she saw what she'd been searching for. He'd feel that same jolt when something would leap out at him from one of his dozens of sketches.

Now he was only preparing, and he was as calm and ordered as his equipment. On an easel he set the canvas, blank and waiting. Carefully, he selected three pieces of charcoal. He'd begin with them. He was going over his first informal sketches when he heard her footsteps.

She paused in the doorway, tossed her head and stared at him. With deliberate care, he set his pad back on the worktable.

Her hair fell loose and rich over the striped silk shoulders. At a movement, the gold hoops at her ears and the half-dozen gold bracelets on her arm jangled. Her eyes, darkened and sooty, still smoldered with temper. Without effort, he could picture her whirling around an open fire to the sound of violins and tambourines.

Aware of the image she projected, Kirby put both hands on her hips and walked into the room. The full scarlet skirt flowed around her legs. Standing in front of him, she whirled around twice, turning her head each time so that she watched him over her shoulder. The scent of wood smoke and roses flowed into the room.

"You want to paint Katrina's picture, eh?" Her voice lowered into a sultry Slavic accent as she ran a fingertip down his cheek. Insolence, challenge, and then a laugh that skidded warm and dangerous over his skin. "First you cross her palm with silver."

He'd have given her anything. What man wouldn't? Fighting her, fighting himself, he pulled out a cigarette. "Over by the east window," he said easily. "The light's better there."

No, he wouldn't get off so easy. Behind the challenge and the insolence, her body still trembled for him. She wouldn't let him know it. "How much you pay?" she demanded, swirling away in a flurry of scarlet and silk. "Katrina not come free."

"Scale." He barely resisted the urge to grab her by the hair and drag her back. "And you won't get a dime until I'm finished."

In an abrupt change, Kirby brushed and smoothed her skirts. "Is something wrong?" she asked mildly. "Perhaps you don't like the dress after all."

He crushed out his cigarette in one grinding motion. "Let's get started."

"I thought we already had," she murmured. Her eyes were luminous and amused. He wanted to choke her every bit as much as he wanted to crawl for her. "You insisted on painting."

"Don't push me too far, Kirby. You have a tendency to bring out my baser side."

"I don't think I can be blamed for that. Maybe you've locked it up too long." Because she'd gotten precisely the reaction she'd wanted, she became completely cooperative. "Now, where do you want me to stand?"

"By the east window."

Tie score, she thought with satisfaction as she obliged him.

He spoke only when he had to—tilt your chin higher, turn your head. Within moments he was able to turn the anger and the desire into concentration. The rain fell, but its sound was muffled against the thick glass windows. With the tower door nearly closed, there wasn't another sound.

He watched her, studied her, absorbed her, but the man and the artist were working together. Perhaps by putting her on canvas, he'd understand her...and himself. Adam swept the charcoal over the canvas and began.

Now she could watch him, knowing that he was turned inward. She'd seen dozens of artists work; the old, the young, the talented, the amateur. Adam was, as she'd suspected, different.

He wore a sweater, one he was obviously at home in, but no smock. Even as he sketched he stood straight, as though his nature demanded that he remain always alert. That was one of the things she'd noticed about him first. He was always watching. A true artist did, she knew, but there seemed to be something more.

She called him conventional, knowing it wasn't quite true. Not quite. What was it about him that didn't fit into the mold he'd been fashioned for? Tall, lean, attractive, aristocratic, wealthy, successful, and...daring? That was the word that came to mind, though she wasn't completely sure why.

There was something reckless about him that appealed to her. It balanced the maturity, the dependability she hadn't known she'd wanted in a man. He'd be a rock to hold on to during an earthquake. And he'd be the earthquake. She was, Kirby realized, sinking fast. The trick would be to keep him from realizing it and making a fool of herself. Still, beneath it all, she liked him. That simple.

Adam glanced up to see her smiling at him. It was disarming, sweet and uncomplicated. Something warned him that Kirby without guards was far more dangerous than Kirby with them. When she let hers drop, he put his in place.

"Doesn't Hiller paint a bit?"

He saw her smile fade and tried not to regret it. "A bit."

"Haven't you posed for him?"

"No."

"Why not?"

The ice that came into her eyes wasn't what he wanted for the painting. The man and artist warred as he continued to sketch. "Let's say I didn't care much for his work."

"I suppose I can take that as a compliment to mine."

She gave him a long, neutral look. "If you like."

Deceit was part of the job, he reminded himself. What he'd heard in Fairchild's studio left him no choice. "I'm surprised he didn't make an issue of it, being in love with you."

"He wasn't." She bit off the words, and ice turned to heat.

"He asked you to marry him."

"One hasn't anything to do with the other."

He looked up and saw she said exactly what she meant. "Doesn't it?"

"I agreed to marry him without loving him."

He held the charcoal an inch from the canvas, forgetting the painting. "Why?"

While she stared at him, he saw the anger fade. For a moment she was simply a woman at her most vulnerable. "Timing," she murmured. "It's probably the most important factor governing our lives. If it hadn't been for timing, Romeo and Juliet would've raised a half-dozen children."

He was beginning to understand, and understanding only made him more uncomfortable. "You thought it was time to get married?"

"Stuart's attractive, very polished, charming, and I'd thought harmless. I realized the last thing I wanted was a polished, charming, harmless husband. Still, I thought he loved me. I didn't break the engagement for a long time because I thought he'd make a convenient husband, and one who wouldn't demand too much." It sounded empty. It had been empty. "One who'd give me children."

"You want children?"

The anger was back, quickly. "Is there something wrong with that?" she demanded. "Do you think it strange that I'd want a family?" She made a quick, furious movement that had the gold jangling again. "This might come as a shock, but I have needs and feelings almost like a réal person. And I don't have to justify myself to you."

She was halfway to the door before he could stop her. "Kirby, I'm sorry." When she tried to jerk out of his hold, he tightened it. "I *am* sorry."

"For what?" she tossed back.

"For hurting you," he murmured. "With stupidity."

Her shoulders relaxed under his hands, slowly, so that he knew it cost her. Guilt flared again. "All right. You hit a nerve, that's all." Deliberately she removed his hands from her shoulders and stepped back. He'd rather she'd slapped him. "Give me a cigarette, will you?"

She took one from him and let him light it before she turned away again. "When I accepted Stuart's proposal—"

"You don't have to tell me anything."

"I don't leave things half done." Some of the insolence was back when she whirled back to him. For some reason it eased Adam's guilt. "When I accepted, I told Stuart I wasn't in love with him. It didn't seem fair otherwise. If two people are going to have a relationship that means anything, it has to start out honestly, don't you think?"

He thought of the transmitter tucked into his briefcase. He thought of McIntyre waiting for the next report. "Yes."

She nodded. It was one area where she wasn't flexible. "I told him that what I wanted from him was fidelity and children, and in return I'd give him those things and as much affection as I could." She toyed with the cigarette, taking one of her quick, nervous drags. "When I realized things just wouldn't work for either of us that way, I went to see him. I didn't do it carelessly, casually. It was very difficult for me. Can you understand that?"

"Yes, I understand that."

It helped, she realized. More than Melanie's sympathy, more even than her father's unspoken support, Adam's simple understanding helped. "It didn't go well. I'd known there'd be an argument, but I hadn't counted on it getting so out of hand. He made a few choice remarks on my maternal abilities and my track record.

Anyway, with all the blood and bone being strewn about, the real reason for him wanting to marry me came out."

She took a last puff on the cigarette and crushed it out before she dropped into a chair. "He never loved me. He'd been unfaithful all along. I don't suppose it mattered." But she fell silent, knowing it did. "All the time he was pretending to care for me, he was using me." When she looked up again, the hurt was back in her eyes. She didn't know it—she'd have hated it. "Can you imagine how it feels to find out that all the time someone was holding you, talking with you, he was thinking of how you could be useful?" She picked up the piece of half-formed wood that would be her anger. "Useful," she repeated. "What a nasty word. I haven't bounced back from it as well as I should have."

He forgot McIntyre, the Rembrandt and the job he still had to do. Walking over, he sat beside her and closed his hand over hers. Under them was her anger. "I can't imagine any man thinking of you as useful."

When she looked up, her smile was already spreading. "What a nice thing to say. The perfect thing." Too perfect for her rapidly crumbling defenses. Because she knew it would take so little to have her turning to him now and later, she lightened the mood. "I'm glad you're going to be there Saturday."

"At the party?"

"You can send me long, smoldering looks and everyone'll think I jilted Stuart for you. I'm fond of petty revenge."

He laughed and brought her hands to his lips. "Don't

change," he told her with a sudden intenseness that had her uncertain again.

"I don't plan on it. Adam, I— Oh, chicken fat, what're you doing here? This is a private conversation."

Wary, Adam turned his head and watched Montique bounce into the room. "He won't spread gossip."

"That isn't the point. I've told you you're not allowed in here."

Ignoring her, Montique scurried over and with an awkward leap plopped into Adam's lap. "Cute little devil," Adam decided as he scratched the floppy ears.

"Ah, Adam, I wouldn't do that."

"Why?"

"You're only asking for trouble."

"Don't be absurd. He's harmless."

"Oh, yes, he is. *She* isn't." Kirby nodded her head toward the doorway as Isabelle slinked through. "Now you're in for it. I warned you." Tossing back her head, Kirby met Isabelle's cool look equally. "I had nothing to do with it."

Isabelle blinked twice, then shifted her gaze to Adam. Deciding her responsibility had ended, Kirby sighed and rose. "There's nothing I can do," she told Adam and patted his shoulder. "You asked for it." With this, she swept out of the room, giving the cat a wide berth.

"I didn't ask him to come up here," Adam began, scowling down at Isabelle. "And there can't be any harm in— Oh, God," he murmured. "She's got me doing it."

Chapter 6

"Let's walk," Kirby demanded when the afternoon grew late and Fairchild had yet to budge from his studio. Nor would he budge, she knew, until the Van Gogh was completed down to the smallest detail. If she didn't get out and forget about her father's pet project for a while, she knew she'd go mad.

"It's raining," Adam pointed out as he lingered over coffee.

"You mentioned that before." Kirby pushed away her own coffee and rose. "All right then, I'll have Cards bring you a lap robe and a nice cup of tea."

"Is that a psychological attack?"

"Did it work?"

"I'll get a jacket." He strode from the room, ignoring her quiet chuckle.

When they walked outside, the fine misting rain fell

over them. Leaves streamed with it. Thin fingers of fog twisted along the ground. Adam hunched inside his jacket, thinking it was miserable weather for a walk. Kirby strolled along with her face lifted to the sky.

He'd planned to spend the afternoon on the painting, but perhaps this was better. If he was going to capture her with colors and brush strokes, he should get to know her better. No easy task, Adam mused, but a strangely appealing one.

The air was heavy with the fragrance of fall, the sky gloomy. For the first time since he'd met her, Adam sensed a serenity in Kirby. They walked in silence, with the rain flowing over them.

She was content. It was an odd feeling for her to identify as she felt it so rarely. With her hand in his, she was content to walk along as the fog moved along the ground and the chilly drizzle fell over them. She was glad of the rain, of the chill and the gloom. Later, there would be time for a roaring fire and warm brandy.

"Adam, do you see the bed of mums over there?"

"Hmm?"

"The mums, I want to pick some. You'll have to be the lookout."

"Lookout for what?" He shook wet hair out of his eyes.

"For Jamie, of course. He doesn't like anyone messing with his flowers."

"They're your flowers."

"No, they're Jamie's."

"He works for you."

"What does that have to do with it?" She put a hand on his shoulder as she scanned the area. "If he catches me, he'll get mad, then he won't save me any leaves. I'll be quick—I've done this before."

"But if you—"

"There's no time to argue. Now, you watch that window there. He's probably in the kitchen having coffee with Tulip. Give me a signal when you see him."

Whether he went along with her because it was simpler, or because he was getting into the spirit of things despite himself, Adam wasn't sure. But he walked over to the window and peeked inside. Jamie sat at a huge round table with a mug of coffee in both frail hands. Turning, he nodded a go-ahead to Kirby.

She moved like lightning, dashing to the flower bed and plucking at stems. Dark and wet, her hair fell forward to curtain her face as she loaded her arms with autumn flowers. She should be painted like this, as well, Adam mused. In the fog, with her arms full of wet flowers. Perhaps it would be possible to capture those odd little snatches of innocence in the portrait.

Idly he glanced back in the window. With a ridiculous jolt of panic, he saw Jamie rise and head for the kitchen door. Forgetting logic, Adam dashed toward her.

"He's coming."

Surprisingly swift, Kirby leaped over the bed of flowers and kept on going. Even though he was running full stride, Adam didn't catch her until they'd rounded the side of the house. Giggling and out of breath, she collapsed against him.

"We made it!"

"Just," he agreed. His own heart was thudding— from the race? Maybe. He was breathless—from the game? Perhaps. But they were wet and close and the fog was rising. It didn't seem he had a choice any longer.

With his eyes on hers, he brushed the dripping hair back from her face. Her cheeks were cool, wet and smooth. Yet her mouth, when his lowered to it, was warm and waiting.

She hadn't planned it this way. If she'd had the time to think, she'd have said she didn't want it this way. She didn't want to be weak. She didn't want her mind muddled. It didn't seem she had a choice any longer.

He could taste the rain on her, fresh and innocent. He could smell the sharp tang of the flowers that were crushed between them. He couldn't keep his hands out of her hair, the soft, heavy tangle of it. He wanted her closer. He wanted all of her, not in the way he'd first wanted her, but in every way. The need was no longer the simple need of a man for woman, but of him for her. Exclusive, imperative, impossible.

She'd wanted to fall in love, but she'd wanted to plan it out in her own way, in her own time. It wasn't supposed to happen in a crash and a roar that left her trembling. It wasn't supposed to happen without her permission. Shaken, Kirby drew back. It wasn't going to happen until she was ready. That was that. Nerves taut again, she made herself smile.

"It looks like we've done a good job of squashing them." When he would've drawn her back, Kirby thrust the flowers at him. "They're for you."

"For me?" Adam looked down at the mums they held between them.

"Yes, don't you like flowers?"

"I like flowers," he murmured. However unintentionally, she'd moved him as much with the gift as with the kiss. "I don't think anyone's given me flowers before."

"No?" She gave him a long, considering look. She'd been given floods of them over the years, orchids, lilies, roses and more roses, until they'd meant little more than nothing. Her smile came slowly as she touched a hand to his chest. "I'd've picked more if I'd known."

Behind them a window was thrown open. "Don't you know better than to stand in the rain and neck?" Fairchild demanded. "If you want to nuzzle, come inside. I can't stand sneezing and sniffling!" The window shut with a bang.

"You're terribly wet," Kirby commented, as if she hadn't noticed the steadily falling rain. She linked her arm with his and walked to the door that was opened by the ever-efficient Cards.

"Thank you." Kirby peeled off her soaking jacket. "We'll need a vase for the flowers, Cards. They're for Mr. Haines's room. Make sure Jamie's not about, will you?"

"Naturally, miss." Cards took both the dripping jackets and the dripping flowers and headed back down the hall.

"Where'd you find him?" Adam wondered aloud. "He's incredible."

"Cards?" Like a wet dog, Kirby shook her head. "Papa brought him back from England. I think he was a spy, or maybe it was a bouncer. In either case, it's obvious he's seen everything."

"Well, children, have you had a nice holiday?" Fairchild bounced out of the parlor. He wore a paint-streaked shirt and a smug smile. "My work's complete, and now I'm free to give my full attention to my sculpting. It's time I called Victor Alvarez," he murmured. "I've kept him dangling long enough."

"He'll dangle until after coffee, Papa." She sent her father a quick warning glance Adam might've missed if he hadn't been watching so closely. "Take Adam in the parlor and I'll see to it."

She kept him occupied for the rest of the day. Deliberately, Adam realized. Something was going on that she didn't want him getting an inkling of. Over dinner, she was again the perfect hostess. Over coffee and brandy in the parlor, she kept him entertained with an in-depth discussion on baroque art. Though her conversations and charm were effortless, Adam was certain there was an underlying reason. It was one more thing for him to discover.

She couldn't have set the scene better, he mused. A quiet parlor, a crackling fire, intelligent conversation. And she was watching Fairchild like a hawk.

When Montique entered, the scene changed. Once again, the scruffy puppy leaped into Adam's lap and settled down.

"How the hell did he get in here?" Fairchild demanded.

"Adam encourages him," Kirby stated as she sipped at her brandy. "We can't be held responsible."

"I should say not!" Fairchild gave both Adam and Montique a steely look. "And if that—that creature threatens to sue again, Adam will have to retain his own attorney. I won't be involved in a legal battle, particularly when I have my business with Senhor Alvarez to complete. What time is it in Brazil?"

"Some time or other," Kirby murmured.

"I'll call him immediately and close the deal before we find ourselves slapped with a summons."

Adam sat back with his brandy and scratched Montique's ears. "You two don't seriously expect me to believe you're worried about being sued by a cat?"

Kirby ran a fingertip around the rim of her snifter. "I don't think we'd better tell him about what happened last year when we tried to have her evicted."

"No!" Fairchild leaped up and shuffled before he darted to the door. "I won't discuss it. I won't remember it. I'm going to call Brazil."

"Ah, Adam…" Kirby trailed off with a meaningful glance at the doorway.

Adam didn't have to look to know that Isabelle was making an entrance.

"I won't be intimidated by a cat."

"I'm sure that's very stalwart of you." Kirby downed the rest of her drink then rose. "Just as I'm sure you'll understand if I leave you to your courage. I really have to reline my dresser drawers."

For the second time that day, Adam found himself alone with a dog and cat.

A half hour later, after he'd lost a staring match with Isabelle, Adam locked his door and contacted McIntyre. In the brief, concise tones that McIntyre had always admired, Adam relayed the conversation he'd overheard the night before.

"It fits," McIntyre stated. Adam could almost see him rubbing his hands together. "You've learned quite a bit in a short time. The check on Hiller reveals he's living on credit and reputation. Both are running thin. No idea where Fairchild's keeping it?"

"I'm surprised he doesn't have it hanging in full view." Adam lit a cigarette and frowned at the Titian across the room. "It would be just like him. He mentioned a Victor Alvarez from Brazil a couple of times. Some kind of deal he's cooking."

"I'll see what I can dig up. Maybe he's selling the Rembrandt."

"He hardly needs the money."

"Some people never have enough."

"Yeah." But it didn't fit. It just didn't fit. "I'll get back to you."

Adam brooded, but only for a few moments. The sooner he had something tangible, the sooner he could untangle himself. He opened the panel and went to work.

In the morning, Kirby posed for Adam for more than two hours without the slightest argument. If he thought her cooperation and her sunny disposition were designed to confuse him, he was absolutely right. She was also keeping him occupied while Fairchild made the final arrangements for the disposal of the Van Gogh.

Adam had worked the night before until after midnight, but had found nothing. Wherever Fairchild had hidden the Rembrandt, he'd hidden it well. Adam's search of the third floor was almost complete. It was time to look elsewhere.

"Hidden with respect and affection," he remembered. In all probability that would rule out the dungeons and the attic. Chances were he'd have to give them some time, but he intended to concentrate on the main portion of the house first. His main objective would be Fairchild's private rooms, but when and how he'd do them he had yet to determine.

After the painting session was over and Kirby went back to her own work, Adam wandered around the first floor. There was no one to question his presence. He was a guest and he was trusted. He was supposed to be, he reminded himself when he became uncomfortable. One of the reasons McIntyre had drafted him for this particular job was because he would have easy access to the Fairchilds and the house. He was, socially and professionally, one of them. They'd have no reason to be suspicious of a well-bred, successful artist whom they'd welcomed into their own home. And the more Adam tried to justify his actions, the more the guilt ate at him.

Enough, he told himself as he stared out at the darkening sky. He'd had enough for one day. It was time he went up and changed for Melanie Burgess's party. There he'd meet Stuart Hiller and Harriet Merrick. There were no emotional ties there to make him feel like a spy and a thief. Swearing at himself, he started up the stairs.

"Excuse me, Mr. Haines." Impatient, Adam turned and looked down at Tulip. "Were you going up?"

"Yes." Because he stood on the bottom landing blocking her way, he stood aside to let her pass.

"You take this up to her then, and see she drinks it." Tulip shoved a tall glass of milky white liquid into his hand. "All," she added tersely before she clomped back toward the kitchen.

Where did they get their servants? Adam wondered, frowning down at the glass in his hands. And why, for the love of God, had he let himself be ordered around by one? When in Rome, he supposed, and started up the steps again.

The *she* obviously meant Kirby. Adam sniffed doubtfully at the glass as he knocked on her door.

"You can bring it in," she called out, "but I won't drink it. Threaten all you like."

All right, he decided, and pushed her door open. The bedroom was empty, but he could smell her.

"Do your worst," she invited. "You can't intimidate me with stories of intestinal disorders and vitamin deficiencies. I'm healthy as a horse."

The warm, sultry scent flowed over him. Glass in hand, he walked through and into the bathroom where the steam rose up, fragrant and misty as a rain forest. With her hair pinned on top of her head, Kirby lounged in a huge sunken tub. Overhead, hanging plants dripped down, green and moist. White frothy bubbles floated in heaps on the surface of the water.

"So she sent you, did she?" Unconcerned, Kirby rubbed a loofah sponge over one shoulder. The bubbles, she concluded, covered her with more modesty than most women at the party that night would claim. "Well, come in then, and stop scowling at me. I won't ask you to scrub my back."

He thought of Cleopatra, floating on her barge. Just how many men other than Caesar and Antony had she driven mad? He glanced at the long mirrored wall behind the sink. It was fogged with the steam that rose in visible columns from her bath. "Got the water hot enough?"

"Do you know what that is?" she demanded, and plucked her soap from the dish. The cake was a pale, pale pink and left a creamy lather on her skin. "It's a filthy-tasting mixture Tulip tries to force on me periodically. It has raw eggs in it and other vile things." Making a face she lifted one surprisingly long leg out of the bath and soaped it. "Tell me the truth, Adam, would you voluntarily drink raw eggs?"

He watched her run soap and fingertips down her calf. "I can't say I would."

"Well, then." Satisfied, she switched legs. "Down the drain with it."

"She told me to see that you drank it. All," he added, beginning to enjoy himself.

Her lower lip moved forward a bit as she considered. "Puts you in an awkward position, doesn't it?"

"A position in any case."

"Tell you what, I'll have a sip. Then when she asks if I drank it I can say I did. I'm trying to cut down on my lying."

Adam handed her the glass, watching as she sipped and grimaced. "I'm not sure you're being truthful this way."

"I said cutting down, not eliminating. Into the sink," she added. "Unless you'd care for the rest."

"I'll pass." He poured it out then sat on the lip of the tub.

Surprised by the move, she tightened her fingers on the soap. It plopped into the water. "Hydrophobia," she muttered. "No, don't bother, I'll find it." Dipping her hand in, she began to search. "You'd think they could make a soap that wasn't forever leaping out of your hands." Grateful for the distraction, she gripped the soap again. "Aha. I appreciate your bringing me that revolting stuff, Adam. Now if you'd like to run along…"

"I'm in no hurry." Idly he picked up her loofah. "You mentioned something about scrubbing your back."

"Robbery!" Fairchild's voice boomed into the room just ahead of him. "Call the police. Call the FBI. Adam, you'll be a witness." He nodded, finding nothing odd in the audience to his daughter's bath.

"I'm so glad I have a large bathroom," she murmured. "Pity I didn't think to serve refreshments." Relieved by the interruption, she ran the soap down her arm. "What's been stolen, Papa? The Monet street scene, the Renoir portrait? I know, your sweat socks."

"My black dinner suit!" Dramatically he pointed a finger to the ceiling. "We'll have to take fingerprints."

"Obviously stolen by a psychotic with a fetish for formal attire," Kirby concluded. "I love a mystery. Let's list the suspects." She pushed a lock of hair out of her eyes and leaned back—a naked, erotic Sherlock Holmes. "Adam, have you an alibi?"

With a half smile, he ran the damp abrasive sponge through his hands. "I've been seducing Polly all afternoon."

Her eyes lit with amusement. She'd known he had potential. "That won't do," she said soberly. "It wouldn't take above fifteen minutes to seduce Polly. You have a black dinner suit, I suppose."

"Circumstantial evidence."

"A search warrant," Fairchild chimed in, inspired. "We'll get a search warrant and go through the entire house."

"Time-consuming," Kirby decided. "Actually, Papa, I think we'd best look to Cards."

"The butler did it." Fairchild cackled with glee, then immediately sobered. "No, no, my suit would never fit Cards."

"True. Still, as much as I hate to be an informer, I overheard Cards telling Tulip he intended to take your suit."

"Trust," Fairchild mumbled to Adam. "Can't trust anyone."

"His motive was sponging and pressing, I believe." She sank down to her neck and examined her toes. "He'll crumble like a wall if you accuse him. I'm sure of it."

"Very well." Fairchild rubbed his thin, clever hands together. "I'll handle it myself and avoid the publicity."

"A brave man," Kirby decided as her father strode out of the room. Relaxed and amused, she smiled at Adam. "Well, my bubbles seem to be melting, so we'd better continue this discussion some other time."

Reaching over, Adam yanked the chain and drew the old-fashioned plug out of the stupendous tub. "The time's coming when we're going to start—and finish—much more than a conversation."

Wary, Kirby watched her water level and last defense recede. When cornered, she determined, it was best to be nonchalant. She tried a smile that didn't quite conceal the nerves. "Let me know when you're ready."

"I intend to," he said softly. Without another word, he rose and left her alone.

Later, when he descended the stairs, Adam grinned when he heard her voice.

"Yes, Tulip, I drank the horrid stuff. I won't disgrace you by fainting in the Merrick living room from malnutrition." The low rumble of response that followed was dissatisfied. "Cricket wings, I've been walking in heels for half my life. They're not six inches, they're three. And I'll still have to look up at everyone over twelve. Go bake a cake, will you?"

He heard Tulip's mutter and sniff before she stomped out of the room and passed him.

"Adam, thank God. Let's go before she finds something else to nag me about."

Her dress was pure, unadorned white, thin and floaty. It covered her arms, rose high at the throat, as modest as a nun's habit, as sultry as a tropical night. Her hair fell, black and straight over the shoulders.

Tossing it back, she picked up a black cape and swirled it around her. For a moment she stood, adjusting it while the light from the lamps flitted over the absence of color. She looked like a Manet portrait—strong, romantic and timeless.

"You're a fabulous-looking creature, Kirby."

They both stopped, staring. He'd given compliments before, with more style, more finesse, but he'd never meant one more. She'd been flattered by princes, in foreign tongues and with smooth deliveries. It had never made her stomach flutter.

"Thank you," she managed. "So're you." No longer sure it was wise, she offered her hand. "Are you ready?"

"Yes. Your father?"

"He's already gone," she told him as she walked toward the door. And the sooner they were, the better. She needed a little more time before she was alone with him again. "We don't drive to parties together, especially to Harriet's. He likes to get there early and usually stays longer, trying to talk Harriet into bed. I've had my car brought around." She shut the door and led him to a silver Porsche. "I'd rather drive than navigate, if you don't mind."

But she didn't wait for his response as she dropped into the driver's seat. "Fine," Adam agreed.

"It's a marvelous night." She turned the key in the ignition. The power vibrated under their feet. "Full moon, lots of stars." Smoothly she released the brake, engaged the clutch and pressed the accelerator. Adam was tossed against the seat as they roared down the drive.

"You'll like Harriet," Kirby continued, switching gears as Adam stared at the blurring landscape. "She's like a mother to me." When they came to the main road, Kirby downshifted and swung to the left, tires squealing. "You met Melly, of course. I hope you won't desert me completely tonight after seeing her again."

Adam braced his feet against the floor. "Does anyone notice her when you're around?" And would they make it to the Merrick home alive?

"Of course." Surprised by the question, she turned to look at him.

"Good God, watch where you're going!" None too gently, he pushed her head around.

"Melly's the most perfectly beautiful woman I've ever known." Downshifting again, Kirby squealed around a right turn then accelerated. "She's a very clever designer and very, very proper. Wouldn't even take a settlement from her husband when they divorced. Pride, I suppose, but then she wouldn't need the money. There's a marvelous view of the Hudson coming up on your side, Adam." Kirby leaned over to point it out. The car swerved.

"I prefer seeing it from up here, thanks," Adam told her as he shoved her back in her seat. "Do you always drive this way?"

"Yes. There's the road you take to the gallery," she continued. She waved her hand vaguely as the car whizzed by an intersection. Adam glanced down at the speedometer.

"You're doing ninety."

"I always drive slower at night."

"There's good news." Muttering, he flicked on the lighter.

"There's the house up ahead." She raced around an ess curve. "Fabulous when it's all lit up this way."

The house was white and stately, the type you expected to see high above the riverbank. It glowed with elegance from dozens of windows. Without slackening pace, Kirby sped up the circular drive. With a squeal of brakes, and a muttered curse from Adam, she stopped the Porsche at the front entrance.

Reaching over, Adam pulled the keys from the ignition and pocketed them. "I'm driving back."

"How thoughtful." Offering her hand to the valet, Kirby stepped out. "Now I won't have to limit myself to one drink. Champagne," she decided, moving up the steps beside him. "It seems like a night for it."

The moment the door opened, Kirby was enveloped by a flurry of dazzling, trailing silks. "Harriet." Kirby squeezed the statuesque woman with flaming red hair. "It's wonderful to see you, but I think I'm being gnawed by the denture work of your crocodile."

"Sorry, darling." Harriet held her necklace and drew back to press a kiss to each of Kirby's cheeks. She was an impressive woman, full-bodied in the style Rubens had immortalized. Her face was wide and smooth, dominated by deep green eyes that glittered with silver on the lids. Harriet didn't believe in subtlety. "And this must be your houseguest," she continued with a quick sizing up of Adam.

"Harriet Merrick, Adam Haines." Kirby grinned and pinched Harriet's cheek. "And behave yourself, or Papa'll have him choosing weapons."

"Wonderful idea." With one arm still linked with Kirby's, Harriet twined her other through Adam's. "I'm sure you have a fascinating life story to tell me, Adam."

"I'll make one up."

"Perfect." She liked the look of him. "We've a crowd already, though they're mostly Melanie's stuffy friends."

"Harriet, you've got to be more tolerant."

"No, I don't." She tossed back her outrageous hair. "I've been excruciatingly polite. Now that you're here, I don't have to be."

"Kirby." Melanie swept into the hall in an ice-blue

sheath. "What a picture you make. Take her cloak, Ellen, though it's a pity to spoil that effect." Smiling, she held out a hand to Adam as the maid slipped Kirby's cloak off her shoulders. "I'm so glad you came. We've some mutual acquaintances here, it seems. The Birminghams and Michael Towers from New York. You remember Michael, Kirby?"

"The adman who clicks his teeth?"

Harriet let out a roar of laughter while Adam struggled to control his. With a sigh, Melanie led them toward the party. "Try to behave, will you?" But Adam wasn't certain whether she spoke to Kirby or her mother.

This was the world he was used to—elegant people in elegant clothes having rational conversations. He'd been raised in the world of restrained wealth where champagne fizzed quietly and dignity was as essential as the proper alma mater. He understood it, he fit in.

After fifteen minutes, he was separated from Kirby and bored to death.

"I've decided to take a trek through the Australian bush," Harriet told Kirby. She fingered her necklace of crocodile teeth. "I'd love you to come with me. We'd have such fun brewing a billy cup over the fire."

"Camping?" Kirby asked, mulling it over. Maybe what she needed was a change of scene, after her father settled down.

"Give it some thought," Harriet suggested. "I'm not planning on leaving for another six weeks. Ah, Adam." Reaching out, she grabbed his arm. "Did Agnes Birmingham drive you to drink? No, don't answer. It's written all over your face, but you're much too polite."

He allowed himself to be drawn between her and Kirby, where he wanted to be. "Let's just say I was looking for more stimulating conversation. I've found it."

"Charming." She decided she liked him, but would reserve judgment a bit longer as to whether he'd suit her Kirby. "I admire your work, Adam. I'd like to put the first bid in on your next painting."

He took glasses from a passing waiter. "I'm doing a portrait of Kirby."

"She's posing for you?" Harriet nearly choked on her champagne. "Did you chain her?"

"Not yet." He gave Kirby a lazy glance. "It's still a possibility."

"You have to let me display it when it's finished." She might've been a woman who ran on emotion on many levels, but the bottom line was art, and the business of it. "I can promise to cause a nasty scene if you refuse."

"No one does it better," Kirby toasted her.

"You'll have to see the portrait of Kirby that Philip painted for me. She wouldn't sit for it, but it's brilliant." She toyed with the stem of her glass. "He painted it when she returned from Paris—three years ago, I suppose."

"I'd like to see it. I'd planned on coming by the gallery."

"Oh, it's here, in the library."

"Why don't you two just toddle along then?" Kirby suggested. "You've been talking around me, you might as well desert me physically, as well."

"Don't be snotty," Harriet told her. "You can come,

too. And I... Well, well," she murmured in a voice suddenly lacking in warmth. "Some people have no sense of propriety."

Kirby turned her head, just slightly, and watched Stuart walk into the room. Her fingers tightened on the glass, but she shrugged. Before the movement was complete, Melanie was at her side.

"I'm sorry, Kirby. I'd hoped he wouldn't come after all."

In a slow, somehow insolent gesture, Kirby pushed her hair behind her back. "If it had mattered, I wouldn't have come."

"I don't want you to be embarrassed," Melanie began, only to be cut off by a quick and very genuine laugh.

"When have you ever known me to be embarrassed?"

"Well, I'll greet him, or it'll make matters worse." Still, Melanie hesitated, obviously torn between loyalty and manners.

"I'll fire him, of course," Harriet mused when her daughter went to do her duty. "But I want to be subtle about it."

"Fire him if you like, Harriet, but not on my account." Kirby drained her champagne.

"It appears we're in for a show, Adam." Harriet tapped a coral fingertip against her glass. "Much to Melanie's distress, Stuart's coming over."

Without saying a word, Kirby took Adam's cigarette.

"Harriet, you look marvelous." The smooth, cultured voice wasn't at all like the tone Adam had heard in Fairchild's studio. "Africa agreed with you."

Harriet gave him a bland smile. "We didn't expect to see you."

"I was tied up for a bit." Charming, elegant, he turned to Kirby. "You're looking lovely."

"So are you," she said evenly. "It seems your nose is back in joint." Without missing a beat, she turned to Adam. "I don't believe you've met. Adam, this is Stuart Hiller. I'm sure you know Adam Haines's work, Stuart."

"Yes, indeed." The handshake was polite and meaningless. "Are you staying in our part of New York long?"

"Until I finish Kirby's portrait," Adam told him and had the dual satisfaction of seeing Kirby grin and Stuart frown. "I've agreed to let Harriet display it in the gallery."

With that simple strategy, Adam won Harriet over.

"I'm sure it'll be a tremendous addition to our collection." Even a man with little sensitivity wouldn't have missed the waves of resentment. For the moment, Stuart ignored them. "I wasn't able to reach you in Africa, Harriet, and things have been hectic since your return. The Titian woman has been sold to Ernest Myerling."

As he lifted his glass, Adam's attention focused on Kirby. Her color drained, slowly, degree by degree until her face was as white as the silk she wore.

"I don't recall discussing selling the Titian," Harriet countered. Her voice was as colorless as Kirby's skin.

"As I said, I couldn't reach you. As the Titian isn't listed under your personal collection, it falls among the saleable paintings. I think you'll be pleased with the price." He lit a cigarette with a slim silver lighter. "Myerling did insist on having it tested. He's more interested in investment than art, I'm afraid. I thought you'd want to be there tomorrow for the procedure."

Oh, God, oh, my God! Panic, very real and very strong, whirled through Kirby's mind. In silence, Adam watched the fear grow in her eyes.

"Tested!" Obviously insulted, Harriet seethed. "Of all the gall, doubting the authenticity of a painting from my gallery. The Titian should not have been sold without my permission, and certainly not to a peasant."

"Testing isn't unheard-of, Harriet." Seeing a hefty commission wavering, Stuart soothed, "Myerling's a businessman, not an art expert. He wants facts." Taking a long drag, he blew out smoke. "In any case, the paperwork's already completed and there's nothing to be done about it. The deal's a fait accompli, hinging on the test results."

"We'll discuss this in the morning." Harriet's voice lowered as she finished off her drink. "This isn't the time or place."

"I—I have to freshen my drink," Kirby said suddenly. Without another word, she spun away to work her way through the crowd. The nausea, she realized, was a direct result of panic, and the panic was a long way from over. "Papa." She latched on to his arm and pulled him out of a discussion on Dali's versatility. "I have to talk to you. Now."

Hearing the edge in her voice, he let her drag him from the room.

Chapter 7

Kirby closed the doors of Harriet's library behind her and leaned back against them. She didn't waste any time. "The Titian's being tested in the morning. Stuart sold it."

"Sold it!" Fairchild's eyes grew wide, his face pink. "Impossible. Harriet wouldn't sell the Titian."

"She didn't. She was off playing with lions, remember?" Dragging both hands through her hair, she tried to speak calmly. "Stuart closed the deal, he just told her."

"I told you he was a fool, didn't I? Didn't I?" Fairchild repeated as he started dancing in place. "I told Harriet, too. Would anyone listen? No, not Harriet." He whirled around, plucked up a pencil from her desk and broke it in two. "She hires the idiot anyway and goes off to roam the jungle."

"There's no use going over that again!" Kirby snapped at him. "We've got to deal with the results."

"There wouldn't be any results if I'd been listened to. Stubborn woman falling for a pretty face. That's all it was." Pausing, he took a deep breath and folded his hands. "Well," he said in a mild voice, "this is a problem."

"Papa, this isn't an error in your checkbook."

"But it can be handled, probably with less effort. Any way out of the deal?"

"Stuart said the paperwork had been finalized. And it's Myerling," she added.

"That old pirate." He scowled a moment and gave Harriet's desk a quick kick. "No way out of it," Fairchild concluded. "On to the next step. We exchange them." He saw by Kirby's nod that she'd already thought of it. There was a quick flash of pride before anger set in. The round, cherubic face tightened. "By God, Stuart's going to pay for making me give up that painting."

"Very easily said, Papa." Kirby walked into the room until she stood toe to toe with him. "But who was it who settled Adam in the same room with the painting? Now we're going to have to get it out of his room, then get the copy from the gallery in without him knowing there's been a switch. I'm sure you've noticed Adam's not a fool."

Fairchild's eyebrows wiggled. His lips curved. He rubbed his palms together. "A plan."

Knowing it was too late for regrets, Kirby flopped into a chair. "We'll phone Cards and have him put the painting in my room before we get back."

He approved this with a brief nod. "You have a marvelous criminal mind, Kirby."

She had to smile. A sense of adventure was already spearing through the panic. "Heredity," she told her father. "Now, here's my idea...." Lowering her voice, she began the outline.

"It'll work," Fairchild decided a few moments later.

"That has yet to be seen." It sounded plausible enough, but she didn't underestimate Adam Haines. "So there's nothing to be done but to do it."

"And do it well."

Her agreement was a careless shrug of her shoulders. "Adam should be too tired to notice that the Titian's gone, and after I make the exchange at the gallery, I'll slip it back into his room. Sleeping pills are the only way." She stared down at her hands, dissatisfied, but knowing it was the only way out. "I don't like doing this to Adam."

"He'll just get a good night's sleep." Fairchild sat on the arm of her chair. "We all need a good night's sleep now and again. Now we'd better go back or Melanie'll send out search parties."

"You go first." Kirby let out a deep breath. "I'll phone Cards and tell him to get started."

Kirby waited until Fairchild had closed the doors again before she went to the phone on Harriet's desk. She didn't mind the job she had to do, in fact she looked forward to it. Except for Adam's part. It couldn't be helped, she reminded herself, and gave Cards brief instructions.

Now, she thought as she replaced the receiver, it was too late to turn back. The die, so to speak, had been cast. The truth was, the hastily made plans for the evening would prove a great deal more interesting than a party. While she hesitated a moment longer, Stuart opened the door, then closed it softly behind him.

"Kirby." He crossed to her with a half smile on his face. His patience had paid off now that he'd found her alone. "We have to talk."

Not now, she thought on a moment's panic. Didn't she have enough to deal with? Then she thought of the way he'd humiliated her. The way he'd lied. Perhaps it was better to get everything over with at once.

"I think we said everything we had to say at our last meeting."

"Not nearly everything."

"Redundancy bores me," she said mildly. "But if you insist, I'll say this. It's a pity you haven't the money to suit your looks. Your mistake, Stuart, was in not making me want you—not the way you wanted me." Deliberately her voice dropped, low and seductive. She hadn't nearly finished paying him back. "You could deceive me about love, but not about lust. If you'd concentrated on that instead of greed, you might've had a chance. You are," she continued softly, "a liar and a cheat, and while that might've been an interesting diversion for a short time, I thank God you never got your hands on me or my money."

Before she could sweep around him, he grabbed her arm. "You'd better remember your father's habits before you sling mud."

She dropped her gaze to his hand, then slowly raised it again. It was a look designed to infuriate. "Do you honestly compare yourself with my father?" Her fury came out on a laugh, and the laugh was insult itself.

"You'll never have his style, Stuart. You're second-rate, and you'll always be second-rate."

He brought the back of his hand across her face hard enough to make her stagger. She didn't make a sound. When she stared up at him, her eyes were slits, very dark, very dangerous slits. The pain meant nothing, only that he'd caused it and she had no way to pay him back in kind. Yet.

"You prove my point," Kirby said evenly as she brushed her fingers over her cheek. "Second-rate."

He wanted to hit her again, but balled his hands into fists. He needed her, for the moment. "I'm through playing games, Kirby. I want the Rembrandt."

"I'd take a knife to it before I saw Papa hand it over to you. You're out of your class, Stuart." She didn't bother to struggle when he grabbed her arms.

"Two days, Kirby. You tell the old man he has two days or it's you who'll pay."

"Threats and physical abuse are your only weapons." Abruptly, with more effort than she allowed him to see, Kirby turned her anger to ice. "I've weapons of my own, Stuart, infinitely more effective. And if I chose to drop to gutter tactics, you haven't the finesse to deal with me." She kept her eyes on his, her body still. He might curse her, but Stuart knew the truth when he heard it. "You're a snake," she added quietly. "And you can't stay off your belly for long. The fact that you're stronger than I is only a temporary advantage."

"Very temporary," Adam said as he closed the door at his back. His voice matched Kirby's chill for chill. "Take your hands off her."

Kirby felt the painful grip on her arms relax and

watched Stuart struggle with composure. Carefully he straightened his tie. "Remember what I said, Kirby. It could be important to you."

"You remember how Byron described a woman's revenge," she countered as she rubbed the circulation back into her arms. "'Like a tiger's spring—deadly, quick and crushing.'" She dropped her arms to her sides. "It could be important to you." Turning, she walked to the window and stared out at nothing.

Adam kept his hand on the knob as Stuart walked to the door. "Touch her again and you'll have to deal with me." Slowly Adam turned the knob and opened the door. "That's something else for you to remember." The sounds of the party flowed in, then silenced again as he shut the door at Stuart's back.

"Well," he began, struggling with his own fury. "I guess I should be grateful I don't have an ex-fiancée hanging around." He'd heard enough to know that the Rembrandt had been at the bottom of it, but he pushed that aside and went to her. "He's a poor loser, and you're amazing. Most women would have been weeping or pleading. You stood there flinging insults."

"I don't believe in pleading," she said as lightly as she could. "And Stuart would never reduce me to tears."

"But you're trembling," he murmured as he put his hands on her shoulders.

"Anger." She drew in a deep breath and let it out slowly. She didn't care to show a weakness, not to anyone. "I appreciate the white-knight routine."

He grinned and kissed the top of her head. "Any time. Why don't we…" He trailed off as he turned her to face him. The mark of Stuart's hand had faded to a dull, angry red, but it was unmistakable. When Adam touched his fingers to her cheek, his eyes were cold. Colder and more dangerous than she'd ever seen them. Without a word, he spun around and headed for the door.

"No!" Desperation wasn't characteristic, but she felt it now as she grabbed his arm. "No, Adam, don't. Don't get involved." He shook her off, but she sprinted to the door ahead of him and stood with her back pressed against it. The tears she'd been able to control with Stuart now swam in her eyes. "Please, I've enough on my conscience without dragging you into this. I live my life as I choose, and what I get from it is of my own making."

He wanted to brush her aside and push through the crowd outside the door until he had his hands on Stuart. He wanted, more than he'd ever wanted anything, the pleasure of smelling the other man's blood. But she was standing in front of him, small and delicate, with tears in her eyes. She wasn't the kind of woman tears came easily to.

"All right." He brushed one from her cheek and made a promise on it. Before it was over, he would indeed smell Stuart Hiller's blood. "You're only postponing the inevitable."

Relieved, she closed her eyes a moment. When she opened them again, they were still damp, but no longer desperate. "I don't believe in the inevitable." She took his hand and brought it to her cheek, holding it there a moment until she felt the tension drain from both of them. "You must've come in to see my portrait. It's there, above the desk."

She gestured, but he didn't take his eyes from hers.

"I'll have to give it a thorough study, right after I give my attention to the original." He gathered her close and just held her. It was, though neither one of them had known it, the perfect gesture of support. Resting her head against his shoulder, she thought of peace, and she thought of the plans that had already been put into motion.

"I'm sorry, Adam."

He heard the regret in her voice and brushed his lips over her hair. "What for?"

"I can't tell you." She tightened her arms around his waist and clung to him as she had never clung to anyone. "But I am sorry."

The drive away from the Merrick estate was more sedate than the approach. Kirby sat in the passenger seat. Under most circumstances, Adam would've attributed her silence and unease to her scene with Hiller. But he remembered her reaction at the mention of the sale of a Titian.

What was going on in that kaleidoscope brain of hers? he wondered. And how was he going to find out? The direct approach, Adam decided, and thought fleetingly that it was a shame to waste the moonlight. "The Titian that's been sold," he began, pretending he didn't see Kirby jolt. "Has Harriet had it long?"

"The Titian." She folded her hands in her lap. "Oh, years and years. Your Mrs. Birmingham's shaped like a zucchini, don't you think?"

"She's not my Mrs. Birmingham." A new game, he concluded, and relaxed against the seat. "It's too bad it was sold before I could see it. I'm a great admirer of Titian. The painting in my room's exquisite."

Kirby let out a sound that might have been a nervous giggle. "The one at the gallery is just as exquisite," she told him. "Ah, here we are, home again. Just leave the car out front," she said, half relieved, half annoyed, that the next steps were being put into play. "Cards will see to it. I hope you don't mind coming back early, Adam. There's Papa," she added as she stepped from the car. "He must've struck out with Harriet. Let's have a nightcap, shall we?"

She started up the steps without waiting for his agreement. Knowing he was about to become a part of some hastily conceived plan, he went along. It's all too pat, he mused as Fairchild waited at the door with a genial smile.

"Too many people," Fairchild announced. "I much prefer small parties. Let's have a drink in the parlor and gossip."

Don't look so bloody anxious, Kirby thought, and nearly scowled at him. "I'll go tell Cards to see to the Rolls and my car." Still, she hesitated as the men walked toward the parlor. Adam caught the indecision in her eyes before Fairchild cackled and slapped him on the back.

"And don't hurry back," he told Kirby. "I've had enough of women for a while."

"How sweet." The irony and strength came back into her voice. "I'll just go in and eat Tulip's lemon trifle. All," she added as she swept past.

Fairchild thought of his midnight snack with regret. "Brat," he muttered. "Well, we'll have Scotch instead."

Adam dipped his hands casually in his pockets and watched every move Fairchild made. "I had a chance to see Kirby's portrait in Harriet's library. It's marvelous."

"One of my best, if I say so myself." Fairchild lifted the decanter of Chivas Regal. "Harriet's fond of my brat, you know." In a deft move, Fairchild slipped two pills from his pocket and dropped them into the Scotch.

Under normal circumstances Adam would've missed it. Clever hands, he thought as intrigued as he was amused. Very quick, very agile. Apparently they wanted him out of the way. He was going to find it a challenge to pit himself against both of them. With a smile, he accepted the drink, then turned to the Corot landscape behind him.

"Corot's treatment of light," Adam began, taking a small sip. "It gives all of his work such deep perspective."

No ploy could've worked better. Fairchild was ready to roll. "I'm very partial to Corot. He had such a fine hand with details without being finicky and obscuring the overall painting. Now the leaves," he began, and set down his drink to point them out. While the lecture went on, Adam set down his own drink, picked up Fairchild's and enjoyed the Scotch.

Upstairs Kirby found the Titian already wrapped in heavy paper. "Bless you, Cards," she murmured. She checked her watch and made herself wait a full ten minutes before she picked up the painting and left the room. Quietly she moved down the back stairs and out to where her car waited.

In the parlor, Adam studied Fairchild as he sat in the corner of the sofa, snoring. Deciding the least he could do was to make his host more comfortable, Adam started to swing Fairchild's legs onto the couch. The sound of a car engine stopped him. Adam was at the window in time to see Kirby's Porsche race down the drive.

"You're going to have company," he promised her. Within moments, he was behind the wheel of the Rolls.

The surge of speed added to Kirby's sense of adventure. She drove instinctively while she concentrated on her task for the evening. It helped ease the guilt over Adam, a bit.

A quarter mile from the gallery, she stopped and parked on the side of the road. Grateful that the Titian was relatively small, though the frame added weight, she gathered it up again and began to walk. Her heels echoed on the asphalt.

Clouds drifted across the moon, obscuring the light then freeing it again. With her cape swirling around her, Kirby walked into the cover of trees that bordered the gallery. The light was dim, all shadows and secrets. Up ahead came the low moan of an owl. Tossing back her hair, she laughed.

"Perfect," she decided. "All we need is a rumble of thunder and a few streaks of lightning. Skulking through the woods on a desperate mission," she mused. "Surrounded by the sounds of night." She shifted the bundle in her arms and continued on. "What one does for those one loves."

She could see the stately red brick of the gallery through the trees. Moonlight slanted over it. Almost there, she thought with a quick glance at her watch. In an hour she'd be back home—and perhaps she'd have the lemon trifle after all.

A hand fell heavily on her shoulder. Her cape spread out like wings as she whirled. Great buckets of blood, she thought as she stared up at Adam.

"Out for a stroll?" he asked her.

"Why, hello, Adam." Since she couldn't disappear, she had to face him down. She tried a friendly smile. "What are you doing out here?"

"Following you."

"Flattering. But wasn't Papa entertaining you?"

"He dozed off."

She stared up at him a moment, then let out a breath. A wry smile followed it. "I suppose he deserved it. I hope you left him comfortable."

"Enough. Now what's in the package?"

Though she knew it was useless, she fluttered her lashes. "Package?"

He tapped his finger on the wrapping.

"Oh, this package. Just a little errand I have to run. It's getting late, shouldn't you be starting back?"

"Not a chance."

"No." She moved her shoulders. "I thought not."

"What's in the package, Kirby, and what do you intend to do with it?"

"All right." She thrust the painting into his arms because hers were tiring. When the jig was up, you had to make the best of it. "I suppose you deserve an explanation, and you won't leave until you have one anyway. It has to be the condensed version, Adam, I'm running behind schedule." She laid a hand on the package he held. "This is the Titian woman, and I'm going to put it in the gallery."

He lifted a brow. He didn't need Kirby to tell him that he held a painting. "I was under the impression that the Titian woman was in the gallery."

"No..." She drew out the word. If she could have thought of a lie, a half-truth, a fable, she'd have used it. She could only think of the truth. "This is a Titian," she told him with a nod to the package. "The painting in the gallery is a Fairchild."

He let the silence hang a moment while the moonlight filtered over her face. She looked like an angel… or a witch. "Your father forged a Titian and palmed it off on the gallery as an original?"

"Certainly not!" Indignation wasn't feigned. Kirby bit back on it and tried to be patient. "I won't tell you any more if you insult my father."

"I don't know what came over me."

"All right then." She leaned back against a tree. "Perhaps I should start at the beginning."

"Good choice."

"Years ago, Papa and Harriet were vacationing in Europe. They came across the Titian, each one swearing they'd seen it first. Neither one would give way, and it would've been criminal to let the painting go altogether. They compromised." She gestured at the package. "Each paid half, and Papa painted a copy. They rotate ownership of the original every six months, alternating with the copy, if you get the drift. The stipulation was that neither of them could claim ownership. Harriet kept hers in the gallery—not listing it as part of her private collection. Papa kept it in a guest room."

He considered for a moment. "That's too ridiculous for you to have made up."

"Of course I didn't make it up." As it could, effectively, her bottom lip pouted. "Don't you trust me?"

"No. You're going to do a lot more explaining when we get back."

Perhaps, Kirby thought. And perhaps not.

"Now just how do you intend to get into the gallery?"

"With Harriet's keys."

"She gave you her keys?"

Kirby let out a frustrated breath. "Pay attention, Adam. Harriet's furious about Stuart selling the painting, but until she studies the contracts there's no way to know how binding the sale is. It doesn't look good, and we can't take a chance on having the painting tested—my father's painting, that is. If the procedure were sophisticated enough, it might prove that the painting's not sixteenth-century."

"Harriet's aware that a forgery's hanging in her gallery?"

"An emulation, Adam."

"And are there any other…emulations in the Merrick Gallery?"

She gave him a long, cool look. "I'm trying not to be annoyed. All of Harriet's paintings are authentic, as is her half of the Titian."

"Why didn't she replace it herself?"

"Because," Kirby began and checked her watch. Time was slipping away from her. "Not only would it have been difficult for her to disappear from the party early as we did, but it would've been awkward altogether. The night watchman could report to Stuart that she came to the gallery in the middle of the night carrying a package. He might put two and two together. Yes, even he might add it up."

"So what'll the night watchman have to say about Kirby Fairchild coming into the gallery in the middle of the night?"

"He won't see us." Her smile was quick and very, very smug.

"Us?"

"Since you're here." She smiled at him again, and meant it. "I've told you everything, and being a gentleman you'll help me make the switch. We'll have to work quickly. If we're caught, we'll just brazen it out. You won't have to do anything, I'll handle it."

"You'll handle it." He nodded at the drifting clouds. "We can all sleep easy now. One condition." He stopped her before she could speak. "When we're done, if we're not in jail or hospitalized, I want to know it all. If we are in jail, I'll murder you as slowly as possible."

"That's two conditions," she muttered. "But all right."

They watched each other a moment, one wondering how much would have to be divulged, one wondering how much could be learned. Both found the deceit unpleasant.

"Let's get it done." Adam gestured for her to go first.

Kirby walked across the grass and went directly to the main door. From the deep pocket of her cloak, she drew out keys.

"These two switch off the main alarm," she explained as she turned keys in a series of locks. "And these unbolt the door." She smiled at the faint click of tumblers. Turning, she studied Adam, standing behind her in his elegant dinner suit. "I'm so glad we dressed for it."

"Seems right to dress formally when you're breaking into a distinguished institution."

"True." Kirby dropped the keys back in her pocket. "And we do make a rather stunning couple. The Titian hangs in the west room on the second floor. The watchman has a little room in the back, here on the main floor. I assume he drinks black coffee laced with rum and reads pornographic magazines. I would. He's supposed to make rounds hourly, though there's no way to be certain he's diligent."

"And what time does he make them, if he does?"

"On the hour—which gives us twenty minutes." She glanced at her watch and shrugged. "That's adequate, though if you hadn't pressed me for details we'd've had more time. Don't scowl," she added. She pressed her finger to her lips and slipped through the door.

From out of the depths of her pocket came a flashlight. They followed the narrow beam over the carpet. Together they moved up the staircase.

Obviously she knew the gallery well. Without hesitation, she moved through the dark, turning on the second floor and marching down the corridor without breaking rhythm. Her cape swirled out as she pivoted into a room. In silence she played her light over paintings until it stopped on the copy of the Titian that had hung in Adam's room.

"There," Kirby whispered as the light shone on the sunset hair Titian had immortalized. The light was too poor for Adam to be certain of the quality, but he promised himself he'd examine it minutes later.

"It's not possible to tell them apart—not even an expert." She knew what he was thinking. "Harriet's a respected authority, and she couldn't. I'm not sure the tests wouldn't bear it out as authentic. Papa has a way of treating the paints." She moved closer so that her light illuminated the entire painting. "Papa put a red circle on the back of the copy's frame so they could be told apart. I'll take the package now," she told him briskly. "You can get the painting down." She knelt and began to unwrap the painting they'd brought with them. "I'm glad you happened along," she decided. "Your height's going to be an advantage when it comes to taking down and putting up again."

Adam paused with the forgery in his hands. Throttling her would be too noisy at the moment, he decided. But later… "Let's have it then."

In silence they exchanged paintings. Adam replaced his on the wall, while Kirby wrapped the other. After she'd tied the string, she played the light on the wall again. "It's a bit crooked," she decided. "A little to the left."

"Look, I—" Adam broke off at the sound of a faint, tuneless whistle.

"He's early!" Kirby whispered as she gripped the painting. "Who expects efficiency from hired help these days?"

In a quick move, Adam had the woman, the painting and himself pressed against the wall by the archway. Finding herself neatly sandwiched, and partially smothered, Kirby held back a desperate urge to giggle. Certain it would annoy Adam, she held her breath and swallowed.

The whistle grew louder.

In her mind's eye, Kirby pictured the watchman strolling down the corridor, pausing to shine his light here and there as he walked. She hoped, for the watchman's peace of mind and Adam's disposition, the search was cursory.

Adam felt her trembling and held her tighter. Somehow he'd manage to protect her. He forgot that she'd gotten him into the mess in the first place. Now his only thought was to get her out of it.

A beam of light streamed past the doorway, with the whistle close behind. Kirby shook like a leaf. The light bounced into the room, sweeping over the walls in a curving arch. Adam tensed, knowing discovery was inches away. The light halted, rested a moment, then streaked away over its original route. And there was darkness.

They didn't move, though Kirby wanted to badly, with the frame digging into her back. They waited, still and silent, until the whistling receded.

Because her light trembling had become shudder after shudder, Adam drew her away to whisper reassurance. "It's all right. He's gone."

"You were wonderful." She covered her mouth to muffle the laughter. "Ever thought about making breaking and entering a hobby?"

He slid the painting under one arm, then took a firm grip on hers. When the time was right, he'd pay her back for this one. "Let's go."

"Okay, since it's probably a bad time to show you around. Pity," she decided. "There are some excellent engravings in the next room, and a really marvelous still life Papa painted."

"Under his own name?"

"Really, Adam." They paused at the hallway to make certain it was clear. "That's tacky."

They didn't speak again until they were hidden by the trees. Then Adam turned to her. "I'll take the painting and follow you back. If you go over fifty, I'll murder you."

She stopped when they reached the cars, then threw

him off balance with suddenly serious eyes. "I appreciate everything, Adam. I hope you don't think too badly of us. It matters."

He ran a finger down her cheek. "I've yet to decide what I think of you."

Her lips curved up at the corners. "That's all right then. Take your time."

"Get in and drive," he ordered before he could forget what had to be resolved. She had a way of making a man forget a lot of things. Too many things.

The trip back took nearly twice the time, as Kirby stayed well below the speed limit. Again she left the Porsche out front, knowing Cards would handle the details. Once inside, she went straight to the parlor.

"Well," she mused as she looked at her father. "He seems comfortable enough, but I think I'll just stretch him out."

Adam leaned against the doorjamb and waited as she settled her father for the night. After loosening his tie and pulling off his shoes, she tossed her cape over him and kissed his balding head. "Papa," she murmured. "You've been outmaneuvered."

"We'll talk upstairs, Kirby. Now."

Straightening, Kirby gave Adam a long, mild look. "Since you ask so nicely." She plucked a decanter of brandy and two glasses from the bar. "We may as well be sociable during the inquisition." She swept by him and up the stairs.

Chapter 8

Kirby switched on the rose-tinted bedside lamp before she poured brandy. After handing Adam a snifter, she kicked off her shoes and sat cross-legged on the bed. She watched as he ripped off the wrapping and examined the painting.

Frowning, he studied the brush strokes, the use of color, the Venetian technique that had been Titian's. Fascinating, he thought. Absolutely fascinating. "This is a copy?"

She had to smile. She warmed the brandy between her hands but didn't drink. "Papa's mark's on the frame."

Adam saw the red circle but didn't find it conclusive. "I'd swear it was authentic."

"So would anyone."

He propped the painting against the wall and turned to her. She looked like an Indian priestess—the nightfall of hair against the virgin white silk. With an enigmatic smile, she continued to sit in the lotus position, the brandy cupped in both hands.

"How many other paintings in your father's collection are copies?"

Slowly she lifted the snifter and sipped. She had to work at not being annoyed by the question, telling herself he was entitled to ask. "All of the paintings in Papa's collection are authentic. Excepting now this Titian." She moved her shoulders carelessly. It hardly mattered at this point.

"When you spoke of his technique in treating paints for age, you didn't give the impression he'd only used it on one painting."

What had given her the idea he wouldn't catch on to a chance remark like that one? she wondered. The fat's in the fire in any case, she reminded herself. And she was tired of trying to dance around it. She swirled her drink and red and amber lights glinted against the glass.

"I trust you," she murmured, surprising them both. "But I don't want to involve you, Adam, in something you'll regret knowing about. I really want you to understand that. Once I tell you, it'll be too late for regrets."

He didn't care for the surge of guilt. Who was deceiving whom now? his conscience demanded of him. And who'd pay the price in the end? "Let me worry about that," he stated, dealing with Kirby now and saving his conscience for later. He swallowed brandy and let the heat ease through him. "How many copies has your father done?"

"Ten—no, eleven," she corrected, and ignored his

quick oath. "Eleven, not counting the Titian, which falls into a different category."

"A different category," he murmured. Crossing the room, he splashed more brandy into his glass. He was certain to need it. "How is this different?"

"The Titian was a personal agreement between Harriet and Papa. Merely a way to avoid bad feelings."

"And the others?" He sat on a fussily elegant Queen Anne chair. "What sort of arrangements did they entail?"

"Each is individual, naturally." She hesitated as she studied him. If they'd met a month from now, would things have been different? Perhaps. Timing again, she mused and sipped the warming brandy. "To simplify matters, Papa painted them, then sold them to interested parties."

"Sold them?" He stood because he couldn't be still. Wishing it had been possible to stop her before she'd begun, he started to pace the room. "Good God, Kirby. Don't you understand what he's done? What he's doing? It's fraud, plain and simple."

"I wouldn't call it fraud," she countered, giving her brandy a contemplative study. It was, after all, something she'd given a great deal of thought to. "And certainly not plain or simple."

"What then?" If he'd had a choice, he'd have taken her away then and there—left the Titian, the Rembrandt and her crazy father in the ridiculous castle and taken off. Somewhere. Anywhere.

"Fudging," Kirby decided with a half smile.

"Fudging," he repeated in a quiet voice. He'd forgotten she was mad as well. "Fudging. Selling counterfeit paintings for large sums of money to the unsuspecting is fudging? Fixing a parking ticket's fudging." He paced another moment, looking for answers. "Damn it, his work's worth a fortune. Why does he do it?"

"Because he can," she said simply. She spread one hand, palm out. "Papa's a genius, Adam. I don't say that just as his daughter, but as a fellow artist. With the genius comes a bit of eccentricity, perhaps." Ignoring the sharp sound of derision, she went on. "To Papa, painting's not just a vocation. Art and life are one, interchangeable."

"I'll go along with all that, Kirby, but it doesn't explain why—"

"Let me finish." She had both hands on the snifter again, resting it in her lap. "One thing Papa can't tolerate is greed, in any form. To him greed isn't just the worship of money, but the hoarding of art. You must know his collection's constantly being lent out to museums and art schools. Though he has strong feelings that art belongs in the private sector, as well as public institutions, he hates the idea of the wealthy buying up great art for investment purposes."

"Admirable, Kirby. But he's made a business out of selling fraudulent paintings."

"Not a business. He's never benefited financially." She set her glass aside and clasped her hands together. "Each prospective buyer of one of Papa's emulations is first researched thoroughly." She waited a beat. "By Harriet."

He nearly sat back down again. "Harriet Merrick's in on all of this?"

"All of this," she said mildly, "has been their joint hobby for the last fifteen years."

"Hobby," he murmured and did sit.

"Harriet has very good connections, you see. She makes certain the buyer is very wealthy and that he or she lives in a remote location. Two years ago, Papa sold an Arabian sheik a fabulous Renoir. It was one of my favorites. Anyway—" she continued, getting up to freshen Adam's drink, then her own "—each buyer would also be known for his or her attachment to money, and/or a complete lack of any sense of community spirit or obligation. Through Harriet, they'd learn of Papa's ownership of a rare, officially undiscovered artwork."

Taking her own snifter, she returned to her position on the bed while Adam remained silent. "At the first contact, Papa is always uncooperative without being completely dismissive. Gradually he allows himself to be worn down until the deal's made. The price, naturally, is exorbitant, otherwise the art fanciers would be insulted." She took a small sip and enjoyed the warm flow of the brandy. "He deals only in cash, so there's no record. Then the paintings float off to the Himalayas or Siberia or somewhere to be kept in seclusion. Papa then donates the money anonymously to charity."

Taking a deep breath at the end of her speech, Kirby rewarded herself with more brandy.

"You're telling me that he goes through all that, all the work, all the intrigue, for nothing?"

"I certainly am not." Kirby shook her head and leaned forward. "He gets a great deal. He gets satisfaction, Adam. What else is necessary after all?"

He struggled to remember the code of right and wrong. "Kirby, he's stealing!"

Kirby tilted her head and considered. "Who caught

your support and admiration, Adam? The Sheriff of Nottingham or Robin Hood?"

"It's not the same." He dragged a hand through his hair as he tried to convince them both. "Damn it, Kirby, it's not the same."

"There's a newly modernized pediatric wing at the local hospital," she began quietly. "A little town in Appalachia has a new fire engine and modern equipment. Another, in the dust bowl, has a wonderful new library."

"All right." He rose again to cut her off. "In fifteen years I'm sure there's quite a list. Maybe in some strange way it's commendable, but it's also illegal, Kirby. It has to stop."

"I know." Her simple agreement broke his rhythm. With a half smile, Kirby moved her shoulders. "It was fun while it lasted, but I've known for some time it had to stop before something went wrong. Papa has a project in mind for a series of paintings, and I've convinced him to begin soon. It should take him about five years and give us a breathing space. But in the meantime, he's done something I don't know how to cope with."

She was about to give him more. Even before she spoke, Adam knew Kirby was going to give him all her trust. He sat in silence, despising himself, as she told him everything she knew about the Rembrandt.

"I imagine part of it's revenge on Stuart," she continued, while Adam smoked in silence and she again swirled her brandy without drinking. "Somehow Stuart found out about Papa's hobby and threatened exposure the night I broke our engagement. Papa told me not to worry, that Stuart wasn't in a position to make waves. At the time I had no idea about the Rembrandt business."

She was opening up to him, no questions, no hesitation. He was going to probe, God help him, he hadn't a choice. "Do you have any idea where he might've hidden it?"

"No, but I haven't looked." When she looked at him, she wasn't the sultry gypsy or the exotic princess. She was only a daughter concerned about an adored father. "He's a good man, Adam. No one knows that better than I. I know there's a reason for what he's done, and for the time being, I have to accept that. I don't expect you to share my loyalty, just my confidence." He didn't speak, and she took his silence for agreement. "My main concern now is that Papa's underestimating Stuart's ruthlessness."

"He won't when you tell him about the scene in the library."

"I'm not going to tell him. Because," she continued before Adam could argue, "I have no way of predicting his reaction. You may have noticed, Papa's a very volatile man." Tilting her glass, she met his gaze with a quick change of mood. "I don't want you to worry about all this, Adam. Talk to Papa about it if you like. Have a chat with Harriet, too. Personally, I find it helpful to tuck the whole business away from time to time and let it hibernate. Like a grizzly bear."

"Grizzly bear."

She laughed and rose. "Let me get you some more brandy."

He stopped her with a hand on her wrist. "Have you told me everything?"

With a frown, she brushed at a speck of lint on the bedspread. "Did I mention the Van Gogh?"

"Oh, God." He pressed his fingers to his eyes. Somehow he'd hoped there'd be an end without really believing it. "What Van Gogh?"

Kirby pursed her lips. "Not exactly a Van Gogh."

"Your father?"

"His latest. He's sold it to Victor Alvarez, a coffee baron in South America." She smiled as Adam said nothing and stared straight ahead. "The working conditions on his farm are deplorable. Of course, there's nothing we can do to remedy that, but Papa's already allocated the purchase price for a school somewhere in the area. It's his last for several years, Adam," she added as he sat with his fingers pressed against his eyes. "And really, I think he'll be pleased that you know all about everything. He'd love to show this painting to you. He's particularly pleased with it."

Adam rubbed his hands over his face. It didn't surprise him to hear himself laughing. "I suppose I should be grateful he hasn't decided to do the ceiling in the Sistine Chapel."

"Only after he retires," Kirby put in cheerfully. "And that's years off yet."

Not certain whether she was joking or not, he let it pass. "I've got to give all this a little time to settle."

"Fair enough."

He wasn't going back to his room to report to McIntyre, he decided as he set his brandy aside. He wasn't ready for that yet, so soon after Kirby shared it all with him without questions, without limitations. It wasn't possible to think about his job, or remember outside obligations, when she looked at him with all her trust. No, he'd find a way, somehow, to justify what he chose to do in the end. Right and wrong weren't so well defined now.

Looking at her, he needed to give, to soothe, to show her she'd been right to give him that most precious of gifts—unqualified trust. Perhaps he didn't deserve it, but he needed it. He needed her.

Without a word, he pulled her into his arms and crushed his mouth to hers, no patience, no requests. Before either of them could think, he drew down the zipper at the back of her dress.

She wanted to give to him—anything, everything he wanted. She didn't want to question him but to forget all the reasons why they shouldn't be together. It would be so easy to drown in the flood of feeling that was so new and so unique. And yet, anything real, anything strong, was never easy. She'd been taught from an early age that the things that mattered most were the hardest to obtain. Drawing back, she determined to put things back on a level she could deal with.

"You surprise me," she said with a smile she had to work at.

He pulled her back. She wouldn't slip away from him this time. "Good."

"You know, most women expect a seduction, no matter how perfunctory."

The amusement might be in her eyes, but he could feel the thunder of her heart against his. "Most women aren't Kirby Fairchild." If she wanted to play it lightly, he'd do his damnedest to oblige her—as long as the result was the same. "Why don't we call this my next spontaneous act?" he suggested, and slipped her dress down her shoulders. "I wouldn't want to bore you with a conventional pursuit."

How could she resist him? The hands light on her skin, the mouth that smiled and tempted? She'd never hesitated about taking what she wanted...until now. Perhaps the time had come for the chess game to stop at a stalemate, with neither winning all and neither losing anything.

Slowly she smiled and let her dress whisper almost soundlessly to the floor.

He found her a treasure of cool satin and warm flesh. She was as seductive, as alluring, as he'd known she'd be. Once she'd decided to give, there were no restrictions. In a simple gesture she opened her arms to him and they came together.

Soft sighs, low murmurs, skin against skin. Moonlight and the rose tint from the lamp competed, then merged, as the mattress yielded under their weight. Her mouth was hot and open, her arms were strong. As she moved under him, inviting, taunting, he forgot how small she was.

Everything. All. Now. Needs drove them both to take without patience, and yet... Somehow, beneath the passion, under the heat, was a tenderness neither had expected from the other.

He touched. She trembled. She tasted. He throbbed. They wanted until the air seemed to spark with it. With each second both of them found more of what they'd needed, but the findings brought more greed. Take, she seemed to say, then give and give and give.

She had no time to float, only to throb. For him. From him. Her body craved—*yearn* was too soft a word. She required him, something unique for her. And he, with a kiss, with a touch of his hand, could raise her up to planes she'd only dreamed existed. Here was the completion, here was the delight, she'd hoped for without truly believing in. This was what she'd wanted so desperately in her life but had never found. Here and now. Him. There was and needed to be nothing else.

He edged toward madness. She held him, hard and tight, as they swung toward the edge together. Together was all she could think. Together.

Quiet. It was so quiet there might never have been such a thing as sound. Her hair brushed against his cheek. Her hand, balled into a loose fist, lay over his heart. Adam lay in the silence and hurt as he'd never expected to hurt.

How had he let it happen? Control? What had made him think he had control when it came to Kirby? Somehow she'd wrapped herself around him, body and mind, while he'd been pretending he'd known exactly what he'd been doing.

He'd come to do a job, he reminded himself. He still had to do it, no matter what had passed between them. Could he go on with what he'd come to do, and protect her? Was it possible to split himself in two when his road had always been so straight? He wasn't certain of anything now, but the tug-of-war he'd lose whichever way the game ended. He had to think, create the distance he needed to do so. Better for both of them if he started now.

But when he shifted away, she held him tighter. Kirby lifted her head so that moonlight caught in her eyes and mesmerized him. "Don't go," she murmured. "Stay and sleep with me. I don't want it to end yet."

He couldn't resist her now. Perhaps he never would.

Saying nothing, Adam drew her close again and closed his eyes. For a little while he could pretend tomorrow would take care of itself.

Sunlight woke her, but Kirby tried to ignore it by piling pillows on top of her head. It didn't work for long. Resigned, she tossed them on the floor and lay quietly, alone.

She hadn't heard Adam leave, nor had she expected him to stay until morning. As it was, she was grateful to have woken alone. Now she could think.

How was it she'd given her complete trust to a man she hardly knew? No answer. Why hadn't she evaded his questions, skirted her way around certain facts as she was well capable of doing? No answer.

It wasn't true. Kirby closed her eyes a moment, knowing she'd been more honest with Adam than she was being with herself. She knew the answer.

She'd given him more than she'd ever given to any man. It had been more than a physical alliance, more than a few hours of pleasure in the night. The essence of self had been shared with him. There was no taking it back now, even if both of them would have preferred it.

Unknowingly, he'd taken her innocence. Emotional virginity was just as real, just as vital, as the physical. And it was just as impossible to reclaim. She, thinking of the night, knew that she had no desire to go back. Now they would both move forward to whatever waited for them.

Rising, she prepared to face the day.

Upstairs in Fairchild's studio, Adam studied the rural landscape. He could feel the agitation and drama.

The serene scene leaped with frantic life. Vivid, real, disturbing. Its creator stood beside him, not the Vincent van Gogh who Adam would've sworn had wielded the brush and pallette, but Philip Fairchild.

"It's magnificent," Adam murmured. The compliment was out before he could stop it.

"Thank you, Adam. I'm fond of it." Fairchild spoke as a man who'd long before accepted his own superiority and the responsibility that came with it.

"Mr. Fairchild—"

"Philip," Fairchild interrupted genially. "No reason for formality between us."

Somehow Adam felt even the casual intimacy could complicate an already hopelessly tangled situation. "Philip," he began again, "this is fraud. Your motives might be sterling, but the result remains fraud."

"Absolutely." Fairchild bobbed his head in agreement. "Fraud, misrepresentation, a bald-faced lie without a doubt." He lifted his arms and let them fall. "I'm stripped of defenses."

Like hell, Adam thought grimly. Unless he was very much mistaken, he was about to be treated to the biggest bag of pure, classic bull on record.

"Adam…" Fairchild drew out the name and steepled his hands. "You're an astute man, a rational man. I pride myself on being a good judge of character." As if he were very old and frail, Fairchild lowered himself into a chair. "Then, again, you're imaginative and open-minded—that shows in your work."

Adam reached for the coffee Cards had brought up. "So?"

"Your help with our little problem last night—and

your skill in turning my own plot against me—leads me to believe you have the ability to adapt to what some might term the unusual."

"Some might."

"Now." Accepting the cup Adam handed him, Fairchild leaned back. "You tell me Kirby filled you in on everything. Odd, but we'll leave that for now." He'd already drawn his own conclusions there and found them to his liking. He wasn't about to lose on other points. "After what you've been told, can you find one iota of selfishness in my enterprise? Can you see my motive as anything but humanitarian?" On a roll, Fairchild set down his cup and let his hands fall between his bony knees. "Small, sick children, and those less fortunate than ourselves, have benefited from my hobby. Not one dollar have I kept, not a dollar, a franc, a sou. Never, never have I asked for credit or honor that, naturally, society would be anxious to bestow on me."

"You haven't asked for the jail sentence they'd bestow on you, either."

Fairchild tilted his head in acknowledgment but didn't miss a beat. "It's my gift to mankind, Adam. My payment for the talent awarded to me by a higher power. These hands…" He held them up, narrow, gaunt and oddly beautiful. "These hands hold a skill I'm obliged to pay for in my own way. This I've done." Bowing his head, Fairchild dropped them into his lap. "However, if you must condemn me, I understand."

Fairchild looked, Adam mused, like a stalwart Christian faced by pagan lions: firm in his belief, resigned to his fate. "One day," Adam murmured, "your halo's going to slip and strangle you."

"A possibility." Grinning, he lifted his head again. "But in the meantime, we enjoy what we can. Let's have one of those Danishes, my boy."

Wordlessly, Adam handed him the tray. "Have you considered the repercussions to Kirby if your...hobby is discovered?"

"Ah." Fairchild swallowed pastry. "A straight shot to my Achilles' heel. Naturally both of us know that Kirby can meet any obstacle and find a way over, around or through it." He bit off more Danish, enjoying the tang of raspberry. "Still, merely by being, Kirby demands emotion of one kind or another. You'd agree?"

Adam thought of the night, and what it had changed in him. "Yes."

The brief, concise answer was exactly what Fairchild had expected. "I'm taking a hiatus from this business for various reasons, the first of which is Kirby's position."

"And her position as concerns the Merrick Rembrandt?"

"A different kettle of fish." Fairchild dusted his fingers on a napkin and considered another pastry. "I'd like to share the ins and outs of that business with you, Adam, but I'm not free to just yet." He smiled and gazed over Adam's head. "One could say I've involved Kirby figuratively, but until things are resolved, she's a minor player in the game."

"Are you casting as well as directing this performance, Papa?" Kirby walked into the room and picked up the Danish Fairchild had been eyeing. "Did you sleep well, darling?"

"Like a rock, brat," he muttered, remembering the

confusion of waking up on the sofa under her cape. He didn't care to be outwitted, but was a man who acknowledged a quick mind. "I'm told your evening activities went well."

"The deed's done." She glanced at Adam before resting her hands on her father's shoulders. The bond was there, unbreakable. "Maybe I should leave the two of you alone for a while. Adam has a way of digging out information. You might tell him what you won't tell me."

"All in good time." He patted her hands. "I'm devoting the morning to my hawk." Rising, he went to uncover his clay, an obvious dismissal. "You might give Harriet a call and tell her all's well before you two amuse yourselves."

Kirby held out her hand. "Have you any amusements in mind, Adam?"

"As a matter of fact…" He went with the impulse and kissed her as her father watched and speculated. "I had a session of oils and canvas in mind. You'll have to change."

"If that's the best you can do. Two hours only," she warned as they walked from the room. "Otherwise my rates go up. I have my own work, you know."

"Three."

"Two and a half." She paused at the second-floor landing.

"You looked like a child this morning," he murmured, and touched her cheek. "I couldn't bring myself to wake you." He left his hand there only a moment, then moved away. "I'll meet you upstairs."

Kirby went to her room and tossed the red dress on

the bed. While she undressed with one hand, she dialed the phone with the other.

"Harriet, it's Kirby to set your mind at rest."

"Clever child. Was there any trouble?"

"No." She wiggled out of her jeans. "We managed."

"We? Did Philip go with you?"

"Papa was snoozing on the couch after Adam switched drinks."

"Oh, dear." Amused, Harriet settled back. "Was he very angry?"

"Papa or Adam?" Kirby countered, then shrugged. "No matter, in the end they were both very reasonable. Adam was a great help."

"The test isn't for a half hour. Give me the details."

Struggling in and out of clothes, Kirby told her everything.

"Marvelous!" Pleased with the drama, Harriet beamed at the phone. "I wish I'd done it. I'll have to get to know your Adam better and find some spectacular way of showing him my gratitude. Do you think he'd like the crocodile teeth?"

"Nothing would please him more."

"Kirby, you know how grateful I am to you." Harriet's voice was abruptly serious and maternal. "The situation's awkward to say the least."

"The contract's binding?"

"Yes." She let out a sigh at the thought of losing the Titian. "My fault. I should've explained to Stuart that the painting wasn't to be sold. Philip must be furious with me."

"You can handle him. You always do."

"Yes, yes. Lord knows what I'd do without you, though. Poor Melly just can't understand me as you do."

"She's just made differently." Kirby stared down at the floor and tried not to think about the Rembrandt and the guilt it brought her. "Come to dinner tonight, Harriet, you and Melanie."

"Oh, I'd love to, darling, but I've a meeting. To-morrow?"

"Fine. Shall I call Melly, or will you speak with her?"

"I'll see her this afternoon. Take care and do thank Adam for me. Damn shame I'm too old to give him anything but crocodile teeth."

With a laugh, Kirby hung up.

The sun swept over her dress, shooting it with flames or darkening it to blood. It glinted from the rings at her ears, the bracelets on her arms. Knowing the light was as perfect as it would ever be, Adam worked feverishly.

He was an artist of subtle details, one who used light and shadow for mood. In his portraits he strove for an inner reality, the truth beneath the surface of the model. In Kirby he saw the essence of woman—power and frailty and that elusive, mystical quality of sex. Aloof, alluring. She was both. Now, more than ever, he understood it.

Hours passed without him giving them a thought. His model, however, had a different frame of mind.

"Adam, if you'll consult your watch, you'll see I've given you more than the allotted time already."

He ignored her and continued to paint.

"I can't stand here another moment." She let her arms drop from their posed position, then wiggled them from the shoulders down. "As it is, I'll probably never pole-vault again."

"I can work on the background awhile," he muttered. "I need another three hours in the morning. The light's best then."

Kirby bit off a retort. Rudeness was something to be expected when an artist was taken over by his art. Stretching her muscles, she went to look over his shoulder.

"You've a good hand with light," she decided as she studied the emerging painting. "It's very flattering, certainly, rather fiery and defiant with the colors you've chosen." She looked carefully at the vague lines of her face, the tints and hues he was using to create her on canvas. "Still, there's a fragility here I don't quite understand."

"Maybe I know you better than you know yourself." He never looked at her, but continued to paint. In not looking, he didn't see the stunned expression or the gradual acceptance.

Linking her hands together, Kirby wandered away. She'd have to do it quickly, she decided. It needed to be done, to be said. "Adam…"

An inarticulate mutter. His back remained to her.

Kirby took a deep breath. "I love you."

"Umm-hmm."

Some women might've been crushed. Others would've been furious. Kirby laughed and tossed back her hair. Life was never what you expected. "Adam, I'd like just a moment of your attention." Though she continued to smile, her knuckles turned white. "I'm in love with you."

It got through on the second try. His brush, tipped in coral, stopped in midair. Very slowly, he set it down and turned. She was looking at him, the half smile on her face, her hands linked together so tightly they hurt. She hadn't expected a response, nor would she demand one.

"I don't tell you that to put pressure on you, or to embarrass you." Nerves showed only briefly as she moistened her lips. "It's just that I think you have a right to know." Her words began to spill out quickly. "We haven't known each other for long, I know, but I suppose it just happens this way sometimes. I couldn't do anything about it. I don't expect anything from you, permanently or temporarily." When he still didn't speak, she felt a jolt of panic she didn't know how to deal with. Had she ruined it? Now the smile didn't reach her eyes. "I've got to change," she said lightly. "You've made me miss lunch as it is."

She was nearly to the door before he stopped her. As he took her shoulders, he felt her tense. And as he felt it, he understood she'd given him everything that was in her heart. Something he knew instinctively had never been given to any other man.

"Kirby, you're the most exceptional woman I've ever known."

"Yes, someone's always pointing that out." She had to get through the door and quickly. "Are you coming down, or shall I have a tray sent up?"

He lowered his head to the top of hers and wondered how things had happened so quickly, so finally. "How many people could make such a simple and unselfish declaration of love, then walk away without asking for anything? From the beginning you haven't done one thing I'd've expected." He brushed his lips over her hair, lightly, so that she hardly felt it. "Don't I get a chance to say anything?"

"It's not necessary."

"Yes, it is." Turning her, he framed her face with his hands. "And I'd rather have my hands on you when I tell you I love you."

She stood very straight and spoke very calmly. "Don't feel sorry for me, Adam. I couldn't bear it."

He started to say all the sweet, romantic things a woman wanted to hear when love was declared. All the traditional, normal words a man offered when he offered himself. They weren't for Kirby. Instead he lifted a brow. "If you hadn't counted on being loved back, you'll have to adjust."

She waited a moment because she had to be certain. She'd take the risk, take any risk, if she was certain. As she looked into his eyes, she began to smile. The tension in her shoulders vanished. "You've brought it on yourself."

"Yeah. I guess I have to live with it."

The smile faded as she pressed against him. "Oh, God, Adam, I need you. You've no idea how much."

He held her just as tightly, just as desperately. "Yes, I do."

Chapter 9

To love and to be loved in return. It was bewildering to Kirby, frightening, exhilarating. She wanted time to experience it, absorb it. Understanding it didn't matter, not now, in the first rush of emotion. She only knew that although she'd always been happy in her life, she was being offered more. She was being offered laughter at midnight, soft words at dawn, a hand to hold and a life to share. The price would be a portion of her independence and the loyalty that had belonged only to her father.

To Kirby, love meant sharing, and sharing had no restrictions. Whatever she had, whatever she felt, belonged to Adam as much as to herself. Whatever happened between them now, she'd never be able to change that. No longer able to work, she went down from her studio to find him.

The house was quiet in the early-evening lull with the staff downstairs making the dinner preparations and gossiping. Kirby had always liked this time of day—after a long, productive session in her studio, before the evening meal. These were the hours to sit in front of a roaring fire, or walk along the cliffs. Now there was someone she needed to share those hours with. Stopping in front of Adam's door, she raised a hand to knock.

The murmur of voices stopped her. If Adam had her father in another discussion, he might learn something more about the Rembrandt that would put her mind at ease. While she hesitated, the thumping of the front door knocker vibrated throughout the house. With a shrug, she turned away to answer.

Inside his room, Adam shifted the transmitter to his other hand. "This is the first chance I've had to call in. Besides, there's nothing new."

"You're supposed to check in every night." Annoyed, McIntyre barked into the receiver. "Damn it, Adam, I was beginning to think something had happened to you."

"If you knew these people, you'd realize how ridiculous that is."

"They don't suspect anything?"

"No." Adam swore at the existence of this job.

"Tell me about Mrs. Merrick and Hiller."

"Harriet's charming and flamboyant." He wouldn't say harmless. Though he thought of what he and Kirby had done the night before, he left it alone. Adam had already rationalized the entire business as having nothing to do with his job. Not specifically. That was enough to justify his keeping it from McIntyre. Instead, Adam would tell him what Adam felt applied and nothing more. "Hiller's very smooth and a complete phony. I walked in on him and Kirby in time to keep him from shoving her around."

"What was his reason?"

"The Rembrandt. He doesn't believe her father's keeping her in the dark about it. He's the kind of man who thinks you can always get what you want by knocking the other person around—if they're smaller."

"Sounds like a gem." But he'd heard the change in tone. If Adam was getting involved with the Fairchild woman... No. McIntyre let it go. That they didn't need. "I've got a line on Victor Alvarez."

"Drop it." Adam kept his voice casual, knowing full well just how perceptive Mac could be. "It's a wild-goose chase. I've already dug it up and it doesn't have anything to do with the Rembrandt."

"You know best."

"Yeah." McIntyre, he knew, would never understand Fairchild's hobby. "Since we agree about that, I've got a stipulation."

"Stipulation?"

"When I find the Rembrandt, I handle the rest my own way."

"What do you mean your own way? Listen, Adam—"

"My way," Adam cut him off. "Or you find someone else. I'll get it back for you, Mac, but after I do, the Fairchilds are kept out of it."

"Kept out?" McIntyre exploded so that the receiver crackled with static. "How the hell do you expect me to keep them out?"

"That's your problem. Just do it."

"The place is full of crazies," McIntyre muttered. "Must be contagious."

"Yeah. I'll get back to you." With a grin, Adam switched off the transmitter.

Downstairs, Kirby opened the door and looked into the myopic, dark-framed eyes of Rick Potts. Knowing his hand would be damp with nerves, she held hers out. "Hello, Rick. Papa told me you were coming to visit."

"Kirby." He swallowed and squeezed her hand. Just the sight of her played havoc with his glands. "You look mar-marvelous." He thrust drooping carnations into her face.

"Thank you." Kirby took the flowers Rick had partially strangled and smiled. "Come, let me fix you a drink. You've had a long drive, haven't you? Cards, see to Mr. Potts's luggage, please," she continued without giving Rick a chance to speak. He'd need a little time, she knew, to draw words together. "Papa should be down soon." She found a club soda and poured it over ice. "He's been giving a lot of time to his new project; I'm sure he'll want to discuss it with you." After handing him his drink, she gestured to a chair. "So, how've you been?"

He drank first, to separate his tongue from the roof of his mouth. "Fine. That is, I had a bit of a cold last week, but I'm much better now. I'd never come to see you if I had any germs."

She turned in time to hide a grin and poured herself a glass of Perrier. "That's very considerate of you, Rick."

"Have you—have you been working?"

"Yes, I've nearly done enough for my spring show-ing."

"It'll be wonderful," he told her with blind loyalty. Though he recognized the quality of her work, the more powerful pieces intimidated him. "You'll be stay-ing in New York?"

"Yes." She walked over to sit beside him. "For a week."

"Then maybe—that is, I'd love to, if you had the time, of course, I'd like to take you to dinner." He gulped down club soda. "If you had an evening free."

"That's very sweet of you."

Astonished, he gaped, pupils dilating. From the doorway, Adam watched the puppylike adulation of the lanky, somewhat untidy man. In another ten sec-onds, Adam estimated, Kirby would have him at her feet whether she wanted him there or not.

Kirby glanced up, and her expression changed so subtly Adam wouldn't have noticed if he hadn't been so completely tuned in to her. "Adam." If there'd been relief in her eyes, her voice was casual. "I was hoping you'd come down. Rick, this is Adam Haines. Adam, I think Papa mentioned Rick Potts to you the other day."

The message came across loud and clear. Be kind. With an easy smile, Adam accepted the damp hand-shake. "Yes, Philip said you were coming for a few days. Kirby tells me you work in watercolors."

"She did?" Nearly undone by the fact that Kirby would speak of him at all, Rick simply stood there a moment.

"We'll have to have a long discussion after din-ner." Rising, Kirby began to lead Rick gently toward the door. "I'm sure you'd like to rest a bit after your drive. You can find the way to your room, can't you?"

"Yes, yes, of course."

Kirby watched him wander down the hall before she turned back. She walked back to Adam and wrapped her arms around him. "I hate to repeat myself, but I love you."

He framed her face with his hands and kissed her softly, lightly, with the promise of more. "Repeat yourself as often as you like." He stared down at her, suddenly and completely aroused by no more than her smile. He pressed his mouth into her palm with a restraint that left her weak. "You take my breath away," he murmured. "It's no wonder you turn Rick Potts to jelly."

"I'd rather turn you to jelly."

She did. It wasn't an easy thing to admit. With a half smile, Adam drew her away. "Are you really going to tell him I'm a jealous lover with a stiletto?"

"It's for his own good." Kirby picked up her glass of Perrier. "He's always so embarrassed after he loses control. Did you learn any more from Papa?"

"No." Puzzled, he frowned. "Why?"

"I was coming to see you right before Rick arrived. I heard you talking."

She slipped a hand into his and he fought to keep the tension from being noticeable. "I don't want to press things now." That much was the truth, he thought fiercely. That much wasn't a lie.

"No, you're probably right about that. Papa tends to get obstinate easily. Let's sit in front of the fire for a little while," she said as she drew him over to it. "And do nothing."

He sat beside her, holding her close, and wished things were as simple as they seemed.

Hours went by before they sat in the parlor again, but they were no longer alone. After an enormous meal, Fairchild and Rick settled down with them to continue the ongoing discussion of art and technique. Assisted by two glasses of wine and half a glass of brandy, Rick began to heap praise on Kirby's work. Adam recognized the warning signals of battle—Fairchild's pink ears and Kirby's guileless eyes.

"Thank you, Rick." With a smile, Kirby lifted her brandy. "I'm sure you'd like to see Papa's latest work. It's an attempt in clay. A bird or something, isn't it, Papa?"

"A bird? A bird?" In a quick circle, he danced around the table. "It's a hawk, you horrid girl. A bird of prey, a creature of cunning."

A veteran, Rick tried to soothe. "I'd love to see it, Mr. Fairchild."

"And so you will." In one dramatic gulp, Fairchild finished off his drink. "I intend to donate it to the Metropolitan."

Whether Kirby's snort was involuntary or contrived, it produced results.

"Do you mock your father?" Fairchild demanded. "Have you no faith in these hands?" He held them out, fingers spread. "The same hands that held you fresh from your mother's womb?"

"Your hands are the eighth wonder of the world,"

Kirby told him. "However…" She set down her glass, sat back and crossed her legs. Meticulously she brought her fingers together and looked over them. "From my observations, you have difficulty with your structure. Perhaps with a few years of practice, you'll develop the knack of construction."

"Structure?" he sputtered. "Construction?" His eyes narrowed, his jaw clenched. "Cards!" Kirby sent him an easy smile and picked up her glass again. "Cards!"

"Yes, Mr. Fairchild."

"Cards," Fairchild repeated, glaring at the dignified butler, who stood waiting in the doorway.

"Yes, Mr. Fairchild."

"Cards!" He bellowed and pranced.

"I believe Papa wants a deck of cards—Cards," Kirby explained. "Playing cards."

"Yes, miss." With a slight bow, Cards went to get some.

"What's the matter with that man?" Fairchild muttered. In hurried motions, he began to clear off a small table. Exquisite Wedgwood and delicate Venetian glass were dumped unceremoniously on the floor. "You'd think I didn't make myself clear."

"It's so hard to get good help these days," Adam said into his glass.

"Your cards, Mr. Fairchild." The butler placed two sealed decks on the table before gliding from the room.

"Now I'll show you about construction." Fairchild pulled up a chair and wrapped his skinny legs around its legs. Breaking the seal on the first deck, he poured the cards on the table. With meticulous care, he leaned one card against another and formed an arch. "A steady hand and a discerning eye," Fairchild mumbled as he began slowly, and with total intensity, to build a house of cards.

"That should keep him out of trouble for a while," Kirby declared. Sending Adam a wink, she turned to Rick and drew him into a discussion on mutual friends.

An hour drifted by over brandy and quiet conversation. Occasionally there was a mutter or a grumble from the architect in the corner. The fire crackled. When Montique entered and jumped into Adam's lap, Rick paled and sprang up.

"You shouldn't do that. She'll be here any second." He set down his glass with a clatter. "Kirby, I think I'll go up. I want to start work early."

"Of course." She watched his retreat before turning to Adam. "He's terrified of Isabelle. Montique got into his room when he was sleeping and curled on his pillow. Isabelle woke Rick with some rather rude comments while she stood on his chest. I'd better go up and make sure everything's in order." She rose, then bent over and kissed him lightly.

"That's not enough."

"No?" The slow smile curved her lips. "Perhaps we'll fix that later. Come on, Montique, let's go find your wretched keeper."

"Kirby…" Adam waited until both she and the puppy were at the doorway. "Just how much rent does Isabelle pay?"

"Ten mice a month," she told him soberly. "But I'm going to raise it to fifteen in November. Maybe she'll be out by Christmas." Pleased with the thought, she led Montique away.

"A fascinating creature, my Kirby," Fairchild commented.

Adam crossed the room and stared down at the huge, erratic card structure Fairchild continued to construct. "Fascinating."

"She's a woman with much below the surface. Kirby can be cruel when she feels justified. I've seen her squash a six-foot man like a bug." He held a card between the index fingers of both hands, then slowly lowered it into place. "You'll notice, however, that her attitude toward Rick is invariably kind."

Though Fairchild continued to give his full attention to his cards, Adam knew it was more than idle conversation. "Obviously she doesn't want to hurt him."

"Exactly." Fairchild began to patiently build another wing. Unless Adam was very much mistaken, the cards were slowly taking on the lines of the house they were in. "She'll take great care not to because she knows his devotion to her is sincere. Kirby's a strong, independent woman. Where her heart's involved, however, she's a marshmallow. There are a handful of people on this earth she'd sacrifice anything she could for. Rick's one of them—Melanie and Harriet are others. And myself." He held a card on the tops of his fingers as if weighing it. "Yes, myself," he repeated softly. "Because of this, the circumstances of the Rembrandt are very difficult for her. She's torn between separate loyalties. Her father, and the woman who's been her mother most of her life."

"You do nothing to change it," Adam accused. Irrationally he wanted to sweep the cards aside, flatten the meticulously formed construction. He pushed his hands into his pockets, where they balled into fists. Just how much could he berate Fairchild, when he was deceiving Kirby in nearly the same way? "Why don't you give her some explanation? Something she could understand?"

"Ignorance is bliss," Fairchild stated calmly. "In this case, the less Kirby knows, the simpler things are for her."

"You've a hell of a nerve, Philip."

"Yes, yes, that's quite true." He balanced more cards, then went back to the subject foremost in his mind. "There've been dozens of men in Kirby's life. She could choose and discard them as other women do clothing. Yet, in her own way, she was always cautious. I think Kirby believed she wasn't capable of loving a man and had decided to settle for much, much less by agreeing to marry Stuart. Nonsense, of course." Fairchild picked up his drink and studied his rambling card house. "Kirby has a great capacity for love. When she loves a man, she'll love with unswerving devotion and loyalty. And when she does, she'll be vulnerable. She loves intensely, Adam."

For the first time, he raised his eyes and met Adam's. "When her mother died, she was devastated. I wouldn't want to live to see her go through anything like that again."

What could he say? Less than he wanted to, but still only the truth. "I don't want to hurt Kirby. I'll do everything I can to keep from hurting her."

Fairchild studied him a moment with the pale blue eyes that saw deep and saw much. "I believe you, and hope you find a way to avoid it. Still, if you love her, you'll find a way to mend whatever damage is done. The game's on, Adam, the rules set. They can't be altered now, can they?"

Adam stared down at the round face. "You know why I'm here, don't you?"

With a cackle, Fairchild turned back to his cards. Yes, indeed, Adam Haines was sharp, he thought, pleased. Kirby had called it from the beginning. "Let's just say for now that you're here to paint and to...observe. Yes, to observe." He placed another card. "Go up to her now, you've my blessing if you feel the need for it. The game's nearly over, Adam. Soon enough we'll have to pick up the pieces. Love's tenuous when it's new, my boy. If you want to keep her, be as stubborn as she is. That's my advice."

In long, methodical strokes, Kirby pulled the brush through her hair. She'd turned the radio on low so that the hot jazz was hardly more than a pulse beat. At the sound of a knock, she sighed. "Rick, you really must go to bed. You'll hate yourself in the morning."

Adam pushed open the door. He took a long look at the woman in front of the mirror, dressed in wisps of beige silk and ivory lace. Without a word, he closed and latched the door behind him.

"Oh, my." Setting the brush on her dresser, Kirby turned around with a little shudder. "A woman simply isn't safe these days. Have you come to have your way with me—I hope?"

Adam crossed to her. Letting his hands slide along the silk, he wrapped his arms around her. "I was just passing through." When she smiled, he lowered his mouth to hers. "I love you, Kirby. More than anyone, more than anything." Suddenly his mouth was fierce, his arms were tight. "Don't ever forget it."

"I won't." But her words were muffled against his mouth. "Just don't stop reminding me. Now…" She drew away, inches only, and slowly began to loosen his tie. "Maybe I should remind you."

He watched his tie slip to the floor just before she began to ease his jacket from his shoulders. "It might be a good idea."

"You've been working hard," she told him as she tossed his jacket in the general direction of a chair. "I think you should be pampered a bit."

"Pampered?"

"Mmm." Nudging him onto the bed, she knelt to take off his shoes. Carelessly she let them drop, followed by his socks, before she began to massage his feet. "Pampering's good for you in small doses."

He felt the pleasure spread through him at the touch that could almost be described as motherly. Her hands were soft, with that ridge of callus that proved they weren't idle. They were strong and clever, belonging both to artist and to woman. Slowly she slid them up his legs, then down—teasing, promising, until he wasn't certain whether to lay back and enjoy, or to grab and take. Before he could do either, Kirby stood and began to unbutton his shirt.

"I like everything about you," she murmured as she tugged the shirt from the waistband of his slacks. "Have I mentioned that?"

"No." He let her loosen the cuffs and slip the shirt from him. Taking her time, Kirby ran her hands up his rib cage to his shoulders. "The way you look." Softly she pressed a kiss to his cheek. "The way you feel." Then the other. "The way you think." Her lips brushed over his chin. "The way you taste." Unhooking his slacks, she drew them off, inch by slow inch. "There's nothing about you I'd change."

She straddled him and began to trace long, lingering kisses over his face and neck. "Once when I wondered about falling in love, I decided there simply wasn't a man I'd like well enough to make it possible." Her mouth paused just above his. "I was wrong."

Soft, warm and exquisitely tender, her lips met his. Pampering…the word drifted through his mind as she gave him more than any man could expect and only a few might dream of. The strength of her body and her mind, the delicacy of both. They were his, and he didn't have to ask. They'd be his as long as his arms could hold her and open wide enough to give her room.

Knowing only that she loved, Kirby gave. His body heated beneath hers, lean and hard. Disciplined. Somehow the word excited her. He knew who he was and what he wanted. He'd work for both. And he wouldn't demand that she lose any part of what she was to suit that.

His shoulders were firm. Not so broad they would overwhelm her, but wide enough to offer security when she needed it. She brushed her lips over them. There were muscles in his arms, but subtle, not something he'd flex to show her his superiority, but there to protect if she chose to be protected. She ran her fingers over them. His hands were clever, elegantly masculine. They wouldn't hold her back from the places she had to go, but they would be there, held out, when she returned. She pressed her mouth to one, then the other.

No one had ever loved him just like this—patiently, devotedly. He wanted nothing more than to go on feeling those long, slow strokes of her fingers, those moist, lingering traces of her lips. He felt each in every pore. A total experience. He could see the glossy black fall of her hair as it tumbled over his skin and hear the murmur of her approval as she touched him.

The house was quiet again, but for the low, simmering sound of the music. The quilt was soft under his back. The light was dim and gentle—the best light for lovers. And while he lay, she loved him until he was buried under layer upon layer of pleasure. This he would give back to her.

He could touch the silk, and her flesh, knowing that both were exquisite. He could taste her lips and know that he'd never go hungry as long as she was there. When he heard her sigh, he knew he'd be content with no other sound. The need for him was in her eyes, clouding them, so that he knew he could live with little else as long as he could see her face.

Patience began to fade in each of them. He could feel her body spring to frantic life wherever he touched. He could feel his own strain from the need only she brought to him. Desperate, urgent, exclusive. If he'd had only a day left to live, he'd have spent every moment of it there, with Kirby in his arms.

She smelled of wood smoke and musky flowers, of woman and of sex, ripe and ready. If he'd had the power, he'd have frozen time just then, as she loomed above him in the moonlight, eyes dark with need, skin flashing against silk.

Then he drew the silk up and over her head so that he could see her as he swore no man would ever see her again. Her hair tumbled down, streaking night against her flesh. Naked and eager, she was every primitive fantasy, every midnight dream. Everything.

Her lips were parted as the breath hurried between them. Passion swamped her so that she shuddered and rushed to take what she needed from him—for him. Everything. Everything and more. With a low sound of triumph, Kirby took him inside her and led the way. Fast, furious.

Her body urged her on relentlessly while her mind exploded with images. Such color, such sound. Such frenzy. Arched back, she moved like lightning, hardly aware of how tightly his hands gripped her hips. But she heard him say her name. She felt him fill her.

The first crest swamped her, shocking her system then thrusting her along to more, and more and more. There was nothing she couldn't have and nothing she wouldn't give. Senseless, she let herself go.

With his hands on her, with the taste of her still on his lips, Adam felt his system shudder on the edge of release. For a moment, only a moment, he held back. He could see her above him, poised like a goddess, flesh damp and glowing, hair streaming back as she lifted her hands to it in ecstasy. This he would remember always.

The moon was no longer full, but its light was soft and white. They were still on top of the quilt, tangled close as their breathing settled. As she lay over him, Adam thought of everything Fairchild had said. And everything he could and couldn't do about it.

Slowly their systems settled, but he could find none of the answers he needed so badly. What answers would there be based on lies and half-truths?

Time. Perhaps time was all he had now. But how much or how little was no longer up to him. With a sigh, he shifted and ran a hand down her back.

Kirby rose on an elbow. Her eyes were no longer clouded, but saucy and clear. She smiled, touched a fingertip to her own lips and then to his. "Next time you're in town, cowboy," she drawled as she tossed her hair over her shoulder, "don't forget to ask for Lulu."

She'd expected him to grin, but he grabbed her hair and held her just as she was. There was no humor in his eyes, but the intensity she'd seen when he held a paintbrush. His muscles had tensed, she could feel it.

"Adam?"

"No, don't." He forced his hand to relax, then stroked her cheek. It wouldn't be spoiled by the wrong word, the wrong move. "I want to remember you just like this. Fresh from loving, with moonlight on your hair."

He was afraid, unreasonably, that he'd never see her like that again—with that half smile inches away from his face. He'd never feel the warmth of her flesh spread over his with nothing, nothing to separate them.

The panic came fast and was very real. Unable to stop it, Adam pulled her against him and held her as if he'd never let her go.

Chapter 10

After thirty minutes of posing, Kirby ordered herself not to be impatient. She'd agreed to give Adam two hours, and a bargain was a bargain. She didn't want to think about the time she had left to stand idle, so instead tried to concentrate on her plans for sculpting once her obligation was over. Her *Anger* was nearly finished.

But the sun seemed too warm and too bright. Every so often her mind would go oddly blank until she pulled herself back just to remember where she was.

"Kirby." Adam called her name for the third time and watched as she blinked and focused on him. "Could you wait until the session's over before you take a nap?"

"Sorry." With an effort, she cleared her head and smiled at him. "I was thinking of something else."

"Don't think at all if it puts you to sleep," he muttered, and slashed scarlet across the canvas. It was right, so right. Nothing he'd ever done had been as right as this painting. The need to finish it was becoming obsessive. "Tilt your head to the right again. You keep breaking the pose."

"Slave driver." But she obeyed and tried to concentrate.

"Cracking the whip's the only way to work with you." With care, he began to perfect the folds in the skirt of her dress. He wanted them soft, flowing, but clearly defined. "You'd better get used to posing for me. I've already several other studies in mind that I'll start after we're married."

Giddiness washed over her. She felt it in waves—physical, emotional—she couldn't tell one from the other. Without thinking, she dropped her arms.

"Damn it, Kirby." He started to swear at her again when he saw how wide and dark her eyes were. "What is it?"

"I hadn't thought… I didn't realize that you…" Lifting a hand to her spinning head, she walked around the room. The bracelets slid down to her elbow with a musical jingle. "I need a minute," she murmured. Should she feel as though someone had cut off her air? As if her head was three feet above her shoulders?

Adam watched her for a moment. She didn't seem quite steady, he realized. And there was an unnaturally high color in her cheeks. Standing, he took her hand and held her still. "Are you ill?"

"No." She shook her head. She was never ill, Kirby reminded herself. Just a bit tired—and, perhaps for the first time in her life, completely overwhelmed. She took a deep breath, telling herself she'd be all right in a moment. "I didn't know you wanted to marry me, Adam."

Was that it? he wondered as he ran the back of his hand over her cheek. Shouldn't she have known? And yet, he remembered, everything had happened so fast. "I love you." It was simple for him. Love led to marriage and marriage to family. But how could he have forgotten Kirby wasn't an ordinary woman and was anything but simple? "You accused me of being conventional," he reminded her, and ran his hands down her hair to her shoulders. "Marriage is a very conventional institution." And one she might not be ready for, he thought with a quick twinge of panic. He'd have to give her room if he wanted to keep her. But how much room did she need, and how much could he give?

"I want to spend my life with you." Adam waited until her gaze had lifted to his again. She looked stunned by his words—a woman like her, Adam thought. Beautiful, sensuous, strong. How was it a woman like Kirby would be surprised to be wanted? Perhaps he'd moved too quickly, and too clumsily. "Any way you choose, Kirby. Maybe I should've chosen a better time, a better place, to ask rather than assume."

"It's not that." Shaky, she lifted a hand to his face. It was so solid, so strong. "I don't need that." His face blurred a moment, and, shaking her head, she moved away again until she stood where she'd been posing. "I've had marriage proposals before—and a good many less binding requests." She managed a smile. He wanted her, not just for today, but for the tomorrows, as well. He wanted her just as she was. She felt the tears well up, of love, of gratitude, but blinked them back. When wishes came true it was no time for tears. "This is the one I've been waiting for all of my life, I just didn't expect to be so flustered."

Relieved, he started to cross to her. "I'll take that as a good sign. Still, I wouldn't mind a simple yes."

"I hate to do anything simple."

She felt the room lurch and fade, then his hands on her shoulders.

"Kirby— Good God, there's gas leaking!" As he stood holding her up, the strong, sweet odor rushed over him. "Get out! Get some air! It must be the heater." Giving her a shove toward the door, he bent over the antiquated unit.

She stumbled across the room. The door seemed miles away, so that when she finally reached it she had only the strength to lean against the heavy wood and catch her breath. The air was cleaner there. Gulping it in, Kirby willed herself to reach for the knob. She tugged, but it held firm.

"Damn it, I told you to get out!" He was already choking on the fumes when he reached her. "The gas is pouring out of that thing!"

"I can't open the door!" Furious with herself, Kirby pulled again. Adam pushed her hands away and yanked himself. "Is it jammed?" she murmured, leaning against him. "Cards will see to it."

Locked, he realized. From the outside. "Stay here." After propping her against the door, Adam picked up a chair and smashed it against the window. The glass cracked, but held. Again, he rammed the chair, and again, until with a final heave, the glass shattered.

Moving quickly, he went back for Kirby and held her head near the jagged opening.

"Breathe," he ordered.

For the moment she could do nothing else but gulp fresh air into her lungs and cough it out again. "Someone's locked us in, haven't they?"

He'd known it wouldn't take her long once her head had cleared. Just as he knew better than to try to evade. "Yes."

"We could shout for hours." She closed her eyes and concentrated. "No one would hear us, we're too isolated up here." With her legs unsteady, she leaned against the wall. "We'll have to wait until someone comes to look for us."

"Where's the main valve for that heater?"

"Main valve?" She pressed her fingers to her eyes and forced herself to think. "I just turn the thing on when it's cold up here…. Wait. Tanks—there are tanks out in back of the kitchen." She turned back to the broken window again, telling herself she couldn't be sick. "One for each tower and for each floor."

Adam glanced at the small, old-fashioned heater again. It wouldn't take much longer, even with the broken window. "We're getting out of here."

"How?" If she could just lie down—just for a minute… "The door's locked. I don't think we'd survive a jump into Jamie's zinnias," she added, looking down to where the chair had landed. But he wasn't listening to her. When Kirby turned, she saw Adam running his hand over the ornate trim. The panel yawned open. "How'd you find that one?"

He grabbed her by the elbow and pulled her forward. "Let's go."

"I can't." With the last of her strength, Kirby braced her hands against the wall. Fear and nausea doubled at the thought of going into the dark, dank hole in the wall. "I can't go in there."

"Don't be ridiculous."

When he would've pulled her through, Kirby jerked away and backed up. "No, you go. I'll wait for you to come around and open the door."

"Listen to me." Fighting the fumes, he grabbed her shoulders. "I don't know how long it'd take me to find my way through that maze in the dark."

"I'll be patient."

"You could be dead," he countered between his teeth. "That heater's unstable—if there's a short this whole room would go up! You've already taken in too much of the gas."

"I won't go in!" Hysteria bubbled, and she didn't have the strength or the wit to combat it. Her voice rose as she stumbled back from him. "I can't go in, don't you understand?"

"I hope you understand this," he muttered, and clipped her cleanly on the jaw. Without a sound, she collapsed into his arms. Adam didn't hesitate. He tossed her unceremoniously over his shoulder and plunged into the passageway.

With the panel closed to cut off the flow of gas, the passage was in total darkness. With one arm holding Kirby in place, Adam inched along the wall. He had to reach the stairs, and the first mechanism. Groping, testing each step, he hugged the wall, knowing what would happen to both of them if he rushed and plunged them headlong down the steep stone stairway.

He heard the skitter of rodents and brushed spider-webs out of his face. Perhaps it was best that Kirby was unconscious, he decided. He'd get her through a lot easier carrying her than he would dragging her.

Five minutes, then ten, then at last his foot met empty space.

Cautiously, he shifted Kirby on his shoulder, pressed the other to the wall, and started down. The steps were stone, and treacherous enough with a light. In the dark, with no rail for balance, they were deadly. Fighting the need to rush, Adam checked himself on each step before going on to the next. When he reached the bottom, he went no faster, but began to trace his hand along the wall, feeling for a switch.

The first one stuck. He had to concentrate just to breathe. Kirby swayed on his shoulder as he maneuvered the sharp turn in the passage. Swearing, Adam moved forward blindly until his fingers brushed over a second lever. The panel groaned open just enough for him to squeeze himself and his burden through. Blinking at the sunlight, he dashed around dust-covered furniture and out into the hall.

When he reached the second floor and passed Cards, he didn't break stride. "Turn off the gas to Kirby's studio from the main valve," he ordered, coughing as he moved by. "And keep everyone away from there."

"Yes, Mr. Haines." Cards continued to walk toward the main stairway, carrying his pile of fresh linens.

When Adam reached her room, he laid Kirby on the bed, then opened the windows. He stood there a moment, just breathing, letting the air rush over his face and soothe his eyes. His stomach heaved. Forcing himself to take slow, measured breaths, he leaned out. When the nausea passed, he went back to her.

The high color had faded. Now she was as pale as the quilt. She didn't move. Hadn't moved, he remembered, since he'd hit her. With a tremor, he pressed his fingers to her throat and felt a slow, steady pulse. Quickly he went into the bathroom and soaked a cloth with cold water. As he ran it over her face, he said her name.

She coughed first, violently. Nothing could've relieved him more. When her eyes opened, she stared at him dully.

"You're in your room," he told her. "You're all right now."

"You hit me."

He grinned because there was indignation in her voice. "I thought you'd take a punch better with a chin like that. I barely tapped you."

"So you say." Gingerly she sat up and touched her chin. Her head whirled once, but she closed her eyes and waited for it to pass. "I suppose I had it coming. Sorry I got neurotic on you."

He let his forehead rest against hers. "You scared the hell out of me. I guess you're the only woman who's received a marriage proposal and a right jab within minutes of each other."

"I hate to do the ordinary." Because she needed another minute, she lay back against the pillows. "Have you turned off the gas?"

"Cards is seeing to it."

"Of course." She said this calmly enough, then began to pluck at the quilt with her fingers. "As far as I know, no one's tried to kill me before."

It made it easier, he thought, that she understood and accepted that straight off. With a nod, he touched a hand to her cheek. "First we call a doctor. Then we call the police."

"I don't need a doctor. I'm just a little queasy now, it'll pass." She took both his hands and held them firmly. "And we can't call the police."

He saw something in her eyes that nearly snapped his temper. Stubbornness. "It's the usual procedure after attempted murder, Kirby."

She didn't wince. "They'll ask annoying questions and skulk all over the house. It's in all the movies."

"This isn't a game." His hands tightened on hers. "You could've been killed—would've been if you'd been in there alone. I'm not giving him another shot at you."

"You think it was Stuart." She let out a long breath. Be objective, she told herself. Then you can make Adam be objective. "Yes, I suppose it was, though I wouldn't have thought him ingenious enough. There's no one else who'd want to hurt me. Still, we can't prove a thing."

"That has yet to be seen." His eyes flashed a moment as he thought of the satisfaction he'd get from beating a confession out of Hiller. She saw it. She understood it.

"You're more primitive than I'd imagined." Touched, she traced her finger down his jaw. "I didn't know how nice it would be to have someone want to vanquish dragons for me. Who needs a bunch of silly police when I have you?"

"Don't try to outmaneuver me."

"I'm not." The smile left her eyes and her lips. "We're not in the position to call the police. I couldn't answer the questions they'd ask, don't you see? Papa has to resolve the business of the Rembrandt, Adam. If everything came out now, he'd be hopelessly compromised. He might go to prison. Not for anything," she said softly. "Not for anything would I risk that."

"He won't," Adam said shortly. No matter what strings he'd have to pull, what dance he'd have to perform, he'd see to it that Fairchild stayed clear. "Kirby, do you think your father would continue with whatever he's plotting once he knew of this?"

"I couldn't predict his reaction." Weary, she let out a long breath and tried to make him understand. "He might destroy the Rembrandt in a blind rage. He could go after Stuart single-handed. He's capable of it. What good would any of that do, Adam?" The queasiness was passing, but it had left her weak. Though she didn't know it, the vulnerability was her best weapon. "We have to let it lie for a while longer."

"What do you mean, let it lie?"

"I'll speak to Papa—tell him what happened in my own way, so that he doesn't overreact. Harriet and Melanie are coming to dinner tonight. It has to wait until tomorrow."

"How can he sit down and have dinner with Harriet when he has stolen something from her?" Adam demanded. "How can he do something like this to a friend?"

Pain shot into her eyes. Deliberately she lowered them, but he'd already seen it. "I don't know."

"I'm sorry."

She shook her head. "No, you have no reason to be. You've been wonderful through all of this."

"No, I haven't." He pressed the heels of his hands to his eyes.

"Let me be the judge of that. And give me one more day." She touched his wrists and waited until he lowered his hands. "Just one more day, then I'll talk to Papa. Maybe we'll get everything straightened out."

"That much, Kirby. No more." He had some thinking of his own to do. Perhaps one more night would give him some answers. "Tomorrow you tell Philip everything, no glossing over the details. If he doesn't agree to resolve the Rembrandt business then, I'm taking over."

She hesitated a minute. She'd said she trusted him. It was true. "All right."

"And I'll deal with Hiller."

"You're not going to fight with him."

Amused, he lifted a brow. "No?"

"Adam, I won't have you bruised and bloodied. That's it."

"Your confidence in me is overwhelming."

With a laugh, she sat up again and threw her arms around him. "My hero. He'd never lay a hand on you."

"I beg your pardon, Miss Fairchild."

"Yes, Cards." Shifting her head, Kirby acknowledged the butler in the doorway.

"It seems a chair has somehow found its way

through your studio window. Unfortunately, it landed in Jamie's bed of zinnias."

"Yes, I know. I suppose he's quite annoyed."

"Indeed, miss."

"I'll apologize, Cards. Perhaps a new lawn mower... You'll see to having the window repaired?"

"Yes, miss."

"And have that heater replaced by something from the twentieth-century," Adam added. He watched as Cards glanced at him then back at Kirby.

"As soon as possible, please, Cards."

With a nod, the butler backed out of the doorway.

"He takes his orders from you, doesn't he?" Adam commented as the quiet footsteps receded. "I've seen the subtle nods and looks between the two of you."

She brushed a smudge of dirt on the shoulder of his shirt. "I've no idea what you mean."

"A century ago, Cards would've been known as the queen's man." When she laughed at the term, he eased her back on the pillows. "Rest," he ordered.

"Adam, I'm fine."

"Want me to get tough again?" Before she could answer, he covered her mouth with his, lingering. "Turn the batteries down awhile," he murmured. "I might have to call the doctor after all."

"Blackmail." She brought his mouth back to hers again. "But maybe if you rested with me..."

"Rest isn't what would happen then." He drew away as she grumbled a protest.

"A half hour."

"Fine. I'll be back."

She smiled and let her eyes close. "I'll be waiting."

* * *

It was too soon for stars, too late for sunbeams. From a window in the parlor, Adam watched the sunset hold off twilight just a few moments longer.

After reporting the attempt on Kirby's life to McIntyre, he'd found himself suddenly weary. Half lies, half truths. It had to end. It would end, he decided, tomorrow. Fairchild would have to see reason, and Kirby would be told everything. The hell with McIntyre, the job and anything else. She deserved honesty along with everything else he wanted to give her. Everything else, he realized, would mean nothing to Kirby without it.

The sun lowered further and the horizon exploded with rose-gold light. He thought of the Titian woman. She'd understand, he told himself. She had to understand. He'd make her understand. Thinking to check on her again, Adam turned from the window.

When he reached her room, he heard the sound of running water. The simple, natural sound of her humming along with her bath dissolved his tension. He thought about joining her, then remembered how pale and tired she'd looked. Another time, he promised both of them as he shut the door to her room again. Another time he'd have the pleasure of lounging in the big marble tub with her.

"Where's that wretched girl?" Fairchild demanded from behind him. "She's been hiding out all day."

"Having a bath," Adam told him.

"She'd better have a damn good explanation, that's all I have to say." Looking grim, Fairchild reached for the doorknob. Adam blocked the door automatically.

"For what?"

Fairchild glared at him. "My shoes."

Adam looked down at Fairchild's small stockinged feet. "I don't think she has them."

"A man tugs himself into a restraining suit, chokes himself with a ridiculous tie, then has no shoes." Fairchild pulled at the knot around his neck. "Is that justice?"

"No. Have you tried Cards?"

"Cards couldn't get his big British feet in my shoes." Then he frowned and pursed his lips. "Then again, he did have my suit."

"I rest my case."

"The man's a kleptomaniac," Fairchild grumbled as he wandered down the hall. "I'd check my shorts if I were you. No telling what he'll pick up next. Cocktails in a half hour, Adam. Hustle along."

Deciding a quiet drink was an excellent idea after the day they'd put in, Adam went to change. He was adjusting the knot in his own tie when Kirby knocked. She opened it without waiting for his answer, then stood a moment, deliberately posed in the doorway— head thrown back, one arm raised high on the jamb, the other at her hip. The slinky jumpsuit clung to every curve, falling in folds from her neck and dispensing with a back altogether. At her ears, emeralds the size of quarters picked up the vivid green shade. Five twisted, gold chains hung past her waist.

"Hello, neighbor." Glittering and gleaming, she crossed to him. Adam put a finger under her chin and studied her face. As an artist, she knew how to make use of the colors of a makeup palette. Her cheeks were tinted with a touch of bronze, her lips just a bit darker. "Well?"

"You look better," he decided.

"That's a poor excuse for a compliment."

"How do you feel?"

"I'd feel a lot better if you'd stop examining me as though I had a rare terminal disease and kiss me as you're supposed to." She twisted her arms around his neck and let her lashes lower.

It was them he kissed first, softly, with a tenderness that had her sighing. Then his lips skimmed down, over her cheeks, gently over her jawline.

"Adam…" His name was only a breath on the air as his mouth touched hers. She wanted it all now. Instantly. She wanted the fire and flash, the pleasure and the passion. She wanted that calm, spreading contentment that only he could give to her. "I love you," she murmured. "I love you until there's nothing else but that."

"There is nothing else but that," he said, almost fiercely. "We've a lifetime for it." He drew her away so he could bring both of her hands to his lips. "A lifetime, Kirby, and it isn't long enough."

"Then we'll have to start soon." She felt the giddiness again, the light-headedness, but she wouldn't run from it. "Very soon," she added. "But we have to wait at least until after dinner. Harriet and Melanie should be here any minute."

"If I had my choice, I'd stay with you alone in this room and make love until sunrise."

"Don't tempt me to tarnish your reputation." Because she knew she had to, she stepped back and finished adjusting his tie herself. It was a brisk, womanly gesture he found himself enjoying. "Ever since I told Harriet about your help with the Titian, she's decided you're the greatest thing since peanut butter. I wouldn't want to mess that up by making you late for dinner."

"Then we'd better go now. Five more minutes alone with you and we'd be a lot more than late." When she laughed, he linked her arm through his and led her from the room. "By the way, your father's shoes were stolen."

To the casual observer, the group in the parlor would have seemed a handful of elegant, cosmopolitan people. Secure, friendly, casually wealthy. Looking beyond the sparkle and glitter, a more discerning eye might have seen the pallor of Kirby's skin that her careful application of makeup disguised. Someone looking closely might have noticed that her friendly nonsense covered a discomfort that came from battling loyalties.

To someone from the outside, the group might have taken on a different aspect if the canvas were stretched. Rick's stuttering nerves were hardly noticed by those in the parlor. As was Melanie's subtle disdain for him. Both were the expected. Fairchild's wolfish grins and Harriet's jolting laughter covered the rest.

Everyone seemed relaxed, except Adam. The longer it went on, the more he wished he'd insisted that Kirby postpone the dinner party. She looked frail. The more energy she poured out, the more fragile she seemed to him. And touchingly valiant. Her devotion to Harriet hadn't been lip service. Adam could see it, hear it. When she loved, as Fairchild had said, she loved completely. Even the thought of the Rembrandt would be tearing her in two. Tomorrow. By the next day, it would be over.

"Adam." Harriet took his arm as Kirby poured after-dinner drinks. "I'd love to see Kirby's portrait."

"As soon as it's finished you'll have a private viewing." And until the repairs in the tower were complete, he thought, he was keeping all outsiders away.

"I'll have to be content with that, I suppose." She pouted a moment, then forgave him. "Sit beside me," Harriet commanded and spread the flowing vermilion of her skirt on the sofa. "Kirby said I could flirt with you."

Adam noticed that Melanie turned a delicate pink at her mother's flamboyance. Unable to resist, he lifted Harriet's hand to his lips. "Do I need permission to flirt with you?"

"Guard your heart, Harriet," Kirby warned as she set out drinks.

"Mind your own business," Harriet tossed back. "By the way, Adam, I'd like you to have my necklace of crocodile teeth as a token of my appreciation."

"Good heavens, Mother." Melanie sipped at her blackberry brandy. "Why would Adam want that hideous thing?"

"Sentiment," she returned without blinking an eye. "Adam's agreed to let me exhibit Kirby's portrait, and I want to repay him."

The old girl's quick, Adam decided as she sent him a guileless smile, and Melanie's been kept completely in the dark about the hobby her mother shares with Fairchild. Studying Melanie's cool beauty, Adam decided her mother knew best. She'd never react as Kirby did. Melanie could have their love and affection, but secrets were kept within the triangle. No, he realized, oddly pleased. It was now a rectangle.

"He doesn't have to wear it," Harriet went on, breaking into his thoughts.

"I should hope not," Melanie put in, rolling her eyes at Kirby.

"It's for good luck." Harriet sent Kirby a glance, then squeezed Adam's arm. "But perhaps you have all the luck you need."

"Perhaps my luck's just beginning."

"How quaintly they speak in riddles." Kirby sat on the arm of Melanie's chair. "Why don't we ignore them?"

"Your hawk's coming along nicely, Mr. Fairchild," Rich hazarded.

"Aha!" It was all Fairchild needed. Bursting with good feelings, he treated Rick to an in-depth lecture on the use of calipers.

"Rick's done it now," Kirby whispered to Melanie. "Papa has no mercy on a captive audience."

"I didn't know Uncle Philip was sculpting."

"Don't mention it," Kirby said quickly. "You'll never escape." Pursing her lips, she looked down at Melanie's elegant dark rose dress. The lines flowed fluidly with the flash of a studded buckle at the waist. "Melly, I wonder if you'd have time to design a dress for me."

Surprised, Melanie glanced up. "Oh course, I'd love to. But I've been trying to talk you into it for years and you've always refused to go through the fittings."

Kirby shrugged. A wedding dress was a different matter, she mused. Still, she didn't mention her plans with Adam. Her father would know first. "I usually buy on impulse, whatever appeals at the time."

"From Goodwill to Rive Gauche," Melanie murmured. "So this must be special."

"I'm taking a page from your book," Kirby evaded. "You know I've always admired your talent, I just knew I wouldn't have the patience for all the preliminaries." She laughed. "Do you think you can design a dress that'd make me look demure?"

"Demure?" Harriet cut in, pouncing on the word. "Poor Melanie would have to be a sorceress to pull that off. Even as a child in that sweet little muslin you looked capable of battling a tribe of Comanches. Philip, you must let me borrow that painting of Kirby for the gallery."

"We'll see." His eyes twinkled. "You'll have to soften me up a bit first. I've always had a deep affection for that painting." With a hefty sigh, he leaned back with his drink. "Its value goes below the surface."

"He still begrudges me my sitting fee." Kirby sent her father a sweet smile. "He forgets I never collected for any of the others."

"You never posed for the others," Fairchild reminded her.

"I never signed a release for them, either."

"Melly posed for me out of the goodness of her heart."

"Melly's nicer than I am," Kirby said simply. "I like being selfish."

"Heartless creature," Harriet put in mildly. "It's so selfish of you to teach sculpture in the summer to those handicapped children."

Catching Adam's surprised glance, Kirby shifted uncomfortably. "Harriet, think of my reputation."

"She's sensitive about her good deeds," Harriet told Adam with a squeeze for his knee.

"I simply had nothing else to do." With a shrug, Kirby turned away. "Are you going to Saint Moritz this year, Melly?"

Fraud, Adam thought as he watched her guide the subject away from herself. A beautiful, sensitive fraud. And finding her so, he loved her more.

By the time Harriet and Melanie rose to leave, Kirby was fighting off a raging headache. Too much strain, she knew, but she wouldn't admit it. She could tell herself she needed only a good night's sleep, and nearly believe it.

"Kirby." Harriet swirled her six-foot shawl over her shoulder before she took Kirby's chin in her hand. "You look tired, and a bit pale. I haven't seen you look pale since you were thirteen and had the flu. I remember you swore you'd never be ill again."

"After that disgusting medicine you poured down my throat, I couldn't afford to. I'm fine." But she threw her arms around Harriet's neck and held on. "I'm fine, really."

"Mmm." Over her head, Harriet frowned at Fairchild. "You might think about Australia. We'll put some color in your cheeks."

"I will. I love you."

"Go to sleep, child," Harriet murmured.

The moment the door was closed, Adam took Kirby's arm. Ignoring her father and Rick, he began to pull her up the stairs. "You belong in bed."

"Shouldn't you be dragging me by the hair instead of the arm?"

"Some other time, when my intentions are less

peaceful." He stopped outside her door. "You're going to sleep."

"Tired of me already?"

The words were hardly out of her mouth when his covered it. Holding her close, he let himself go for a moment, releasing the needs, the desires, the love. He could feel her heart thud, her bones melt. "Can't you see how tired I am of you?" He kissed her again with his hands framing her face. "You must see how you bore me."

"Anything I can do?" she murmured, slipping her hands under his jacket.

"Get some rest." He took her by the shoulders. "This is your last opportunity to sleep alone."

"Am I sleeping alone?"

It wasn't easy for him. He wanted to devour her, he wanted to delight her. He wanted, more than anything else, to have a clean slate between them before they made love again. If she hadn't looked so weary, so worn, he'd have told her everything then and there. "This may come as a shock to you," he said lightly. "But you're not Wonder Woman."

"Really?"

"You're going to get a good night's sleep. Tomorrow." He took her hands and the look, the sudden intenseness, confused her. "Tomorrow, Kirby, we have to talk."

"About what?"

"Tomorrow," he repeated before he could change his mind. "Rest now." He gave her a nudge inside. "If you're not feeling any better tomorrow, you're going to stay in bed and be pampered."

She managed one last wicked grin. "Promise?"

Chapter 11

It was clear after Kirby had tossed in bed and fluffed up her pillow for more than an hour that she wasn't going to get the rest everyone seemed to want for her. Her body was dragging, but her mind refused to give in to it.

She tried. For twenty minutes she recited dull poetry. Closing her eyes, she counted five hundred and twenty-seven camels. She turned on her bedside radio and found chamber music. She was, after all of it, wide awake.

It wasn't fear. If Stuart had indeed tried to kill her, he'd failed. She had her own wits, and she had Adam. No, it wasn't fear.

The Rembrandt. She couldn't think of anything else after seeing Harriet laughing, after remembering how Harriet had nursed her through the flu and had given her a sweet and totally unnecessary woman-to-woman talk when she'd been a girl.

Kirby had grieved for her own mother, and though she'd died when Kirby had been a child, the memory remained perfectly clear. Harriet hadn't been a substitute. Harriet had simply been Harriet. Kirby loved her for that alone.

How could she sleep?

Annoyed, Kirby rolled over on her back and stared at the ceiling. Maybe, just maybe, she could make use of the insomnia and sort it all out and make some sense out of it.

Her father, she was certain, would do nothing to hurt Harriet without cause. Was revenge on Stuart cause enough? After a moment, she decided it didn't follow.

Harriet had gone to Africa—that was first. It had been nearly two weeks after that when Kirby had broken her engagement with Stuart. Afterward she had told her father of Stuart's blackmail threats and he'd been unconcerned. He'd said, Kirby remembered, that Stuart wasn't in any position to make waves.

Then it made sense to assume they'd already begun plans to switch the paintings. Revenge was out.

Then why?

Not for money, Kirby thought. Not for the desire to own the painting himself. That wasn't his way— she knew better than anyone how he felt about greed. But then, stealing from a friend wasn't his way, either.

If she couldn't find the reason, perhaps she could find the painting itself.

Still staring at the ceiling, she began to go over everything her father had said. So many ambiguous comments, she mused. But then, that was typical of him. In the house—that much was certain. In the house, hidden with appropriate affection and respect. Just how many hundreds of possibilities could she sort through in one night?

She blew out a disgusted breath and rolled over again. With a last thump for her pillow, she closed her eyes. The yawn, she felt, was a hopeful sign. As she snuggled deeper, a tiny memory probed.

She'd think about it tomorrow…. No, now, she thought, and rolled over again. She'd think about it now. What was it her father had been saying to Adam when she'd walked into his studio the night after the Titian switch? Something… Something…about involving her figuratively.

"Root rot," she muttered, and squeezed her eyes shut in concentration. "What the devil was that supposed to mean?" Just as she was about to give up, the idea seeped in. Her eyes sprang open as she sprang up. "It'd be just like him!"

Grabbing a robe, she dashed from the room.

For a moment in the hall she hesitated. Perhaps she should wake Adam and tell him of her theory. Then again, it was no more than that, and he hadn't had the easiest day of it, either. If she produced results, then she'd wake him. And if she was wrong, her father would kill her.

She made a quick trip to her father's studio, then went down to the dining room.

On neither trip did she bother with lights. She wanted no one to pop out of their room and ask what she was up to. Carrying a rag, a bottle and a stack of newspapers, she went silently through the dark. Once she'd reached the dining room, she turned on the lights. No one would investigate downstairs except Cards. He'd never question her. She worked quickly.

Kirby spread the newspapers in thick pads on the dining room table. Setting the bottle and the rag on them, she turned to her own portrait.

"You're too clever for your own good, Papa," she murmured as she studied the painting. "I'd never be able to tell if this was a duplicate. There's only one way."

Once she'd taken the portrait from the wall, Kirby laid it on the newspaper. "Its value goes below the surface," she murmured. Isn't that what he'd said to Harriet? And he'd been smug. He'd been smug right from the start. Kirby opened the bottle and tipped the liquid onto the rag. "Forgive me, Papa," she said quietly.

With the lightest touch—an expert's touch—she began to remove layers of paint in the lower corner. Minutes passed. If she was wrong, she wanted the damage to be minimal. If she was right, she had something priceless in her hands. Either way, she couldn't rush.

She dampened the rag and wiped again. Her father's bold signature disappeared, then the bright summer grass beneath it, and the primer.

And there, beneath where there should have been only canvas, was a dark, somber brown. One letter, then another, appeared. It was all that was necessary.

"Great buckets of blood," she murmured. "I was right."

Beneath the feet of the girl she'd been was Rembrandt's signature. She'd go no further. As carefully as she'd unstopped it, Kirby secured the lid of the bottle.

"So, Papa, you put Rembrandt to sleep under a copy of my portrait. Only you would've thought to copy yourself to pull it off."

"Very clever."

Whirling, Kirby looked behind her into the dark outside the dining room. She knew the voice; it didn't frighten her. As her heart pounded, the shadows moved. What now? she asked herself quickly. Just how would she explain it?

"Cleverness runs in the family, doesn't it, Kirby?"

"So I'm told." She tried to smile. "I'd like to explain. You'd better come in out of the dark and sit down. It could take—" She stopped as the first part of the invitation was accepted. She stared at the barrel of a small polished revolver. Lifting her gaze from it, she stared into clear, delicate blue eyes. "Melly, what's going on?"

"You look surprised. I'm glad." With a satisfied smile, Melanie aimed the gun at Kirby's head. "Maybe you're not so clever after all."

"Don't point that at me."

"I intend to point it at you." She lowered the gun to chest level. "And I'll do more than point it if you move."

"Melly." She wasn't afraid, not yet. She was confused, even annoyed, but she wasn't afraid of the woman she'd grown up with. "Put that thing away and sit down. What're you doing here this time of night?"

"Two reasons. First, to see if I could find any trace of the painting you've so conveniently found for me. Second, to finish the job that was unsuccessful this morning."

"This morning?" Kirby took a step forward then

froze when she heard the quick, deadly click. Good
God, could it actually be loaded? "Melly..."

"I suppose I must have miscalculated a bit or you'd
be dead already." The elegant rose silk whispered as
she shrugged. "I know the passages very well. Remember, you used to drag me around in them when we were
children—before you went in with a faulty flashlight.
I'd changed the batteries in it, you see. I'd never told
you about that, had I?" She laughed as Kirby remained
silent. "I used the passages this morning. Once I was
sure you and Adam were settled in, I went out and
turned on the gas by the main valve—I'd already broken the switch on the unit."

"You can't be serious." Kirby dragged a hand through
her hair.

"Deadly serious, Kirby."

"Why?"

"Primarily for money, of course."

"Money?" She would've laughed, but her throat was
closing. "But you don't need money."

"You're so smug." The venom came through. Kirby
wondered that she'd never heard it before. "Yes, I need
money."

"You wouldn't take a settlement from your ex-hus-
band."

"He wouldn't give me a dime," Melanie corrected.
"He cut me off, and as he had me cold on adultery, I
wasn't in a position to take him to court. He let me
get a quiet, discreet divorce so that our reputations
wouldn't suffer. And except for one incident, I'd been
very discreet. Stuart and I were always very careful."

"Stuart?" Kirby lifted a hand to rub at her temple. "You and Stuart?"

"We've been lovers for over three years. Questions are just buzzing around in your head, aren't they?" Enjoying herself, Melanie stepped closer. The whiff of Chanel followed her. "It was more practical for us if we pretended to be just acquaintances. I convinced Stuart to ask you to marry him. My inheritance has dwindled to next to nothing. Your money would have met Stuart's and my tastes very nicely. And we'd have got close to Uncle Philip."

She ignored the rest and homed in on the most important. "What do you want from my father?"

"I found out about the little game he and Mother indulged in years ago. Not all the details, but enough to know I could use it if I had to. I thought it was time to use your father's talent for my own benefit."

"You made plans to steal from your own mother."

"Don't be so self-righteous." Her voice chilled. The gun was steady. "Your father betrayed her without a murmur, then double-crossed us in the bargain. Now you've solved that little problem for me." With her free hand, she gestured to the painting. "I should be grateful I failed this morning. I'd still be looking for the painting."

Somehow, some way, she'd deal with this. Kirby started with the basics. "Melly, how could you hurt me? We've been friends all our lives."

"Friends?" The word sounded like an obscenity. "I've hated you for as long as I can remember."

"No—"

"Hated," Melanie repeated, coldly this time and with

the ring of truth. "It was always you people flocked around, always you men preferred. My own mother preferred you."

"That's not true." Did it go so deep? Kirby thought with a flood of guilt. Should she have seen it before? "Melly—" But as she started forward, Melanie gestured with the gun.

"'Melanie, don't be so stiff and formal.... Melanie, where's your sense of humor?'" Her eyes narrowed into slits. "She never came right out and said I should be more like you, but that's what she wanted."

"Harriet loves you—"

"Love?" Melanie cut Kirby off with a laugh. "I don't give a damn for love. It won't buy what I need. You may have taken my mother, but that was a minor offense. The men you snatched from under my nose time and time again is a bigger one."

"I never took a man from you. I've never shown an interest in anyone you were serious about."

"There have been dozens," Melanie corrected. Her voice was as brittle as glass. "You'd smile and say something stupid and I'd be forgotten. You never had my looks, but you'd use that so-called charm and lure them away, or you'd freeze up and do the same thing."

"I might've been friendly to someone you cared for," Kirby said quickly. "If I froze it was to discourage them. Good God, Melly, I'd never have done anything to hurt you. I love you."

"I've no use for your love any longer. It served its purpose well enough." She smiled slowly as tears swam in Kirby's eyes. "My only regret is that you didn't fall for Stuart. I wanted to see you fawn over him, knowing he preferred me—married you only because I wanted it. When you came to see him that night, I nearly came out of the bedroom just for the pleasure of seeing your face. But…" She shrugged. "We had long-range plans."

"You used me," Kirby said quietly when she could no longer deny it. "You had Stuart use me."

"Of course. Still, it wasn't wise of me to come back from New York for the weekend to be with him."

"Why, Melanie? Why have you pretended all these years?"

"You were useful. Even as a child I knew that. Later, in Paris, you opened doors for me, then again in New York. It was even due to you that I spent a year of luxury with Carlyse. You wouldn't sleep with him and you wouldn't marry him. I did both."

"And that's all?" Kirby murmured. "That's all?"

"That's all. You're not useful any longer, Kirby. In fact, you're an inconvenience. I'd planned your death as a warning to Uncle Philip, now it's just a necessity."

She wanted to turn away, but she needed to face it. "How could I have known you all my life and not seen it? How could you have hated me and not shown it?"

"You let emotions rule your life, I don't. Pick up the painting, Kirby." With the gun, she gestured. "And be careful with it. Stuart and I have been offered a healthy sum for it. If you call out," she added, "I'll shoot you now and be in the passage with the painting before anyone comes down."

"What are you going to do?"

"We're going into the passage. You're going to have a nasty spill, Kirby, and break your neck. I'm going to take the painting home and wait for the call to tell me of your accident."

She'd stall. If only she'd woken Adam… No, if she'd woken him, he, too, would have a gun pointed at him. "Everyone knows how I feel about the passages."

"It'll be a mystery. When they find the empty space on the wall, they'll know the Rembrandt was responsible. Stuart should be the first target, but he's out of town and has been for three days. I'll be devastated by the death of my oldest and dearest friend. It'll take months in Europe to recover from the grief."

"You've thought this out carefully." Kirby rested against the table. "But are you capable of murder, Melly?" Slowly she closed her fingers around the bottle, working off the top with her thumb. "Face-to-face murder, not remote-control like this morning."

"Oh, yes." Melanie smiled beautifully. "I prefer it. I feel better with you knowing who's going to kill you. Now pick up the painting, Kirby. It's time."

With a jerk of her arm, Kirby tossed the turpentine mixture, splattering it on Melanie's neck and dress. When Melanie tossed up her hand in protection, Kirby lunged. Together they fell in a rolling heap onto the floor, the gun pressed between them.

"What do you mean Hiller's been in New York since yesterday?" Adam demanded. "What happened this morning wasn't an accident. He had to have done it."

"No way." In a few words McIntyre broke Adam's theory. "I have a good man on him. I can give you the name of Hiller's hotel. I can give you the name of the restaurant where he had lunch and what he ate while you were throwing chairs through windows. He's got his alibi cold, Adam, but it doesn't mean he didn't arrange it."

"Damn." Adam lowered the transmitter while he rearranged his thinking. "It gives me a bad feeling, Mac. Dealing with Hiller's one thing, but it's a whole new story if he has a partner or he's hired a pro to do his dirty work. Kirby needs protection, official protection. I want her out."

"I'll work on it. The Rembrandt—"

"I don't give a damn about the Rembrandt," Adam tossed back. "But it'll be in my hands tomorrow if I have to hang Fairchild up by his thumbs."

McIntyre let out a sigh of relief. "That's better. You were making me nervous thinking you were hung up on the Fairchild woman."

"I am hung up on the Fairchild woman," Adam returned mildly. "So you'd better arrange for—" He heard the shot. One, sharp and clean. It echoed and echoed through his head. *"Kirby!"* He thought of nothing else as he dropped the open transmitter on the floor and ran.

He called her name again as he raced downstairs. But his only answer was silence. He called as he rushed like a madman through the maze of rooms downstairs, but she didn't call back. Nearly blind with terror, his own voice echoing back to mock him, he ran on, slamming on lights as he went until the house was lit up like a celebration. Racing headlong into the dining room, he nearly fell over the two figures on the floor.

"Oh, my God!"

"I've killed her! Oh, God, Adam, help me! I think

I've killed her!" With tears streaming down her face, Kirby pressed a blood-soaked linen napkin against Melanie's side. The stain spread over the rose silk of the dress and onto Kirby's hand.

"Keep the pressure firm." He didn't ask questions, but grabbed a handful of linen from the buffet behind him. Nudging Kirby aside, he felt for a pulse. "She's alive." He pressed more linen to Melanie's side. "Kirby—"

Before he could speak again, there was chaos. The rest of the household poured into the dining room from every direction. Polly let out one squeal that never ended.

"Call an ambulance," Adam ordered Cards, even as the butler turned to do so. "Shut her up, or get her out," he told Rick, nodding to Polly.

Recovering quickly, Fairchild knelt beside his daughter and the daughter of his closest friend. "Kirby, what happened here?"

"I tried to take the gun from her." She struggled to breathe as she looked down at the blood on her hands. "We fell. I don't—Papa, I don't even know which one of us pulled the trigger. Oh, God, I don't even know."

"Melanie had a gun?" Steady as a rock, Fairchild took Kirby's shoulders and turned her to face him. "Why?"

"She hates me." Her voice shook, then leveled as she stared into her father's face. "She's always hated me, I never knew. It was the Rembrandt, Papa. She'd planned it all."

"Melanie?" Fairchild glanced beyond Kirby to the unconscious figure on the floor. "She was behind it." He fell silent, only a moment. "How bad, Adam?"

"I don't know, damn it. I'm an artist, not a doctor." There was fury in his eyes and blood on his hands. "It might've been Kirby."

"Yes, you're right." Fairchild's fingers tightened on his daughter's shoulder. "You're right."

"I found the Rembrandt," Kirby murmured. If it was shock that was making her light-headed, she wouldn't give in to it. She forced herself to think and to speak clearly.

Fairchild looked at the empty space on the wall, then at the table where the painting lay. "So you did."

With a cluck of her tongue, Tulip pushed Fairchild aside and took Kirby by the arm. Ignoring everyone else, she pulled Kirby to her feet. "Come with me, lovie. Come along with me now, that's a girl."

Feeling helpless, Adam watched Kirby being led away while he fought to stop the bleeding. "You'd better have a damn good explanation," he said between his teeth as his gaze swept over Fairchild.

"Explanations don't seem to be enough at this point," he murmured. Very slowly he rose. The sound of sirens cut through the quiet. "I'll phone Harriet."

Almost an hour had passed before Adam could wash the blood from his hands. Unconscious still, Melanie was speeding on her way to the hospital. His only thought was for Kirby now, and he left his room to find her. When he reached the bottom landing, he came upon an argument in full gear. Though the shouting was all one-sided, the noise vibrated through the hall.

"I want to see Adam Haines and I want to see him immediately!"

"Gate-crashing, Mac?" Adam moved forward to stand beside Cards.

"Adam, thank God." The small, husky man with the squared-off face and disarming eyes ran a hand through his disheveled mat of hair. "I didn't know what'd happened to you. Tell this wall to move aside, will you?"

"It's all right, Cards." He drew an expressionless stare. "He's not a reporter. I know him."

"Very well, sir."

"What the hell's going on?" McIntyre demanded when Cards walked back down the hall. "Who just got carted out of here in an ambulance? Damn it, Adam, I thought it might be you. Last thing I know, you're shouting and breaking transmission."

"It's been a rough night." Putting a hand on his shoulder, Adam led him into the parlor. "I need a drink." Going directly to the bar, Adam poured, drank and poured again. "Drink up, Mac," he invited. "This has to be better than the stuff you've been buying in that little motel down the road. Philip," he continued as Fairchild walked into the room, "I imagine you could use one of these."

"Yes." With a nod of acknowledgment for McIntyre, and no questions, Fairchild accepted the glass Adam offered.

"We'd better sit down. Philip Fairchild," Adam went on as Fairchild settled himself, "Henry McIntyre, investigator for the Commonwealth Insurance company."

"Ah, Mr. McIntyre." Fairchild drank half his Scotch in one gulp. "We have quite a bit to discuss. But first,

Adam, satisfy my curiosity. How did you become involved with the investigation?"

"It's not the first time I've worked for Mac, but it's the last." He sent McIntyre a quiet look that was lined in steel. "There's a matter of our being cousins," he added. "Second cousins."

"Relatives." Fairchild smiled knowingly, then gave McIntyre a charming smile.

"You knew why I was here," Adam said. "How?"

"Well, Adam, my boy, it's nothing to do with your cleverness." Fairchild tossed off the rest of the Scotch, then rose to fill his glass again. "I was expecting someone to come along. You were the only one who did." He sat back down with a sigh. "Simple as that."

"Expecting?"

"Would someone tell me who was in that ambulance?" McIntyre cut in.

"Melanie Burgess." Fairchild looked into his Scotch. "Melly." It would hurt, he knew, for a long time. For himself, for Harriet and for Kirby. It was best to begin to deal with it. "She was shot when Kirby tried to take her gun away—the gun she was pointing at my daughter."

"Melanie Burgess," McIntyre mused. "It fits with the information I got today. Information," he added to Adam, "I was about to give you when you broke transmission. I'd like it from the beginning, Mr. Fairchild. I assume the police are on their way."

"Yes, no way around that." Fairchild sipped at his Scotch and deliberated on just how to handle things. Then he saw he no longer had McIntyre's attention. He was staring at the doorway.

Dressed in jeans and a white blouse, Kirby stood just inside the room. She was pale, but her eyes were dark. She was beautiful. It was the first thing McIntyre thought. The second was that she was a woman who could empty a man's mind the way a thirsty man empties a bottle.

"Kirby." Adam was up and across the room. He had his hands on hers. Hers were cold, but steady. "Are you all right?"

"Yes. Melanie?"

"The paramedics handled everything. I got the impression the wound wasn't as bad as it looked. Go lie down," he murmured. "Forget it for a while."

"No." She shook her head and managed a weak smile. "I'm fine, really. I've been washed and patted and plied with liquor, though I wouldn't mind another. The police will want to question me." Her gaze drifted to McIntyre. She didn't ask, but simply assumed he was with the police. "Do you need to talk to me?"

It wasn't until then he realized he'd been staring. Clearing his throat, McIntyre rose. "I'd like to hear your father's story first, Miss Fairchild."

"Wouldn't we all?" Struggling to find some balance, she walked to her father's chair. "Are you going to come clean, Papa, or should I hire a shady lawyer?"

"Unnecessary, my sweet." He took her hand and held it. "The beginning," he continued with a smile for McIntyre. "It started, I suppose, a few days before Harriet flew off to Africa. She's an absentminded woman. She had to return to the gallery one night to pick up some papers she'd forgotten. When she saw the light in Stuart's office, she started to go in and scold him for working late. Instead she eavesdropped on his phone conversation and learned of his plans to steal the Rembrandt. Absentminded but shrewd, Harriet left and let Stuart think his plans were undetected." He grinned and squeezed Kirby's hand. "An intelligent woman, she came directly to a friend known for his loyalty and his sharp mind."

"Papa." With a laugh of relief, she bent over and kissed his head. "You were working together, I should've known."

"We developed a plan. Perhaps unwisely, we decided not to bring Kirby into it." He looked up at her. "Should I apologize?"

"Never."

But the fingers brushing over her hand said it for him. "Kirby's relationship with Stuart helped us along in that decision. And her occasional shortsightedness. That is, when she doesn't agree with my point of view."

"I might take the apology after all."

"In any case." Rising, Fairchild began to wander around the room, hands clasped behind his back. His version of Sherlock Holmes, Kirby decided, and settled back for the show. "Harriet and I both knew Stuart wasn't capable of constructing and carrying through on a theft like this alone. Harriet hadn't any idea whom he'd been talking to on the phone, but my name had been mentioned. Stuart had said he'd, ah, 'feel me out on the subject of producing a copy of the painting.'" His face fell easily into annoyed lines. "I've no idea why he should've thought a man like me would do something so base, so dishonest."

"Incredible," Adam murmured, and earned a blinding smile from father and daughter.

"We decided I'd agree, after some fee haggling. I'd then have the original in my possession while palming the copy off on Stuart. Sooner or later, his accomplice would be forced into the open to try to recover it. Meanwhile, Harriet reported the theft, but refused to file a claim. Instead she demanded that the insurance company act with discretion. Reluctantly she told them of her suspicion that I was involved, thereby ensuring that the investigation would be centered around me, and by association, Stuart and his accomplice. I concealed the Rembrandt behind a copy of a painting of my daughter, the original of which is tucked away in my room. I'm sentimental."

"Why didn't Mrs. Merrick just tell the police and the insurance company the truth?" McIntyre demanded after he'd worked his way through the explanation.

"They might have been hasty. No offense," Fairchild added indulgently. "Stuart might've been caught, but his accomplice would probably have gotten away. And, I confess, it was the intrigue that appealed to both of us. It was irresistible. You'll want to corroborate my story, of course."

"Of course," McIntyre agreed, and wondered if he could deal with another loony.

"We'd have done things differently if we'd had any idea that Melanie was involved. It's going to be difficult for Harriet." Pausing, he aimed a long look at McIntyre that was abruptly no-nonsense. "Be careful with her. Very careful. You might find our methods unorthodox, but she's a mother who's had two unspeakable shocks tonight: her daughter's betrayal and the possibility of losing her only child." He ran a hand over Kirby's hair as he stopped by her. "No matter how deep the hurt, the love remains, doesn't it, Kirby?"

"All I feel is the void," she murmured. "She hated me, and I think, I really think, she wanted me dead more than she wanted the painting. I wonder... I wonder just how much I'm to blame for that."

"You can't blame yourself for being, Kirby." Fairchild cupped her chin. "You can't blame a tree for reaching for the sun or another for rotting from within. We make our own choices and we're each responsible for them. Blame and credit belong to the individual. You haven't the right to claim either from someone else."

"You won't let me cover the hurt with guilt." After a long breath she rose and kissed his cheek. "I'll have to deal with it." Without thinking, she held out a hand for Adam before she turned to McIntyre. "Do you need a statement from me?"

"No, the shooting's not my jurisdiction, Miss Fairchild. Just the Rembrandt." Finishing off the rest of his Scotch he rose. "I'll have to take it with me, Mr. Fairchild."

All graciousness, Fairchild spread his arms wide. "Perfectly understandable."

"I appreciate your cooperation." If he could call it that. With a weary smile, he turned to Adam. "Don't worry, I haven't forgotten your terms. If everything's as he says, I should be able to keep them out of it officially, as we agreed the other day. Your part of the job's over, and all in all you handled it well. So, I'll be sorry if you're serious about not working for me anymore. You got the Rembrandt back, Adam. Now I've got to get started on untangling the red tape."

"Job?" Going cold, Kirby turned. Her hand was still linked in Adam's, but she felt it go numb as she drew it slowly away. "Job?" she repeated, pressing the hand to her stomach as if to ward off a blow.

Not now, he thought in frustration, and searched for the words he'd have used only a few hours later. "Kirby—"

With all the strength she had left, all the bitterness she'd felt, she brought her hand across his face. "Bastard," she whispered. She fled at a dead run.

"Damn you, Mac." Adam raced after her.

Chapter 12

Adam caught up to her just as Kirby started to slam her bedroom door. Shoving it open, he pushed his way inside. For a moment, they only stared at each other.

"Kirby, let me explain."

"No." The wounded look had been replaced by glacial anger. "Just get out. All the way out, Adam—of my house and my life."

"I can't." He took her by the shoulders, but her head snapped up, and the look was so cold, so hard, he dropped his hands again. It was too late to explain the way he'd planned. Too late to prevent the hurt. Now he had to find the way around it. "Kirby, I know what you must be thinking. I want—"

"Do you?" It took all of her effort to keep her voice from rising. Instead it was cool and calm. "I'm going to tell you anyway so we can leave everything neat and tidy." She faced him because she refused to turn her back on the pain or on the betrayal. "I'm thinking that I've never detested anyone more than I detest you at this moment. I'm thinking Stuart and Melanie could take lessons on using people from you. I'm thinking how naive I was, how stupid, to have believed there was something special about you, something stable and honest. And I wonder how I could've made love with you and never seen it. Then again, I didn't see it in Melanie, either. I loved and trusted her." Tears burned behind her eyes but she ignored them. "I loved and trusted you."

"Kirby…"

"Don't touch me." She backed away, but it was the tremor in her voice, not the movement, that stopped him from going to her. "I don't ever want to feel your hands on me again." Because she wanted to weep, she laughed, and the sound was as sharp as a knife. "I've always admired a really good liar, Adam, but you're the best. Every time you touched me, you lied. You prostituted yourself in that bed." She gestured toward it and wanted to scream. She wanted to fling herself on it and weep until she was empty. She stood, straight as an arrow. "You lay beside me and said all the things I wanted to hear. Do you get extra points for that, Adam? Surely that was above and beyond the call of duty."

"Don't." He'd had enough. Enough of her cold, clear look, her cold, clear words. "You know there was no dishonesty there. What happened between us had nothing to do with the rest."

"It has everything to do with it."

"No." He'd take everything else she could fling at

him, but not that. She'd changed his life with hardly more than a look. She had to know it. "I should never have put my hands on you, but I couldn't stop myself. I wanted you. I needed you. You have to believe that."

"I'll tell you what I believe," she said quietly, because every word he spoke was another slice into her heart. She'd finished with being used. "You came here for the Rembrandt, and you meant to find it no matter who or what you had to go through. My father and I were means to an end. Nothing more, nothing less."

He had to take it, had to let her say it, but there'd be no lies between them any longer. "I came for the Rembrandt. When I walked through the door I only had one priority, to find it. But I didn't know you when I walked through the door. I wasn't in love with you then."

"Is this the part where you say everything changed?" she demanded, falling back on fury. "Shall we wait for the violins?" She was weakening. She turned away and leaned on the post of the bed. "Do better, Adam."

She could be cruel. He remembered her father's warning. He only wished he believed he had a defense. "I can't do better than the truth."

"Truth? What the hell do you know about truth?" She whirled back around, eyes damp now and shimmering with heat. "I stood here in this room and told you everything, everything I knew about my father. I trusted you with his welfare, the most important thing in my life. Where was your truth then?"

"I had a commitment. Do you think it was easy for me to sit here and listen, knowing I couldn't give you what you were giving me?"

"Yes." Her tone was dead calm, but her eyes were

fierce. "Yes, I think it was a matter of routine for you. If you'd told me that night, the next day or the next, I might've believed you. If I'd heard it from you, I might've forgiven you."

Timing. Hadn't she told him how vital timing could be? Now he felt her slipping away from him, but he had nothing but excuses to give her. "I was going to tell you everything, start to finish, tomorrow."

"Tomorrow?" Slowly she nodded. "Tomorrows are very convenient. A pity for us all how rarely they come."

All the warmth, all the fire, that had drawn him to her was gone. He'd only seen this look on her face once before—when Stuart had backed her into a corner and she'd had no escape. Stuart had used physical dominance, but it was no prettier than the emotional pressure Adam knew he used. "I'm sorry, Kirby. If I'd taken the risk and told you this morning, it would've been different for all of us."

"I don't want your apology!" The tears beat her and poured out. She'd sacrificed everything else, now her pride was gone, as well. "I thought I'd found the man I could share my life with. I fell in love with you in the flash of an instant. No questions, no doubts. I believed everything you said to me. I gave you everything I had. In all my life no one's been allowed to know me as you did. I entrusted you with everything I am and you used me." Turning, she pressed her face into the bedpost.

He had, he couldn't deny it even to himself. He'd used her, as Stuart had used her. As Melanie had used her. Loving her made no difference, yet he had to hope it made all the difference. "Kirby." It took all the strength he had not to go to her, to comfort her, but he'd only be comforting himself if he put his arms around her now. "There's nothing you can say to me I haven't said to myself. I came here to do a job, but I fell in love with you. There wasn't any warning for me, either. I know I've hurt you. There's nothing I can do to turn back the clock."

"Do you expect me to fall into your arms? Do you expect me to say nothing else matters but us?" She turned, and though her cheeks were still damp, her eyes were dry. "It all matters," she said flatly. "Your job's finished here, Adam. You've recovered your Rembrandt. Take it, you earned it."

"You're not going to cut me out of your life."

"You've done that for me."

"No." The fury and frustration took over so that he grabbed her arm and jerked her against him. "No, you'll have to adjust to the way things are, because I'm coming back." He ran his hands down her hair, and they weren't steady. "You can make me suffer. By God, you can do it. I'll give you that, Kirby, but I'll be back."

Before his anger could push him too far, he whirled around and left her alone.

Fairchild was waiting for him, sitting calmly in the parlor by the fire. "I thought you'd need this." Without getting up, he gestured to the glass of Scotch on the table beside him. He waited until Adam had tossed it back. He didn't need to be told what had passed between them. "I'm sorry. She's hurt. Perhaps in time the wounds will close and she'll be able to listen."

Adam's knuckles whitened on the glass. "That's what I told her, but I didn't believe it. I betrayed her."

His glance lowered and settled on the older man. "And you."

"You did what you had to do. You had a part to play." Fairchild spread his hands on his knees and stared at them, thinking of his own part. "She would've dealt with it, Adam. She's strong enough. But even Kirby has a breaking point. Melanie... It was too soon after Melanie."

"She won't let me comfort her." It was that anguish that had him turning to stare out of the window. "She looks so wounded, and my being here only makes it harder for her." Steadying himself, he stared out at nothing. "I'll be out as soon as I can pack." He turned, his head only, and looked at the small, balding man in front of the fire. "I love her, Philip."

In silence Fairchild watched Adam walk away. For the first time in his six decades he felt old. Old and tired. With a deep, deep sigh he rose and went to his daughter.

He found her curled on her bed, her head cradled by her knees and arms. She sat silent and unmoving and, he knew, utterly, utterly beaten. When he sat beside her, her head jerked up. Slowly, with his hand stroking her hair, her muscles relaxed.

"Do we ever stop making fools of ourselves, Papa?"

"You've never been a fool."

"Oh, yes, yes, it seems I have." Settling her chin on her knees, she stared straight ahead. "I lost our bet. I guess you'll be breaking open that box of cigars you've been saving."

"I think we can consider the extenuating circumstances."

"How generous of you." She tried to smile and failed. "Aren't you going to the hospital to be with Harriet?"

"Yes, of course."

"You'd better go then. She needs you."

His thin, bony hand continued to stroke her hair. "Don't you?"

"Oh, Papa." Tears came in a flood as she turned into his arms.

Kirby followed Cards downstairs as he carried her bags. In the week since the discovery of the Rembrandt she'd found it impossible to settle. She found no comfort in her art, no comfort in her home. Everything here held memories she could no longer deal with. She slept little and ate less. She knew she was losing touch with the person she was, and so she'd made plans to force herself back.

She opened the door for Cards and stared out at the bright, cheery morning. It made her want to weep.

"I don't know why a sensible person would get up at this ridiculous hour to drive to the wilderness."

Kirby forced back the gloom and turned to watch her father stride down the stairs in a ratty bathrobe and bare feet. What hair he had left was standing on end. "The early bird gathers no moss," she told him. "I want to get to the lodge and settle in. Want some coffee?"

"Not while I'm sleeping," he muttered as she nuzzled his cheek. "I don't know what's wrong with you, going off to that shack in the Himalayas."

"It's Harriet's very comfortable cabin in the Adirondacks, twenty miles from Lake Placid."

"Don't nitpick. You'll be alone."

"I've been alone before," she reminded him. "You're annoyed because you won't have anyone but Cards to shout at for a few weeks."

"He never shouts back." But even as he grumbled, Fairchild was studying Kirby's face. The shadows were still under her eyes and the loss of weight was much too apparent. "Tulip should go with you. Someone has to make you eat."

"I'm going to do that. Mountain air should make me ravenous." When he continued to frown at her, she touched his cheek. "Don't worry, Papa."

"I am worried." Taking her shoulders, he held her at arm's length. "For the first time in your life, you're causing me genuine concern."

"A few pounds, Papa."

"Kirby." He cupped her face in his strong, thin hand. "You have to talk to Adam."

"No!" The word came out violently. With an effort, she drew a steadying breath. "I've said all I want to say to Adam. I need time and some solitude, that's all."

"Running away, Kirby?"

"As fast as I can. Papa, Rick proposed to me again before he left."

"What the hell does that have to do with anything?" he demanded. "He always proposes to you before he leaves."

"I nearly said yes." She lifted her hands to his, willing him to understand. "I nearly said yes because it seemed an easy way out. I'd have ruined his life."

"What about yours?"

"I have to glue the pieces back together. Papa, I'll be fine. It's Harriet who needs you now."

He thought of his friend, his oldest and closest friend. He thought of the grief. "Melanie's going to Europe when she's fully recovered."

"I know." Kirby tried not to remember the gun, or the hate. "Harriet told me. She'll need both of us when Melly's gone. If I can't help myself, how can I help Harriet?"

"Melanie won't see Harriet. The girl's destroying herself with hate." He looked at his own daughter, his pride, his treasure. "The sooner Melanie's out of the hospital and thousands of miles away, the better it'll be for everyone."

She knew what he'd done, how he'd fought against his feelings about Melanie to keep from causing either her or Harriet more grief. He'd comforted them both without releasing his own fury. She held him tightly a moment, saying nothing. Needing to say nothing.

"We all need some time," she murmured. When she drew away, she was smiling. She wouldn't leave him with tears in her eyes. "I'll cloister myself in the wilderness and sculpt while you pound on your hawk."

"Such a wicked tongue in such a pretty face."

"Papa…" Absently she checked the contents of her purse. "Whatever painting you do will be done under your own name?" When he didn't answer, she glanced up, narrowing her eyes. "Papa?"

"All my paintings will be Fairchilds. Haven't I given you my word?" He sniffed and looked injured. Kirby began to feel alarmed.

"This obsession with sculpting," she began, eyeing

him carefully. "You don't have it in your head to attempt an emulation of a Rodin or Cellini?"

"You ask too many questions," he complained as he nudged her toward the door. "The day's wasting away, better get started. Don't forget to write."

Kirby paused on the porch and turned back to him. "It'll take you years," she decided. "If you ever acquire the talent. Go ahead and play with your hawk." She kissed his forehead. "I love you, Papa."

He watched her dart down the steps and into her car. "One should never interfere in the life of one's child," he murmured. Smiling broadly, he waved goodbye. When she was out of sight, he went directly to the phone.

The forest had always appealed to her. In mid-autumn, it shouted with life. The burst of colors were a last swirling fling before the trees went into the final cycle. It was an order Kirby accepted—birth, growth, decay, rebirth. Still, after three days alone, she hadn't found her serenity.

The stream she walked past rushed and hissed. The air was brisk and tangy. She was miserable.

She'd nearly come to terms with her feelings about Melanie. Her childhood friend was ill, had been ill for a long, long time and might never fully recover. It hadn't been a betrayal any more than cancer was a betrayal. But it was a malignancy Kirby knew she had to cut out of her life. She'd nearly accepted it, for Melanie's sake and her own.

She could come to terms with Melanie, but she had yet to deal with Adam. He'd had no illness, nor a lifetime of resentments to feed it. He'd simply had a job to do. And that was too cold for her to accept.

With her hands in her pockets, she sat down on a log and scowled into the water. Her life, she admitted, was a mess. She was a mess. And she was damn sick of it.

She tried to tell herself she'd put Adam out of her life. She hadn't. Yes, she'd refused to listen to him. She'd made no attempt to contact him. It wasn't enough. It wasn't enough, Kirby decided, because it left things unfinished. Now she'd never know if he'd had any real feelings for her. She'd never know if, even briefly, he'd belonged to her.

Perhaps it was best that way.

Standing, she began to walk again, scuffing the leaves that danced around her feet. She was tired of herself. Another first. It wasn't going to go on, she determined. Whatever the cost, she was going to whip Kirby Fairchild back into shape. Starting now. At a brisk pace, she started back to the cabin.

She liked the way it looked, set deep in the trees by itself. The roof was pitched high and the glass sparkled. Today, she thought as she went in through the back door, she'd work. After she'd worked, she'd eat until she couldn't move.

Peeling off her coat as she went, she walked directly to the worktable she'd set up in the corner of the living room. Without looking around, she tossed the coat aside and looked at her equipment. She hadn't touched it in days. Now she sat and picked up a formless piece of wood. This was to be her *Passion*. Perhaps now more than ever, she needed to put that emotion into form.

There was silence as she explored the feel and life

of the wood in her hands. She thought of Adam, of the nights, the touches, the tastes. It hurt. Passion could. Using it, she began to work.

An hour slipped by. She only noticed when her fingers cramped. With a sigh, she set the wood down and stretched them. The healing had begun. She could be certain of it now. "A start," she murmured to herself. "It's a start."

"It's *Passion*. I can already see it."

The knife slipped out of her hand and clattered on the table as she whirled. Across the room, calmly sitting in a faded wingback chair, was Adam. She'd nearly sprung out of the chair to go to him before she stopped herself. He looked the same, just the same. But nothing was. That she had to remember.

"How did you get in here?"

He heard the ice in her voice. But he'd seen her eyes. In that one instant, she'd told him everything he'd ached for. Still, he knew she couldn't be rushed. "The front door wasn't locked." He rose and crossed to her. "I came inside to wait for you, but when you came in, you looked so intense; then you started right in. I didn't want to disturb your work." When she said nothing, he picked up the wood and turned it over in his hand. He thought it smoldered. "Amazing," he murmured. "Amazing what power you have." Just holding it made him want her more, made him want what she'd put into the wood. Carefully he set it down again, but his eyes were just as intense when he studied her. "What the hell've you been doing? Starving yourself?"

"Don't be ridiculous." She stood and walked away from him, but she didn't know where to go.

"Am I to blame for that, too?"

His voice was quiet, serious. She'd never be able to resist that tone. Gathering her strength, she turned back to him. "Did Tulip send you to check up on me?"

She was too thin. Damn it. Had the pounds melted off her? She was so small. How could she be so small and look so arrogant? He wanted to go to her. Beg. He was nearly certain she'd listen now. Yet she wouldn't want it that way. Instead, he tucked his hands in his pockets and rocked back on his heels. "This is a cozy little place. I wandered around a bit while you were out."

"Glad you made yourself at home."

"It's everything Harriet said it would be." He looked at her again and smiled. "Isolated, cozy, charming."

She lifted a brow. It was easiest with the distance between them. "You've spoken to Harriet?"

"I took your portrait to the gallery."

Emotion came and went again in her eyes. Picking up a small brass pelican, she caressed it absently. "My portrait?"

"I promised her she could exhibit it when I'd finished." He watched her nervous fingers run over the brass. "It wasn't difficult to finish without you. I saw you everywhere I looked."

Quickly she turned to walk to the front wall. It was all glass, open to the woods. No one could feel trapped with that view. Kirby clung to it. "Harriet's having a difficult time."

"The strain shows a bit." In her, he thought, and in

you. "I think it's better for her that Melanie won't see her at this point. With Stuart out of the way, the gallery's keeping Harriet busy." He stared at her back, trying to imagine what expression he'd find on her face. "Why aren't you pressing charges, Kirby?"

"For what purpose?" she countered. She set the piece of brass down. A crutch was a crutch, and she was through with them. "Both Stuart and Melanie are disgraced, banished from the elite that means so much to them. The publicity's been horrid. They have no money, no reputation. Isn't that punishment enough?"

"Melanie tried to kill you. Twice." Suddenly furious at the calm, even tone, he went to her and spun her around. "Damn it, Kirby, she wanted you dead!"

"It was she who nearly died." Her voice was still even, but she took a step back, from him. "The police have to accept my story that the gun went off accidentally, even if others don't. I could have sent Melly to jail. Wouldn't I feel avenged watching Harriet suffer?"

Adam forced back the impatience and stared through the glass. "She's worried about you."

"Harriet?" Kirby shrugged. "There's no need. When you see her, tell her I'm well."

"You can tell her yourself when we get back."

"We?" The lightest hint of temper entered her voice. Nothing could have relieved him more. "I'm going to be here for some time yet."

"Fine. I've nothing better to do."

"That wasn't an invitation."

"Harriet already gave me one," he told her easily. He gave the room another sweeping glance while Kirby smoldered. "The place looks big enough for two."

"That's where you're wrong, but don't let me spoil your plans." She spun on her heel and headed for the stairs. Before she'd gotten five feet, his fingers curled around her arm and held her still. When she whirled, he saw that his gypsy was back.

"You don't really think I'd let you leave? Kirby, you disappoint me."

"You don't *let* me do anything, Adam. Nor do you prevent me from doing anything."

"Only when it's necessary." While she stood rigid, he put his hands on her shoulders. "You're going to listen to me this time. And you're going to start listening in just a minute."

He pressed his mouth to hers as he'd needed to for weeks. She didn't resist. Nor did she respond. He could feel her fighting the need to do both. He could press her, he knew, and she'd give in to him. Then he might never really have her. Slowly their gazes locked; he straightened.

"You're nearly through making me suffer," he murmured. "I've paid, Kirby, in every moment I haven't been with you. Through every night you haven't been beside me. When are you going to stop punishing me?"

"I don't want to punish you." It was true. She'd already forgiven him. Yet, her confidence, that strong, thin shield she'd always had, had suffered an enormous blow. This time when she stepped back he didn't try to stop her. "I know we parted badly. Maybe it'd be best if we just admitted we'd both made a mistake and left it at that. I realize you did what you had to do. I've always done the same. It's time I got on with my life and you with yours."

He felt a quick jiggle of panic. She was too calm, much too calm. He wanted emotion from her, any kind she'd give. "What sort of life would either of us have without the other?"

None. But she shook her head. "I said we made a mistake—"

"And now you're going to tell me you don't love me?"

She looked straight at him and opened her mouth. Weakening, she shifted her gaze to just over his shoulder. "No, I don't love you, Adam. I'm sorry."

She'd nearly cut him off at the knees. If she hadn't looked away at the last instant, it would've been over for him. "I'd've thought you could lie better than that." In one move he closed the distance between them. His arms were around her, firm, secure. The same, she thought. Nothing had changed after all. "I've given you two weeks, Kirby. Maybe I should give you more time, but I can't." He buried his face in her hair while she squeezed her eyes shut. She'd been wrong, she remembered. She'd been wrong about so many things. Could this be right?

"Adam, please…"

"No, no more. I love you." He drew away, barely resisting the need to shake her. "I love you and you'll have to get used to it. It isn't going to change."

She curled her hand into a fist before she could stroke his cheek. "I think you're getting pompous again."

"Then you'll have to get used to that, too. Kirby…" He framed her face with his hands. "How many ways would you like me to apologize?"

"No." Shaking her head she moved away again. She

should be able to think, she warned herself. She had to think. "I don't need apologies, Adam."

"You wouldn't," he murmured. Forgiveness would come as easily to her as every other emotion. "Your father and I had a long talk before I drove up here."

"Did you?" She gave her attention to a bowl of dried flowers. "How nice."

"He's given me his word he'll no longer…emulate paintings."

With her back to him, she smiled. The pain vanished without her realizing it, and with it, the doubts. They loved. There was so little else in life. Still smiling, Kirby decided she wouldn't tell Adam of her father's ambition with sculpting. Not just yet. "I'm glad you convinced him," she said with her tongue in her cheek.

"He decided to concede the point to me, since I'm going to be a member of the family."

With a flutter of her lashes, she turned. "How lovely. Is Papa adopting you?"

"That wasn't precisely the relationship we discussed." Crossing to her, he took her into his arms again. This time he felt the give and the strength. "Tell me again that you don't love me."

"I don't love you," she murmured, and pulled his mouth to hers. "I don't want you to hold me." Her arms wound around his neck. "I don't want you to kiss me again. Now." Her lips clung to his, opening, giving. As the heat built, he groaned and drew her in.

"Obstinate, aren't you?" he muttered.

"Invariably."

"But are you going to marry me?"

"On my terms."

When her head tilted back, he ran kisses up the length of her throat. "Which are?"

"I may come easy, but I don't come free."

"What do you want, a marriage settlement?" On a half laugh, he drew away. She was his, whoever, whatever she was. He'd never let her go again. "Can't you think of anything but money?"

"I'm fond of money—and we still have to discuss my sitting fee. However…" She drew a deep breath. "My terms for marriage are four children."

"Four?" Even knowing Kirby, he'd been caught off guard. "Four children?"

She moistened her lips but her voice was strong. "I'm firm on that number, Adam. The point's non-negotiable." Then her eyes were young and full of needs. "I want children. Your children."

Every time he thought he loved her completely, he found he could love her more. Still more. "Four," he repeated with a slow nod. "Any preference to gender?"

The breath she'd been holding came out on a laugh. No, she hadn't been wrong. They loved. There was very little else. "I'm flexible, though a mix of some sort would be nice." She tossed her head back and smiled up at him. "What do you think?"

He swept her into his arms then headed for the stairs. "I think we'd better get started."

* * * * *